Reclaiming Arabella

The Agron Realm Trilogy, Book 1

DianaKay Abraham

Copyright © 2024 DianaKay Abraham

Reclaiming Arabella: Book 1 of the Agron Realm Trilogy

ISBN: 979-8338013656 (Paper Back)
ISBN: 979-8338032589 (Hard Back)

Cover design by: DianaKay Abraham

Edited by: Maurie A Pollock and Holly Smith

Printed in the United States of America

To anyone that has ever felt undervalued or marginalized: Don't give up, there IS a light and you will find your way out of the darkness.

"Beyond the East the sunrise, beyond the West the sea.
And the East and West my wander-thirst, that will not let me be.

It works in me like madness, Dear, to bid me say good-bye;
For the seas call, and the stars call, and oh! the call of the sky!"

GERALD GOULD

Contents

The Agron Realm Playlist

Devils Don't Fly
Natalia Kills
Storms a Coming
Pat Kenny
Wild Horses
Grace Power
Shadows
Ryan Jesse
Rise
Carolyn Jones
Redemption
Besomorph, Cooper and Riell
Devil Doesn't Bargain
Alex Benjamin
Fighter
Fearless Soul
All Eyes on You
Smash Into Pieces
Middle Finger
Bohnes
My Jolly Sailor Bold
Ashley Serena
Birds of a Feather
Lilith Max
Six Feet Deep
Royalle Lynn
Goddess
Written by Wolves
Hate Me
Eurielle

The Agron Realm Map

THE AGRON REALM

THE MEADOWS

KING PEMATER'S CASTLE

THE TORRENT KINGDOM

THE BRUME

THE AGRON KEEP

THE SUMMIT

SUMMER

THE JORDANT FALLS

ZEUS HOME

COLLORK RIVER

QUEEN CLARK'S CASTLE

MIDELPORT

THE DAEMON KINGDOM

THE EASTERN SHALLOWS

THE WESTERN SHADOWS

NEERIA

DESIPORE

PARADISLAKE

Prologue

Uriah

"She'll be your bride one day when you're older and she reaches maturity," my father said in a soft whisper as he bent his tall, broad frame slightly to peer over my shoulder.

In the sunlight cast through the window, my father, the Lord of the Shallows, Peter to those closest to him, looked every bit as if his hair was about to combust. The gray stone walls were adorned with hunter green and gold velvet curtains and plush chairs. A bedchamber with more of the same and added sage tones were through a door to the far side of the room.

The Agron Keep lay in the middle of the realm where the king held the throne, his court of advisors and ruled the land beyond. The Keep was a central point and the stronghold was located West of the Summit region which bordered the rest of the continent currently occupied by humans. It was a bustling and busy place full of life. Small villages surrounded the Keep and the forested lands, leaving the grounds of the castle for those employed by the crown and the royal military.

I'd never been in this wing before. It was meant for a neighboring regions ruling class but not unlike my own. Though we were part of the crowns employ, we held our station at home mostly. My family's wing in the Keep was adorned with deep royal blue and silver silks. We normally stayed on the South side of the continent facing the sea in the Western Shallows. So, when visiting the keep, we naturally were given a wing in the South of the castle.

The North side faced a great mountain flanked by rolling meadows that butted up to the grounds. The snow capped peaks in the distance were visible when I looked out over the lush flowering gardens below—a beautiful backdrop to our otherwise ruthless world. We only stayed here for special occasions, like this one, which meant we are a full days ride Northeast of our home in the Shallows Western Estate.

Normally we kept to the Shallows as the region was vast and constant vigilance to approaching attacks from the human military was necessary. The ancient magical wards protecting the Agron realm grew weaker every year as Agron's magical force continued to decline. Patrols never ceased, lest the human armies and navy manage to break through.

"What will she be called?" I asked, staring down at the beautiful fae baby before me. Her skin was palest porcelain and she had plump rosy cheeks with rounded ears. Unusual for a fae but not unheard of. My own ears came to a slight point, though rounded more than most older fae. A wisp of golden blonde hair laced with hints of red crowned her head and her soft eyelashes fluttered as she slept nestled in the small cradle.

She had only been born the day before. My father and I had come to secure our line as soon as we received word that Arabella, the Lady of the Meadows was in labor. This baby was to be my betrothed. The union between her and I would bring the North and South together, an alliance that would build over the next eighteen years with the promise that when she reached maturity, she'd become my bride. We would marry with the intent to produce an heir that would then become the next King or Queen of the Agron Realm.

The Lord of Summit, John, ruled over the Eastern region of the realm. The Summit ran along the entirety of the Couloir River—its sheer cliff faces dividing the fae half of the continent from the humans Eastern half. John's eldest daughter was only months old. The Brume region, which lay to the west of the Agron Keep was governed by Ulysses, Lord of the Brume. Ulysses' son was still toddling but their children were betrothed as soon as the girl had been born.

It was decided by King Astros' council that the East and West would join as would the North and South. The Lords of each region offered up their children for these unions to benefit the dying magic in the realm, barring mating bonds.

Mating bonds were rare and strong, a deep magic that could not be denied by those bound by them. Their magic would rebel until the pair united or it destroyed them in mind and body. It signified a perfect, most coveted match by the fae, for the legends were told generation after generation.

Those with mating bonds would bring greater magic back to the realm. I'd been waiting for the region of the Meadows, North of the Agron Keep to produce an heir. I had a sizable age gap with whomever they paired me with, but I'd had to wait regardless.

After my child's birth from my union with the North, my child's counterpart would come from the union of the East and West, creating balance in all things. In the event two males were born, the first born would become next in line for the throne and would then choose a female from any of the four Lords' lines when he reached maturity.

Our small realm had a bright future ahead considering our magic was suffering. As a lord's son, it would become my duty to help restore that power to its former glory—that is, if all went according to plan. It was thought that if the strongest families, like mine, that currently held lordships over the four regions wed and bred, those unions would restore the most power to where it belonged in Agron's Keep with the central governing seat, currently held by King Reuben Astros.

King Astros himself was still young, in his fifth decennial but his family line hadn't produced well for his people. He had no magic and the deep magic was thinning across the land. Deep magic was passed from generation to generation from the fae of old, each year losing a bit more as its potency waned. The fae grew weaker, many relying on modern methods of living rather than embracing their given magic. Being a mindful king, he promised to pass the power to stronger fae families that held the old magics for the better of all the people. As such, he vowed to never sire an heir. With no heir the crown would pass to a new line with stronger magic. Our survival as a species depended on it. The dilution of fae blood intermingling with humans, would be the reckoning of the old ways.

I reached down into the wood cradle I was knelt before, tentatively sweeping my finger down one side of her small feathered wings. *Lovely.*
She was only a baby but her beauty would blossom over time and she would grow strong. The sunlight landed on the tip of her wings and I could see the rainbow effect as the sun highlighted the green, gold and purple hues to her otherwise black feathers.

Her father, Lionel, the Lord of the Meadows, watched me. His long blond hair swept back in a tight braid that ran down his back. His hard glare nearly unnerved me as I watched his newborn daughter sleep.

"Arabella. She'll be called Arabella, after her late mother," her father said, pursing his lips as he studied my face. He had massive white wings with tawny spots speckled throughout. I'd never have the nerve to touch *those* wings. It was rude by any standard to touch a faery's wings but I couldn't help myself with the baby's. They were tiny and perfect.

Her mother passed away shortly after the birth yesterday. Complications occurred and the healing fae had to choose which to save. They chose the new life. The Lord of Meadows looked exhausted and the spark was dull in his green eyes.

It was said that he commanded the rare gift of light though none was shining in this moment. His normally otherworldly glow was dimmed, leaving his skin pale and washed out. I wondered if Arabella would yield light too or if she'd inherit her mothers powers. She'd been a great seer. *I wonder if she knew she would die,* I thought to myself.

I recently began wielding shadows. *It would be poetic to*

see her stands of lights intertwined with my shadow. About a year ago, I discovered the shadows would do my bidding if I concentrated a little bit. I'll turn ten in a few months' time, it feels as if I'd had my shadows for company my whole life, much like my wings. The shadows spoke to me in ways I couldn't explain. It was more of an intuition than anything.

My wings were unusual and said to be shadows turned solid, something no one had seen in nearly a millennium when it was common across the fae of the Shallows. The nearly transparent black flesh of them rippled over my shoulders. They were only truly opaque under the moonlight. The always reminded me of dragonfly wings. *Arabella and I will be a lovely pair, in time, of course,* I thought to myself. Until then, our fathers would do what they could to keep our lands safe. Fae matured much faster than humans intellectually so we knew war was not the answer. We could obliterate them, but at what cost to the future?

The humans on the Eastern side of the continent always sought to destroy us. I scoffed as I thought of them. *Stupid humans. They're the piss ants of the world, but our magic is dying and they have learned to live without it.*

The Summit was constantly in battle. The Navy of the Shallows was always on guard. A natural reef blocked most of the humans exploits as did the wards in place, but there was still a mile wide stretch that lay unguarded by the ancient rocks so regular patrols were necessary. The humans had never been able to breach the Shallows. *Thank the King!*

Frightened of the magics we were born with, the humans' jealous hatred of our kind drove them to constant attempts to rid the world of us. Most of the fae of the Realm paid them little mind. We might all prosper if only the humans would set aside their forefathers pronouncement of war so we could help them.

My father placed his hand on my shoulder, my own dark auburn hair brushing to the side in the process. I needed a hair cut. I preferred my hair short while most Fae plated it and kept it long. I found it cumbersome.

"I'm sorry for the loss. Your Lady will be missed by all. If there's anything you should need, please, send word and I'll answer the call," my father said addressing Lionel, *Lord of the Meadows*. The older generations always seemed to prefer titles when available. He nodded, now staring at his baby, asleep in the cradle—all that was left of his mate. "Uriah, it's time we return to the Shallows. You'll see her again soon enough," my father concluded as he turned me away from Arabella, pushing his palm into my shoulder before giving a light squeeze. He swept out of the room with me striding after him.

I tipped my head to Arabella and her father and then I hurried after my own. *I'll see her at holidays. She won't be a boring baby for long. Year after next she will be able to visit the Shallows and I shall take her flying.*

Part One: Revelation

Twenty-Five Years Later

"Oh, curse it," I muttered to myself. My long copper colored braid had snagged a rock in this forsaken, never ending, pit of despair, pitch black cave. When I wandered in I'd been looking for a place to lay low just for a few hours while the human soldiers that searched for me gave up.

But oh no, one wrong step and I tumbled into this second branch that ran concurrently only below the first, and it apparently never ended but continued to take me West. I think it's West. *Who the hell knows at this point?* I wondered to myself. I tugged at the amber necklace I wore. It felt too tight. *Why does this thing have to itch at a time like this?*

I had been outside of Neera, doing what I do best— assassinating assholes. I'd found my mark, only to realize he was a prominent military man. Oops. Either way I had my proof and I'd be collecting payment shortly, if I could get out here. *Come on!* I yanked at my hair.

It was stiflingly hot and sweat trickled between my breasts and down my back, pooling around my middle underneath my tight leather top. *The air is so thick, I could chew it.* I kicked myself for not wearing the tank top I'd considered this morning. The short sleeved leather vest I'd cinched myself into left little room for air to enter but protected my skin.

My vest stuck horribly to the scars on my back and torso, gifts of my forsaken childhood, and I wanted nothing more than to strip down to my flesh. However, for the sake of *just in case* I weathered the heat. My silk lined leather pants had fused themselves to my ample behind hours ago so I'd probably never get them off on my own anyway. I'd stopped feeling my toes hours before as well. I cursed my new boots and my mouth felt like sandpaper. I desperately needed to find water.

I'd sent out tendrils of my powers, but they never reported back, which was unusual. Hopefully that doesn't mean I've stumbled upon my own grave. My powers felt weaker here. My cords of light dimmer without the sun to help fuel them. It made me uneasy and off kilter. It was pitch black in the cave save for the small ball of light I'd conjured for myself. It only lit the way for a few feet before being snatched up by the never-ending darkness.

I couldn't even follow an echo; the sandy bottom of the tunneled cave system absorbed all the sound around me, which was a blessing and a curse. If I happen to run into anyone or anything, they won't hear me coming except with the ball of light, they could *see* me coming and that would be worse.

Working my hair free, I examined the crevice that had snagged it. Odd lines of silver, deep purple and smooth gray weaved their way through the red natural rock of the cave. I'd never seen anything like it. I wasn't exactly a geologist though. Almost everything consisted of red dirt around here. Though I suppose being this close to the Southern sea might have something to do with it. The land was rich with iron ore and the salt marshes were vast.

I frequented the Daemon Kingdom in the South East of the continent. Queen Opal Clawin was usually amenable with a little prodding. It was easy for me to find work in the towns inhabited by humans surrounding her castle. She didn't call on me nearly as often as I assumed she would at first.

A few years ago, I'd been caught leaving her castle by a member of her personal guard after killing a nobles son. He had raped a maid in the castle and her mother had hired me. After being held and tortured for a few weeks, I was told in no uncertain terms that I either belonged to her now, or I could face decapitation in her courtyard. The only real benefit was that it helped me to hide in plain sight from those that would wish me harm. *No one wants to piss off the Queen's personal assassin.*

It was a delicate balance. I'd managed to keep myself free for the last seven years since my escape from servitude in the Northern Kings castle. The Torrent Kingdom was off limits for me. So the Daemon Kingdom has become my refuge. King Gralton Plavlock was monstrous and though I'd vowed to take his head, he wasn't someone I could fight. Yet. With time I could complete my vow. I just had to be patient. It was a virtue after all.

The border to the Agron Realm wouldn't be too far from here, presumably. No one crossed that though. The fae were not to be underestimated with their trickery and magic. It was said they were to be cruel and unyielding when they captured an enemy. I often wondered if I had fae blood in me. *I am most definitely unyielding. What human can cast light and bend it to her will? How many humans enjoy hurting miscreants?*

Aside from my attitude, I was the only one in the human lands that seemed to have magic. I hid my strange abilities for the most part and stayed away from people. It was easier that way. Either I'd begin to make them uncomfortable with my mere presence after a short while or they'd try to harm me. Life was unforgiving that way and I had no intention of being enslaved by King Plavlock again.

My hair hung down my back. *I need to pin my hair up.* I wrapped it around the top of my head into a crown and dug a pin out of my front pants pocket to secure it. That helped with the heat a little too. I swear it was getting hotter. I tugged on the cord of my necklace again. *Maybe I should just take it off.* I felt a tingle shoot down my spine. *Why does it do that? What was I doing? Forward, right. Get out of the cave.*

I continued along the sandy path through the darkness. I'd considered turning back but, I'd been walking in this direction for hours at this point. To turn around would mean walking hours back and who knows? I may just be a few turns from freedom. Or death. If I didn't find water soon that would surely be the case. I took small sips to ration what little I had in my canteen, but it ran dry over an hour before and the heat was...ugh. I needed a real plan, instead, I trudged on. *I'm so dizzy. How much further?*

I paused again, panting. I'd gone down a steep hill for what felt like hours only to have it level out and quickly begin a steep incline. My legs were heavily muscled as I was constantly on the move, rarely resting for a day or two. I wasn't thin by any means, either as I relied heavily on carbs to get me through. *I can never buy enough meat. I need to find more marks.* Add in the heat and I was ready for respite.

This wretched path had just leveled out again, although there were less natural formations. It was more like a tunnel than a cave on this side of the subterranean valley.

After another hour or so in my unproductive march through darkness, I rounded a corner. I sent out three beams of my power. I didn't want to drain myself completely of power, but I needed them to show me the way out. If a beam found a way back to the Daemon Kingdom, it would double back and fade slowly as I followed it to my horse, Knightmare.

I stopped and watched. The light trailed down the long path, stalactites and stalagmites lighting up along the way. As my light zoomed past one in particular, it made an odd shadow flicker up the wall. The hair raised on the back of my neck. *I am not alone.*

"Friend or foe?" I called down the way, mentally preparing myself for a fight. I could fight if the alternative was dying by an enemy's hand. I placed a hand over the dagger strapped to my left thigh. I was good at single hand to hand combat but the odds weren't in my favor if there were many opponents.

The lack of proper fuel for my body coupled with a bit of a kerfuffle earlier left me mostly spent, my powers dwindling every second. I had room to run, I suppose, but for how long and with how many in pursuit? The tendrils of light I'd sent faded. My magic was not normal down here. I needed sunlight. Even moonlight would be beneficial at this point.

I sent another tendril of light toward the shadow, only the shadow had moved and was now only six or so feet from me, just barely out of reach of my ball of light. He was watching me and I couldn't see him. *Shit!* I blanched, clutching my throat and giving a bit of a winded giggle. *You sound like a schoolgirl. Although...*

Perhaps if he thought I was just some silly lost girl this could go my way. "Oh! You startled me. How'd you move from there to here so fast?" He took one step forward into my light. His piercing stare was a sight to behold.

His brow creased in clear confusion, and he crossed his heavily muscled arms across his chest. I noted several daggers within arms reach strapped to both thighs, and a sword sheathed at his side. He was wearing leather pants, he left his chest bare.

Shadows flickered in my light highlighting his rippling abs and muscled chest. My eye's followed his body up searching for his face again. He was much taller than me, I barely came to his shoulder. If I weren't stuck in a cave, I might have let my eyes linger a moment. His shirt had been tucked into a back pocket.

Clearly, he'd found it stifling in here too. He had a tattoo that snaked up his left forearm. It looked like swirls of water that were moving. *Must be a trick of the shadows around us.* It felt like they had come to life since his approach. I could feel them testing and tasting me, like a soft breeze had joined us in the cave. I wanted to bat them away as it tickled, but dared myself not to. *How odd and yet, familiar?*

"I move how I wish to move. How did you get here?" he asked. He still hadn't answered my question; friend or foe? *I guess I'll go with foe.* I shifted my feet into more of a fighting stance.

"One foot in front of the other usually works best," I answered. If he wanted to play a game to feel each other out, then so be it. "Are you familiar with the area? I'm finding myself a bit...in the dark." He just stared. So I waited. After what felt like eons I heard him sigh.

"You're in a restricted area," he snipped, clearly irritated that he was even talking to me. "To what purpose are you here?" He uncrossed his arms. His wrist twitched, ready to grab a dagger if I dare move. *Okay, not so friendly indeed.*

"I'm not trying to be 'in a restricted area,' I'm trying to get out of it. Got any insight? You clearly don't want me here and I don't want to stay, so if you'll just point me in the right direction to get out of your way, I'll kindly do so." I held the ball of light in my right hand. I was ready to toss it in the air and pull my khopesh free from my side. I was left handed, which came as an advantage as well.

My blade was unconventional for these parts of the world having been made on another continent. It had a crescent shaped moonstone built in to the grip. It flared to life when I pushed my light into it accidentally one day. I'd never seen another stone like the one adorning my favorite weapon. I felt invincible with it in my hand. It's proven to be highly effective and afforded me room to rip down shields and slice with the sickle.

It was a lovely bit of steel. It came to a slight curve at the tip, making it a good slashing weapon, but I could also gut someone quickly and rip away shields and other weapons efficiently. It took me awhile to really get the hang of it. The handle was what had drawn me to it in the beginning.

I'd challenged a group of sailors to a game of cards seven years prior and won it after I took all their money. It didn't hurt that I was drinking water out of a gin bottle and giving them all double shots of rum. I got a few nice daggers too, but my khopesh is my favorite.

The dark stranger pinched the bridge of his nose with two fingers. He had big hands. "Well, actually, I guess you and I have that in common. How long have you been trying to get out of here?"

Interesting. *Perhaps a friend after all?* I studied him in my dim light for a moment. His eyes softened, and the shadows around us receded a bit. His short hair flopped forward a little as he dropped his hand from his face. That's when I noticed his pointed ears. He...he was fae. My breath caught and my eyes flared wide as I realized that it wasn't a breeze that controlled the shadows—he was. I was standing in a dark cave, lost with no way out, and trapped with a stone cold predator. *Keep it together. You have tricks too.*

I took a step back as shock washed over me. He hadn't attacked, but he was fast enough to do so. He was nearly twice my size yet he silently moved down the tunnel in mere seconds after my magic had highlighted him. *How did he get down here?*

"How long have *you* been down here?" I inquired. My guard doubled after my realization that I definitely crossed into where I shouldn't be. The humans had been at war with the fae for so long. I'm not sure anyone remembered when or why it had started in the first place. I very much looked human, even if I didn't feel like one or particularly act like one most of the time. *Don't think about it.*

He stepped forward slowly, raising his palms as he spoke. "Is this what we're doing? Look, I'm not going to hurt you. I would like to know why you're on my land though. Where did you begin from? *I* found this little cave about four hours ago. I didn't know it existed but I would like to know how *you* found it and how often you come here."

"I wasn't trying to find it. I was in a different cave and fell into this one." I tipped my head to the side. He looked interested, so I continued. "I was at the Western most edge of Neera. I needed..." I sighed. "I needed a place to hide from the men chasing me. I was lost in the woods. I ran into a cave, and it seemed deep so I kept running. I could hear them behind me so I didn't stop." *What do school girls sound like?*

"The next thing I knew I was falling and then I ended up on this path. There were only two directions I could go. I continued the way I'd been running before I fell. I didn't really stop long enough to see what was behind me," I said while we stared each other down.

8

I wasn't about to volunteer that I'd felt pressure in my middle to continue this way. Something pulled me forward, but I also had a growing sense of unease as I moved further away from the cave opening. Those first moments entering the cave, I could feel anxiety building inside me, but the curiosity over whatever drew me forward won. I could still feel the tug in my middle. It was stronger now than it had been, but I couldn't place where it was coming from. I felt compelled to answer the mystery.

Getting out of here in one piece is more important, but I always liked a good mystery. The old woman in the kitchen I was forced to work in always said I was too nosy for my own good. Perhaps she was right. I do tend to get myself into some tough spots.

"You fell...into this cave?" He sounded skeptical at best as he raised a brow and cocked his head slightly to the side. His hair flopped over his brow. He brushed it back casually.

"Well, I did my best not to stutter. I speak my mind and mind what I speak. Old habits, you know," I answered letting irritation coat my voice. "Yes. As I just explained, I was running and then I fell from one cave system into this cave system. I've been wandering in the dark for about six hours now, if I had to guess. I can't see the sun...I don't know what time it is," I mused as I shook my head from side to side and pursed my lips.

"You can't see the sun? I suppose that's one way to tell time. A pocket watch is simpler. Are you from Neera, then?" he asked.

"No. That just happened to be where I was when I found the cave. Do you know where we are? You said I was on your land? Where might that be?" I questioned, though, I didn't need the answer. He was fae. I'd walked myself across the border somehow. I already knew I was either in the Summit or the Shallows.

The question I had now was could I get out. It seemed that anyone that passed over the treacherous mountains separating the human Kingdoms from the Agron Realm never returned. This cave must run right under the massive divide and swift river just over the territory lines. Crossing this divide had been easier than climbing up the sheer face of the cliffs surrounding the Summit. This was not good.

"I think you already know," he whispered. "I think, perhaps, you came on purpose. I just don't know the reason a seemingly human female would want to come here." He paused. "How is it you smell like and appear to be a human but you clearly have magic? I saw the tendrils of light you released and you're clearly producing a ball of light, both of which are inherently fae."

"Ask me no questions and I'll tell you no lies," I quipped. *Don't think about it. Ouch!* A zing shot down my back again and I adjusted my necklace. That'd been my strategy for as long as I could remember. I in fact *couldn't remember*. I'd been a slave at the kings castle in the Torrent Kingdom and I was forced to drink a potion every morning and evening for as long as I could think back. I always felt foggy and listless for awhile afterward. It dimmed me and made it so that I had no choice other than to do as I was told. *I was weak. I was nothing. They told me daily. They were right.*

"Okay." The frustration was heavy in his voice. "What's your name then? You could tell me that at least. I'm Uriah, I think if we work together we may be able to get above ground."

"They call me Raven," I stared at him for a moment. *Unusual name. Uriah...I know that name.* A trickle of sweat ran down his forehead onto his brow. We were both drenched. "Did the cave split anywhere from the direction you came? Mine has been a straight shot, so short of walking six hours back to explore the other side of the cave in, I don't think there's an exit behind me."

"Hello Raven. That's an interesting name. To answer your question, yes. There was a split a ways back behind me. I thought I'd heard noises so I came this way to see what it might be."

"Brave of you..." I remarked. He smirked at my reply, both of his eyebrows rising at my tenacity. He had a handsome face, clearly clean shaven, with a strong chin and high cheekbones. His skin was light and I could just make out a few freckles across the bridge of his straight nose. The light I had conjured was too dim to see his hair color, but it looked dark in the faded light. His shaggy hair was cut short at the nape of his neck. *I thought all fae wore their hair long?*

"Perhaps you'd like to accompany me? We can go to the split and see if there's a way out. Unless, of course, you'd rather stay down here, in the dark, with this oppressive heat." He turned slightly and put a hand out as an invitation to walk forward. *Friend?* It was at that moment I realized he had wings. They blended into the darkness surrounding us, just the slightest shimmer showing their full width. *Why does that seem familiar?*

He had them tucked tightly close to his body. I hadn't even seen them until he'd turned and then they faded into the pitch black of the cave surrounding us. Flawless. Beautiful. *Like a dream from long ago.* Something made my heart ache at the sight. *How strange?*

Chapter 2

Uriah

She slowly stepped toward me. Tentative. Alert. On Guard. Smart, but odd. She looked human but had magic. There's more to this I haven't seen yet. Perhaps she was half fae? She was short and thicker than the fae females I was surrounded by daily. They were all stick thin and bony, tall. Boring. Not that it mattered much since, I wasn't looking. My betrothed had been taken as a child. I didn't want anyone else. She never had the chance to grow into a female I could truly love, but the idea of something so precious being stolen from me, our future being snuffed out in an instant, hurt my soul.

Arabella was stolen by her nanny in the middle of the night, mere days before her fourth birthday. The Meadows manor in the North had been bathed in blood. Half the staff were murdered and left wherever they had been. She was never seen again. Gone! Not a hide nor hair of her to be found. Her bed had been soaked in blood, enough to leave her drained. The only other fae unaccounted for was her caretaker Everlee. Her bags had been hastily packed, but left behind. I was fourteen and the memory still wakes me nearly every night. My dreams for the future turned into nightmares.

The memory of the messenger coming in the dead of night to tell my father the tragedy still haunted me. He'd ridden straight through—a two day journey. Our family's opportunity to secure the crown was taken from us as well. It was a double blow, but I cared more about Arabella, our future and what we would become for the realm.

She had been delightful, alert and intelligent from the

time she could walk. Advanced, even for fae who matured in the mind before their bodies could catch up. Everything seemed to come easy for her. I never looked at her as more than a growing female at the time. She was a child, but over time, she would have been my wife. I delighted in watching her play her harp, she'd been a natural. She loved to climb trees and swim in the pond on her father's estate. She was funny and quick witted for barely more than a toddler. Arabella was mature for her age. She was left alone far too much.

It's been twenty one years, and I still wonder. The King is still in his prime, nowhere close to relinquishing the throne, but the Lord of Meadows refused to remarry after the death of his mate. The agreements behind the arrangements were meant to stand. He had to yield his seat as Lord of Meadows to a new family line or produce another female heir.

After he was forced to remarry a decade ago, he had his newest child, Arianna. She is supposed to replace what was taken from us. A child, for fuck's sake, and they expected me to marry her, bed her. *She's only six, the sick fucks.* By the time she turns eighteen, I'll be forty seven. The thought turned my stomach. The nearly ten year gap between Arabella and I had taken some getting used to. As a child myself, it was easier to stomach then.

I'd been enthralled the moment I met her. She'd only been a day old, her beautiful little feathered wings tucked gently under her. As she grew, her hair had darkened and turned into soft ringlets cascading down her back between her wings. I spent a week at her estate every season. The idea was we would grow accustomed to each other, even if it was only platonic given the age gap.

I shake my head to clear the errant thoughts. I hadn't thought of Arabella in awhile. Shame washed over me. She was supposed to be my best friend, then my bride. My love. Mine. *Stolen.*

"How is it you made that ball of light?" I asked as our footsteps drew even. She smelled of cinnamon and strawberries. *That's an odd combination. Where have I scented that before?* She held the light out in front of her, illuminating the way a little at a time as we began to walk back the way I'd come.

I didn't want to tell her the branch I'd seen was about a two hour walk back. She hadn't asked, but the omission may get me in trouble. She seemed like a fire ball. *Quick witted.* Her scythe looked well used and she was clearly dressed for engaging in hand to hand combat. A dagger was strapped to her thigh in clear reach.

She looked up to my face. She was tiny. I noticed she lifted her hand higher to illuminate my face better, gauging me. She's every bit a warrior in her own right. *I wonder what her cause is? Who does she fight for?* I bent my head forward, waiting for a response. She was calculating, and I could see the gears grinding through her mind. *Tell him, don't tell him.* This was turning into an interesting day.

"It's just something I figured out how to do when I was younger. I needed light. I wished for it over and over again and suddenly, I had it," she said thoughtfully. "You're not bothered by it? The darkness, I mean? How were you navigating with no light source?"

"No. The darkness doesn't bother me. My shadows guide me. I can't see minute details, however, I can see big shapes clear enough," I replied. She paused mid step, and her brow crinkled as if in deep thought again. *What's that look for?* I wanted to reach over and smooth it out, but I stopped myself. *Hands to yourself. She might bite.* Instead, I tilted my head to the side. "Do you know any other magic? I can't say I've ever come across someone so very *human* in appearance that could wield a fae light." *If she is human.*

"That's a very personal question," she began walking again speeding up a bit. Silence fell around us as we walked through the cave. After about five minutes, she volunteered, "I've found that I can do several things, should a *true* need arise. It's rarely the same thing twice and only with dire need.

14

It tends to...creep people out if I'm around anyone when it happens. So, I try to limit when it occurs. I have a fair bit of control over some things, like light, generally speaking." She lifted the ball of light in her hand. "Most of the time, I even surprise myself."

Interesting. *This girl is a mystery.* "Can I ask for an example other than the ball of light? I'll volunteer one for you. I wield shadows. I can manipulate them to bring me things, tell me secrets they hear whispered in the wind..."

"That's technically three..." Raven's voice trailed off as she raised an eyebrow. I noticed then, that her nose had a small crystal piercing in the left side. Taking in more of her appearance, she also had several piercings in her rounded ears and she wore a leather cord around her neck, the pendant resting on her cleavage. She kept tugging on the necklace as if it were uncomfortable. She was well proportioned, and it was becoming difficult *not* to notice. *Maybe she's not a warrior?* Piercings were easily ripped out in hand to hand combat so most avoided them if they engaged regularly.

We were walking side by side now. The cave was open just enough that neither of us were in danger of smashing into anything in the semi darkness. Her fae light bobbed with each step, and she added, "Like I said, it comes with need. I needed light once and I figured out how to get it. I've wished to find objects before, like say, a knife or rope, and they've suddenly appeared in my hand, although that never works for things like food or water." She licked her lips. They were dry. I could see it now. She'd been down here for hours. *Perhaps she isn't lying about running from men.*

"I see, it's a handy bit of magic, but there are magical laws. That's why food won't appear, and, for water to appear you have to have had the gift passed down to you," I said, pulling a canteen out of a void in the air.

I could store things in a small pocket of space in the *between*. The between was a magical tear in the folds of time, devoid of substance where one could keep something almost infinitely if it lay undisturbed. The more magic a fae had, the bigger their void could be in the between. My magic was stronger alone than some of the more prominent families altogether, even I could no longer do some of the things I'd grown up doing while core magic in our world dissipated. My father had always warned me against the give and take of our magic. *Use it or lose it. The fools that ignore their calling will be the death of us.*

At thirty five, I shouldn't have to worry about such things, but here we are. As I offered her the canteen, I blurted, "You're looking at me like I have two heads. It's only water, nothing more. With the heat down here, I'm sure you need it." She continued to stare at me as I unfastened the top of it and took a deep draw. "I promise I mean you no harm."

She nodded, took the canteen, and sniffed it. She was intelligent indeed. Not having sensed anything by smell, she took a tiny taste, and then she waited a moment. *Very smart, indeed.* Having had no ill effect from the small taste, she said, "Thank you. Forgive me for checking. I found that those who say they mean me no harm generally mean to do the most harm to me." She took a deep draw off the canteen. She clearly did not want to take all of it, but she needed to hydrate some of what she'd lost. A pang of worry struck me. *Now who's being odd? Why do I care if she's hydrated?*

"That's quite a statement coming from someone appearing so young. Does your family not look after you?" It might be a bold question, but perhaps she'll answer it.

"I look after myself." Her brow pinched together again, assessing me. "How far until the split off?"

"Ah, that's the question, isn't it? Well, we've been walking for say, thirty minutes? So probably, hmm, I mean to say, that is…" I began rambling like an idiot. *Will she be angry I've led her further from her home? Why am I so nervous?!*

"There *is* a branch in the path? Another tunnel or section to the cave this way?" She sounded slightly alarmed.

"Yes! Yes. There is. My apologies. It is a bit further perhaps an hour walk if we stay brisk. From there, it's another two hours to the way I came in or we can take the branch and see where we end up," I say quickly. *Fuck. I'm an idiot. She's kind of fun to be around, and I'm going to mess it all up. But why do I care?* The thoughts plagued my conscience. The look on her face is murderous.

"So, were you just hoping I wouldn't notice that we were walking and walking without a seeming end to this... darkness?" She asked incredulously. "Congratulations. My middle finger wants to give you a standing ovation." My mouth dropped open, then closed. "Right. Okay. And what happens when we find a way out? We shake hands and go on our merry way?" she mused. *Mad, she's definitely angry, but she's got some sass. Interesting.* She tugged on her necklace again.

"In theory that would be the idea." *I need to proceed cautiously.* "I must admit though, I find you rather amusing to talk to, even when you threaten crude gestures." I shot a lopsided smile at her. "I dare say I may want to chat a bit longer. Assuming we come out where I think we will, you may want to rest before you try to journey back to Neera. I'll offer accommodation in my estate, of course," I finished. She stopped dead in her tracks.

"Why?" She looked me in the eye, or what she could see of my eyes through the pale fae light ensconcing us.

"I just told you. I'm enjoying talking to you. I don't meet many new people, fae or human, and you, my dear, are quite an enigma." *She seems so familiar. I need to know. I can't let her leave until I have answers.* "And after the day we've both had, rest would be wise. There's a pass into the Daemon Kingdom that I can show you, but it tends to be quite a hike. Starting fresh tomorrow would be the safest way. Night will likely be nearly upon us by the time we get out of here as well." My heart was pounding in my throat. How did I bring the conversation here? Why? *Shut up, moron! I'll scare her away if I come on too heavy.*

Chapter 3

Raven

"I'm an enigma? That's why you offered me water and now accommodations? Are you sure you didn't just want to use the fancy word?" I huffed a laugh. *All men want is sex. If he thinks he'll get me back to his house just to fuck me, then he has another thing coming to him.* "Okay, we met less than an hour ago. Let's just say we don't owe each other anything and get out of this mess. From there I can get myself back to…" I trailed off. I didn't really have anywhere to go but that wasn't the point. I appreciated the water. *Needed* the water even. This male fae was over the top too nice. *What is his deal? Is he just trying to get laid? He keeps staring at my ass.*

"I'm sorry if that's off putting. I can't say I've ever met anyone in a circumstance such as this. I suppose I don't know the formality, if any, about the next step. That said, I can feel the exhaustion rolling off you in waves. Even keeping a fae light going is costing you. It's to my benefit as well for you to 'keep the light on' so to speak. I don't have the ability to make one, and even seeing the big things coming with my limited vision in the dark, navigation is difficult. More so, we can't both see through my shadows. I could guide you along in the dark but I expect you'd rather me not touch you. So, as a compromise, I'm proposing I provide you shelter while you recuperate before you try to travel whence you've come," Uriah replied. He loosened a big breath.

Huh. A kind fae. Maybe he's not trying to get in my pants. This guy is hard to read. At least at first glance. Today was certainly a break in monotony. "I guess I can consider it. I'll reserve an answer until after I see where we come out. I can usually shift a decent distance, so pass or no pass, getting back shouldn't be a problem. Although when I tried to shift myself out of the cave, it wouldn't work. Perhaps there are wards at play here," I confessed giving him a side glace as we continued on. *Maybe it was wards. Shifting through time and space, from one location to another, took concentration and a push of magic. Maybe I'm just to tired?*

He looked at me, deeper, more focused than before in the dim light. *Tell me your secrets big boy. I know you have them.* Choosing to ignore the inquiry about wards he asked, "You can shift? That's... are you fae?" Uriah asked, seeming to ignore everything else I just said.

"If we're being honest, I don't know what I am. I was raised in the Torrent Kingdom as an orphan servant of sorts. I was given minimal orders and expected to keep my mouth shut and work. Questions were forbidden and when I broke that rule, well, the consequences were harsh," I divulged. *Don't tell him that. What are you doing? Get his secrets, don't spill your own.*

I immediately didn't know why I said it. *What is wrong with me?!* The tug increased in my middle as I turned toward Uriah, but it had stopped pulling me when we began walking together. The water he shared had been clean. I know he didn't slip me anything. He drank it too. I didn't know him but I was sharing far more than I ought to. What was *I* thinking?

The two of us fell into an awkward silence as we continued walking for a few more minutes. The sand was making my calves burn with the effort. After awhile, Uriah asked, "Why were the men chasing you?"

"What?" I asked, confused for a moment. "Ah, you caught that," I said, catching up. Our earlier conversation had come back to haunt me. I absentmindedly tugged on the leather cord holding my pendant again. "I was running from the men because..." *Well, shit, how do I answer that?* My voice trailed off as I sighed a long deep sigh. "Do you really need to know?" He shot me a curious look, his brow arching high. "Never mind, you wouldn't have asked if you didn't." *How should I phrase this?* "I'm a debt collector of sorts. I collected a debt, and they didn't appreciate my efforts."

He returned my side eye glance, not stopping this time, "Collected a debt. Like an overdue return, or like stole something back for someone?"

"Stole is a bit of a strong word. I mean, are you really a thief if you've never been prosecuted?" I deflected. He didn't catch my meaning by 'debt collector' and I wasn't sure if I wanted to widen his knowledge of me yet. That, and getting caught is half the crime. "I think at this point we're what, an hour and a half into this shin dig? You haven't attempted to hurt me, and I have no intention of hurting you, does it really matter what we do for a living?"

"When you put it that way, I suppose not," he conceded. He stiffened suddenly, turning to look over his shoulder while he reached for my right arm. "I need you to trust me," he whispered. "Step to me, and put the light out for a moment."

"What? Why?" I asked. Alarm bells began ringing in my mind. We were being watched. I could feel it. Less light was not going to help us. The hair on the back of my neck rose, and a tingle of awareness ran down my sweaty back in my tight leather top, I glanced over my shoulder. My eyes flared in alarm as red eyes peered at us from a ways back. I reached for my khopesh, but I was too slow.

Uriah acted quickly. He grabbed the ball of light from my hand and chucked it as hard as he could behind us. His arm wrapped around my waist, and he pulled me into him. My hands flew up and rested between us on his shoulders. Somehow, the darkness became darker, solid, like we were wrapped in a cocoon. It was cooler than the hot and humid cave.

His damp skin was smooth, his chest hard and sculpted. My top had shifted as he spun me and my cleavage bulged, pressing against him. The sweat dripped off both of us. I should probably be disgusted, except there was—something consolatory about him as goose bumps broke out across my flesh. And his scent, cedar wood and fresh salt air. He smelled of a campfire on the beach. I tried to step back and felt my back press into his velvety soft wings. *We are in a cocoon.*

He spun us so his back was to the creature and I was pressed against the wall of the cave. A heartbeat later, his wings unwrapped us, and he drew his sword as he stepped back, ready to fight off the threat. My magic was weak. I was dehydrated as well as missing a few meals, with no light, I don't know how much help I could be in the pitch black darkness of the cave.

I could see nothing except those red, glowing eyes moving closer to us. The growl that ripped through the air tore the breath from my lungs. Pain seared through me as I slammed myself back against the cave wall. I heard Uriah's sword swing through the air and a guttural scream followed. Slicing and hacking sounds filled the cave tunnel. The red eyes slowly began to dim as the growl turned into a whimper before going silent. Just then, two more pairs of eyes appeared.

It felt like a disadvantage to slam my light into them. It would blind Uriah. I could hear him swing over and over making contact with each blow he mustered, a dance with death in the dark. The sounds flitted around, as if he was moving from side to side in an attempt to maneuver around them without being boxed in. I froze in fear. Adrenaline was pumping wildly through my veins, willing me to try to help him.

I knew I was clearly at a disadvantage with the lack of sight. Still, I tried to stay present, pulling my khopesh with my left hand and my dagger with my right. I took a battle stance, widening my feet and planting myself.

I couldn't see Uriah, but what I could see was a last pair of eyes moving closer. Another growl sounded closer to me yet. I heard a slash through the air, and another pair of glowing eyes dimmed. Uriah was fast and steady, strong. He made fast work of eliminating the threat, but I could not see it in the darkness. The last pair of eyes dimmed, a gurgled whine cutting off at the same time.

I jumped when his hand found my wrist. "Are you ok?" I whispered into the darkness. I could smell the rusty scent of blood in the thick air. I didn't know if it belonged to the beasts or him. "I can't see anything. Are you injured?" I was shaking. Unusual for me, but I didn't like the dark and had never encountered whatever the hell those things had been. I shuddered. *Get it together! You are not weak!*

"No, I'm not injured. I can see in the dark, remember? Those were cadfiends. We used to practice with them when I was younger since we seem to constantly be at war, and they make a good practice opponent. They tend to travel in packs of three, so we should be ok now, but where one pack is, others will follow. We shouldn't linger. The smell of the blood will draw more—" He hesitated a moment. I suspected he scented my fear.

"The light would have blinded me to most of their movements. That's why I tossed it. I'm pretty sure it shattered on impact. Can you make another, Raven?" he inquired as he pulled my dagger out of my hand and slid it home in my thigh holster. I felt the air stir in front of me. He was going for my khopesh next. I sheathed it myself before he could touch it.

I lifted my now empty hand and called for light. A new ball formed in my hand, illuminating us once again, only it was dimmer than before. My body was exhausted from the days activities. I was shaking with the effort of holding my arm up. Uriah tentatively reached out and brushed his calloused hand down my other arm from my shoulder to my elbow, giving a soft squeeze of reassurance. An electric warm tingle spread where his fingers traced. *That was odd.*

I heard my stomach growl. I needed to eat. "Are you hungry? I ran out of water long ago, I still have some food..." My voice trailed off as he looked down at me. His brow furrowed again, and concern etched along his face. I glanced past him and could just make out a heap of sinew and bloody bones. The cadfiends were close. I need to distract myself before I fall apart. *Focus on something.*

Uriah cut them down and wasn't even winded from the effort. Here I stood, shaking when I'd done nothing to even help him except cower against the wall. Sure, I'd drawn my blades, but what good were they if I didn't use them?

"I could use a snack, but you should eat. That light is much dimmer than before. We need to get you out of here." He observed me as he spoke. I felt off and I couldn't place it. I felt like my magic was wilder than before entering the cave, unpredictable. Something was upsetting it. It was taking a lot of effort to control, and it was making me weaker by the minute. *This place gives me the creeps.*

I gave him a hard look, contemplating. *Guess I'm sharing more secrets. But I need to eat. I won't be on my feet much longer if I don't.* I steeled myself then I opened a void in the air. I'd discovered I could hide things in plain sight once when I was in King Plavlock's castle and had stolen food to eat. I could hear someone coming down the hall to the kitchen where I worked, and I wished for a place to hide it, but I was chained to the wall with no where to go. It opened with my need.

I concentrated on opening my void. I stashed things like food, clothes, books, and anything else I needed in there. Since I was always on the move, it was easier to use a bit of magic then it was to be caught with no supplies. I reached in and using the fae light, grabbed the last two apples I had. The juice would help hydrate us as well. I should have eaten one earlier, clearly I wasn't thinking straight.

"You can open a void too? That's definitely a fae thing. You said you didn't know what you were? You're an orphan? Did you ever know your parents?" He looked at me—clearly confused. My utterly human appearance and absolute fae abilities were always a juxtaposition. It threw off the people I came into contact with. *Don't think about it.*

On one hand, I was a petite female, appearing weak and

soft; on the other, I could rip someone's heart out of their chest without even physically touching them. I just had to bid my magic to do it. The dichotomy was strange at best.

I failed just now. I could've taken down all three cadfiends if I'd been alone and needed to. I don't know what it would have cost me. Every bit of magic was a trade, price had to be paid to use it, but in the right circumstance, it was worth it. Energy was always sacrificed so, I would have had just enough to protect myself. *This time. I need to sleep.* I shifted my weight and offered Uriah the larger of the two apples. "No, you need to eat. I'll take the smaller," he stated, accepting the apple. He scrutinized me for a moment, as if not sure he should eat his apple.

I nodded and took a bite. "I don't remember," I said simply as I shrugged my shoulders. "But yes, obviously I can open a void. It's handy."

He bit into his apple. A line of juice ran down his chin, and he wiped it away as we began walking again. We moved swifter this time, both of us more alert, knowing more cadfiends would eventually make their way through. He nodded his head as he chewed. "You don't remember, or you don't want to tell me?"

"A bit of both," I admitted. "Mostly, I don't remember. There's flashes of things, but not much that makes sense. I was little when I began working in King Plavlock's castle. I remember being in the dark, alone and cold for a long time. It felt like forever, but I don't know the true time I spent in the dark. After what seemed to be ages, they put me in the kitchen to work. I remember the dress I wore no longer fit. I was given a flour sack to wear instead. I had to peel the potatoes, make bread, and do whatever grunt work they needed. Then I was excused to go to sleep until it was time to work again. Rinse and repeat. That was my life until my magic grew and began to truly form, and the potion they forced down my throat every day stopped working."

"They drugged you?" Uriah looked at me, the outrage and

anger heaving in his voice as he continued. "So, you were a child at their mercy and they knew to nullify your powers? But you don't remember anything before that?"

"Just wild flowers, and then the dark. I figured out how to summon the ball of light in the dark. It wasn't long after they moved me to the kitchen and made me drink a purple potion every day in the morning and evening," I said before shaking my head. *Why do I keep telling him things? Stop it. It was so long ago. It doesn't matter anymore.* "It was a long time ago, so whatever I am really doesn't matter anymore. I'm just me. For better or worse, that's all I can be."

Chapter 4

Uriah

"You don't truly believe that, do you? You matter. Your powers matter! This world is dying. The *magic* is dying! Every ounce that remains is important. It can be restored; there just has to be balance. It's always give and take. The problem is when we began taking more than we gave. You don't strike me as someone that takes more than necessary. I know we've just met today, but you seem grounded, and rational. Those traits are hard to find anymore. I'm almost certain you're fae too, if not wholly, then at least half. You've held onto a fae light for almost eight hours. That's an immense feat, not to mention the tendril of light you shot out earlier." I paused, not sure what to say next. *Do I divulge? She's shared with me.*

"That was why I came down here. A cord of light appeared in front of me while I was training with my advisors. I followed it, and found the mouth of a cave I never realized existed. Then I found you," I said. She paused. I saw fear flit across her face before she carefully tucked it away and schooled her expression.

"That was quite the confession. You waited this long to tell me. Why tell me at all?" Raven asked, shaking her head, her brow pinching together again. She took a bite of her apple, chewing thoughtfully. She really was lovely. Her hair was braided above her head, fashioned into a crown. I could see it now, a crown upon her head. She was royalty incarnate. I'd never been interested in anyone. I shut that part of me down after Arabella disappeared, vowing to honor her memory until my duty was established for me and I was forced to marry. But with Raven, there was something familiar about her, the wisp of a dream.

"Why tell you? Because you'd figure it out on your own eventually, for starters. Other than that, we're nearly to the branch out. We can take that path, and I'll join you. We can see where it leads together. But, I'm hoping you'll consider just coming back with me the way I came," *It couldn't be, could it? After so long...* I held still as I heard her breath catch. *Too fast. Give her time, she's skittish.* I looked at her. Really looked at her. *So familiar. Maybe, but how?*

"What purpose would I come back with you for? I know you offered accommodations, however, I haven't decided to accept them, as generous as they sound. I can't deny my powers are stunted down here, but I fully believe when I'm in open air again, they'll regain their potency." She relaxed her breath again, breathing normal. "As much as I appreciate what you did back there, please make no mistake that push come to shove, I can protect myself."

"I have no doubt about that," I assured her. "And I can't deny that my motives are partly selfish. I'd like to learn more about you. Perhaps we could share a meal, talk awhile longer. See each other in proper light, not this dim faelight."

"This was a meal," Raven said, waving her apple core. She smirked, tilting her head again. She wasn't outright saying no to my advances. *Go slow. You can win her over. Talk her into spending more time. Get the answers.* She shook her head. "Look, Uriah, I'm sure you're a nice fae. You seem fair from what I've gathered, and you've shown me kindness that many wouldn't consider, especially for a stranger. The thing is, companions aren't something I entertain. I tend to keep a solitary life, and I'm not interested in changing that."

Ouch. She's a tough cookie. Keep trying. "Okay, I'm not asking you to. Just maybe consider staying a few days. I can provide a private suite. I'll instruct that no one is to bother you. Who you see, or don't, can be on your terms. Perhaps I can help you unravel the mystery of your past," I prodded. *I keep putting my foot in my mouth, why stop now?*

We reached the opening of the intersection between the two tunnels. She looked at me but didn't speak. Sadness weighed on her face. Lifting her left hand, she said, "Point me." Tendrils of golden light swirled from her outstretched palm. I'd never seen such magic, and it was utterly beautiful. Majestic. The cord of light started down the entrance to the tunnel where she'd shot it then curved back. It weaved itself between my back and my wings, then looped around her.

As it encircled us, it began to glow brighter. The sheer shock on her face made me freeze. "Oh," she muttered. I swear if I could see better, she would be flushed pink.

The light slowly started to fade as I stepped closer to her. She turned to face me. She was *really* looking at me for the first time, clearly surprised but also curious. "I'm not sure what that means," she said as she tipped her chin to look up at me more fully. This time, my breath caught, the desire to touch her burning within me. *I wonder what she tastes like?*

"I have an idea, but I wouldn't want to tell you how you're supposed to feel," I whispered. The tendril of light was still swirling around us. My shadows latching on and clinging to it as it dissipated. The light was fading, but the feeling left in its absence was undeniable. We'd both been called here. I reached forward and gently tipped her chin up to a better angle, and my fingers tingled where they met her silky smooth skin. The magnetism between us heightened.

She licked her lips, the indecision clear on her face. The internal battle was written on her expression. *She believes all fae to be monsters. Fucking humans. How much have they distorted her thinking? Will she let me show her the truth? Will she believe me? Will she trust the bond?*

Her eyes flickered to my lips for just a moment. I leaned down to her. Our lips were barely apart, apple scented breaths playing on each others faces. I looked into her eyes. *What color are they?* I couldn't see them well in the dim light. Everything had a washed out hue to it. I waited. This would be her decision. *Please, let me be right.*

"Uriah," Raven whispered, "There are several sets of red eyes watching us." Her voice trembled. At that moment the cave exploded with movement. Teeth gnashed and claws ripped as a cadfiend slammed into me, rattling my bones, as I grunted with the effort of shoving it back. Her fae light dropped to the ground.

I heard her khopesh leave its sheath just as I drew my own sword, rebounding on instinct after the impact. Tendrils of light snaked out into the darkness toward the red eyes. She couldn't see well enough to advance on our new enemy, but she could send her magic. I watched as she quickly sent a cord of light bursting towards the beasts and wrapped around a cadfiends neck. It sliced as it tightened. The glow in its eyes snuffed out.

I swung my sword at another as it lunged for us, slicing it clear through the middle. I felt the spray of the blood as my blade cut. Blood and guts flooded the small area, sinking into the sandy bottom. I rebounded and quickly lashed out at another. Raven and I guarded each other's back as we fought in the close space of the light.

Her fae light rolled around on the ground. We were both doing our best not to crush it so she could see in the pitch black cave. She sent out more tendrils of light while I called for my shadows to strangle one beast as I swung at another. I heard the sickly wet splat of her blade as she slashed into a beast. It's whimper and whine echoed in the barely widened cavern.

As suddenly as everything started, it stopped. Heaps of flesh surrounded us. I'm not even sure how many we killed. We'd made a good pair and took them down efficiently. I'm not sure she would ever stop surprising me. *A warrior indeed. She's so petite. I'd never expect how brutal her attack was.*

Breathless she said, "Which is the shorter way out of here, do you think?"

"The way I came is probably another hour and half, maybe two hours that way," I said, pointing to the entrance on the left.

"This one," I continued to say while waving my sword to the right, blood splattering in the dim light. "I've never been down. If I had to guess knowing the geography in the area, it should open up in the Southern tip of the Summit mountains. So, I'd wager maybe a forty five minute walk if we move quickly." *Fuck. There goes that moment. I should have kissed her.* "Are you injured?" I concluded. We were both now covered in gore. *Great. Maybe she'd let me help her wash it off.*

"Just a scratch. Are you ok?" she asked for the second time today. She wiped her sickle on her pants and bent to pick up the fae light. As she turned to bend down I saw the claw marks raking down her left arm. We both sheathed our weapons.

"I'm fine. Let me see your arm,"I said. As I stepped toward her, she stepped back. *Uh oh.* "Please, let me heal it." I held my hands palm up, also for a second time today. She had to see I wouldn't hurt her, *couldn't* hurt her now that I knew what she was to me. *She doesn't understand what just happened.* This was getting confusing. I froze, letting her think for a moment. *Space. She'll need a fair bit of space.*

Finally, after several heart beats she stepped forward. The air felt different inches away from each other. Electricity charged the air, buzzing between us. Our magic was blending, and there would be no stopping it.

I gently turned her upper left arm in my hands, letting my healing magic loose. It caressed and sunk into her flesh as it knitted the wounds closed. Her skin slowly stopped weeping. Her blood smelled sweet, every drop precious. A tightness pulled in my chest at the thought that I had allowed her to be injured. I was too focused on the beasts I'd taken down. I didn't watch enough to help her as she fought. I should have been injured, not her.

After a few moments her skin was finished knitting back together. Her skin felt soft and smooth in my hands, and I could feel the strong muscle underneath. She looked soft and weak, but that was far from the case, a careful deception. From a quick glance, she wouldn't appear to be a threat, but if she wanted to, she could inflict great damage –a perfect weapon. The tension in my shoulders eased. She didn't need me to protect her. She could do that on her own.

"Thank you," Raven whispered. Her voice squeaked out. I opened the void and pulled out the canteen, offering it to her first. She accepted it from me and took a long pull. Thankfully, I had filled it before entering the cave; it was still half full. She gave me a delicate smile and handed it back. "Thank you for that too." She tipped her head to the side and watched me as I took a drink next. *What is she thinking? Does she understand that our magic just bonded?* I made sure to place my lips exactly where hers had been. It might be the only taste of her I got.

"So," I said as I tucked the canteen away, "left or right? I'll leave it up to you."

We were still standing close together. I could feel her breath, calmer now, caressing my bare chest. I was half naked and felt entirely too clothed. *Please. Come home. Please.* "To the right," she answered. I sighed, trying not to give away too much of my disappointment, and started to turn. Resignation was forming like a lead ball in my gut. "Let's see what's down there." She took a step and stopped, reaching for my arm.

Her hands were tiny. She slid her left hand down my right forearm to my hand. Holding it and giving me a small squeeze. "Maybe we'll learn something new." *That's not a no. Maybe I'm not forsaken after all.* I squeezed her hand back, and we started walking in silence. My thoughts were racing and my stomach had turned itself inside out.

We were still hand in hand a half hour later, picking our way through the cave. The path was no longer loose sand. Instead, stalactites and stalagmites littered the way slowing us down. She'd lost her balance a couple times, so now I was determined to keep hold of her. Every time she slipped, she apologized. The light twang of fear lacing through her voice made anger rise in me. She was obviously worried I'd say something about the clumsiness, but I wasn't angered about the blunder. Instead raw ire built for whoever made her feel like she needed to apologize for something like that.

A few minutes later we rounded a tight bend, and light fell from the sky, the cave finally lightening. "Well, look at that!" I exclaimed as cold fresh air washed over us. What a relief. The heat had been relentless. There wasn't a spot on us that wasn't soaked in sweat.

She took a big breath, letting the cool air saturate her lungs. We entered a clearing as we exited the mouth of the cave. I'd never noticed this entrance either. It was covered by heavy vegetation. We picked through the bracken and stepped into a small meadow. The meadow was ripe with wild flowers and, encircled by heavy forest. We were deep in the Southern edge of the Summit, and cliff faces surrounded us on all but one side where the river flowed.

The cut off of my boundary was not far from here. "That must be the Couloir river," I guessed pointing to the deep water running on the right of the meadow. It was very deep in spots and rather wide with varying depth of canyon surrounding it. It served as a natural border.

This side had a gentle slope to the embankment. Across the river rose a sheer cliff with a hundred foot incline straight up.

Raven released my hand. It immediately felt too empty but I let her go. She walked across the meadow to the river bank and sank to her knees. Her hair was copper and the sun shining on it highlighted gold strands. Her leather top was a sandy brown and looked nice against her porcelain skin.

It'd been torn fighting the cadfiends. I could see the slashes across her shoulder, though she didn't appear to be injured anymore, old scars were visible. She was so fair. I joined her and knelt beside her, taking in her lush curves. The amount of scars her body carried was not lost on me. The faint white lines were prominent enough to make my gut twist again. *I'll kill whoever harmed her.*

Scooping water into our hands, we sloshed it about ourselves to wash off the blood from the cadfiends we'd decimated. "That's better. So much better," Raven said as she turned to me with a brilliant smile on her face. She closed her hazel eyes and turned her face to the sun filled September sky. After washing myself, I leaned forward on my knees.

"Is Raven really your name?" I had to know.

"It's what I've always been called for as long as I can remember. So I suppose that would make it my name." She looked at me, confused.

"How old are you?" I asked. My heart was going to beat out of my chest. I couldn't believe my eyes. *How is it so?* I needed confirmation.

"I'm not sure to be honest. I don't know when I was born. No one at the castle knew, and the one time I asked...well, let's just say I never bothered to ask again." Her brow pinched together again. Her hazel eyes found my own. I knew those eyes. I'd dreamed of them often and wished for them to find their way home. I nodded.

"Raven, how did you get the scars on your back? I can just make them out from the edge of your shirt. There, on your shoulders?" I asked gently, barely more than a whisper. She stood up abruptly. *Fuck.*

"I..." She stuttered and shook her head while taking two steps back. "I've always had them." A tear slid down her cheek, and her voice cracked as she answered. She took another step back. Her already pale face had gone even whiter.

"Arabella." I let the name hang on the breeze. "They may have called you Raven, all these years but your name is Arabella." I reached for her as I stood. My love, my betrothed, my fated mate stood mere feet in front of me. "You felt the magic that brought you back to me in the cave. I don't want to overwhelm you or scare you. You must understand, you belong here." I shifted on my feet.

I put my hand out, palm up, yet again. "Not where ever it is that they stole you away to. This is home. Don't you remember me? Uriah, heir to the Shallows. My father passed away two years ago. I'm Lord now. You were meant to be my

Lady."

"My name is Raven," she whispered, as more tears fell down her face and she took another step back. The pain etched into her furrowed brow broke my heart. *She doesn't know who she is anymore. She's tried to repress it.* Her breathing hitched as she gazed at me. Recognition snapped into place. She shook her head. The tears were solid streams pouring down her face now.

"Come home with me. They took twenty one years from us and they don't deserve a moment more," I pleaded as my voice broke.

"I can't," Arabella replied in a barely audible whisper. Agony ripped across her face. She turned and slipped into a shift, disappearing to where it was her heart desired to be. And then she was gone. Again. My heart, my love, my everything. Just...gone.

Chapter 5

Uriah

As soon as my feet hit the ground in the courtyard of my estate, I began bellowing, "Sebastian! Felix! Where are you?" I had to find her. I had her for hours at my finger tips and realized too late. *So funny and quit to wit. So beautiful. All her curves. She's missed some meals, but the way she is built. My Arabella, grown.* As soon as the sunlight washed over her face, the moment I could truly see her eyes, I knew she was mine despite the mating bond snapping when she used her magic in the cave.

My heart still broke at the thought of the scars where her beautiful little wings had been. They took her wings! *My Arabella. Alive.* All these years she'd been in the human lands. King Plavlock took her and locked her away in his castle. *Didn't we send in spies? Father said both kingdoms were thoroughly searched. How did we miss her?*

He cut off her wings. The agony whipped through me. *Wings are sacred. Blessed. Her beautiful wings. No wonder she lost who she was—her essence has been mutilated. The pain she went through. The shame she must still feel, that's the worse thing that could have happened to her, next to death. Her wings. She'll never get to fly, to feel the wind rush around her.*

My breath grew ragged, and I dropped to my knees. Nausea assaulted me. Full sobs broke free of my control. *What did they do to her? How long did they have her? What is keeping her there? There has to be a reason she would flee from me.* My body shook and my hands planted firmly in the sand of the courtyard. I vomited up the apple she'd given me. I'd been with her not ten minutes before. The horror on her face as she shifted away from me was palpable. *I can't. Not I don't want to. I can't.*

She may be free to move around on her own but something was holding her. *Or someone? There has to be a reason. I'll find it and get her to come back to the Agron Realm. She belongs with the fae, with me. I can protect her.* I know it. But what or who, and more importantly, where? My chest tightened, and the world spun. Sweat dripped down my nose into the sandy gravel.

Strong hands grasped my shoulder, and the sun blocked my face as Sebastian's chocolate brown eyes came into view. He knelt beside me, and placed a hand on my back, careful not to touch my wings. "My Lord? Are you injured? What happened?" The stench of blood filled the air from my soaked clothes.

He looked at Felix, who now knelt on the other side of me. Clear alarm plastered to his tanned face as he took in my half-naked sweaty body, vomit and gore all over me.

"Arabella." I gasped. My chest hurt, the bond pulling me back toward the cave. "I found Arabella. The cave we found scouting last week. I went to explore it this morning. She was trapped inside. She fell from another system running above from the human lands into the one leading to our realm. She doesn't know who she is anymore. She thinks she's named Raven. I tried to get her back here, but I spooked her. I came on too strong. Our mating bond snapped." I broke down, choking out the words.

"And the cadfiends…" I continued after another gasp. *We need to act!* My mind was wild with apprehension as I tried to explain everything to my two best friends.

"We ran into a few sets of them. And then when we left the cave, I could see her better in the sunlight. I could really see her and it's Arabella. She shifted away. She's… she's alive. She said she was held as a servant in Torrent. Every time I asked her anything about her past, she said she couldn't remember. All she could remember was darkness and then working in a kitchen." I choked out all I could remember from our conversations earlier in the day.

"She wields light! Beautiful, pure cords of light, like her father. We need to notify him immediately! We have to find her. She entered the other side of the cave in Neera, she was fleeing some threat. Something about collecting a debt and hiding in a cave to escape." I shook my head. "She wouldn't elaborate. We must send word across the realm that she has been found!. She's alive."

I looked at Felix, his dark brows raised and blue eyes wide. "Gather men and supplies. She fell into the cave from another cave running above. It's about a ten hour trek from to the cave system from here, and there's cadfiends running around in there. I want men ready to go in a half hours time. Bring extra water rations." I sat up, my nerves leveling out as I took control back of my body. A plan formulated in my mind.

"Explore any and all branches of the cave. Map them out, and get into the cave where it collapsed." I said as I settled into a crouch and began drawing a basic map in the sand to get them started.

"We need to find out what lies beyond the breach. Queen Clawin could likely bring her forces through it if she wished." I pointed to a figure I'd drawn as Sebastian leaned closer to my diagram.

"The cave is straight shot to both us and the Summit. Secure the line. I want soldiers posted twenty four hours a day. Break up teams so the whole line is occupied sporadically," I continued. "Take imbued fae lights. It's pitch black."

This was more than Arabella. As much as I wanted to focus solely on finding her again, getting her back, I couldn't. The entire realm was at risk. "I want a rider saddled and ready in fifteen minutes. He's to go to the King's Keep first, then on to the Meadows," I was up and moving now.

Sebastian and Felix trotted to keep up as I jogged along the path into my manor perched on a cliff over looking the sea. I'd had it built fifteen years prior. My father had lived in the

Western Shallows Estate.

When I'd grown older, I decided to build a second estate on the Eastern edge of the Shallows, closer to the front lines where I was needed. When my father died and I became Lord two years ago, I moved the seat of power to here, the Eastern Shallows Estate. It was more convenient and held less memories.

We raced down a hallway toward my office. "I'll draft a fast letter with the bullet points to get out." Sebastian was commander of my forces. He worked in tandem with my army and navy commanders to keep our affairs in order. He was shorter than most fae and stocky, a brute really. His short cropped strawberry blonde hair was unusual for a fae. He preferred to keep it short, as I did. I hated nothing more than having hair in my face while trying to swing a sword. It's impractical at best, stupid at worst. It was too easy to grab a fist full of hair in hand to hand.

Sebastian nodded, his stature serious. He Clearly understood the complexity of the situation and my fervor from years of experience and simply knowing me so well. He was calculating the information I'd just spewed at him as he rushed off. His body was rigid and moving quickly as he set off on his task.

Felix looked at me, eye to eye. "You're sure it was her?" he asked carefully as he adjusted his long dark brown braid over his shoulder so it lay down his muscled back. His piercing blue eyes were intense as he assessed what I was saying.

Felix was one of my best friends, as was Sebastian. We'd been raised as brothers. Felix headed my intelligence division, tasked with gathering and collecting information on the human lands to thwart them before they could do any real damage. Somehow he missed a whole tunnel system built and tapped into natural caves.

The human kingdom's had never breached the Summit mountain pass, but there was a first time for everything. The cave I explored today would be an easy entry point for a multitude of reasons.

The largest being that it opened to the Summit valleys on our side of the Couloir River, as well as Neera being a sea port. They could easily move in thousands of soldiers and swarm us. My navy was busy enough holding a cease fire line where the natural reef gave way for merchants. Most of the ships were a precaution. The humans had never been able to breach the wards by sea either.

I'd noticed Arabella—no, *Raven*—had her hair braided up. She was fierce, smart. What the years had done to her... *I have to find her again. She has to be okay.*

"Yes. I'm sure it was her. I think I jogged her memory of me too, whatever is left of it. She was such a small child when she was taken." I froze. *She was so small back then. Does she even remember me? I saw her as often as I could.*

"Our magic bonded," I began again, "as Zeds, foretold it would. I didn't understand what the *old seer* had meant when he said, 'her light will find the path and the bond will ignite in darkness.' I didn't recognize her immediately, all grown up and in the pitch black cave, but after talking to her for awhile and touching her..."

I paused, remembering. *She was so delicate, her skin so smooth and velvety.* "I could feel the bond growing –the attraction building, and then she used her magic as a compass. Only it didn't show her the way out as she requested. It wrapped itself around us and solidified the mating bond. We were attacked by cadfiends, and it ruined the moment," I huffed an exasperated laugh. "Fucking cadfiends." *I should have kissed her. I should have taken the chance.*

"The second we exited the cave and I could see her fully, with her hazel eyes, and copper hair. I knew for sure then. She looks a bit like her father, but her voice is more like I remember her mother's." I half mumbled to myself as I picked through my desk.

"She has a spotty memory, it tracks; she wasn't quite four when she was taken. Doesn't matter, she's my fated mate. The magic has spoken regardless. I *will* find her. The magic calls for it, and our world depends on it," I paused as I began writing on a sheet of stationary.

"They broke her. They cut off her wings and broke her spirit. She's a fighter though, quick with a blade and somehow she's been trained with her magic. Or maybe she figured it out on her own. She's lethal, prudent but still kind in her own way. She contemplated everything she said before she said it. She's not rash. There has to be a valid reason she ran from me. I just have to find out what it is."

I finished jotting down the events of the day quickly. I stacked another sheet of stationary on top of the first and let my shadows wash over it, drawing a copy onto the top sheet with my magic. It would have to do.

"Excuse me sir," a young fae with long brown hair said from the door way. "You requested a rider, urgent delivery?"

"Yes, take one of these to the Agron Keep. Tell them you need to place it in King Astros' hand directly. Request an urgent audience, as ordered by the Lord of Shallows." I paused and looked the rider over, "This is urgent and confidential, be sure it reaches him." I placed a crashing wave seal on the envelop of the first letter with silver wax. "And the second letter is to go to the Lord of Meadows. Check at the Keep for him before you seek him in his region. He spends a great deal of time out of the Meadows."

It would take him a full day to reach the Keep and another to reach the Meadows. Ancient wards prevented fae from shifting across the entirety of the realm. "Make haste. There isn't time to spare. Leave your horse at the Keep and borrow one for the trip to the Meadows. Don't sleep until both letters are delivered,"I said as I handed him a third sheet with instructions.

I signed them as an order so he could produce it if he had a problem. He wouldn't, not with news like this. This was cause for escalating the war. It was the fae approach to leave things a stale mate. For centuries the human's had proven they were incapable of breaching the wards, so we let them keep trying and simply monitored the boundaries, keeping fae in and human's out. It was simplest to ignore them for the most part. Clearly, we'd been underestimating their tenacity to destroy themselves.

Twenty-One Years Earlier

"Come now, darling. It's time you got ready for bed," Everlee called to me from my bed chamber. I was in the upstairs corridor of the Meadows manor between my father's wing and the nursery. She was turning down the sheets like she always did, always at sunset and always before I was done playing. Bugger.

I ran down the soft sage carpet in the oak hallway and hid under my father's large desk in his spacious office. He was gone again. *He hates being here. He never wants to be with me. Why won't he play with me?* My father preferred to spend his time at Agron's Keep in the center of our realm, on official business, as he called it.

I hated going there, but I hated him gone too. There were too many people and I always had to be quiet. The lessons with the other Lords' children were boring. I'd learned them already and found it dull, despite being the youngest—except the harp. I could play the harp all day. The lessons with the other Lords' children were boring. *I miss Uriah. He's funny and takes me flying. Tutors are dumb.*

The Meadows manor was quiet. Our vast meadows were full of wild flowers and there was plenty to do with the horses on the grounds. Our staff had dwindled since my mother died. Father was often cranky when he was home and prone to fits of anger. *Why is he so difficult?* Father always ranted that they only stayed in his employ so long because they cared for her. *I wish he would smile more.*

I never knew my mother. She died when I was born. I'd heard tales of how great a seer she was. Her magic was powerful and far reaching. Many seers could tell you simple things, but my mother could see visions of the future farther out and didn't have to come into direct contact with someone to provide a telling. Often times people from all over the Agron Realm wrote to her. I had a stash of letters I'd stolen from my fathers office hidden under a loose floor board in my room.

I wish I had known my Mother. I'm sure she was a lovely person. I bet she would play with me. I was to birth the next King or Queen, so the healers had saved me instead of her. I didn't really know what that meant, only that it was my purpose.

I thought back to what Father told me. *'You'll marry Uriah when you turn 18. When you move to the Shallows, you'll be the Lady there and provide a babe—"* my father said. It was a high honor, and I should be happy about it.

Everlee called for me again. "Arabella! Get in this room this instance." *Or what? You're not my mother...but you take care of me anyway. I hope Everlee doesn't leave too.* I tucked in tighter underneath the desk, hugging my knees to my chest and carefully tucking my wings behind me. There was a ledge built in it that made a good hiding spot. I could still fit. I was small for my age, but far smarter than most fae children. Everlee said it was because I was only around mature fae. *Boring.* I was almost four. *Will Uriah come for a party? Will Father even plan one? Will he even return in time?*

I bit my lip so I wouldn't giggle. She'd be looking for me for awhile. I started daydreaming of swimming at the pond. I liked to feed the ducks and watch the squirrels leap from tree to tree while looking up at big fluffy clouds in the blue sky laying in the meadow. I always chased the big yellow butterflies as they moved from flower to flower. I always looked forward to flying with Uriah when he came for a visit. *I want to fly. When will my wings be strong enough? Maybe I should jump off the banister and test them?* I felt my eye begin to close and I fought to stay awake. *Is Everlee even looking?*

❀ ❀ ❀ ❀ ❀

I startled awake on the floor under my father's desk. The rug below his desk stuck to my cheek, making creases. When did I fall asleep? Why didn't Everlee come find me? Is it morning? I slid out from under his desk. What's that? There was someone talking loud in the stairwell. I was cold. My little olive colored dress had hitched up and twisted into the bottom of my black feathered wings. I tugged it down as I stood up. The room was dark, and embers burned low in the fireplace as if no one had tended it recently. I thought they kept all the fireplaces lit through the night in winter?

I tiptoed out the open door and down the hallway toward my bedchamber. I moved carefully to stay on the rug so my footsteps would be quiet. I was going to be in trouble. I bit my lip. Everlee will be angry. Maybe. Only if she's still awake. I walked into my dark room. There were voices floating down the hall.

"You dolt, if you had done as you were told, we'd be out of here already. I always have to do everything," the high pitch of a female's voice sounded angry as I skirted into my room. *Who is that? Who is she talking to?*

A book case in the corner housed my favorite stories. A wide chair with emerald and grass green velvet pillows that Everlee read to me was tucked in beside the shelves. Everything was soft shades of green with gold accent. I always liked the shades of blue Uriah was adorned in better. When I was older, I'd be moving to the Shallows. The colors there were blue and silver.

"I'm sorry Judy! This is overwhelming! I'm not like you," a males voice drifted through the door way. I froze, who was that? Is it guard change already? "I can't handle this! You've asked too much of me this time."

"Too much of you! The lengths I've taken to elevate our

family line. Move your ass, we need to finish this and be gone before anyone realizes what we've done," the shrill voice echoed down the hall. *Judy? The lady that pesters Father?* The hair on the back of my neck rose.

I crept to the edge of my bed. *Why is it so cold?* The blankets were pulled back and folded down for me. I kicked my little black shoes off and slipped out of my socks. Climbing up, I scooted into the middle of my spacious bed. I laid on my side so I didn't bend any of my feathers, I tugged on the blanket in the darkened room. *Huh?* I tugged again. *Why won't it move?* It wouldn't flap over to cover me up. I sat up and patted the bed. I touched something sticky and yanked my hand back in disgust.

I sniffed my hand. *What is that?* It smelled like an old metal can that had been left out in the rain. I patted again and felt something smooth and stringy. *Hair?* I kept feeling around the bed and the tip of an ear came to my hand. I jerked my arm back again. "Everlee?" I said softly. Goosebumps erupted down my arm, and my heart beat fast. *What happened?*

I snapped my fingers. and fae lights ignited next to me in both lamps flanking my bed. I looked down at my hand. Sticky red blood covered my finger tips, like when I'd cut my hands jumping off the banister and landed on a big vase. I shattered it while trying to fly before my wings could hold me. I looked at Everlee and she wasn't moving. The sheets were stained red with her life leaking from her severed throat. I screamed.

The male fae from the hallway stepped into the room. I froze. I didn't recognize him as one of my guards, but he was wearing our colors. *Did more of Father's men quit?* He held a dagger dripping blood to the carpet. *Is that Everlee's blood?* I screamed again and backed up against my ornate oak headboard, the flowers in the pattern pressing into my wings.

"Now child, it's time to be quiet. No one can hear you anymore," he said, as he cleared the room in a few paces. He grabbed my small wrist in his big hand and tucked his bloody dagger into its sheath. He took Everlee's dead hand in its stead.

I'm going to throw up. I felt the room spin and he shifted us through time and space. *No. No. No. But the wards. They don't allow that! Daddy! Where are you?* Tears leaked down my face, a fast and warm trickle, as we shifted and stopped again. The air grew more frigid with each bound.

We landed somewhere outside in a forested woodland, and I felt the shift begin again. We leaped though space four times before we landed. Each time the air grew colder. I could see my breath as I sobbed. *I need a coat. My shoes! I need my shoes.* I prepared myself again for another shift, but it never came.

I looked over, and at some point he'd left Everlee behind. *Did he leave her in the woods? That's one way to hide a body. Who will take care of me? How will they find me? Is he going to hurt me too? Who else did they hurt?* A biting, frigid air hit my bare arms and legs. I shivered against the cold as he dragged me along behind him, his black hair blowing in the wind.

I couldn't keep up with his brisk walk, and I stumbled. Holding my wrist tighter, he dragged me behind him. "Get up," he growled. He kept moving as my knees scraped on the ground leading to a drawbridge. "Move it. We're already late," he said as he pulled me along. We crossed the moat into the landing of a castle. He stopped at a door off to the side of the wall. I whimpered as the cold stung my skin, snow flakes floating on the air around us.

I found my feet again as he slowed to approach the door. He thumped it three times in quick succession. The wind blew snow and ice around me. My exposed skin began to sting, raw with ice burns from being dragged.

A small window opened. "Speak your business," a gruff voice inquired.

"I have a gift for King Plavlock," the fae stated, gesturing toward the ground where I was half sprawled again, trying to get my footing as he held my arm at an awkward angle. My bare feet slid on the icy ground, and the ice cut into the tender soles of my feet. The man in the window nodded, a metallic clinking began rumbling into the night as a small door made of metal thatch work began to lift.

The fae grabbed my arm firmly and pushed me through the now open archway into the castle. Guards were scattered about with mall bonfires here and there to take a little chill off their hands as they worked their shift.

"Keep up," he snapped at me again. Tears began to form anew and ran down my chubby cheeks until they froze. My wild copper curls blew around my face making it hard to see. My knee was bleeding from being dragged, and my teeth chattered with the cold.

My feet burned. *Why is this happening? Who are these people? Are they from another region? He doesn't look like anyone I know. Are they humans? Humans are stupid and violent.* Layers of ice lay all around everything inside the rock brick castle. Everything was adorned with purple and white against the gray brickwork. Soldiers stood on post as we began to ascend the outside stair cases. I slid with every step never fully getting my bearings.

We climbed flight after flight. I couldn't count how many steps we took. The man that held my wrist followed a soldier. My feet and legs burned. My teeth audibly chattered. The wind was bitter against my bare skin, and I swayed in the strong breeze. We came to a heavy oak door at the top of the last flight and it opened as we approached. There was a long hallway with suits of human armor lining it. *I should have gotten in bed like Everlee told me.* I trembled.

It was warm inside the hall. The floors were smooth and I left bloody footprints as I stepped. I still shivered as my muscles began to loosen. Great tapestries with visions of humans slaughtering fae hung from ceiling to floor. *As if that were possible. Father says they can't get through the wards of ancient magic.* "Sit. Do not move," the dark haired fae said pushing me into a wood chair along the wall by the door at the end of the corridor. I looked around. The beams making the ceiling had cobwebs clustered throughout them and the room smelled of burnt tobacco like in my Father's pipe. *Gross. What are they going to do with me?*

Some time passed. I don't know how long. My stomach rumbled. I wished I would have eaten more of my dinner, but it had been turnip greens and boiled quail eggs. *Yuck.* The last time I'd eaten turnip greens, it made me throw up, so I'd stuffed most of it in my napkin.

I began to nod off and my head drooped to the side. At the same time, I tried to also sit up in the chair so the male fae didn't get angry with me again. He had squinted, angry eyes and kept his lips turned down in a sneer.

Finally, a door to the left of us opened. The fae stood and brushed his hands down his thighs before grabbing hold of my arm again. It was already bruised from earlier, but he squeezed harder ripping me from the seat as I failed to move fast enough. "Stop, it hurts," I cried as I tried to pull back out of his grip.

We walked down the thick purple carpet on the white marble floor. The room was nearly empty and large enough to echo. High beams made of more marble arched over head. Stained glass filled every bit of wall space to filter in as much light as possible during the day.

Flames flickered from lit torches as we walked toward the throne at the end of the room. *I bet it's pretty during the day. It's still so dark. What if no one comes? What will happen to me?*

At the end of the carpet on the dais sat a large throne and a human male. His hair was brightest white, as were his silk clothes. A thick white fur lay draped over his shoulders. He was adorned with diamonds the size of the quail eggs I'd had for dinner and he had a silver crown crusted in blue and purple stones upon his head. The light flickered off his aged face, leaving deep grooves making him appear alarming. He had dark circles under his eyes and he looked to be half awake as well. He scowled as we approached. "What is this nonsense? Why have you woken me, Fae?" He all but growled. Then, I noticed his rounded ears. *Human.* My muscles tensed and goosebumps ran down the length of me.

Tears began to fall from my face again. I couldn't stop them if I tried. This human was going to kill me. I could feel it. Everlee's blood now dried on my hands, I knew mine would mingle with hers tonight. I could feel it in my bones. I could feel the ghost of the future swirling in the cold air around me.

"Your Majesty, I present to you the only daughter of the Lord of Meadows from the Agron Realm. As decreed by King Astros and his council, she's to bear the next King or Queen of the Agron Realm when she comes of age, if she comes of age that is." He glanced down at me and adjusted his stance. "She's been betrothed to the heir of the Lord of Shallows. Their union will be a strong one if she were to survive until then," the male fae said, shifting nervously again.

The fae's eyes were so dark they were nearly black. They matched the jet black hair that was braided down his back, his pointed ears just peaking through his hair. His skin was tanned and stood out against the white marble. His dark forest green tunic had patches of blood soaked into it. *He has no blood on his hands. I do though.*

I want Everlee. He hurt Everlee!

The king sat up straighter on his throne and peered down at me. "Why are her ears round? I thought all you fae had pointy ones?" the King demanded, he glanced at the fae's pointy ears and searched his dark eyes for the lie. Terror flooded through me and the thought of being hurt. I pulled against the fae with all my strength, trying to break free. The fae easily scooped me up, kicking and screaming now, and held me as they talked.

"She was born with rounded ears," the fae said, digging his arm into my middle angrily as I continued to kick and hit him. "It's my understanding her mother was half human and half fae, so she would be a quarter human, hence the wings, but also the rounded ears. I believe the only outwardly fae identifier she has are the wings." He pinned my arms down as he answered, and I shook in his grasp. Warm pee ran down my legs and dripped into a puddle at our feet as he wrapped a hand across my mouth. I tried to bite him, but he held my jaw closed.

"Good, good. Well enough. What is your price?" King Plavlock surveyed the fae male that had stolen me and killed Everlee. Tears dripped off his hand as the fae held my face. *Wait until my father finds you. Oh Everlee. Help me! Someone help me!*

"I want to take a human bride for my own. She lives in this castle. A maiden. Her name is Piper," the fae explained. The King nodded as he studied me.

"Very well. Guards! Go and collect this Piper. Take her and this fae and toss them out of my castle. Leave the child and send in the Sculptor." Movement immediately began. The fae quickly turned and walked down the carpet, without so much as a glance back as I watched him go. My fate now laid in the hands of a cruel human king.

"What is your name child?" The King was talking to me. My throat went dry, and I stopped screaming for all the good I was doing in saving myself. My eyes widened in surprise.

"Arabella," I answered quietly, my voice cutting out. *I'm thirsty.*

"Hmm, not anymore." The King Stared down at me, studying me for a moment. "I shall call you Raven, like those little feathers you have there. And I think I'd like them for my collection." He stated it so matter of fact as he smiled down at me. *What does that mean? For his collection?*

"But they're mine," I said. The king simply pursed his lips.

A door banged open on the back side of the throne. The King looked over his shoulder as a male walking in. "Ah, Sculptor. Thank you for coming so quickly."

"Your Majesty." A man with greasy dark hair and a scarred face bowed his head as he knelt beside me, avoiding the puddle of now cooling piss. "What service can I provide for you at this late hour?" He was winded and speaking quickly, he seemed annoyed to have been called. His hands were covered in black leather gloves, and he wore a black cloak that looked to have melting snow flakes clinging to it.

"Take the child down to the block. See to it that she can't get loose. This one likes to kick, try to break her of that habit. I want her wings preserved. After that, tuck her away somewhere until she can be of use. We may need her at some point. Until then, keep her alive."

He stared at me coldly. "Yes, beautiful wings, my dear Raven. Don't forget your new name. The wings. Yes...They shall make a lovely trophy."

✾✾✾✾✾

I woke with cold sticky blood pooled around my face, neck and head. My hands and feet were numb from the cold underneath and around me. The room smelled of wet hay and mildew. Thunder pounded in my ears and searing pain lanced down my shoulder blades. The potion they'd made me drink was wearing off. I'd gone completely numb as soon as he tipped it down my throat earlier. I fought to keep my eyes open but couldn't.

What did he do to me? I promised to be good. I promised I wouldn't fight anymore. Where's Father? Is he coming to get me?

I was stripped to my underwear and strapped face down on a stone table. A gag had been tied around my mouth and acted as a bit wedged between my teeth. My hands and ankles were tied down tightly with sharp metal chains. They dug in, increasing my misery. I wiggled, but couldn't shift them much.

Cold air drafted through the small room. It was made of stone blocks, stained red from years of blood covering them, and a low ceiling hovered just above the man standing at my side. I imagine if he stood on his toes, his dark hair would touch the ceiling. There were no windows, just a handful of candles for light that wavered in the drafts of chilly air.

"Almost done, little Raven," the Sculptor crooned. "This was more complicated than I thought it would be. You have so many little tendons. You're strong. I haven't had the pleasure of a fae to play with for years." He finished doing something to my back and stepped around the stone table in front of me.

He bent, squatting down to look me in the face. "You and I will get to know each other well. I have many trials I'd like for you to try to conquer. Some you may even come to enjoy. As for these wings of yours, I'm nearly done. If Gralton hadn't specified to keep you alive, I'd already have them off of you," the Sculptor prattled on about his process. *Who's Gralton? Is that the King's name? Does he dare to call a King by his given name?*

He stood and moved back around the table. A mist of smoke wafted in front of my face and my eyes instantly grew heavy. Before I fell asleep again, I felt his knife swipe across my back, a small pop sounded as a tendon popped loose. I let out a blood curdling scream as flames of pain rolled up and down my spine before blackness took me again. Tears mixed with the blood and a new gush of warmth covered my shoulder as my consciousness faded.

❀❀❀❀❀

I don't know how long it was before I woke again. I shuddered in agony. I could feel something moving over my back but the room I lay in was dark. No, no, no. What did he do to me? My wings! I need my wings!

"I can't be me without my wings. How will I fly?" I whispered into the dark.

The straw under me was stuck to my skin, and I was propped up on my side. Rough fabric bunched against my bare skin. I reached back to try to feel what was on my back, but moving my shoulder was excruciating. I stifled a cry. *What will he do if he hears me?* I bit into my lip, tasting blood. *It's so dark. I wish I had light.*

I swiped at something and pinched it between two fingers bringing it forward to look at it in the stream of light that barely laid out the room. My eyes were only partially adjusted to the darkness that seemed to be my whole world now. There was a beam of light coming from under the door across the small stone room.

I held my hand out to see what squishy thing lay in my palm. I squinted in the dark and cringed when I realized what I was holding. My hand jerked, and I threw myself back against the wall the bed was pushed up against. *Maggots.* My ruined back was infested with maggots. My wings—gone . *My beautiful wings. My wings...*

I closed my eyes again. The room began to spin and my breath hitched. *Father? Daddy? Where are you?*

No tears came this time. I refused to give them more. I was always warned by the guards not to wander too far from the manor, that someone may wish to steal me away. *I thought they were just trying to keep me close to the house.*

My empty stomach contracted as I tried not to throw up. I willed blackness to take me and I wished I'd never wake again. As far as I was concerned, Arabella was dead. *I'm Raven now. Raven. Raven. Raven.*

Chapter 7

Raven

It'd been a week since I met Uriah. *Or found my way back to him.* When he'd said my given name, the memories began flooding back to me. I cried for days after I shifted away, keeping it together long enough to collect my bounty for the man I'd killed. I provided his head for payment after retrieving it from a section of the void. That head was the whole reason I ended up in that cave in the first place. I'd needed the coin though.

I may be indentured into Queen Clawin's service, but she only paid me if she hired me for a specific task, and usually not well, as long as she doesn't hold me again. Images flashed through my mind; hanging in a damp dungeon, my arms stretched over my head, my toes barely scraping the floor. A pipe dripped above me, splattering me with boiling water directly from the boiler room. My skin was raw and angry from the constant assault. She left me there so long my shoulders dislocated before offering me a chance at freedom. *It took weeks to heal.*

I didn't mind working for myself. I used the money I made to buy some supplies, like more food and staples to store in the void and a new book. I'd read the ones I carried too many times for it to be interesting. So, I'd traded the three I had for two new ones and bought an additional one. Then I tucked myself away and cried it out. *Maybe it will all work out? Is he looking for me?*

It had been years since I allowed myself to wallow in such misery. I remembered him. *Uriah.* He belonged to the

Shallows, the region of sea and marsh in the southern half of the Agron Realm, and I belonged... nowhere. Not anymore. I was nothing. I didn't have a home. *I don't belong.* I did have a job needed to finish though. Queen Clawin had offered the contract just a few days before I went into that cave. More like volunteering for a pittance of pay, or death. Charming. *I'm no less a slave now than I was before.*

Had I been doing the job I was supposed to be doing, I'd be no where near here. I should have been inland, hunting down the heads Queen Clawin wanted. But, coin. A girl needed to eat, and the soldier was easy picking. Money couldn't buy happiness, but it sure makes misery easier to live with. I took the job of killing a rapist for enough to restock my food supplies. Who could blame me? A little cleavage and I roped him in with mere minutes of my time. A moth to flame. I got more than I bargained for. And now? *Now what do I do?*

Uriah had said twenty one years were stolen from me. I didn't know how long it'd been. That would make me twenty five. I could have sworn I was closer to twenty, but who knows how much time I lost in the darkness of that dungeon? No one ever came to rescue me, so how important was I really?

The fae from the cave was so handsome and gone was the adolescent awkwardness. *His wings, oh his wings!* They had that smoky shimmer I'd always marveled at. He used to scoop me up when I was a toddler and fly us to the pond on the edge of my father's estate. My father. He never looked for me. *He never had time for me either.*

Uriah found me, or was it that our magic pulled us together? He was handsome and seemed kind. His dark auburn hair was cut short still, and the soft slope of his straight nose perfectly aligned with his strong chin. Those deep hazel eyes, the whiskey brown interwoven with the light blue gray like the feathers of a heron, and the interspersed green of a pine. I couldn't see his eyes well in the cave. My light just wasn't bright enough, and he was a full head taller than me.

When he said that name, *Arabella,* I thought my heart

would stop. She died. I let her. I was such a small child and it was easier to pretend that she never existed so I could survive, so Raven could survive. I didn't allow myself to think of home. I knew I'd never get back there, so what was the point? And now? Even though I escaped, I doubted anyone would believe it was me. My wings were gone.

A shadow fell over my shoulder. *"Don't get lost in your thoughts. You'll find only strangers there,"* my horse Knightmare said into my mind as he walked up to me. He started to stamp his foot in the sand of the dune I was sitting on. I'd perched myself among the fronds of tall grass and had a book in my lap. I had the habit of fingering the pendant around my neck like a worry stone as I read.

We stayed in the coastal areas as frequently as possible. *I wonder if that is because of Uriah. Maybe I can belong to the Shallows. I always liked blue.*

"I don't know how he recognized me," I said to Knightmare. He was a jet black stallion. I found Knightmare four years after I left the kitchen and escaped the Torrent Kingdom in the North. I rescued him from a burning barn. I'd been leaving a bar after completing a job. I liked to drink on the nights I killed. Sleep often evaded me, and the liquor helped.

Knightmare was weak at first from his injuries, but we made it together. He'd been badly burned and maimed. His right eye was blinded and most of his flank had cooked. I nursed him back to health. It took months and months. Still, a third of his body was host to deep scars. We were both survivors.

"You don't know your impact. Any fool worth knowing would remember you," Knightmare said. *Uriah does remember me. He saw me for who I am before I dared to acknowledge it myself.* Knightmare's voice was deep and somber, wise beyond what most would think for a horse. He was a faehorse imbued with his own kind of magic, stolen as well, a decade ago. *He's my only friend.*

He could speak into my mind and he'd figured out how

to shift us larger distances too. He hadn't been able to shift at all when we met, but after I shifted him a few times, he figured it out. His magic was a little different, but still useful all the same. He had a knack for knowing when someone was dishonest, not to mention he looked like he was ready to trample at any moment. He was a grouch but he was mine. We took care of each other.

"Do you think once we work this contract, finish it I mean, you'd want to go back to the Agron Realm?" I asked as I tucked a chunk of my long curly hair behind my ear. I kept it braided when I was working, but in our off time I liked it loose.

We were staying in a makeshift camp by the sea. I set wards with my magic so we'd know if anyone approached, but it was a quiet area. My small canvas tent offered a little privacy and reprieve from the wind, though I preferred to sleep under the stars. It was the last week of September. The night had started to cool significantly, so shelter was necessary.

In the colder months, I'd located a few caves that we frequented. They were big enough I could walk Knightmare in so he had shelter too. It wasn't glamorous by any means, but it got us through okay. With a few strong wards and a good fire, we were fine.

"I think the better question is 'what do you want to do?'" Knightmare swung his head over to me, nuzzling my neck where I sat on a boulder facing the sea. The wind gently blew my hair, but it stayed tucked behind my ear. I still had a book in my lap and he had been grazing on the small patch of grass by the tent.

I pondered a bit. I was so conflicted. On one hand, I didn't need anyone other than Knightmare. On the other, I had mourned my life all these years. I missed my father and Uriah. Everlee. *Don't do that. I'm going to make myself cry again.* I sighed. There Uriah had been, in the flesh, begging for me to come home.

I left him with his hand out, reaching for me. I watched his heart break as I shifted away. *Will he even forgive me? How can I face him after fleeing like that? Will he even want me once he knows me?*

The first time I left him by force, the second by fear. Queen Clawin would hunt me down and put me back in her dungeon or kill me if I didn't complete my task. I owed her five heads. I collected one the first day, but the other four were still in the wind. *Find them fast.* I told myself. *Maybe Uriah will still accept me and Knightmare.* I needed to start my search. I had a lead on the brothers I was searching for. Hopefully they would lead me to the other two. I just had to follow this through.

The brothers frequented a bar in the sketchy side of Palomora in the Daemon Kingdom, just to the East of Neera. I was on the coast between the two villages now. I plan to go tomorrow night. Friday was usually a good day to find people.

"The bond... I can feel it, Knightmare. Every time I call on my magic, I can feel it tugging me to him. I wonder if he feels the same?" *I hope. I don't know if he wants me back.*

Chapter 8

Raven

Friday had been fruitful. Three of the slime balls I was searching for were sitting at a table next to the wall near the back exit. The pub they frequented was in a sketchy neighborhood. I slit the throat of one the moment I walked into the noisy and crowded bar.

Smoke filled the room. It was dark with dimly lit candle chandeliers hanging from the old birch beams along the ceiling. Scarlet and black painted walls made it feel moody. High tables were scattered about, all filled with humans smoking who knows what and drinking to their heart's content. *Must be nice to not have a care in the world.* The acrid smell made my nose twitch. I moved quickly before anyone noticed my presence.

Recognition danced across the younger looking brother's face as he noted my blade, my dagger already flicked across the table buried deep in his chest. *Such idiots. Who leaves their back open to a doorway? The arrogance is poetic.*

I wasn't fast enough to end the other, but I did manage to grab a trace of his magic. A fae nonetheless, running around with a bunch of humans. *What's his story? Why is a fae abusing humans with other humans? Weird. Is he not strong enough to fuck with his own kind?* He shifted where he sat, fleeing the bloody scene. I'd find him. His kind never stayed hidden for long. Whispers would travel through towns he frequented. *If gossip fails me, the trace from his magic will tell me when and where he used his magic anyway. It always feels off.* Maybe he'd be a fool and lead me to their friend as well.

I noticed I could sense when magic had been near after the cave. It made me feel different, wilder. I'd never pinned down exactly what it was until a week ago while walking through a marketplace in Neera. I had seen a dark haired fae, and I could have sworn he was following me. He wore a cloak, but I just caught sight of the tip of his ear as I looked back rounding a corner. *I learn more about myself everyday. Focus!* I reprimanded myself as my mind began to wander.

All hell broke loose when people began to realize what was happening. They always scream. *Do they have to be so loud?* I quickly sheathed my bloody khopesh and grabbed the hand of the now gurgling younger brother and then a fist full of the short cropped, curly blonde hair of the one I'd practically decapitated, quickly severing most of the way through his neck as I had approached from behind. *One swipe. I'm getting more efficient.*

Blood ran down the front of his tunic soaking into his pants and on the leather bench he sat upon, his head wobbled as I pulled on his arm.

I shifted us away, taking us to the dock of a deserted fishery. Good enough. I ripped my dagger out of the second ones chest. He'd landed half sat up and fell back against the grimy, peeling wall of the building. It was dilapidated and should probably be condemned, but as far as I knew, it still operated. I let go of him, satisfied that he was too far gone to run. He immediately started to tilt toward the fish scale covered dock.

The younger brother was bleeding out. His imminent death was a few breaths away; now that the removed dagger released the flow. He was not fighting it, but I'd delivered a death blow so there wasn't much he *could* do. His chest cavity was rapidly filling with blood. Soon enough his lungs wouldn't be able to inflate from all the excess pressure. *Nearly three down. Progress. I just have to finish this one off and collect their heads.*

Remorse flitted across his face. He gaped at his older

brothers dead body laying on the dock in front of him, a line of blood running from his mouth and his mostly detached head. They would get no mercy from me.

The five miscreants I hunted had raped and murdered three young girls outside Queen Clawin's palace. It caused quite the commotion for all the elite that resided in or around the castle.

As Knightmare put it, *"'Some days you are the bird flying high in the sky with no worries, and some days, you are the statue on the ground getting shit on.'"* I'd laughed so hard when Knightmare had given me the snarky after I'd returned to him and told him what was going on. He always puts a good spin on things for me.

As fear sprang up and uneasiness grew in the village, the Queen had summoned me to find them and exact justice. *How does she always know where I am?* No trial necessary. They didn't show those girls mercy, so why should she? *I may hate her for hurting me, but I can't argue with that. The Queen's still a bitch. My shoulder still pops in and out of place from hanging in her dungeon. Over one measly rapist...*I shook my head, shaking off the memory.

I quickly severed the older brothers neck. I couldn't stay on this dock for very long, even I didn't want witnesses. *It smells so bad. Fish guts are stuck to everything. I*t was relatively easy work with my khopesh. Over the years, I'd figured out that spinal vertebrae popped apart fairly easily if I paid attention to where I was cutting. The sinew was barely held together after the force of shifting ten miles.

The five criminals I hunted were suspected of having done it before, but this time there was a witness. I made her talk to me in the Queens stable where Knightmare had been boarded while I attended to the summons. With his mind reading magic he confirmed for me that she wasn't lying. Good enough for me. With descriptions of the five, I asked around and got a list of names. They were often seen together and had a penchant for violence against the vulnerable.

Not anymore.

"I'm so cold," the younger brother said with a gurgle. He shuddered and fell over the rest of the way. His face turned out, and fish scales stuck to his blood splattered cheek. His gray eyes opened wide but no longer seeing. *Three down, two to go.*

I set the head on the dock by its body and went to work on the younger brother. His sandy blonde hair was about the same shade as his brothers.

"Dumb ass, you should have made your own way in life instead of following him." I mumbled to myself. He wouldn't be dead right now if he'd stayed off his brother's wretched path.

I remembered the first time I learned that lesson. "'Villains aren't born, they're made,'" the Sculptor always told me as he washed all the blood off himself after he 'sculpted' me. So many cuts. So many burns. "'I'm creating a masterpiece out of you, my little dove. I can't wait to see how you'll turn out, Raven.'"

Who made these assholes? Am I really any better then they are? After all, I'm known as the *"Sculptor's apprentice."*

Blood pooled under my knees as I sliced into the younger brothers neck, cutting through the sinew, and pulled his head free from his shoulders. I set it next to the first one and loosened my grip on my magic, letting it flow from me.

Cords of light wrapped around the first body and lifted it over the edge of the dock. Water splashed, making the blood splatter about. After releasing the first body, my magic wrapped itself around the second body and dropped it into the water. *Here, fishy fishy! Time for dinner.*

I stood and looked myself over. *Ugh! Gross.* Blood didn't really bother me anymore, however I didn't like to be saturated in it. I'd seen enough of my own leak out of me frequently growing up. Other people's blood meant nothing. The smell was what bothered me. *Rusty tin cans, just like that time in my bedroom as a child. Oh Everlee. You didn't deserve that fate.* Images of a blood soaked bed and a man with a knife flashed in my memory. *Push it back. Don't think about it.*

I needed to change; these clothes were toast. I opened a second void separate from the main one I used. I had several depending on the need. Picking up the older brother's head I tucked it inside. The first of the five head's I had collected was already in there, mostly preserved. There was no air inside the void, so decay would be greatly delayed. Aside from opening it to add new heads, they would be suspended in time.

After adding the third head, I closed the void. I walked down the dock and knelt. Bending over the side, I splashed water up my arms to clear the blood away. I opened my everyday void and pulled out a small metal bucket before I closed it. Scooping up water, I went back and rinsed the blood from the dock. After several buckets, it was a much better scene, no more disgusting than the average day. The fisherman would see what was left of the carnage floating in the sea soon enough. *Hopefully they aren't too traumatized.*

I opened the void again and put the bucket back, grabbing fresh clothes in the process. As the void closed, I looked over my shoulder. I couldn't see anyone, but a tingle ran up my spine as if someone was watching. I tugged on my necklace as it suddenly felt tight.

The docks were deserted, save for a few small boats at port but no lights or movement. The sun had set hours before, and the full moon was the only light shining on the water. It was enough to see what I needed.

I picked up my pace as I walked away. Skirting down an alley way, I dipped into a deep doorway, quickly kicking off my boots and peeling off my pants. The drying blood made the thick leather hard to slide down. After losing my balance and nearly toppling over, I achieved my task and put on fresh leathers. I stripped off my now ruined top and put on a fresh one. *I'll steal more shirts later.*

This one, a white off the shoulder shirt with ruffles and cornflower and lavender flowers I'd hand embroidered on it, it looked nice with my tan leathers. *My clothes are loose. I need to eat more. Rosie's has the best meat pie.*

My job done for the evening, I laced up my boots, shoved the bloodied clothes into a trashcan and headed to Rosie's. My favorite pub in Palomora, I didn't go often, but I stopped when I could afford it. *The music is so good!*

After shifting across town, I stood in front of the small building. It was quieter here. A much safer side of town. I opened my void and tucked away my khopesh. I'd keep my dagger on me, but I wouldn't need anything more than that.

I always thought I was just stronger than most. How could the Sculptor experiment on me for so long if I wasn't? Uriah was right. I am fae. At least part fae. No wonder they all seem so weak. *No wonder I don't fit in. No wonder I'm different. I don't belong here. Where do I belong?*

I looked to my left down the street, Knightmare and I were on the edge of town where the city met the mountain side. The air was crisp and smelled of honeysuckle. It was dark and I could just make out Knightmare right where I'd asked him to stay before going for my marks. He stood under a small group of trees near the edge of the forest, munching on the tender grass beneath. He blended in well, being jet black and it being dark. *No one will bother him. He'll bite if they do.*

"Go, have some fun. I'll be fine here and take us back to camp when you're drunk enough," he said into my mind. *"You worked hard tonight. All will be as it should be, soon enough. Until then, go eat. You love the fiddle music, but maybe don't dance on the bar this time."* I swear he was laughing at me. He knew I liked to dance and that's exactly where I was headed. I planned to get a shot—or six—of spirits. My favorite was brown sugar bourbon, and they had the best home distillery around. *I earned it tonight.*

Chapter 9

Felix

"I found her. I didn't approach, like you ordered," I said to Uriah as I walked into his dim office. The only light filtered in from the open curtains on the window in front of his desk. A fire burned low under the marbled fireplace in the middle of the room, and the stark white marble stood out against the cherry wood all over the manor. Midnight blue velvet chairs sat facing a small table in the middle. Cherry wood was his favorite, so of course, he'd insisted it be used for nearly everything in the manor. Such a creature of habit.

He'd lost his spark over the last week. He'd been skipping meals and crankier than usual. I don't think he'd been sleeping. He had been obsessing over Arabella, drawing her on every scrap of paper lying around. He really is quite the artist. Why doesn't he draw more?He was heart broken that she hadn't made it back to him yet. He understood that he had to wait for her and, give her space or the whole thing would implode, but it was hard for him. He likes to be in control. Lord was the perfect job for him.

She is his mate. He is pining. *At least he found her. More than I can say for myself. Or Sebastian.*

The King ordered troops from the western most region, the Brume, to come support ours. Ulysses, the Lord of the Brume, was not pleased with the news and sent us soldiers that lacked training. We'd had to create separate camps for them and begin drills immediately. The help was needed, but it'd been stressful organizing everything.

The Summit region was in chaos. John, the Lord of

Summit had spent a great amount of time in the Eastern Shallows Estate using our main wing to organize his troops. John was currently in his own region personally overseeing his army. *He should be back in a few days.*

They'd been unknowingly infiltrated through the cave systems, and we didn't know to what extent yet. Everyone was on high alert. Humans themselves were weak, but like bugs, they could easily overwhelm with numbers. *Thank the King our wards are strong.*

On top of that, Uriah was in a dark place. To have found his lost love *and* have the mating bond snap into place only to just lose her again—*I can't imagine the pain he's in.*

Males were always affected more deeply by the magic of the mating bond. It drove an inherent need to protect and keep their mate close by, not just for procreation, but for self preservation. The two were bonded so deeply, two halves of one whole.

Lionel had arrived two days ago, and that wasn't going well either. He demanded to know more about Arabella. As her father, he was due answers. *Answers we don't have yet.* Lionel demanded to know why Uriah had let her simply shift away. He wanted proof that she actually existed, how he was certain it was her. There were so many questions the surly lord had fired at him.

The older Lord had taken to talking to him as if Uriah was a child. Lionel even went so far as to say Uriah had invented the encounter to avoid his betrothal to Arianna. The child was six, for goodness sake.

What does he expect? Uriah to marry her now? Clearly his eldest is the best match. Why doesn't he believe she is alive? Is his disgusting wife involved? Lionel is a creep. His priorities are so twisted, he never searched for her then, of course he would deny it now. To think, Uriah has to chain himself to that family. Lionel is a heartless bastard. It never seemed he cared, other than collecting the sympathy from the realms nobles.

Uriah reminded Lionel that they were now equals and to

speak to another lord like that was not prudent. *Good for him. I would have thrown Lionel out on his ass.* Lionel had wisely silenced after that, seething with silent rage, his faced flushed. Uriah boldly told him the betrothal to Arianna would never come to pass as the magic had chosen his mate, regardless of whether or not he believed it was Arabella.

To add to Lionel's discomfort, I had chosen that moment to walk in with his wife, Judith, having caught her riffling through the drawers in an office reserved for the Lord of Summit's use.

Lionel turned in an outburst of profanity and left for his assigned quarters on the other half of the estate. We had a visitors' wing with several unoccupied rooms available for the Agron Realms lords and their families. I nodded to several soldiers then; a silent command to watch him and his party.

It didn't help that his wretched harpy of a wife was snooping around. Far from pleasant, she had a habit of looking down her nose at everyone. Clearly she thought her shit didn't stink. I could still hear her shrill voice from when I caught her spying earlier, '*I am the Lady of the Meadows and you will address me as such.*'

Judith, was a piece of work. Ugly inside and out. The prettiest jewels and dresses couldn't cover the evil spewing from her contemptuous eyes. She was upset that Uriah would even consider Arabella as a wife when he could wait for Arianna and have, as she had remarked, 'a young fresh fae ripe for the picking.'

I thought Uriah was going to vomit. Thank the King he declared the betrothal invalid. It had to be adjudicated by the King himself to be formally eradicated, but that would only require a short trip to the Agron Keep.

The bigger problem, was Uriah would need Arabella with him. The two would have to demonstrate the power of the mating bond. A simple kiss would make their magic flare, and it would be apparent to everyone with the influx of their power. The tricky part would be getting her in front of the King when Uriah couldn't get her in front of himself.

Uriah was hunched over his desk, going over maps that had been delivered the day before. Everything we had for current landscaping had to be updated, the new threat assessed fully. The updated subterranean landscape, now mapped out by soldiers and cartographers, was being reissued in new maps across the Realm. The Lord of Summit began searching for similar cave systems and found another. Both came from Queen Clawin's territories in the Southern half of the continent.

Uriah had found the one in the South tip, but it's twin in the North where the river was shallow right along the boundary of the Torrent Kingdom was in the Northern half of the human territories. The cliff faces may make a formidable border, but not if one was willing to go below ground. There was talk about sealing the caves, and plugging for meters on either end to create solid dams before flooding the tunnels.

We would just have to locate the spot in the river above the tunnel section and drill holes. It would be more effective than leaving soldiers to guard it. Now the lords were arguing whether or not it would create flood zones and other issues with erosion. What if the mountain collapsed from the force of water rushing in? They were researching it now while a decision and action would be on the horizon. As the river swelled with fall rains, it'd be an ideal time to engage the maneuver.

"I found her in Palomora. She appeared to be working and in good health. She was, um, well...that is...I mean..." I fidgeted. *Fuck, just spit it out.*

"Uriah, the thing is, I'm not entirely sure you want to know," I leveled with him. "I really don't think you'll like it, and I don't want to report something that may be upsetting to you. Less knowledge may be better in this situation."

He was my best friend. He may be my superior, but I knew him well and how deeply he cared. *He's going to be crushed to see what she became, how much the humans perverted the kind soul she'd been before.*

"She what? Out with it already." Uriah's hazel eyes pierced into mine, his mouth turning down into a grim expression. Worry creased his brow. I always marveled that his hair was such a dark auburn inside verses the natural maroon highlights that lit like flame in the sun. Mine was boring. *Too bad he doesn't like males. Focus Felix!*

"Well, it seems that she would be some sort of dispatcher. An assassin...of sorts. She's called the '*Sculptor's apprentice,*' on the streets. She's fairly well known around Neera and Palomora. She doesn't charge outrageous prices and is willing to trade, not just for goods, but for additional skills. Sewing, masonry, gardening, whatever they have to offer, no matter how insignificant. She tends to find work avenging those who can't fight for themselves. You mentioned she said she collected debts? She kills a lot of rapists and those heavily involved in general debauchery. She's particularly well tasked," I reported.

His eyebrows lifted, a bemused grin crossing his face as realization hit him and what she'd told him clicked into place. He huffed a quiet laugh. "Of course, I'd expect nothing less of my Arabella. She was very cryptic, but I see what she was alluding to now. Smart. She's got an amusing sense of humor —dark, but funny. And I suppose you witnessed some of her... debt collection?"

"You could say that. I watched her enter a sleazy looking dilapidated pub. I went in after her since it seemed busy. The windows were full of people and I saw several enter and exit before I went in. I didn't think she'd notice me and she didn't." *The room was dark and smokey, the floor sticky and gross, but she was focused from what I could see.* "She easily picked out her marks, and she didn't hesitate to make a scene," I said. *Bold. She's swift and ruthless.*

"She took out two of them before they even realized she was there without using her magic at first. Just good old fashioned steel and good aim," I added as Uriah cocked his head looking absolutely amazed. "The scene erupted in screams as realization dawned on the patrons closest to their table. I managed to get close enough in the commotion to get a trace on her magic before she shifted," I assured him.

It was simple, really, I just had to be close enough to focus on someone's aura, their essence. It was like a finger print and flared to life when magic was used. Part of the give and take required for use of that magic.

When magic was called, the aura expanded, and if I threw out my magic at just the right moment, I could latch onto someone else. A quick tug on my magic and the trace was set. By focusing on it, I could determine where she might be. Sort of like a beacon.

"She approached quickly from behind the biggest human, and put a dagger in the heart of another using the shadows as cover. There was a third at the table, a younger fae with long dark hair, he shifted away the moment he saw what she had done to his cronies, but as he did she captured his trace, and I captured hers," I explained.

"She took the two humans to a dock in Palomora, infrequently used from the appearance of it. She proceeded to decapitate them and toss their bodies into the bay. She kept their heads. I presume as proof of her labor. She has enough magic to keep at least two voids open. When she was done with the bodies, she cleaned up and shifted away," I concluded my report. Uriah's mouth gaped open. He stared at me a minute more. *You found her, but can you stomach what she became?*

"She's an assassin? For whom? There must be more to it than that," he said, the corner of his cheek twitching. He clearly wasn't sure what to make of it either. "She can't just be ridding the streets of vermin, there must be a bigger cause..." *Of course, he's always looked for the good in people. Motives matter, but what if she's just a monster?*

"I'm not entirely sure yet. She seems to be doing fairly honest work for what it is. Aside from that, she has a horse that's seen better days and I'm not sure where it is she's staying yet," I said, wishing I could give him more, something to set him at ease. "Perhaps once she finds that fae and collects his head, she'll come find you."

"Let's hope. Try to find out who she's working for and where her allegiances lie, anything you can find. Where she lives, what cities she spends the most time in and any friends she might turn to. Anything. I want to know as much about her life as possible," Uriah ordered.

"On it," I said. "I'm sorry its not easier news to hear." I was taxed this last week trying to help secure our borders, updating my own data, and then using my tracking skills to relocate Arabella. I had a feeling it wasn't going to get any easier. I nodded and backed to the doorway, turning as I reached the door jam and briskly walking down the hall. *Arabella was going to be the death of him.*

"Any news is good news, unless she's dead," I heard him growl as I rounded the corner.

Chapter 10

Uriah

He found her, Felix found her! I hoped she would stay near Neera. Palomora wasn't far from there. She preferred the coast. Maybe that was a good sign. I glanced in the mirror. My hair was shaggier than usual; I needed to shave. I leaned against the dresser in my bedchamber, my vanity mocking me. Dark circles laid under my eyes. I hadn't been sleeping well since the cave. When I did, I dreamed of her, following her but, never catching her. I ran all night, soaked in sweat, and she was always just out of reach. *My new worst nightmare.*

You look like shit. You'd better get it together or she won't want you when she's done doing whatever it is she's doing –an assassin, of all things. I shook my head and glanced toward my bedside table. She deserves so much more. Luxury and comfort. Not hunting down scum. Even if she's good at it, she can't possible enjoy it. Can she? *No, that's not my Arabella. There's so much more to her. There has to be.*

I walked to the edge of my large bed and looked down at the sketches of her I'd made. I spent hours on them that first evening. I wanted to see her again. After I issued orders and sent the rider's out, I needed a distraction, so I started to sketch her. I pulled in all the art supplies I could find across the manor then sent a courier into Marelitor, the sleepy seaside town inland a few miles to buy as many supplies as he could find. It'd been years since I felt like drawing. Now the room is littered with broken pencils and scraps of paper. *My father always used to draw and sketch too. He was quite the artist.*

I remember her copper hair was laced with golden

strands in the sunlight and pinned into the braided crown on her head and the way she knelt with her matching leathers on the river's edge. I barely noticed the blood and refused to draw it. The image of her looking up at me with her brilliant smile full of straight white teeth imprinted forever on my brain. Her full breasts swelled under the edge of her fitted top, and the amber amulet rested between them.

She was lovely. Little flowers and vines were embroidered along her outfit, as if she felt compelled to add her own touch. She's every bit as pretty as I imagined she'd be after she'd come to age, perhaps more so than I could have imagined.

She'll make a beautiful Lady. I'll buy her as many flowered things as she could possibly want. I wonder if we'll have a female together. I hope she looks like her if we do. A perfect mother for the next Queen of the Agron Realm.

My pants tightened at the thought of being with Arabella. The thought of running my hands over her body, kissing her pouty lips, playing with her curls. Her full tits would fit perfectly in my big hands. *She smells like strawberries, I wonder if she tastes like them too.*

I dropped my trousers as I stood shirtless by the bed. It was late, nearly midnight, and I was still awake. My cock was already hard and throbbing. I need some sort of friction. I wonder what she and I could enjoy together? I'd had plenty of the knob gobbling whores chasing after me due to my status, but I'd never taken anyone to bed. I had all the opportunity, but none of the want. Most women just didn't turn me on. I wanted what I couldn't have. I'd enjoyed a few of them, but not fully. *I wonder if Arabella is still a virgin.*

I let my underwear fall to the floor, and I lay down on the bed. My soft mattress should beckon me to sleep, but no such luck was found. I was too wound up. Still staring at her portrait, I spit on my palm and called for my shadows. I slid my hand down my pulsing dick.

Grasping firmly, I began pumping myself. Thick and throbbing, I willed my shadows to flicker at the head of my cock. Slowly at first until a little cum added to the moisture. Shadows wrapped firmly around me, like a mouth but deeper, and began to work me. I willed them to surrender and massage me. I bit my lip as the pressure increased, holding back a moan.

I looked at the lines I drew of her face and closed my eyes. I concentrated on the feel of her hot body pressed against mine in the cave. Gripping harder now, the shadows caressed and built the pressure at the crown of my cock, my hand working me in tandem. I slid my hand up and down more steadily as I remembered her small hand wrapped around mine, wishing she were pumping me instead.

I thought of the scent of cinnamon and strawberries laced with the apples we'd eaten. Her pouty lips...*I wonder if she'd swallow? Would she want to fuck me as badly as I want her?* My breath was ragged as I came in a hot burst, my seed leaking through the fingers I'd wrapped around my cock still pumping.

The shadows I'd called swirled and caressed my balls, working up my shaft to squeeze it all out. I wished every bit of it was filling her. I let my shadows ease off and dissipate. *Soon. I just have to be patient. Give her the time she needs. She said, 'I can't.' Not, 'I don't want to.' Something is keeping her from me, from our life together. Felix will find out what it is and we'll fix it. That's all. It just has to be fixed. I can do that.*

I lay there, cum dripping beneath my balls for a moment before I collected myself and walked into my bathing chamber. Filling the claw footed tub in the spacious room, I got in. An array of soaps were waiting on the window seal by the tub overlooking the sea. I began rinsing myself and the day away. I took a hand mirror off the ledge as I lathered and shaved my face for the first time in a week. I needed to get my shit together. *I miss you, Arabella.*

Chapter 11

Raven

"I told you, he was definitively fae. He shifted away. His ears were covered by his hair, so I didn't register that immediately, I can't argue with the shifting though. What human can do that?" *I feel so dumb. Uriah saw it immediately, and I've never seen myself for what I am.*

"He just hasn't used his magic, or we'd be wherever he is now. We'll find him. Eventually he'll slip up. I heard from that old lady down by the fountain in the market that he visits his girlfriend every month. We'll watch her. He'll come eventually," I said to Knightmare as I knitted my hands through my hair, untangling it.

It'd been three weeks since I'd added the brother's heads to my collection. They were holding up in the void, but even with a lack of air, nothing lasts forever. Time was of the essence. I hadn't been able to locate either the fae that had shifted away or the fourth human—if he was human. Never did I think that I'd be chasing down a fae, not in the human lands at least.

"*Yes, yes, I know. But to be idle this long is boring. This can't remain a pattern. We need to be more productive, especially if you intend to return to the Agron Realm,*" he reminded me. "*Queen Clawin readies an army, and she will attack soon. That cave you ended up in was only the beginning of her attack; just a means of delivery. The treachery she and King Plavlock are planning won't wait. More importantly, from where do they intend to strike? In Plavlock's Torrent Kingdom or Clawin's Daemon Kingdom? The Summit region in the Agron realm runs the length of the continent.*

They could attack anywhere..." Knightmare trailed off as he turned his head away from me. "If you don't hurry, you may have nothing to go to. They're moving the Torrent navy South already. Is it a ruse, or are they staging?"

"I'm sure they'll be fine since Uriah knows about the cave system now. He was bred and born to be the Lord of Shallows. I'm sure that comes with study and logic. He's a warrior and has trained for years by now. I watched him fight, and humans are slow, fragile," I pointed out dropping my hands from my hair and twiddling with my necklace.

Worry still bunched my eyebrows. We walked along a sandy stretch of beach. The sand was soft, and the heel of my boots sunk. My calves needed a rest, but I really did prefer the sea to a valley. I could walk along the beach all day and never grow tired of the scenery. I pulled a long piece of grass from the edge of a dune as Knightmare and I meandered down the coast line to no where in particular.

Weaving the grass through my fingers, I turned to Knightmare before he could answer. *I can't keep my hands still today. Why am I so nervous?* "Do you think I should write to Uriah? I mean, just in case..." My voice trailed off. *Stupid. If Uriah can't protect himself, is he worth dealing with? If I return to the Agron Realm, King Plavlock will certainly be up in arms and pissing off Queen Clawin—the whole continent could be back at war. The stalemate has lasted ages. So far, the Queen had stayed out of it, but it hadn't stopped her finding a way past the Summits anyway. The bigger question was why? What was her motivation?*

Last week, I'd flirted my way into information from a few big mouthed soldiers. A low cut tank top, short skirt and a couple beers while playing cards on the edge of an encampment outside Demplore had yielded me quite a bit of information.

The Queen was gradually moving her armies around and a rumor had started that King Plavlock had pulled his navy war ships together. The two of them teaming up might be the push the humans needed to over run the fae.

I thought of Uriah's promises. *Even if I am fae, would the people even accept me? Becoming the Lady of Shallows. It sounds too good to be true. I don't deserve anything like that. What kind of Lady walks around assassinating the dregs of the kingdom? How would I even learn everything? Surely, Uriah would need me to undertake things while he was away, but I've never even had a home!*

The Torrent Kingdom's forces were sailing South. There was only one way into the Agron Realm by water. The Southern tip of the Shallows hosted a mile wide break in the reef that other wise ran the entirety of that side of the continent. That, coupled with the two hundred foot cliffs around the Brume and Meadows, meant trying to scale them would be futile and a waste of resources.

There wouldn't be any fae left without the natural barriers. They didn't have the soldiers. Humans were a plague on the planet that could overrun them, despite the magic they held. Fae had begun dying out a hundred or so years ago. Less and less born every year and the unions had weaker magic. The whole world knew it was only a matter of time before the day of the Fae would be over.

"Humans are a disease." Knightmare nudged my shoulder with his moist nose, echoing my thoughts. *"It's okay to want a normal life. You've never had security. It's fair to want that. Write to him when we get back to camp. I'll deliver it. It'll take me an hour to shift there and back. They won't know what to expect when they see me. I'll find the one that was watching you at the dock. In any case, the mating bond will pull you together or tear you apart."*

I nodded. *Just in case. What if he really doesn't know what's headed his way? Could I forgive myself if he was injured as a result of not warning him?*

"I think I would sleep better if I did. Are you sure you want to go?" I asked. "I could hire a courier or something." Couriers were the only ones that routinely traveled back and forth between the two worlds of human and fae. It was illegal on both sides of the divide to harm a noted courier. The punishment was swift—death. It didn't matter which side. It was just unheard of. It was the most dangerous and also the most protected job on the continent.

I'd often wondered if I should become a courier instead of a killer, but the latter suited me better. I was judicious in which jobs I chose. I wasn't trying to get rich, we didn't even have a home for goodness sake.

Nomadic life seemed to be okay for the most part. We just moved around depending on the weather. Caves made good shelter and the continent was abundant with them. I touched my necklace again. It felt heavier when I considered having a home base rather than roaming.

"Will you be okay here for a bit if I shift into town and buy some stationary and a pen set? I'll get you some sugar cubes," I tried to sweeten the deal.

"Save the coin and get yourself what you need. We'll both feel better if you sleep enough. You've kept me awake with all your mumbling the last few nights. I'll pass on the sugar if we both get a decent night's sleep," Knightmare said with his head turned to me. I was by his flank, the good side. It made him nervous if I walked on his right. He was afraid with his blind eye he'd accidentally step on me.

I'm not sure either one of us will fully recover from our scars. I rolled my shoulders. They always stung, a tightness and pressure that I couldn't seem to escape. Sometimes, I dreamed that I had wings again and I could fly for miles. I'd only ever flown with Uriah. My wings had been too little when I was a child to fly anywhere. I had been looking forward to my fourth birthday so much. These blasted memories won't stop.

Usually around the age of four or five, a fae's powers began to show, and the ones with wings would be taught to fly. They called it the Reveal. I was just shy of four, so I never got to learn to fly, and my powers hadn't come in. When they did, they were stunted immediately because of that wretched potion. I'd rather eat slugs for the rest of my life than drink that again.

My powers out grew it at least. I learned to make my own

rules. I was strong. I knew it, and Knightmare knew it too. I walked with Knightmare into a small dip in the dunes. High grasses encircled us and blocked a lot of the wind. "Will this do for tonight?" I asked.

"It feels like it'll be clear enough," he said looking into the pale sky just as a warm breeze washed over us. The blades of the high grass on the dunes bent with the wind. For October it really wasn't so bad.

"Okay then, I'll leave you here under magical wards with some hay and be back in a bit. It won't take me long if I shift. I'll try to hurry, then I'll set up camp when I get back," I patted his side, giving him a good scratch and kiss on the nose. "Be a good boy and bite anyone that tries to steal you."

Chapter 12

Uriah

The autumn sun was shining down on me as I stood in the field near my estate holding a piece of stationary with buttercups and daisies hand drawn into the top right corner. With great anticipation, I opened the envelope:

To the Lord of the Shallows

Dear Uriah,

I'm sorry to only be writing. I shouldn't have left you by the river the way I did. It's been eating me up. I was thrown off. No one had said that name in so very long. I panicked. It doesn't happen often but you seem to bring a lot of emotion out of me. I'm trying to sort things through. I let Arabella die two decades ago. I'm trying to resurrect her, but it's not easy for me. There are so many ghosts in my past. I hope you can understand. I have things I can't walk away from just now. I'll come to you after I've handled my responsibilities.

I've pondered it greatly this past month. I've had the nudging of a good friend to guide me. He has a mischievous streak, so it's taken me a bit to come around but I know it would be best for everyone. Mostly, I'm writing now to tell you that there is a plan brewing to breach the Agron Realm through the Summit and Shallows.

Queen Clawin has used more caves to tunnel below the Couloir River. I don't know how many in total, just that they exist. I don't know if King Plavlock has followed suit in the North, but he is moving his navy in its entirety to the South, with a promise from Queen Clawin to supply them and allow entry to the caves through her lands. She's amassing soldiers and nearly doubled her navy as well. Hopefully, it can be rectified before things come to a head.

I'm sure you've already addressed the cave we found ourselves in. You've likely already checked the rest of your border. I've been losing sleep worrying about it, so I thought I should just write. Even with the miles short between us, we're worlds apart, but every time I use my magic, it tugs me toward you. I've taken to not using it much as it makes it harder to not just come your way., but also mostly so the fae you sent after me can't track us.

Soon, I'll be done with my tasks. I can't explain it all in a letter, but please call the dark haired fae off. He's distracting. Please trust me in this. I've had a lot of years to take care of myself. This is something I won't fail in. I hope this finds you well. I've thought of you constantly since we realized what we were to each other. Wait for me...

Always yours,

Raven

P.S. Knightmare bites. If you try to hold him, you will get hurt.

"Well, good thing she warned me," I said to the large black stallion before me. His right eye has clouded over, and he was badly scarred down his right flank as well. He looked well fed and taken care of, so she obviously treasured him. "Please, don't bite me," I said. "Sebastian, bring water and oats for the horse," I finished, glancing over my shoulder to where Sebastian and Felix stood in front of the training ring.

Sebastian set down the sword he'd been working on and pivoted on his heel headed toward the stable in the distance. His muscles flexing as he went. *He seems annoyed that I asked him.* He, Felix and I had been making jokes and sharpening all manor of steel outside on the grounds near a training ring, honing our trove of weapons for any upcoming battles. *We're all tense. We can feel the restless energy from our soldiers.* A skirmish was coming and it felt imminent.

Like Arabella had written, armies were on the move. We'd only found the two cave systems, but I'd be dispatching more rangers to search again. It seemed this was going to be a bigger problem than anticipated. *But she cared enough to write and to warn us. That must be a good sign. 'Wait for me,' she'd wrote. She feels it too. I know it. I will wait. I did wait.*

"Felix, can you run into my office and grab stationary

and a pen? Don't forget ink," I asked. He nodded and headed off toward the manor in the opposite direction of Sebastian. Gravel crunched under his feet as he crossed from the grassy plain onto the driveway and trotted up the road to the manor.

"What do you say ole boy? Stick around for a snack while I write a return letter? I dare say I wouldn't know where to send a reply," I said to the horse. *Not that he understands me. How did she send him here? Nightmare. That's quite a name.* "Why she would name you nightmare, is beyond me." I muttered.

"It's Knightmare with a 'K' because she considers me her knight in shining armor. But yes, of course, I shall wait for your reply but no longer. She and I have urgent business to attend to. This detour seemed necessary for all parties, or I wouldn't be here," the horse spoke into my mind. I startled, and my eyes flew wide as I looked at him. Astonishment rang clear in my head. *A faehorse? Of course she would find a faehorse.*

"Apologies, I hadn't realized you were a faehorse. Please excuse my poor manners," I said to Knightmare. Shock laced through my voice. *How embarrassing.* "Are oats to your liking? I can have Sebastian bring something else if you prefer?"

"Oats are fine. I really don't need a snack. Raven and I ate just before I came, and she feeds me before she feeds herself," he said, looking at me with his left eye.

"Do you mind me asking what happened? To cause the scars along your flank and face? Both you and Ara- er, I mean, Raven, seem to have quite a few between the two of you," I asked delicately, hoping for insight.

"She saved me from a barn fire. I spooked a human. I thought it was one I could trust. I was wrong, obviously, and he tried to kill me. I threw my pleas into any mind near me, and she answered my call," he began to explain.

"She suffered several burns in the process of breaking down the door to get me out of the flaming stable, but she took care of me. She healed me as much as she could. She doesn't have healing powers, but she understands herbal medicine. She provided poultices, fresh food, and water. She sheltered us in a cave while we

healed together," he told me.

"As far as her scars, those are her stories to tell. Most of them she can barely remember. Years of torture by the Sculptor, has greatly effected her memory. You would do well to stop calling her Arabella though. It does more damage than good. I'd never seen her cry the way she did when she returned to me after meeting you. It stirs things from the past. I think it causes her physical pain as well." Knightmare leveled his good eye on me.

I nodded. Why is she holding to a made up name? Arabella was her mothers name. Wouldn't she want that honor back? What did they do to the poor girl? *She can't keep using the name her captives gave her.* "I'll try to change my mindset. It's just, she was named after her mother. Her mother loved her more than herself and sacrificed her life so she could live," I tried to explain. "I miss her horribly. I know I don't really know much about her anymore. She was only a child. We both were. We'll have to learn about each other again. If she gives me a chance, that is. Though by this letter it sounds as if she might be missing me just as much."

Knightmare stared me down. A tingle washed over me and pulled my breath out of my lungs. A flash of gold circled his left eye before fading away. *That was interesting. What magic does* he *have?*

"Here you are," Sebastian said, coming up to us from the left with a bucket in each hand. He'd had the good sense to stay on the horses good side. "Our finest oats and fresh water," he said as he set the buckets in front of the faehorse.

Knightmare finally broke eye contact with me, dipping his head to eat some of the oats. He whinnied in satisfaction.

"Knightmare, would you mind if I tried to heal your eye? I think the burns on your flank are too severe given the time lapse. However, I may be able to bring some of your vision back," I said, hoping maybe I could ease some discomfort that may still linger. I didn't have enough time to thoroughly repair burns like that, not after they had set. It would take numerous sessions and an immense amount of power if it was productive at all.

"If you have healing magic, you may try. Raven did what she could with physical medicine, but she doesn't have healing powers," Knightmare answered, still chewing the oats.

Permission granted. I rubbed my hands together and placed them over his right eye. Feeling for the damage, my magic searched through his eye socket, threading and repairing what connections could still be made. There was a fair bit to hope for.

Felix came up beside me, but I ignored him for the moment. I willed my magic to help the majestic creature. Neither fae nor horse, he was rare and beautiful. *Just like Arabella.* Healing him took several minutes and drained a significant portion of my powers. I would require a nap before dinner. He was nearly finished eating the oats by the time I had worked my magic.

"Thank you. I hadn't expected it to work, but I can see from both eyes now, better than I had before. I'll be more useful to Raven now," Knightmare told me. The flash of gold circled both eyes this time. I nodded to him.

"Glad I could help. I'll make haste with the letter so you can return to Raven," I assured him. I took the paper, pen and ink well from Felix and headed over to a bench overlooking the sea. It was a short walk but would provide me a little privacy. *What do I even say to her?*

Dearest Raven,

I've just been acquainted with Knightmare. He's incredible. I'm glad you have such a good friend to keep you company and help keep you safe. I tried to heal his eye for him. It sounds like you both take great care to love and protect one another. Hopefully, soon you and I can say that about each other too. Knightmare will always have a place in the Shallows as well.

I appreciate you sending word. We knew troops were moving but knowing where they will be headed is helpful.

84

One additional cave system was found in the lower Summit.
They are searching for more. The two we have located will
be rendered useless. I trust that information won't end up
in enemy hands.

It seems you still have loose ends to tie up, so I
will try to be patient and ask Felix to give you space. If
there comes a time I fear for your safety or even question
it, I shall send him to check on you. I don't know if feels
the same for you, but I can feel your bigger emotions.
He'll keep his distance unless dire need should arise. I
don't want you to feel smothered. If you need help, call
out for Felix. He will answer, even if he is far. I myself
have been worrying constantly.

I feel the bond growing, and I think you're having
a similar experience. I shall sleep better tonight having
heard from you. I want nothing more than for you to be
safe. If you need anything, please send word. I'll send it
with Knightmare if necessary. I only want for your safety
and happiness. I think our ideas of that may be a little
different, but I'm sure we can come to a compromise with
time. I hope that will lead you to standing by my side. I
miss you so very much.

With love,
Uriah

I folded the letter and pressed a kiss to it. Please come
home soon. I only hoped it wouldn't scare her away. She said I
brought out emotions in her. Well, I was a mess. I jogged back
to Knightmare, Felix and Sebastian. Knightmare had finished
his oats and water and was looking restless, as he shifted
his feet, he clearly didn't care for Sebastian and kept blowing
snot on him. Ornery isn't he? I chuckled at my observation.
Of course, Arabella would own a contemptuous faehorse. If
anyone could tame one it would be her.

"Thank you, Knightmare," I said as I approached. I
stepped up to his side and put the letter in his side satchel.
It was smaller than a saddle bag, but was perfect for carrying
the letter and small items. *I wish I had something else to send*

her. "Before you go, is there anything else you may need? Food, coin, anything we can pull together quickly for you?"

"We always need coin. Raven has been taking side jobs to get it. She's short on supplies. It's slowing us down on the five for the Queen," Knightmare answered.

Five for the Queen? The heads? Five heads at the Queen's request? *That's who she's working for. Where does her allegiance stand? Did I just tell the enemy my plans? Was this all a set up? Are there really troops moving?* My mind was racing.

Felix must have understood what was said, and pulled a bag of coin from his pocket before he handed it to me. I pulled one from mine and added Felix's to it. I tucked it in with the letter. I would pay Felix back later tonight. Hopefully, the coin would keep Arabella focused on her task for a few weeks. Unless she squandered it, but that was doubtful. It wasn't a lot of coin, but it would keep a reasonable person comfortable for a few months at least. "That should keep you for awhile if you're careful," I said as I stepped away.

"Your kindness is noted, young Lord. I shall take the letter and coin now, thank you for my vision," Knightmare answered. He immediately shifted. We all stared at the space of ground he'd been standing in.

"He just shifted right out of my wards!" I exclaimed.

He hadn't shifted directly into the estate when he'd arrived. He came through a thick wood to the west. Felix had about jumped out of his skin when the horse bolted toward us, stopping inches from him. Nose to nose, he simply turned his head toward his left flank until Felix looked at the side satchel and approached cautiously to retrieve the letter addressed to me.

I looked at the letter in my hand. *What a day. But she wrote to me. She wants to come back. She thinks of me often.* I ran my other hand through my hair while I thought about Arabella.

The tightness in my chest eased just a little bit. I opened the letter again and began rereading it as I silently turned from my best friends and walked back to the manor. By the time

I reached the front door, I heard metal on metal and glanced back to see Sebastian and Felix sparring. Just then, Sebastian sidestepped Felix and sent him flying backward. Sebastian was exceptionally strong and fast for a fae. It wasn't often he was outmatched in the training ring. *Good. A broader war is coming. I can't afford to lose either of them.*

Chapter 13

Arabella

"Ahh!" I cradled my arms over my head as I oriented myself to the new day. *It burns so bad.* I'd just been kicked in the ribs as a wake up call. My ribs stung where the old ladies boot had slammed into my relaxed body; my ankle bothered me more. *I wish I could get this wretched chain off. It's too tight!*

I was covered in bruises, cuts, scrapes, and healing scars on a daily basis. My body had hurt for so long, the new hurts barely registered anymore.

I yanked on this blasted chain around my ankle. The shackle had grown tight as I grew. It'd been on my leg for several years at this point, and though it used to annoy me for being too loose but not loose enough to pry my foot out of, now I had the opposite problem. Bloody scabs wrapped around my ankle. Those itched something fierce.

"Drink this. Now. I haven't got all day. There's chores to do," Clara, the old bat snapped at me. Her breath smelled rotten as she leaned in front of me. I half sat up but lurched back when she put her face in mine. Most of her teeth, what was left of them, were black and stubby. The silver chalice with purple pungent liquid sloshed toward my face. Wisps of gray scraggly hair filled my sight as she bent down. Her hand connected with my face as she slapped my chin up, forcing my head back. "Drink it!" she yelled at me.

I half sat up again and opened my mouth so she could tip it in. She poured too fast, and I sputtered. She slapped me in the back of the head this time. "Don't waste it you little brat," she warned, tipping the rest down my throat. I shuddered. It was like drinking fire and ice combined. She'd learned long ago not to hand me that cup because I'd surely throw it at her. Consequences be damned. *What could they possibly do that they haven't already?*

I felt the effect immediately. My eyes grew heavy. and I felt the tingle of numbness washing all over me. My ankle stopped itching. I stopped caring. The ache in my ribs where she'd just kicked me lessened. Unfortunately, so did my resolve to get out of here. *One day. Just wait.*

Clara wandered back toward the ovens where she'd been working. I slept on a cleared out shelf on the side wall of the kitchen. Pots and pans were stacked above me. I didn't have a bed, but the chain I was attached to just reached enough so I could at least get off the floor. The conditions were better for me, and it made it easier for no one to trip on me. I could care less if *they* tripped on the chain. The shelf used to house deep pots, so I at least had a little head room, though I couldn't stretch out.

My thick curly hair fell in front of my face as I rolled on my knees to the floor and started to stand. I pulled the small piece of leather scrap I'd scrounged and began braiding my mane of hair into a more manageable arrangement. With that accomplished, I walked four paces to a metal bucket that had been placed in the corner.

I wasn't afforded any privacy, even though I desperately needed to pee. I squatted over the bucket and held up my ragged little dress. It was more of a gunny sack. An order of flour had come in it, and I pilfered it to wear. I didn't have undergarments or shoes of any sort and I rarely had the privilege of a bath.

No one ever gave me new clothes, and the dress I'd arrived in all those years ago had been ruined in the dungeons. It would be far too small now. I wasn't a little girl anymore. I hadn't reached maturity, but I was no longer a small child.

I fashioned clothing out of whatever scraps I could find. Once I finished peeing, I stretched the chain on my left ankle to my work station. Something like thirty pounds of potatoes waited for me in a tub of water.

It was my job to peel them one by one, cut out any bad spots, then place them back in the water so they stayed fresh. The cooks would pull what they needed from it. I picked up my small pairing knife and set to work.

They wouldn't dare give me anything more than the dull little knife. Even with the potion, I'd begun growing restless. For a time, I only had to have the potion once a day, but lately they'd been forcing me to drink it both morning and night. *Maybe it'll quit working, and I can get out of here.*

Clara glared at me. *Now what?* "You stupid girl! Not the potatoes, we have to finish this cake first. Take that butter there and that sugar there, the powdery one, and start blending it in that big bowl," she said, pointing to the other ingredients to the side of my work station. *Buttercream, right. King Plavlock's birthday.*

"Sorry ma'am, I forgot," I said, setting a potato down and moving to the frosting ingredients. I whipped the unsalted butter, sugar, milk, vanilla and a spot of blue dye in the large bowl. It came out the whitest white, just like the King would want. He wanted White and purple for everything. Even that damned purple potion.

Thirty minutes had passed since I began my task, and my stomach rumbled. I tried to ignore it. "Here you are, then," I said to Clara, turning to her with the finished buttercream.

"Good, you made a small use of yourself today," she muttered, taking the bowl. She set it in her work station across the small kitchen from me. "Now do the potatoes."

I went back to work on the potatoes. Clara worked to finish the cake and put it in a walk through chamber. The outside was full of ice blocks to keep the inside cool. That was someone else's job though; we never handled the ice and my chain didn't stretch that far anyway.

After a couple hours, I finished the potatoes. One of the male workers in the kitchen came for the tub and replaced it with one full of carrots and radishes. I was to trim the tops and wash away any dirt that may lay on them. With Clara's back facing me, I snitched a small carrot. I chewed quietly, careful not to move my jaw too much lest she notice.

"Are you done with those yet?" she asked after awhile had passed.

"Nearly," I answered. "Clara, do you know when my birthday is?" I dared to ask as I turned to look at her.

Her face turned a deep crimson and I thought she may strike me again. "Why would you ask such a thing?" she said, clutching her throat, the cord of her amber pendant necklace pulling tight at the action. Shock and fear shot across her face and she stumbled for a moment. *What an odd reaction.*

Gathering her wits, she crossed the room and grabbed both my upper arms, shaking me. "Why would you ask such a thing!" she yelled in my face. She shoved me to the stone floor. "I'll finish up here. Go back to bed."

"I can help. I'm not tired. I've only been awake a few hours," I said, confused at her reaction. "I'm sorry I asked. I didn't mean anything by it."

"Finish the carrots. I'll return in a bit, and I want them done when I do return," she said, wiping her hands on her apron, her plump frame shifting under her loose dress. With that, she stormed from the kitchen.

I finished the carrots and radishes, eating several of them while Clara was gone. It must have been an hour since she left. I snitched a small piece of cheese, a burnt roll, and a piece of venison jerky left on the counter barely in reach as well. Hopefully, they didn't notice. It was the most I'd had to eat in awhile.

"She's just through here..." Clara's voice rang out down the corridor leading to the kitchen. *Uh oh.* I turned to look at a man in head to toe black leather covered with scars and short jet black hair as he entered the kitchen behind Clara. *The Sculptor.*

"Hello there little dove. It seems you and I are overdue for a visit," he crooned at me with his deep voice—the voice of my nightmares. My stomach fell. I shouldn't have asked. Asking questions about myself was dangerous. I was Raven. That was it. I was nothing. No one. It didn't matter. Nothings needed no answers. Nothings were just nothing, happy to be alive.

He leered at me as I began to tremble. Pulling a key out of his black leather jacket pocket, he unlocked the shackle at my ankle. Grabbing my upper arm, he jerked me forward as he stood tall towering over me. "It seems you need reminding about the rules of your stay. Let's go have a chat, shall we?" He pulled me along beside him.

"No, no, no. Please. I didn't mean anything by it. Please!" I began to plead as he dragged me from the kitchen into the corridor and into the stairwell at the end of the hallway. "Please! I won't ask again. I don't need to know."

❀❃❀❃❀

Over and over, the Sculptor had made me repeat the lines, "I am nothing. I am no one," Until it sounded like nonsense. Like they weren't really words anymore. Like I wasn't real anymore. Just some made up idea that no longer existed.

"Say it until you know it to be true and I'll let you go," he promised. He wouldn't let me go. It'd been years. No one came. No one cared. I was no one. I was nothing. He was right. I didn't exist. I was nothing more than a ghost, a half dead, powerless girl trapped in purgatory. Just kill me. I wished for light and to die. At some point, I shivered my broken body back to sleep.

When I woke again, I had fresh cuts across my shoulders and back. Blood dripped off my swollen finger tips. My fingernails had been pulled out and my hair sheared off. I shivered, since I was stripped naked in the small, pitch black dungeon cell. Why did it always have to be so dark? I wished for light again and again until I passed out.

When I woke next, I found a ball of light in my hand—

precious, beautiful light. *Hello old friend. It's been quite some time.*

I stared at it for hours, watching it dimly light the murky cell. Rats lingered just out of its path. *How long have I been here?*

I heard someone coming and willed it away so I wouldn't be caught. It blink out to my astonishment. I stared at my hand where it had been, then quickly pretended to be asleep.

"Get up and eat this," someone said as they slapped my bare ass with their hand. "Put your rags back on." A pile of cold material hit my back. I played dead.

As I heard the door slam shut the male said, "The Sculptor really worked that one over this time. Two weeks and she's not healed yet..." His voice floated away. I waited a few minutes to be sure. I didn't want the rats to get the food.

I sat up and wished for light. The ball appeared in my hand again. *Oh, Thank the King.* I paused. *Odd. I haven't said that since I was...a child. Hmm.*

I picked up the food. Lumpy cold stew on a tin plate with day old bread. A cup of—purple *potion.* I dumped the potion down the drain by the wall and ate the stew. *I wonder what would happen if I threw up even one of the two doses. I could puke up the night dose they make me drink before leaving. Why didn't I ever consider it before?*

Chapter 14

Raven

I woke with a start. *Fucking nightmares.* It was still early dawn, the mist and fog swirling around the small patch of trees we'd camped in last night. The tent did little to keep me warm, and the ragged cotton blanket I had was practically useless once the fire burned down. *I need to get a new blanket, but I don't want to use too much coin. Maybe I can steal one.*

I struck a match and lit the candle beside me. Knightmare was still asleep. I could just see him through the tent flap bedded down at the base of a tree. *Let him rest.*

I exited the canvas tent I toted around. It wasn't well made, but it kept the rain off me when needed. I'd stolen it from a military camp some time ago. Bringing the candle with me, I stood up. It was still pretty dark, though I could just make out the sun beginning to brighten the horizon. *Another dawn approaching.* I let the first morning rays soak into my face. I could feel my power reaching for it, as if it needed the extra energy from the sun.

I squatted down next to the fire ring I'd built with rocks from the small clearing. I'd collected a bunch of branches last evening when we made camp here. The pile was growing low after burning for several hours. I spotted more low branches, and I wanted to get one quietly so I didn't disturb Knightmare. *I was waking him up often these past few weeks, I hope Knightmare isn't too angry with me.*

I piled small branches and a bit of tinder I'd stored away and got the fire going again. I sat back on a small boulder to the side of the tent and put on my hole-filled socks and beat up boots and I need to fix that hole in my sock. I'll do it later. I opened my void and pulled out a small pot and some oats. I grabbed a harness feed bag out for Knightmare and poured a few scoops of oats into it and set it aside. Then, I took some for myself and added it to the pot with a pinch of salt. Dumping water from my canteen, I mixed the oatmeal with a spoon and balanced it on two bigger sticks in the fire. I tucked the oats away and closed the void.

As I sat back and waited for breakfast to cook, I pulled out Uriah's letter again. I kept it neatly folded in my pocket. It'd been nearly a month since we'd written each other. I'd been over the moon that he took the time to write back at that moment and beyond grateful for him healing Knightmare's eye. *Such powers! I wonder what other magic he has? I've seen the shadows and healing. I know Uriah healed my arm in the cave, but to heal an injury so old? Incredible.*

Knightmare had been far less grouchy these past few weeks. We were still camped outside of Demplore. The weasel had never shown up, so we were back to the drawing board. I still watched the city center and frequented the market just in case I glimpsed him but I would be lying if I said I wasn't frustrated.

I'd been careful with the coin Uriah had sent back with Knightmare. It was a thoughtful gesture, but I wasn't sure if I should use it or not. *What will he demand in return? Nothing is free. There's always a debt left behind when something is received.* I shook my head. *Don't think like that, he wants to take care of us. He seems like a kind fae. It's not as if we just met.*

My memories flashed to Uriah flying the two of us over a pond. The sun was warm and his hair was lit like flame in the rays. His arms wrapped under my legs and behind my back, with my wings tucked in carefully. *No. No more memories. I need to stay on task if I'll ever be able to return to the Agron Realm.* I flip flopped constantly.

I reread the letter again. *My love.* He seemed to be sure of his feelings. I'd still been careful of using my magic. If I did,

Felix, could pop up at any moment. So, we'd been traveling the old fashion way. Opening and closing my void didn't seem to trigger the trace. If it had, then perhaps he'd held to his word and called Felix off like I'd asked him to do.

Either way, I'd garnered a lead on the fourth human, so we'd be packing up in a few hours and traveling to Stanzley in the North Eastern part of the Daemon Kingdom. It was closer to the border with the Torrent Kingdom, so I didn't travel that way often. Still these were desperate times and it was vital I find at least one of the two, soon.

I'd sent a report via courier just last week with an update to Queen Clawin promising that three were already dead and that I was working to locate the other two. It'd already been almost nine weeks since I accepted the job. Defeat was not really an option. If I didn't supply their heads, she'd take mine instead. *I have to do this. There's no other way. She'd hunt me down for defying her.*

My oats had begun to boil. I took them carefully off the heat and set them to the side. Refolding Uriah's letter, I put it in my pants pocket. Opening my void again, I pulled out a thicker cream colored sweater and pulled it over the gray one I already wore. I pulled my hair back out of my face, and I piled it on top of my head in a messy bun of wild curls. *I wonder if Uriah would prefer my hair up or down?*

My leather pants were no longer silk lined; I'd put those away and traded them for fur lined ones. It was the very end of October and had grown much colder. Snow would soon be upon on the ground and I needed to make some progress. At the rate I was headed, it'd be spring before I was free to decide whether to stay wandering around or return to Uriah. *I already know what I want. Stop pretending.*

Everything in my being was calling me back to the Agron Realm. It was as if acknowledging where I had begun from unlocked a door to my soul, and it was screaming to return, if not to Uriah, then to the Meadows. I'd considered writing my father; he had to know I was alive at this point. Uriah would have notified the Realm, but still, I'd heard not a whisper of him looking for me. *How does he lose a child and not search for them?*

Knightmare began to stir at the smell of my cooked oatmeal. I opened the void again and grabbed a handful of raisins out of a small glass jar. I plopped them in the pot. Next, I added a small scoop of brown sugar. Grabbing the spoon, I closed the void and stirred my oatmeal. I waited for it to cool.

"Good morning, Knightmare," I said, trying to be cheerful. The sun was cresting over the hill side now. It filtered through the trees, fog swirling through it as the rays began to warm the near frozen ground. *That's pretty.*

A nice blanket of dew stuck to the grass as I walked to Knightmare with the feed sack in hand. The tiny beads of water looked like shiny crystals scattered about. "Care for a bite?" I asked, setting it down and opened a third void. I kept several bales of hay in it. I pulled out three leaves and broke them apart in front Knightmare.

"Just leave it beside the hay for now," he said in a sleepy voice. *"I'll have some after the hay."* He lowered his head and began on the hay. He was not a morning person. I turned and moved a bucket of water closer to him. The top was iced over. I pushed on one side and pulled the round block of ice out. *"Great, ice soup,"* he grumbled.

I chuckled to myself and went back to my breakfast, using the spoon to shovel a bite in my mouth. The warm oats hit the spot in the chilly air. I took a swig of water out of my canteen and began in earnest on my sugary sweet breakfast.

When we were done eating, I took the pot through the trees to a small stream we'd passed on our way to the clearing. I sank to my knees and scooped up water. I washed up a bit. Next, I washed the pan, making sure to rinse all the food residue, and then tucked it into the void. I heard Knightmare call my name from the camp. I let out a long sigh. *I bet he knocked his oats over. Silly boy.*

I filled my canteen and walked back to our camp. To my

horror, a man stood next to Knightmare looking him over. He was rather pudgy looking. He looked awkwardly built with a tall, barrel chested figure. Brown hair with gray at the temples was pulled back into a pony tail that just reached his shoulders. His outfit was filthy—dark jeans which had something that suspiciously looked like shit all down one side of them. A thick black wool coat was covering a gray shirt with little holes down the front. I bet he smoked and had dropped ashes down them. His boots were pealing and had seen better days.

I looked past him to the tent. Another scrawnier man stood bent over, rifling through my things. He looked skinnier, younger looking. He had short burnt orange hair. A ginger with freckles that covered his face and hands. He had on a navy blue jacket, buttoned closed to keep the morning chill out. Blue jeans and mismatched boots. *What in the what? These damn ragamuffins. Oh, hell no!*

I pulled my dagger from my thigh sheath. "Good morning, gentlemen," I said, stepping out of the thick tree line into the small clearing. A smile crept across my face. Once I made my presence known, I prepared to unleash fury. "It's okay, Knightmare. She who smiles in a crisis has someone to blame. Good day to die, isn't it?" I questioned as I assessed the scene. Both had a rough look to them. I could smell booze hanging in the air around them.

"Hello beautiful. Quite the horse ya got here," said the man looking over Knightmare. He reached up to stroke his mane, and Knightmare snapped his teeth, stomping his foot in warning as well.

"I'd slap you for touching him, but that would be animal abuse," I replied sharply. I glared at the brute, and my magic began to build in my core, begging for me to unleash it.

"If your looking for coin I haven't got any," I said while I sized them up.

"Do you think they are always this stupid, or are they making a special effort just for us? You take the little one, and I'll handle this big oaf. They were talking before you came back. They don't

really have a plan, but it sounds like they frequent the rougher parts of Demplore," Knightmare said to me. I offered him one curt nod.

"They may have information we can use," I said to Knightmare. I sneered at the scraggly men. *I'm starting to understand what the Fae hate about the humans.*

"Good point. This one seems to be the boss, and the little one is a follower. I'm not sure how much brain power is between them, but it's worth a try. I don't think there is much going on in their heads though." Knightmare told me. We'd kill the ginger and play with the old one.

"What's that, love?" Freckles asked. As he stepped around the campfire closer to me, a knife glinted in his hand. I looked past him, quickly surveying the tree line. *Are there more than these two?*

"What would you be doing, all alone, in these woods?" He leered at me. His eyes washed over my figure as he licked his lips. His smile was disturbing—his teeth were brown and cracked. I grimaced. My gut twisted at the thought of anyone kissing that mouth. "Come now, we could be friends. Have you ever fucked two men at once?"

He glanced at the man by Knightmare. My eyes flicked his way. He was watching me intently and his leering smile was filled with blackened broken teeth. *Do these guys know how to brush their teeth?*

I looked past the ginger. "Shit," I whispered to myself. Through the smoke of the dying fire I could just make out my khopesh on the floor in the tent. Greenhorn mistake. I'd been sharpening it the night before as I bedded down for the night on my thin bedroll.

I called on my magic to deliver it to me as I kept eye contact. Magic swirled at my finger-tips and my hand warmed. Glancing down, my khopesh was now flush with my skin and ready for blood. So much for avoiding Felix. Hopefully Uriah can't sense this. I don't need a distraction—I need whatever information they may have.

"What the? Where'd you get that?" Pudgy asked, his eyes flying wide and his mouth gaping open in astonishment. I nodded to Knightmare, never taking my eyes off of Freckles. Freckles had the good sense to look uneasy and shuffle his feet. *Yes, you've made a huge error today. Your last, in fact.*

"You see, I don't know if you are aware of who *I* am, but you seem to have lost your way and stumbled upon the Sculptor's Apprentice. I'll tell you right now I have no intention of sleeping with anyone in this clearing. I also have no intention of letting you go. A victim can either stay a victim, or they can become the perpetrator. I prefer the latter," I whispered softly, my voice carrying through the campsite. A big smile stretched across my face and I waved them forward with a *come and get me* invitation.

"Well, lovely, if that's how you like it, we can go rough for you," Freckles said. With a laugh he continued, "The 'Sculptor's Apprentice.' Funny little bitch, ain't you. We've heard the tales of that freak. There's no way you're him." This time it was my turn to laugh.

"Aw, it's so cute when you try to talk about things you don't understand." I tilted my head to the side. I sucked in a breath and let it out slowly. "If you're not scared, then let's play a game."

He gawked at me and then lunged toward me, lurching forward with his knife palmed and ready to strike. He covered the ten or so paces between us. I slashed into him with my khopesh as he approached. My magic wrapped around him to stop his momentum and allow me to strike repeatedly. My fae strength and speed was much faster than his pitiful human muster. Warm blood sprayed across my face and cream sweater as he fell to the ground in the heap.

"Ugh, did you have to ruin my sweater?" I pulled my khopesh free of his neck and collarbone. He wasn't going to to get up. I turned to Knightmare who had bitten into the shoulder of Pudgy. He was screaming and swatting at my horse. His knife was on the ground. *Dumb ass.* He hadn't even bothered trying to stab Knightmare. Knightmare stamped his front feet shaking the man. Blood dripped down Pudgy's fingertips as it ran through his sleeve.

I called on my magic again, and cords of golden light burst from my hands. They crossed the short distance and wrapped around Pudgy's middle, binding his arms to him. A second cord wrapped around his mouth making a good gag. A third cord wrapped his ankles and as Knightmare released his bite from his shoulder. He fell to the ground. My magic felt different though. Weird, like in the cave. Weaker? I walked over and quickly sliced through his Achilles tendons with my khopesh. This idiot was going nowhere. He began screaming and thrashing about on the ground. *More blood. Why is there always such a mess?*

"*Well, that was fun. At least we got breakfast first. I think your sweater has seen better days,*" Knightmare sounded off as I crossed to stand next to him. I gently massaged his neck where Pudgy had hit him. *No one touches my horse.*

I squatted down and leaned over Pudgy's face. I tilted my head as I looked at him, anger flared in my face. The necklace around my neck shifted under my sweater. It felt warm against my skin in the chilly autumn morning mist. His eyes were wide, and he was clearly scared as blood began to pool around his ruined ankles. "Here's the deal. You came into my camp. I didn't invite you, and you bit off more than you can chew. It's too late for your friend over there. But maybe you can save yourself."

Chapter 15

Raven

"I can't believe you didn't set wards! What were you thinking? How long have you left us unprotected?" Knightmare was exceptionally angry with me. After the docks, I had stopped warding us routinely, afraid of the trace I knew was on my magic.

"Felix was following us. How was I to know who it was?" I shot Knightmare a glare. With the wards we wouldn't be in this mess. "I get it was pointless, I've used more magic in the last hour than I did for the last month combined." *Hindsight...always twenty-twenty.*

I sighed, "I'm sorry Knightmare. I didn't know if Uriah would be true to his word and send that dark haired fae after us again or not. I can't fight everyone. I just can't. We don't know them yet." Defeat coated my voice. Killing humans was one thing, taking on trained fae was a complete other. The necklace under my sweaters was becoming uncomfortably hot. I tugged at the cord, pulling it free of my layers. The amber glinted in the fire burning bright in the stone ring of my campsite.

Knightmare grumbled and fluttered his lips. *"If you don't trust Uriah, why are you trying so hard to go back there? Huh? We both know you need each other. Your magic is already weaker. Your heart hurts without him. Why fight it so? He's your mate, you'll find no one better suited to put up with you."*

"I—don't know why," I said, twisting the amulet on my necklace round my finger. "I just... it's complicated, like everything in life. I don't know where I belong. I'm not sure

I've ever known. It just always seems to be where ever it is that I'm not." I picked up the spare dagger I'd dug out. "It's not like I hate people. I just feel better when they aren't around."

Pudgy was still corded with my magic. I'd set heavy wards around us after the camp intrusion—sound wards and a ward to confuse whoever tried to come this way. They'd forget what they were doing and wander off in the opposite direction if they got too close.

I'd knocked Pudgy in the head with the dull end of my khopesh and went to gather more firewood. We'd be here for a while, after all. The sleazy ones usually knew what the other grease balls were up to. Knightmare would confirm if he was telling the truth, but maybe he'd need motivation. *He can at least confirm what I already know.*

"It's only complicated if you make it complicated. The mating bond is in play. Your magic has already begun the pull, you won't be able to resist for much longer. You'll need to see him soon at the very least. You and I both know only proximity will quell it. Together your magics will blossom and grow. If you'd only take that necklace off you might be able to feel it the way I can sense it on you. You're holding yourself back, staying away will be catastrophic for both of you," Knightmare warned me of what I already knew.

If a mated pair stayed away from their mate—made the choice to reject the bond—it would drive both parties mad and break their magic. I'd found a book on fae lore after the cave. Education was the most valuable thing I could give myself. I rolled my eyes at Knightmare. He hated my necklace and often blamed it on our bad luck, but to insinuate it had something to do with the bond was just silly.

I couldn't think about it right now. I had a new task at hand, and we needed to locate the fae and human we sought. "I'll send another letter tomorrow, I do miss him, but we need to do this. Maybe he'll meet with me and promise not to try to hold me. Maybe we could spend a few hours together, and then... I don't know. I'll finish this and decide," I said.

I picked up a bucket of water at my feet and dumped it on Pudgy to wake him, I got my mind ready to work. Decide to keep my magic and help his grow, or damn us both. The choice should be easy, but it wasn't just my choice. It's his too. I am a monster. He is a kind fae that takes the time to heal injured animals. *Uriah and I are not the same.*

Knightmare looked at me, sorrow filled his eyes. It was strange to see both his chestnut brown eyes intact. I'd gotten so used to the clouded eye that when he returned with his eyesight repaired I thought my heart would burst at the kindness he'd been offered. Healing magic was a deep magic upon itself. It offered the chance at regeneration. The ability to save someone on the brink of devastation, that was a true power. Not my fancy light tricks.

"Wakey, wakey. Looks like I get to be karma today and I'm all yours. So, now you have my undivided attention," I said, prodding Pudgy with my foot. He grunted, and his eyes fluttered open. The water had barely rinsed any of the deplorable stench off him. I'd moved him to a flat spot to the left side of the tent after I'd knocked him out.

"Time to play." I gave him a mocking look as I leaned over him. I pulled on my magic cord, it went taught and it forced him to sit up. I willed him to stay upright, my cords of light obeying. "What's your name, stinky?" I raised an eyebrow and twitched my nose.

He spit at my feet. I cocked my head and asked again, "What. Is. Your. Name?" His lip curled into a scowl. "Look, you and I both know how this is going to go. We're two pieces of the same pie. You can tell me what I want to know, or you can bleed for a while then tell me anyway. Save us both some time and yourself some agony."

He pursed his lips, and I picked up a pair of leather gloves, sliding one on. I picked up the red hot dagger. It was hot even through the leather. "Your name?" I asked, boredom lacing my voice. "No one will hear your screams," I said simply, as I turned the dagger in my hand, appearing to inspect it. If he wants to play games, I was taught all of them by the Sculptor.

He gulped. His Adam's apple bobbed up and down, and a line of sweat trickled from his gray haired temple. "Re-Reginald. They call me Reg-g-gie though," he stuttered, eyeing the dagger. I glanced at Knightmare who confirmed with a bob of his head that he told the truth. His eyes flashed gold as he used his faehorse magic. *Good. Now we can begin.*

Memories of the dungeon under the Sculptor's hand flashed in my mind, and I pushed them back. The tables were turned now, and I needed answers. My necklace burned at my throat, but I disregarded it.

"Good. Where are you from?" I asked while adjusting my stance. The heat from the fire behind me was becoming intense. Sweat trickled down the small of my back.

"Why do you need to know?" Reggie fired back, spit dribbled down his chin. He really didn't understand his position here. I pulled the cord around his middle tighter. Perhaps he was too comfortable.

"Curiosity killed the cat. Are you the cat, Reggie? I always wondered whose cat was selected to die in that old saying," I mused. "Please Reggie, don't be so difficult. I really don't *feel* like playing games today, although we started all this with you thinking I was the mouse in your game. Turns out I'm the big bad wolf that eats kitty cats for lunch." I said whimsically, with a chuckle at my own tenacity. *I need to get my mood straight today.*

I brought the dagger closer to Reggie, stopping just short of his cheek. I'm sure he could feel the heat. "But, it's a little early for lunch, and I don't eat humans, so if you please." I pressed the tip into his cheek, the scent of burning flesh wafting up to my nose on the breeze.

He tried to lean back. I could feel my cords slipping and tightened them. *That's not good, is my magic losing it's grip?*

"Palomora, I'm from Palomora," Reggie finally answered. *I'm just getting started, old man. I learned from the most twisted fucker of all. He never gave me mercy, now I don't lose when I play this game. I learned every terrifying lesson.*

I glanced at Knightmare. *"Yes, he seems to be telling the truth,"* he confirmed. *"He's not very smart. We were right about that. Apparently big and mean does not equate to exceptional brain power. Work faster. He's lost a lot of blood already. You'll have to get answers from him before he bleeds to death."* I laughed. Brutes usually didn't think with their head up top. One track mind, only I'm not a defenseless female.

"How did you meet your friend?" I asked, using the dagger to point at Freckles where he laid on the ground covered in his own gore. Reggie fought to pull away from me, his eyes wide in terror. The fire burned merrily between his dead friend and us. If it were other circumstances, this might be more enjoyable.

"A bar. We met at a bar I go to most nights." He answered faster this time. He was beginning to understand.

"How long ago?" I asked. I didn't look at Knightmare this time. He'd speak if I was off track or if he lied to us. Hopefully all this wouldn't be for nothing. It definitely wasn't the highlight of my day. So far, that'd been my oatmeal, which now churned in my stomach. I shifted. The dirt was mixed with blood and clung to my boots. *Why's he got to bleed so much. I barely cut him. Just a couple swipes on his ankles.*

"Um..." His eyes darted between Knightmare and I. Knightmare took a step closer, clacking his teeth and stamping his foot on the ground. He was as impatient as I was. "Um, we met...we met, um...last year. In the spring. I don't know," Reggie panted. The welt forming on his face must be painful.

"I'm looking for two individuals. A fae and a human. They run in the same scene you seem to enjoy. I'm wondering if maybe you two idiots crossed their path at some point recently. Would you happen to know Seamus Brandt or Finnigan Altmore?"

He immediately paled. His fair complexion lost every sense of color, and I swear it tinged green. Oh yes, he knows of them. From what I gather, their reputation is as far stretching as my own. He shook his head, "I can't." He began blubbering, and tears leaked down his dirty face. The five o'clock shadow he sported caught them as they began to stream in earnest. "Please, no one walks away from them. They're—they're sick, cruel for the sake of it. Just let me go. I'm sorry. I'm sorry!"

He thrashed as much as he could still coiled in my magic. *Oh, shit.* It had loosened again. I tightened it and pushed more effort into the strands. *Fuck, that's not good. I'll have to hurry this up. My magic, isn't holding.* My heart began to race. Is it the mating bond calling? Is this happening to Uriah too? My eyes flicked to Knightmare. He studied me, having noticed my magic was not doing as I commanded.

"Really? Well, you're not walking away from me either." I smiled broadly and tilted my head as I pointed to his ruined ankles. "So you might as well tell me where I can find them. Maybe they'll kill me and you'll be avenged," I said, my lip curling in frustration.

I tipped the dagger down and brushed it across his cheek, wiping a tear away. He screamed and jerked his head back. Then I sliced it down his arm, opening him up. Beads of blood dotted along his skin as I cut into his jacket letting it fall open and let the tip burn the remaining material to his arm. The smell of rotten material was worse than the burning flesh. I smiled another big smile as he shook, and his eyes flew wide again. Setting the dagger down, I ripped open his gray shirt. Reggie began screaming; if there weren't a sound ward I'd be concerned someone could hear.

"You know what happens when someone is preyed upon? Something breaks in their mind. Something critical. Let's just say that though I may appear to be a small, frail, easily broken human, I'm not. Are you familiar with King Plavlock's pet? I was schooled by the Sculptor himself." I picked the dagger up again. It was cooling, but somehow Reggie didn't seem to be very scared of the fire.

"Where can I find Finnigan and Seamus? I promise I'll make them hurt just as bad. Tell me now, and this can be over quickly. Lie to me, and I'll draw it out. I promise, it'd be better for me and you, if I was in a hurry." He shook his head. *Okay then, if you insist.* I went to work.

Six Weeks Earlier

"What are you doing here?" I whispered in a hiss, quickly ducking into the darkened stable. "You're not supposed to be anywhere near this estate—Aaron has already caught you before." The entirety of the Meadows region was as good as mine now. Decades worth of plans had fallen into place leaving me in control, but the lead guardsman was troublesome. I had a feeling he was suspicious of me. I often found him just out of my sight.

What if he's lurking now? My eyes swept the stable. *How dare Killian come back here. What if we missed someone that night and they recognized him, even after all these years?* Paranoia swept over me. Aaron was hired after, but he's too nosy. Lionel always agrees to send him to the border, but the blasted potion makes him forget before he actually does it.

"I know, but this is urgent." A dark haired man stepped out of the shadows, his dark shoulder length hair just sweeping the collar of his tweed jacket. *When did my brother cut his hair?* He was smartly dressed in light trousers, a crisp white shirt, and clean leather shoes. His hooded eyes darkened in the shade of the unlit stable. Sunlight filtered in through the open doorway, but it didn't reach this far.

"Urgent, you dolt! What's urgent is that you told me Arabella was dead twenty years ago. We've received word she is. in fact, very much alive. Would you like to explain that?" I spat at my brother. "What if she remembers you? What if she connects you to me?" I said, first poking him in the chest and then tapping my collarbone. *This could undo everything I've worked for.*

"I know I messed up. I sold her to King Plavlock. I couldn't think of another way to keep Piper," he said, his voice pleading. "That's why I'm here now. The child has grown into a monster. When I sold her, I figured they would kill her. I found out that now she hunts Finnigan, and she's been searching continuously. He was accused of some crime in the Daemon Kingdom. Queen Clawin has put a bounty on his head, and the girl is after him. The stupid boy never had any sense, and now I have to stop her—for real this time. You have to help me. There has to be a way to get to her before she gets to my son!"

"Your son is a goon, badly bred, and ill tempered. There's been something wrong with him since he was born eighteen years ago. I have no doubt if he has a price upon his head, it is well deserved," I huffed.

My mind whirled. *Arabella knows too much. She'll tell everyone it was me. And that seer, Zeds, he has given prophecy about her to the Lord of Shallows. The old fae knows too much too. So many problems.* My nephew, if I dare call the half human, half fae abomination my blood, was in trouble more often than not.

She can kill the brat. Maybe we can use him to lure her into a trap, kill her in turn.

I walked deeper into the stable with Killian following me. Horses shifted their feet and the smell of dung hung in the hot summer air. One sniffed at my hair. I slapped its nose, and it stepped back in it's stall blowing snot into the stall. *Stupid beast.* I adjusted my layered dress. The corset was digging into my side wrong, but it's a small price to pay for being Lady of the Meadows.

"The child has grown now. It's not a simple manner of just handing her over. I can kill her no more now than I could stomach it then. Surely you must know that," Killian said. He was such a desperate fool. *What can he give me that I don't already have…I bet I can rope him into killing Zeds so I don't have to.*

"But stealing her, that was fine? Selling her—fair game?" I questioned, though I knew he was right. He hadn't been able to kill any of the servants in the manor. His hand shook when he took the bloody knife from me. *Weak, pathetic excuse of a male. Oh no, it was me.* All that delicious blood. I'd soaked in it as I bathed the next morning. I had to look decent for the news to arrive, after all. I always was a good actress. Lionel never suspected.

I was the only one strong enough to carry out the plan. It was simple as they didn't expect the visiting niece of a Lord to slash them to pieces.

Our father was brother to the Lord of the Brume—second oldest, the title went to his older brother. He was left with scraps—money. and property, but no title. I would never have been a Lady had Arabella been available to take her place with Uriah.

Lionel was happy to stay single after his mate had died birthing his child. The hollow shell of a man still pined for her. Thank the King the bitch died. Arabella. She was so perfect in his eyes. Oddly he never cared much about the child named for her *precious* mother. The child, she only reminded him that he'd lost the last connection to his wife. It was best to just be rid of her. I'll have to remedy that somehow. My buffoon of a brother can't do anything right. Selfish and stupid. I'll have to distract Lionel. *Perhaps a new potion? I'll have to visit the sorcerer in the Brume again. What can I bargain?* My thoughts trailed off as I formulated a plan. I have to be careful.

This will cause more uproar, like when I convinced him to marry me. I'd had to use a strong ancient magic to do it, mimicking a mating bond, like he'd been blessed with a second mate. It was unheard of, and it took time, but slowly people accepted it. What know one knew was that I feed him a special blend of *tea* from time to time when I feel him grow distant. I trade favors for the concoction, secrets and information about our troops with the old sorcerer in the Brume—the Musician, he calls himself. He's delighted to make deals with me and what did I care? They're soldiers. They can take care of themselves.

The bigger issue is that when Arianna was grown, her child would be wed to the new heir produced by the Brume and Summit, a boy born just a few months ago. He was her blood cousin. Marrying into incest was a small price to pay for power. By the time Arianna turns eighteen and Uriah impregnates her, well, the timeline was highly inconvenient for everyone.

With Arabella resurfaced though, the King would surely insist she and Uriah wed. She was the logical choice, but not the one I could allow. No, not after all the work I put in to get rid of her, bedding Lionel, killing all those people. No, no. It had to be my daughter. My line was destined to be royalty. There simply was no other way. Maybe if Killian acted from afar? If he didn't see the blood, he wouldn't be so damn squeamish.

"What are you thinking? You have that look, Judy." Killian crossed his arms over his chest. I could see his fast pulse in his neck despite the darkness.

Killian was weak. Piper is kind, but she's a human. How impressive could she ever be? She was aging rapidly and looked like it. We may age slower, but we don't live hundreds of years like our forefathers did. The magic was dying and that perk with it. My daughter would set that right, if we could get rid of Arabella once and for all.

"None of it was right, what you did the night we stole Arabella, what you asked of me. I will always regret it, but I must protect my son. Whatever the King of Torrent did to her; the Sculptor he set loose on her has addled her brain. She's sick, twisted and every bit as cruel as the next fiend. As cruel as you are." Killian said as he shot me a look of loathing. Shaking his head he rubbed the nose of the horse I'd slapped. Easing the creatures discomfort. I rolled my eyes. *He's too soft to be male.*

"Then go... do something about it. I can't do everything. Find her before she can find him," I said, all patience lost. "Find your balls while you're at it! And don't come back here sulking around in the shadows. It's not my fault your magic is weak. At least you can shift, if nothing else. Use it, and find the girl."

I started to turn away and stopped. I sighed, pinching

the bridge of my nose. Two birds, one stone. The old seer, he knows too much, has seen too far into the future. Zeds, yes. Cantankerous old male. *I keep finding his correspondence with Arabella in the manor from all those years ago.* "Come back to this stable after dark. I'll help you save your son, but you have to help me in turn. I'll leave you the means to take care of your problem. You can do me a favor while you're at it, and I'll leave instructions for you. We can prevent more issues from developing."

I turned, my long straight black hair swaying behind me as it fluttered with the air. My dress was cumbersome. I lifted the edge of the silk and cotton and carried it as I walked across the meadow in front of the manor and into my home, the greens and gold shining in the late summer sun.

Chapter 17

Raven

We were a week into November, and I had found a cave on the outskirts of Stanzley in the northeastern part of the Daemon Kingdom to weather out the storm while it snowed. I wanted to be moving on, but even with magic, no one else would be out and about in this blizzard. Most of the continent was forced to hunker down from the weather. It was already a foot deep and not letting up anytime soon.

The last ten days had been a long trudge through the Kingdom. Reggie, my pudgy playmate, had finally divulged that Seamus had indeed been holed up in the city of Stanzley with some of their sleaze ball friends.

Stanzley is one of the biggest cities in the Kingdom. It seems dear Reggie hadn't been willing to narrow things down very much. I helped him remember which neighborhood we should focus our attention on. From what we'd learned Seamus was staying in an industrial district. A lot of machinists, black smiths, carvers and weavers worked in the area. Many of them rented the rooms above their workhouses for cheap since it was ideal for someone that needed short term housing. I've stayed in similar lodgings now and then.

It'd taken us days to work our way here. Tomorrow, we'd pay the area a visit if the weather paused for a moment. I shivered and my stomach growled. *We're almost out of food again.*

We'd risk a shift in the morning, though Knightmare said he'd do it so I didn't have to use my magic. I was furious with

Uriah. I'd barely finished questioning Reggie when Felix came into view. He'd walked right through my wards. The trace had likely given away how I'd weaved them, or he was inside the perimeter already when I cast them. It had been stupid to think a ward would protect us. My magic was weakening, but —Uriah's magic was likely weakening as well.

Thankfully, I'd packed most of our things the third time Reggie passed out from my tinkering. I gave him a little reprieve before waking him again and I put the tent away, made a quick lunch for myself and a snack of apples and carrots for Knightmare. I'd worked Reggie pretty hard. I'd barely had time to slice his ruined throat. His corpse was full of cuts and burns, broken bones...he held out for a long time. They always talk in the end. *How many times did The Sculptor break me?*

I thought back to the scene ten days ago. I had just finished and was cleaning up when Felix stepped in the clearing.

"Was all that really necessary? Felix asked, looking around at the carnage, his black cloak blew in the breeze that had picked up since we began. The crisp air berated his black leathers. Blue waves were visible on his shoulder, his long brown hair braided down his back.

"Yes. I needed the information and I had a good feeling he would have it. I was not wrong." I said, the tinge of frustration coating my voice. Now I had an address, a list of their favorite pubs, and a solid idea of when I could find them at each. Criminals always keep tabs on the ones that made themselves nervous. From the sound of it, Seamus and Finnigan were demented little fuckers. I fully intended to rectify that situation.

"There are better ways, Raven. Surely, you must realize that? Uriah will help you with whatever you need. Anything. I'll help you. You don't have to walk this path alone." Felix took a tentative step toward me.

"Right, help me? When Uriah won't even honor my wishes and order you to leave me be?" I shot back at him, anger rising. The necklace around my neck burning through my sweaters and I felt my blood rise in angst.

"Uriah doesn't know that I'm here. I came on my own. I heard the screaming, like a faint echo. Your magic is growing weaker—I was curious why you were using it all of a sudden when you haven't in weeks. When your wards continued to fail, I decided to come have a peak of what was going on." Felix licked his lips, like he was nervous. His blue eyes darting around, taking in our surroundings.

"He's lying," Knightmare said, the gold ring flashing in his eyes. *"He's been tracking us. He's followed us all along. He was just careful enough to keep his distance."*

"Knightmare can tell if someone is being honest. Lie to me again, Felix. I'd been contemplating writing Uriah, perhaps coming for a visit. I think that notion has gone to flames. Why don't you report *that* to your Lord of Shallows." I turned at once, hopping on Knightmare's back and he shifted us out of camp.

I left Felix with the two dead bodies, a bunch of gore and a mostly dead fire. Felix can clean up the mess. We shifted into the Jordane Forest to the East of the continent.

We ended up South of where we needed to be, so we set off immediately. We had a lot of ground to cover. There were a string of caves we frequented through here. When we near the city, I dismounted. The trees were much thicker in this part of the forest.

We walked along in silence for a half hour until we came upon a cave we'd slept in before. I slipped between the well hidden fissure in the rock. It was a tight squeeze, but the cavern was vast inside and let off rolling echos. There really wasn't a big opening and it only went a little way back before it became a solid wall with no exit.

I lit a candle and checked the caves' furthest corners. It

was clear of any threats or critters. I called Knightmare, and he shifted inside the cave. We'd been stuck here since. I was worried about him as he didn't like to be confined for long periods.

Shortly after we settled in for the evening, it started snowing in earnest. This particular cave blocked most of the wind, but allowed for a fire, so it was our best bet to survive the frigid temperatures.

I set heavy wards, weaving the magic much more intricately than usual to hopefully keep Felix out. *Bastard. If I wanted help, I'd ask for it. But is my magic really failing or did he unwind it? Or is he stronger than me? He tailing us already, was he close enough to fall inside the ward? How am I ever going to sleep tonight? What magic does he have?* My mind raced.

The amber necklace around my neck had turned to ice, making it all the more miserable. Knightmare and I tucked in for the duration of the storm. Thankfully we were used to rationing, so I'd have enough supplies for a few more days. I'd lost a fair bit of weight since summer. My pants were loose, and I had needed to go down a few sizes.

Tears streaked my cheeks. Do I look the same? Will Uriah ever listen to me? I stared at my canvas bag. I'd haphazardly tossed it in the corner of the cave.

We'd used some of the coin from Uriah to restock the staples we needed. I hated the idea of him providing for us, but we had the coin so we might as well use it. I'd counted and recorded it when it came with the letter. I marked it in a ledger so I could pay him back. I don't like owing anyone anything— even a bit of coin. Another lesson from The Sculptor, '*Leverage, never give someone leverage. Once a debt is owed, it's never really repaid.*' I hugged my knees and cried in earnest.

❀ ❀ ❀ ❀ ❀

Early the next morning, we woke to a frozen world. The crevice I'd entered was frozen solid. It filled with snow in the night, but the cave was cozy and relatively warm. It was hard to vacate, however, we needed to get moving. Besides, I wanted to look around before we exited to make sure there wouldn't be any surprises.

I mounted Knightmare and he shifted. I dismounted outside the cave to look around. Knightmare wasn't above me riding him for short distances. Usually he preferred to keep some of his Fae dignity so I walked often. He'd carry things for us if I didn't have space in any of the voids. We tried to be respectful of each other.

"You can't be fucking serious?" I nearly shouted. My voice echoed across the snow.

We took about two steps when Felix stepped forward from behind the tree line. Looking very cold, his black leather encrusted with snow and ice, he held his leather gloved hands palm out. "Please, don't shift away!" he said quickly. He stopped moving and waited.

"Oh, for fuck's sake, why are you here?" I asked, the exasperation thick in my voice. I spun to my left as he took one more step toward us. Drawing my khopesh from my sheath, I glared at him. I was not in the mood for this. *It's fucking freezing and he wants to chat. I groaned internally.*

"Well, first I'd like to apologize. Uriah told me to come *only* if I thought you were in danger. I came anyway, against orders—back at that camp. I wasn't trying to over step—it was simply out of curiosity," he explained. "But it was absolutely against my standing orders. Please don't punish Uriah for my stupidity."

"He speaks the truth this time," Knightmare said, shifting his feet in the deep snow. It was nearly knee high and increasingly becoming miserable. I doubted we would find

either Seamus or Finnigan moving about in this crap. *"He seems to be earnest. Perhaps we should hear him out. He's the only connection you have to Uriah."*

"Why did you follow us now?" I demanded.

"I wanted to apologize while also offering my assistance, if I can help at all. It's been a couple months, and Uriah isn't doing well with the extended separation. Your magic is likely suffering more than you realize as well. I noticed your wards fell moments after you set them. You haven't been using your magic consistently, so you likely haven't noticed, but his are strained. The bond you share? It's getting greedy. It needs you two together," he finished. Worry filled his blue eyes, I cursed him in my mind. *Fuck. I know. I was going to go to him last week, then you showed up.*

"I told you this could happen. We should detour, just for a few hours. I can shift us in two or three leaps. I'll need to rest in between. You can see Uriah while I do. The human and fae likely won't be spotted out in this, and to enter their hovel; with unknown occupants wouldn't be wise if your magic is acting up," Knightmare chimed in.

"We thought something like this might happen. I've been desperately trying to finish this contract. My life is forfeit if I don't. And I'm not sure it'll count if I'm not the one to take their heads specifically," I shared. "So, I don't know how you could help. Queen Clawin has some sort of magic of her own. It's not widely known, however it was in my best interest as the time to make a deal with her, and I can't negate it."

"Clawin has magic? Interesting. We had no idea. That explains some things, also complicates others. What kind of contract is it? Perhaps I can help thwart it?" he asked.

I shook my head. "She is not to be thwarted or I would have already. We'll come for a few hours. Maybe until dawn, but I need assurance that we'll be able to leave. If I'm not actively searching for the last two souls, her magic will notify her. She doesn't need to be near me to kill me," I finished.

Snow crusted Felix's wet brown hair. He nodded. "I can shift us there," he said putting, a hand out. He seemed too eager, or maybe that was just the freezing temperature talking. Desperate. *Is Uriah okay or is this a trap?*

"*I will take you. I don't think he's lying necessarily, but he sounds too keen to get you there.*" Knightmare agreed with my assumption. "*If we shift in and it's a trap, don't hesitate to get away as fast as you can. I'll take care of myself. Don't stay if you can go without me.*"

My brow creased. It felt off, and I couldn't turn off the warning in my head. "Has something happened to Uriah?" I asked.

Felix shifted his feet. "Nothing happened in a physical sense, but he's been depressed. He doesn't think you'll ever come home to him. The magic is taking a toll on him. His shadows have all but abandoned him... He never stopped looking for you, you know. And he refused to consider other brides, even the child he would have been forced to wed later, your half sister. He's always waited and hoped to find you. Having you in front of him and losing you all over again destroyed him."

"Destroyed him?" I asked, a pang reverberated in my chest at his words.

"It's...It's... he needs you," Felix said. Hope and despair etched into his face. "I've known him since we were boys, before you were taken—I've never seen him like this, even in the aftermath, it was never this bad."

I nodded. I looked to Knightmare, he gave me a nod. "*Males are generally affected by the magic more deeply. The most primal of instincts are unlocked. The distance will drive him mad and stifle his magic all the same.*"

My mind spun and my heart ached. *Does he truly love me? I don't know if I can love anyone. If I'm even capable anymore. But if he wants me…it doesn't matter with the bond. He'd have to keep me anyway.* "We'll come until sunrise," I shot Felix a stern glare.

"We must come back at dawn, or both Uriah and I will be lost to the world." *If the Queen kills me, it would kill him too. She can't have him. I won't allow it.*

Part Two: Repossession

Chapter 18

Uriah

I was standing behind my desk, looking out at the waves crashing against the cliffs in the distance. My breakfast was still sitting untouched beside me. I had no appetite and lost some weight.

It was getting harder and harder to be patient. Arabella had to come home soon. She had to be feeling it too. *Does she not want me? Is this an outright rejection?* My magic had fizzled of late. The shadows took ages when I called for them, and they held less and less. It was like my magic was dissipating. I stared at my cold eggs, sausage links and strawberries. Her fruity scent was so alluring. Not eating isn't helping. *Is she is doing okay?* I wondered.

I looked back out the window at another gray morning. Snow flakes were beginning to fall. Usually, the salt air kept them at bay but it seemed everything was so much colder this year. Lonelier.

I turned and looked down at my desk. I was sketching her again. It had become an obsession. I sketched her fighting in the cave in the subdued light, washing her hands by the river, her brilliant smile. *I need air.* The atmosphere of my office was suffocating me.

I walked across my office to the open doorway. As I crossed the threshold I heard familiar voices. Sebastian came into view first as he rounded the corner with his strawberry blonde hair.

My office was on the main floor. There were two levels

below ground that had been dug out. The first lower level floor hosted full apartments where staff stayed in their off hours and one below that which was used for storage and...unsavory things. In this wing of the estate at least. I had an entirely different wing for visitors. They could access this wing through a sky bridge or the front door where they would find sentries waiting to allow entry—if they decided you belonged here.

The entirety of the manor was a rich cherry wood, and carpet runners of blue and silver protected the floors-the Shallows official colors. Coats of armor and vases littered the walk way as decorations. Paintings of various land marks hung on the walls. It was very inviting. The smell of wood polish hung in the air mixed with the salty scent of the sea breeze.

My personal residence, was private. Felix and Sebastian had rooms upstairs near mine, but no one else was privileged enough to live here with me. The third floor held an enclosed balcony, making it more of a three season room, a piano room, library, and another ballroom.

It needed a female's touch. I needed a female's touch. With my mind wondering to myself, I wasn't paying much attention as Felix rounded the corner. I heard him say, "Ah, there he is now. My Lord, I've brought you a visitor."

Felix and Sebastian typically were not very formal, but they knew when to ride the balance. I looked up and couldn't believe my eyes. My pulse quickened as my eyes locked onto her hazel eyes, long copper curls and luscious curves. I noticed that she had lost weight too and an alarm flared in my chest. "Arabella!" I exclaimed. It took four long strides to reach her.

She smiled wide, looking up to me as I reached for her. Her hands were like ice. She had on a torn gray jacket that had seen better days, a holey red sweater, black leather pants and the same boots from the cave. *Has she been eating?* The electric pulse we'd briefly felt in the cave returned. "Raven," she said with end edge to her voice. "I go by Raven now."

"I'm sorry. I forgot myself. Raven," I corrected. "Are you home to stay?"My voice filled with hope and I refused to drop her hands. I shifted my weight, and my socks suddenly felt off, my jeans too tight. The collar on my white polo shirt was too imposing. My tattooed forearm felt different, a shift I hadn't felt in weeks.

"Only for a night, if you don't mind having me. I'll explain it all later, but I have to go back and finish a task. It'd be dire if I didn't, and I just caught a break. The snow storm in the East has made it difficult to follow the lead, and your friend here dogged me down," she said, idly waving toward one of my best friends. Her voice was soft and sweet to my ears. A calming melody. Though she had a crease in her brow and looked a bit agitated.

"Did he? I told him not to, I promise," I said, scowling at him. "He clearly doesn't follow orders too well. I'm so very happy to see you though. Are you hungry? I was supposed to have already eaten, but I let it go cold."

"I can usually muster the energy to eat," she said, glancing around. I'd dropped one of her hands, but I kept her right hand in my left. It reminded me of how we held hands while making our way through the last segment of the cave. "Sebastian said he would put Knightmare in the stables. Is it alright if he stays while I'm here?" she asked. She observed a centuries old vase on a stand near us.

"Of course! He always has a place here, the same as you. He's a good friend. It was an interesting visit, and I was thrilled to get a letter. He'll be taken care of. Are you sure you have to leave tomorrow? I can't convince you to stay longer?"—Hope swelled in my chest.

"Ah hem, my Lord," Felix said. "I can verify that it is absolutely necessary that she continue her duty in the morning. It's paramount to both of you that she be allowed to leave. Any break in searching can trigger a disaster." *What the hell does that mean?*

"I see. Well then, I'm passing off my dailies to you and Sebastian," I said to them. "I shall be occupied until the moment Raven has to depart." They both nodded as they received the orders and turned to begin the new tasks I assigned. They knew my daily roster of events.

"Have you traveled far?" I asked, steering Raven down the corridor the way she'd come and taking a right near the main door. An elaborate ballroom opened up before us. I couldn't take my eyes off her, and she seemed to be having the same problem. She fidgeted with her necklace. "Through here," I said, guiding her through a doorway on the far side of the room.

"From Stanzley." Raven said, an edge to her soft voice.

We entered the kitchen area. Two of my best cooks were puttering around as they worked on their chores for the day. As I entered, I said, "Excuse me dears, would you mind if I took over the kitchen for a few minutes?" They stared at me, stunned speechless.

After a moments pause, the younger of the two said, "Yes, yes, of course, my Lord. If you need anything, simply ring the bell," she gestured to a bell with a black handle on the center island. They waved as they left the room through a side door, and Raven gave them a smile and a nod. *So beautiful. Elegant.*

Raven waited for them to leave before saying, "I don't appreciate you sending Felix after me. You wrote that you wouldn't, but you did anyway."

"I promise, my orders were for him to give you space." She pursed her lips. "I understand you need time. I know you have responsibilities, if it's important to you, than it's important to me." I tried to cajole her.

She huffed a sigh. "I want to be mad at you. I had a speech prepared, but now that were face to face, I'm finding it difficult." She shook her head and pulled on the charm around her neck with her free hand. "Make no mistake though, I'll sacrifice both of our magic if you undermine me again." She tugged her hand and I held tight.

"I'd rather not argue. I wasn't even aware of Felix's actions until moments ago. I'll have a talk with him." I rubbed my free hand down my face. "Fuck," I whispered, the moment catching up to me. "I'm sorry." Her hazel eyes softened a bit at the apology. I offered her a small smile. "I've searched for decades to find you. You're the only one I've ever wanted, and if I have to be patient a bit longer, I will. Just try to give all this a chance. I promise, your life here will be worth it." Silence settled around us for what felt like eternity.

She tilted her head, but her arm went slack and she nodded. "You said something about breakfast? If I'm being honest, it's been a while since I have had a proper meal."

"Okay, let's see what we have here." Giving her a small smile, I gestured toward the pantry. I pulled Raven over to a small table pushed against a wall with three chairs and offered her the one on the right. The kitchen was farmhouse style and rather open compared to many. I set to work when she was seated and could still see me. Moving to the walk-in ice box, I began getting out eggs, ham slices, cheese, mushrooms, peppers, onions and some heavy cream. I made us omelets and thick toast with butter. I set some huckleberry jam on the table between us with two full glasses of fresh squeezed orange juice and slid a plate to her.

She'd been quiet while I was cooking, simply taking in the kitchen. I'd let my head cooks design it when the estate was built. I figured if they had to work there, they might as well choose how it looked. I hummed to myself quietly. Exposed beams washed over the ceiling in this room of the house. She liked to observe things, and I didn't want to disturb that. I sat as she said, "This looks and smells amazing. Have you always known how to cook?" She took a bite. "Mmm..."

"I think being in a military position makes it easier to learn the domestic things. Everyone has to pitch in, or we all starve," I said as I took a bite myself. I did pretty well, but it needed salt. I reached for the salt and pepper shakers on the table and offered them to her first. She shook her head.

"I'm okay. This is perfect," she said around another bite. Her cheeks were tinged pink, and it looked lovely against her porcelain skin tone. Once she finished chewing, she said, "I'm sorry it's taking me so long to finish this contract. I'm sure Felix has told you what I meant by debt collecting by now."

She looked up at me through her lashes. She took a sip of juice. Her eyes widened slightly in delight. *My, she is gorgeous.* "I wasn't trying to be coy, calling it that in the cave. I just know it makes people uncomfortable to know my true function. It's not exactly a pretty one to be honest, however it doesn't really bother me. Plus, the particular jobs I take leave the world a better place."

I nodded. I was chewing a big bite of toast smothered in huckleberry jam. Suddenly, I was ravenous. "You don't have to justify anything to me. I want you to know that. I want to give you the finer things in life, but I'd never fault you for finding your own way, especially with everything you've been through. You are a survivor first. You stayed alive. That's all that really matters to me. The rest we can figure out as we go."

She gave me a tentative smile and sorrow etched her brow. "I never knew anyone was looking for me. I knew I was different. Anytime I asked something about myself—well, I saw the inside of a dungeon for months on end. So I stopped asking." Tears welled in her eyes. She used her napkin to wipe them away quickly.

I reached across the small table, and took her hand in mind. "I can't repair all the damage they've done to you, but I promise I will always try to understand."

Once our plates were mostly empty, she said she'd had enough. I set them on the counter by the dirty pan, cutting board, and bowl I'd used. I didn't want to leave too big of a mess for my staff to clean up. "I've been preparing the manor for your arrival. I hope that's not too forward. I've purchased some dresses and outfits if you'd like to change. There's a small village down the way. The shopkeepers were delighted. Perhaps you'd enjoy a soak in the tub? You look chilled—perhaps it'd warm you up a bit as well. I want you to be comfortable here."

"I would love that," she said, looking surprised. "We were holed up in a cave outside of Stanzley. I probably smell like a horse, or worse." She cringed and her cheeks lined themselves with pink again. The blush looked incredibly endearing.

"This way, then," I gestured to a staircase. We had exited the kitchen and were in the ballroom still, but I liked to have multiple exits from the upstairs areas. It was far more convenient than constantly taking laps around the house.

Chapter 19

Raven

We entered a bed chamber halfway down the hall. It was beautiful with satin and silk in shades from navy blue to cerulean and the lightest powder blues. The walls were dark cherry and the offset was perfectly balanced. Everything was stitched with silver thread. The four poster bed had a cover in a deep ocean blue with silver waves embroidered for a pattern. Three layers of pillows with alternating pillow cases of ocean blue, silver and a pale blue that reminded me of the sky covered the bed.

There was a thick lush carpet and a vanity at the far side of the room. A doorway halfway down the wall across from the foot of the bed led to a bathing chamber. On either side of the door stood matching armoires and dressers flanking both. The side with the vanity seemed to hold all manner of female things from lotions to perfume, jewelry, and hair combs, and as I peaked in the armoire, I found an array of lovely dresses in all sorts of styles and colors. There were easily twenty of them. *He did all this? For me?* I nearly cried at the idea.

On the side where we entered stood a dresser next to his armoire. It held a few knickknacks, cologne, several watches, and a blue velvet jewelry sorter of cuff-links for all occasions. Next to the bed side table was a large window and two sitting chairs. On the bedside table was a silver framed sketch of me. *Did he draw that?* I could imagine it now, he and I sitting with books to do light reading, or perhaps he would sketch while I read. Between the chairs tucked into the corner was a fireplace.

A small cherry wood table rested between them. My heart swelled. *He can't mean all this for us. Is it that easy?*

I looked at him leaning against the open doorway. "Do you like it? I rearranged a little. I was hoping you would find this to your liking. If there's anything you don't like, we'll pitch it," he said stepping forward and clasping his hands behind his back. It looked like a comfortable pose for him.

"It's beautiful," I said in nearly a whisper. I was speechless.

"The bathing chamber is through here." He walked to the door way. "There are towels here and a collection of soaps here." He pointed to the window seal. "Take your time. I'll wait." I nodded. We stepped out to the main bedchamber again. "Choose anything you wish. I had to guess sizes. Some may be too loose. Let me know which ones, and we can have them properly tailored. There are dresses here, or if you prefer, there are pants, sweaters and other things in the dresser. I hope it's not too forward, but I begged a couple of the ladies working in the house to buy undergarments as well."

"It looks and sounds like you were very thorough," I said, smiling at him. I couldn't seem to stop smiling. His dark auburn hair was much darker in the inside lighting than it had been on the river bank. Fae lights burned in silver sconces around each room we'd entered. He looked thinner too, as if he hadn't been eating. Worry etched into my brow.

"What's the matter?" he asked while stepping toward me, "Is it not to your liking?" Now his brow scrunched. He reached forward, and rubbed my upper arms. We stood face to face, and as he stepped forward his scent of cedar wood and sea salt wafted into me. *He smells like home should.*

"Not at all. It's lovely, really. It's just, you seem to have been trying to take care of me despite my absence, but have forgotten all about your needs," I admitted. I tilted my head, and looked into his deep hazel eyes. I felt the tug. It had been growing weaker with the distance between us. It was in full force now.

I stepped closer to him. Shock flitted across his face. He was surprised. I could see it now—he was terrified that I meant to reject him, but I couldn't reject him if I wanted to. I'd given him an empty threat in the kitchen. This felt too right, like destiny...no. Safety. He makes me feel safe.

"Uriah, I promise I've been working to come back to you. I won't lie—I debated for a few weeks. Not because I don't want you. Never that. More that I was not sure you really wanted to deal with me. I can see now how very wrong that insecurity was. I have to finish this contract though. I have to collect five heads. I've already collected three, and the last two are, to my knowledge, residing near each other at the moment. The deal I was pushed into? It's me or them. I won't fail. I don't want to lose you again either."

He opened his mouth to speak, but he didn't say anything. He took the last step to close the gap between us, lowering his head, and he wrapped his strong arms around me, before pulling me closer yet. He whispered, "Arabella, you belong here. Always."

I looked up at him, looking into his eyes briefly, I tilted my head back to give him a better angle and accepted my first kiss. Letting my eyes flutter closed, his lips met mine. The mating bond between us swelled. His shadows and my light collided in a dance that spun the world around us. His mouth was soft and gentle but still firm as he commanded my mouth to part more for him. I let him consume me as his tongue massaged mine. Our bodies were pressed tightly together, and I could feel his throbbing erection pressing into me. I let him pull me tighter against him. His wings fluttered in the flow of magic spilling from us. The fae lights flickered dimly in the sconces.

All too soon it ended. We were breathless as we both looked at each other, our arms intertwined as much as our magic. His scent filled the air—sea salt and cedar colliding with a field of strawberries and cinnamon as we combined. The mating bond purred in delight around us, finally getting what it wanted.

Uriah took a step back, though I could see he didn't want to. "I should let you bathe now. I'll be just down the hall. Perhaps a full tour when you're ready?" he asked. His eyes were filled with wonder and joy, as a smile spread across his face. I nodded and watched as he stepped out of the room, gently closing the door behind him.

I went to the armoire. Opening it, I looked at the various colors. He had chosen everything from bright red, to black, the sunniest yellow, and the palest blue. I chose a light pink chiffon dress with small pink and white roses embroidered up the bottom half of the knee length a-line cut. The hanger held a soft cashmere button down sweater to go over the top of the short sleeved dress as well. It had a full back, so I wouldn't be self conscious of my scars if I got too warm. *Perfect!*

I looked through the many pairs of heels on the bottom shelf. *How did he know all my sizes?* I wondered. I picked a strappy pair of silver heels with a wide and thick heel so I wouldn't trip, but also wouldn't be so short. *He's so tall and strong.*

Walking a few paces to the left, I opened the top drawer in the dresser. A lovely rainbow of lace and silk met my eye. I sifted through all the barely there pieces until I found a pale pink that matched the dress I chose. I held it up to my chest in the vanity mirror. I giggled to myself. *He almost knows my sizes.* The bra would barely hold the girls. I'd at least try it on. Thankfully, the dress would cover most of my cleavage anyway.

I took my spoils and went into the bathing chamber. Setting them on the small table to the side of the deep claw-foot copper tub, I turned on the water and pulled a towel out of the linen cupboard. Stripping down, I threw my old clothes in a void unceremoniously and slipped into the water. I began scrubbing a few months dirt off with a vibrantly scented honey lavender soap, anxious to get back to Uriah and explore his manor with him.

Chapter 20

Uriah

I'd done it. I'd kissed her at long last, and it was every bit as enchanting as I wanted it to be. Our magic needed it just as badly as I did. I think she did too. She's so sweet—she tastes just as much like sun ripened strawberries as she smells of them. I'd always thought of myself as a hands-on physical lover, hands that needed the personal touch, but I've always showed my love through gifts. If I was being honest with myself, I'd never been in love with anyone else. I'd allowed myself a certain level of romance through the years, but I ended the relationship exactly three months to the day of the first date, never a moment more.

Zeds' prophecy came to mind again. I'd never really considered the idea that I could have a mate and would ever find her, much less that my mate would be Arabella. I was always content with the idea of only having a betrothed. I still remember his words as Felix, Sebastian and I sat around his kitchen table.

Her light will find the path and the bond will ignite in darkness.

Zeds' words were always hard to discern. I wonder what other things he told me that will come to pass? Maybe Felix has been right to trust him all these years.

My mate. My Love. Zeds told me where to find her, but I never thought to look. I would have searched every dark place on the planet.

Every part of Arabella felt real and felt right. She was

perfect for me, all the way down to the scars on her body. As much as I hate to admit it, they instilled a righteousness in her, a fire I hope never burned out. I'd miss her beautiful wings, but never more than she likely does. *I wonder how much she remembers?*

I paced up and down the corridor. I wanted to give her time to think, and a bath was a good place to do that. She'd seemed pleased at my initiative. Sebastian had warned it would be too big an insinuation. *If he wasn't screwing Gabriella, I might think he was jealous.* We'd argued about it. Felix had sided with me, saying it would help her feel welcome and that she could have a life here.

"It'll show her the possibilities, and home comforts she hasn't had in the past" Felix had agreed. "It doesn't seem she has been allowed comfort in years, it could sway her."

Felix seemed to understand her—proclivities. As my intelligence commander, he was often tasked with the unsavory parts of extracting information from people. Hopefully, the two aren't too much alike. He's seen her the most, under heavy glamours. He'd been her shadow these past weeks, following her from town to town as she stalked her marks. I'd sent him after her the moment Knightmare had left. Felix, being Felix, had pulled from his magical aura and put a trace on the faehorse as well. The faehorse had strong magic, we'd have to be careful around him. There was no telling all his abilities and what he would share with Arabella.

Felix wouldn't be heading my spy forces if he didn't think like that. *I wonder how many tips he's received from Zeds over the years. Is that how he's so good at what he does? Zeds has very much been like a parent to him since his passed away.*

I didn't like going against my word to Arabella, however I needed to know more about her activities. I needed her to have help nearby should she find herself in trouble. Then Felix walked into her camp after hearing hours of screaming. Curiosity got the better of him. I can't really blame him, but he had to have known she was working. I was still angry though. Aside from Felix undermining me and disobeying orders, Arabella placed the blame on me. *A broken promise already. No. There will be no more of that. She's had too many people betray her. I won't be the next.*

As I walked past Felix's bedroom door, he opened it. "Going that well is it?" he asked, cocking his head and smirking. His blue eyes were full of mischief. *Asshole.*

"I'll have you know, it is. I cooked her breakfast, and she even let me kiss her," I said smugly. I flipped my chin, at him beckoning him back into his room and followed him inside. Tossing up a sound ward, I clasp my hands behind my back. My magic is already feeling stronger. "I was thinking, she's hunting two individuals. One human, the other fae. I think the fae is in the Agron Realm. That's why she can't find him. If he's fae, then he would have ties to one of the regions."

"That may be," Felix said. He crossed his arms across the thick cerulean wool sweater he wore, and the realization of my words dawned on him with where my train of thought was going.

Felix's eyebrows shut up, "I think the human is in Stanzley. Based on what I overheard of her latest interrogation, it sounded like the fae is in the wind, but the human? After the snow settles, he'll be easy to locate. Stanzley is a bigger town, but it only has a few rough neighborhoods he might frequent."

"We'll use that to our advantage then, what do you know about the Queen's involvement?" I inquired as I leaned against Felix's bedpost. His bed was a mess of rumpled silver blankets and several wine bottles littered his bedside table. My nose twitched with the overwhelming smell of stale wine.

"I think that Queen Clawin having her own magic tracer on her may be the issue Arabella's having. I had no idea she had magic—from all I know she's human, but perhaps she working with someone. My understanding is that it's the five heads or Arabella's. The Queen's guard caught her a few years ago assassinating a noble in her castle. After a stint in *custody* the Queen offered her a way out. I think the tracer was placed on her then. I need to research it more—I'm not sure what kind of magic is in play. Arabella is at least convinced she's being watched, if anything, so she's taking the constant search serious. According to Arabella, the Queen's magic has reach."

"That is a problem." A plan formed in my mind. "Do you think the magic would recognize it if we were to bring her the bounty? Not harm the human, just relocate him? The fae too, if we can get our hands on him. My thought was to give Arabella a tour, only I'd leave out our lowest floor. I could save that for tomorrow morning. Leave a gift and get some more answers to the conundrum," I said.

The gift of time. If she doesn't have to search, she won't need to leave.

"She would have to do the interrogation, the actual slaying, and beheading. From what I've seen over these past couple months that won't be a problem for her. I can collect him easily enough. Just get a hand on him and shift. If you warp the wards for a short time, I can put him straight in the basement," Felix said, nodding. I could see his own plan of action take form. "It would save her the trouble of going back to the Daemon Kingdom. Maybe she'd consider staying here to search for the fae in the Agron Realm if I proved I could deliver what she sought." Felix rubbed the stubble on his chin before continuing.

"She did say Queen Clawin knew whether or not she was actively seeking them. I don't know whether that magic could make it through the Agron Realms wards. So, maybe we give her a 'welcome home present' tomorrow morning and offer the resources she needs while we help her search, but we could keep her safe in the manor and she can continue her search in other ways. Call it... active research," Felix finished.

"I like the sound of it. If Arabella actively believes she's working, however slightly, it should trigger whatever magic to read it as such. Yes." I nodded. "Take Sebastian with you. If you can get a hold of both of Arabella's marks, please do, but try to come home with at least one of them. Go now. We'll worry about the other things tomorrow. This is more important. I'd like to give her a meaningful gift in the morning. If that gets her closer to ending this and staying with me, then all the better." I smiled a real smile. I felt my mind race with different schemes to keep her with me. *Maybe, I just have to convince her that she'll find the answers here. Queen Clawin's magic can't argue with that. Where better to find a fae than the Agron Realm?*

Chapter 21

Raven

I looked in the mirror. I was practically brand new. The pink dress flattered my curves and fair skin. My copper hair was untangled and spiraling over my shoulders. The cream sweater cut off at just the right spot to make my waist look thinner, the heels were even comfortable. My amber pendant stood out nicely against the pink as well. I looked well put together for the first time since I was a child.

I crossed the bedroom to the door and opened it. Uriah was leaning against the wall across the hall with a book in hand. Upon seeing me, he snapped it shut, and as he looked up his eyes widened. The biggest smile I'd seen from him crossed his face. "You look incredible. I'm glad you found something to your taste." He stood and offered me his arm.

"Thank you." I beamed, slipping my right wrist through and resting my hand on his left forearm. The wave tattoo looked to be swirling again, no trick of the light this time. His shadows were swirling around us as well, dancing and playing as if all was finally right in the world. *Not yet, but it will be.*

"I asked that lunch be brought up to the third floor. I thought we could enjoy the view and catch up some more," he said as we began to climb the wide staircase at the end of the hall.

"Oh! I hadn't realized I'd taken so long. Is it lunch time already?" I said, blushing horribly and glancing around for a clock. Uriah chuckled and patted my hand with his free one.

"No, no, I mean later. Unless you're hungry? If that is the

case, we'll get a snack. I meant to show you around the house first," he said as we reached the top of the stairs. He leaned forward and pushed open a door to our right. Inside was home to a grand piano, and light blue satin chairs adorned with silver legs were scattered around it with small tables. The piano was set in the center, and the floor dropped several steps to where it waited.

"There are several accomplished pianists that visit now and then. We usually book them for birthdays and such to make an evening of it. We did it more before my father passed away. Most of the attendees were his friends. I have my own, but Felix and Sebastian are really the only two I can stand," he said as he lead me to the piano bench. "Please," he offered me a seat.

"I'm afraid I never learned piano. I'm okay with a mandolin or violin, but they're hard to get your hands on," I said as he sat next to me. Our thighs touched ever so slightly, and the electric pulse running through them made my breath unsteady. My necklace was frigid against my skin, I lifted it to give my cleavage a break for a moment. It felt heavy in my hand as I twiddled it in my fingers.

He smiled, turning so our hazel eyes met. It felt odd, I was so short, but when we sat we were face to face. He flipped up the fallboard and steadied his hands on the ivory keys. "Do you recognize this?" He watched my face while he began to press the keys. The melody was soft and sweet with an up-sweep of emotion as the song progressed. His hands flew across the keys and his feet worked the pedals.

Tears sprang to my eyes. He remembered when I'd all but forgotten. I remember this. Everlee wanted me to be occupied, since I was so much further advanced than most children my age, even for a fae. She hired a tutor to teach me to play. "I used to play this on my harp, when I was little. I started lessons when I was two and picked it quickly. I used to sit in my room and play for hours." Sorrow filled my heart. I was such a bright child. It had all been stripped away and replaced by ugliness.

He stopped playing immediately. "Arabella, I'm sorry. I thought it'd be a good memory. I didn't mean to upset you." Tears streamed down my face. I was frozen in place. I needed to make them stop, but they kept coming, dripping off my cheeks and splattering on my dress. I'm ruining this beautiful dress, a gift from Uriah. *No, no. Don't cry. Not right now. How embarrassing! Don't be so weak.*

My breath felt heavy, as if someone had stacked bricks on my chest. I couldn't pull in enough air and the room began to spin. I sputtered and wrapped my arms around myself trying to steady my lungs.

His arms wrapped around me and pulled me close. "Breath with me a moment. In and out, try to slow your breath to match mine." I rested my head on his collar bone, and he gently stroked the side of my head and my hair. He rocked me in his arms, and his shadows flickered around us. He held me as my breaths even out and began to match his. I melted into his warm chest. I'd never allowed myself to cry like this, not even last September when I'd had to leave him after realizing who he was. His wings folded around us. "It's okay. I'm sorry. I didn't mean to evoke so much. I just thought it might help you remember the beautiful things you've had in your life. You've always been so musically inclined, I thought it might be a happy thing."

After some time, he kissed the top of my head. Tingles worked their way down into my scalp. "I know this is hard. I don't want to make it harder, but I want you to know I never gave up. I never stopped looking for you. I have to admit, I never thought you'd be in the Torrent Kingdom, let alone the King's palace, not that we didn't look there too. My father and I sent spies everywhere. We searched the whole continent," he whispered.

The realization dawned on me then. *The Shallows searched for me? Why not the Meadows? What was my father doing? Did he ever care? Or was it convenient that I was gone?*

My tears began to slow. My face was likely splotchy and red. So much for feeling pretty. I must look like a mess. *Oh no, I got snot on his shirt. I wonder if I can wipe it off without him noticing?*

"Is that why you won't call me Raven?" I asked, trying to distract him as I gently moved my hand up to cover the spot I'd left. He stiffened a little at my inquiry, but he kept his arms wrapped around me. I was practically sitting on his lap.

"I will always prefer to call you Arabella because that is your given name. Not the mocking name forced on you by someone that wished for you to disappear, to cease to exist. The person that stripped you of your birth right, and of all the things that made you uniquely you. I can't give them that when they stole you away for so long," he said, sadness coating his voice as it broke on the last word. He tilted my chin up with one finger. "You deserve better. Arabella deserves better. You deserve to bear the name your mother wanted you to have. You're her name-sake. It keeps her alive too."

I sat in stunned silence. *They didn't take my name. I gave it to them that first night when the Sculptor took my wings.* I'd given them everything. That fae had sold me to the King for a bride of his own, and I just accepted it after my wings had been ripped from my back. I let them take everything from a child lost in a world of pain and anguish. My breathing hitched and the world began to swim before me. I swayed, and he held me tighter.

"Breathe, you have to breathe, slow and even," Uriah whispered into my ear. I tried to suck in a breath, but it wouldn't come. Tears stung my eyes again. The next thing I knew, Uriah kissed a tear off my cheek, his mouth moving to mine a moment later. My body acted on instinct and began to move with his. The tightness in my chest loosened, and we broke apart long enough to take a deep breath. He kissed the tears off my cheeks again, then moved back to my lips.

"I promise, all this will turn into a horrible memory with time. You're safe here, in the Shallows. No harm will come to you. I won't allow it." Uriah said, pulling back to look into my eyes. Our hazel eyes were bright with happiness at finally being near each other. Despite the painful memories, I felt safe for the first time in as long as I could remember.

"I'll find away to finish my tasks quickly, so I won't have to come and go, but perhaps I can come back and forth for a while. Visit more frequently?" My voice trailed off and we went quiet— both thinking.

I have to do this. Can the Queen tell that I'm not in her kingdom? Does she know I came to Uriah? There are wards here; can her magic get through it?

The shadows swirling around us thickened as Uriah replied, "As long as you come back. I don't know that I could stand to be in this world alone now that we've found each other again." Tears welled in my eyes. He caught a tear and swiped it away with his thumb as they began to fall once more.

We sat holding each other and kissing for a few minutes. Our magic danced around the room again, black shadows and golden cords of light intertwining and running free.

Will he protect me if I let him? Will he tire of me if I can't keep it together? Will I ever fit in here?

"I'm sorry. I didn't mean to—to—I don't even know what that was," I mumbled. Shame washed over me now that the spell of our magic was waning. "I never considered how much they truly took from me or how much the Sculptor changed me over the years." I looked down.

How could I have lost so much of myself. Who am I, really?

"It's okay. It's going to be okay. You're home now. You're here. It won't be easy, but you'll find yourself again. The things you used to love may not be the things you'll love now, and that's okay. We change as we grow. You're supposed to," he assured me. More tentatively, he added, "I do think it's time you considered giving up a name meant to spite you, to ridicule you. Raven only derides your absent wings. No one had wings like yours. I still remember the beautiful iridescent nature of them."

They took my wings. I nodded feebly. Uriah was right. "I let them strip me of everything," I whispered. "I was so little and so scared. I didn't know how to fight what was happening to me. I was at their mercy, and they took the magic from me before it could even blossom."

"I know. And I promise you if we ever find that nanny, I'll kill her myself," he vowed. "The blood bath she left behind in the Meadows Estate when she took you. Retribution must be paid. She's owes you a great debt."

Everlee would never...she loved me. She took care of me. She was as close to a mother as I ever knew.

I gasped."Everlee didn't take me. She was dead on my bed." I told him the tale of the slaughter that night. Uriah looked aghast as I explained what really happened. Playing hide and seek at bedtime. My bloody sheets. Shifting over and over past the wards on the manor. The ice that cut my feet. The male fae and how he traded me for some human named Piper. The King with white hair. The Sculptor.

By the time I was done, Uriah's eyes had darkened. His face was somber. "No one knew what happened that night. We always assumed your nanny had stolen you, she was unaccounted for. No wonder we couldn't find you. We had no witnesses."

They were looking for Everlee. "She was dropped into the ether by the male fae that took me. Her body could have landed anywhere." I looked at my hands. "I remember her blood on my hands from finding her body on my bed in the dark."

"That changes everything, Arabella. It had to be done from the inside, someone in your father's circle. That would be the only way to manipulate the wards." His brow furrowed and I saw his throat bob up and down, pushing down the emotions building inside him. "I wish my father was still alive. He'd know exactly who that inner circle was made up of at the time. Let's continue the tour. There may be something in the library," he said, letting his hand slide down my back and standing.

Our legs were stiff from sitting still for so long and we both stretched before we walked hand in hand back out of the piano room and down the upper hall. It formed a big square at the top of the stairs. We entered the second door down the landing. *The large manor was built in a labyrinthine manner. It would be easy to get lost were I left on my own.*

A massive room with two floors along the outer walls opened up before us. Stacked inside were rows and rows of leather bound books; the smell was overwhelming. Leather and ink combined with polish on the table sets and chairs that littered the room. The West side wall was stained glass that let colors dance upon the rows of books. Big squishy couches were dotted around the room as well. It was heaven. I could live here. Everything is so comfortable. I thought it would be awkward coming to see Uriah, but it's not. It's like breathing, natural and easy.

Uriah led me to a counter on the far right of the room across from the stained glass. On a counter running the length of it were several books that looked to be ledgers. "What are these?" I inquired.

"These are ledgers of events that my father or I had to attend. There are more like it in every Lord's estate. It's a bit of a record in case there's ever cause to say we aren't doing our jobs." He laughed a quiet laugh. "These days, our jobs are basically guiding our military commanders. We sealed the caves, by the way. Flooded them with the river. We found seven of them up and down the Summit mountains in all. They stretched from both Kingdoms," he said eyeing me with pride.

"I'm glad my letter helped a little." I looked at him, giving him a small smirk. My face felt tight from all the crying. I was glad to be by his side though. Everything seemed so easy. Even in the cave, I felt it, though I hadn't wanted to then.

He pulled a ledger toward us. "This would have been from around the time you were born. I was just a boy. I had all the families' ledgers combined here when my father died. I didn't bring much from the Western Shallows, but these have always been important to me," he divulged.

I looked at him as he read. His face was lightly freckled amongst his natural tan, weathered by the wind and sea. He was so handsome. It felt like a disparity that he could want me —Raven.

No. Not Raven. Not anymore. Arabella. I won't give them anything else.

Chapter 22

Uriah

She was watching me as I flipped through the ledger. I looked for the dates around the time of her fourth birthday. We had been at Agron's Keep when it happened. Everyone that was in attendance would be listed here. It wasn't until a few days later when Lionel had returned home that the massacre was discovered. On her birthday, though he had been willing to miss it. *Asshole.*

"Ah, here it is. My father, Peter. Your father, Lionel, then Ulysses of Brume, and there's John of the Summit. I don't see anything that looks odd right off the mark." I reached for a box of stationary sheets. Inside was a pen with an inkwell. "I'm writing the names down so we can see who usually accompanied your father and who wasn't there, This won't take long Raven."

"Call me Arabella," she stated clearly, cold and devoid of feeling.

I paused writing a moment. I'm getting through to her; aren't I. *Thank the King. Thank the King.*

"If you're sure. I don't want to influence you if…" I trailed off. She turned and looked at me. The pen was still in my hand, poised to finish the word I was writing.

"I'm sure. I can't keep letting them dictate *my* life, which is exactly what I allowed all these years. Even after I broke free, I was still in their clutches. I can't allow that anymore. Not now that you made your point and I understand the bigger picture." She looked close to tears again, shaking her head in disgust at herself.

I reached with my free hand and cupped her cheek. Her skin was so soft under my calloused fingertips. "You're the bravest being I know," I said simply.

After a couple heart-beats, I went back to the ledger. Some time passed as I flipped through page after page, examining the names and dates, looking for patterns. "Oh, oh dear no. Surely not," I looked at her as I felt the blood drain from my face. "Your stepmother, Judith—She was suppose to travel with her uncle, Ulysses. There's a note here that says she was in the Meadows."

"I didn't know my father remarried. I thought that you would have alerted the Realm after finding me in the cave. I expected some sort of summons or something to come from my father. Surely, he would have at the least sent criers to Neera. I listened in the town square a few times to see if any of the messages might be for me." I leaned into where he pointed in the massive book, searching for the names myself.

"Lionel seemed shaken when I told him. He arrived here a few days later wanting all the information I had, Judith was with him. She's insufferable. How she ever became a lady is beyond me. She was more distracting than anything, expecting to be coddled and pampered. Within reason, sure, as far as comforts go, but she wanted to be hand fed! The audacity," he continued, shaking his head in both bemusement and outrage.

"What's interesting about this is that if she was in the Meadows when you were taken, how is she alive? Every soul in the house had been butchered and accounted for, save for you and Everlee. Everlee's bags were hastily packed in her room, left behind, and blood was all over your bed. We thought she'd killed you and taken your body for ransom," I explained.

"That name, it's familiar. I can't place it." I shook my head, searching my memory. "Judy." The memory came flooding back. "He called her Judy, the fae that took me. In the hallway, just before I turned the light on, he had a bloody knife." Uriah and I starred at each other. He sucked in a big breath.

"Were there any other events she's been at that she shouldn't have been?" Arabella asked. We were both leaning close now. This might be something. "Wait. There—that name, Altmore." She pointed it out. "The fae I'm hunting? His name is Finnigan Altmore. I was going to ask if you might have heard the family name." The hairs on my neck stood on end. *What the fuck?*

"Altmore is Judith's family name." I flipped the ledger back a few pages. "Their father, Judd, is brother to Ulysses, the current Lord of Brume. His heir and the heir of Summit just welcomed a son last May," I said, clearing my throat. I hadn't broached *that* topic yet. We were betrothed and expected to produce an heir still. I wasn't about to bring it up though. I need to her settle first. That's far too heavy. To fast.

Let her lead. She owes you nothing. She owes the Agron Realm nothing. She was abandoned by it.

"His brother's children are listed here, um, older brother named Killian and a younger sister named Judith," I said, flipping a few pages, I pointed again, "And here, Killian married about a year after you disappeared. Piper is her name, and they welcomed a son a year after that," I looked at her. "He'd be about nineteen." I said, her head already nodding with hard agreement.

"That's Finnigan, the fae that the Queen has sent me after," Arabella stated. "So, Killian and Judith slaughtered a household, Killian sold me to King Plavlock in trade for a bride named Piper, and then Judith wormed her way into my fathers bed." I couldn't understand it. *There has to be something more to it. How could Lionel do this to his daughter? He always seemed— different when we were younger, reclusive. Then all of a sudden he agreed to remarry.*

Chapter 23

Uriah

We made a detour back downstairs to my bedchamber after the library. I smirked as I thought about it. *Our bedchamber. She doesn't seem unwilling.* We were astonished at what we uncovered. We searched the ledgers more, and it seemed that Judith had been stalking Arabella's father for at least two years before she made her move to rid the manor of Arabella so she could convince Lionel to wed her and produce a new heir.

We needed to save the evidence, so after she stepped into the room, I shut the door, locked it, warded it against sound, and crossed the room to a large painting hanging on the wall by the fireplace next to the mantle. Drift wood lay across it. The art covered an in-room safe built into the wall. The thickness of the wall between the rooms was used to hide it. Sebastian's room was next door, and if he'd ever noticed the measurements being off, he'd never said anything.

I unlocked the solid steel vault. Leaning in before she could see, I quickly grabbed a small silver box and let my shadows cover it, putting it quickly in my pants' pocket. I turned to her, having moved a few things over, as she reached into a void she'd opened to retrieve the ledgers we'd placed inside. Our magic was much stronger now. The closer we got to each other, the more it flourished. We stacked the ledgers in the safe and locked it.

She begged my pardon for a moment and entered the bathing chamber to relieve herself. I heard the water come on as she washed her hands, and then we traded places. When I exited, she had rearranged her hair a bit, pulling it half back in a braid. *Still a perfect picture of beauty.*

After I unwound the wards I'd set, we left. I went to a wall box and pressed a button. It would chime in the kitchen to tell them I wanted food brought up. While she was washing earlier, I'd set up the days and evening plans with the staff and asked them to be scarce.

"Are your feet okay in those?" I inquired, as I took in that she had chosen heels. I had definitely noticed her well rounded calves and thick curves. *Thick thighs; save lives. Keep it together. Don't fuck this up.*

"I'm okay. I never really have a reason to dress up, so it's a nice change. You selected beautiful clothes. You didn't have to do that, but you know, I appreciate it all the same," she said as we reached the top again.

"All the way around to the other side this time," I said, running my hand down the thick banister. "I think you'll enjoy this."

As we came around the corner of the staircase, she gasped. Her eyes widened, and a smile spread across her face as she took in the view of the ocean beaches and cliff face in the distance as we looked out to sea.

There were three large picture windows facing a balcony. We'd turned into the library before she could glimpse them earlier. The doorway between two windows was glass. As we stepped through, we were met with a fresh breeze of salt air. The air was crisper even though the room had a cherry floor and ceiling tiles, it was otherwise constructed of panels of glass and wood beams.

I had it set for us. A small wicker love seat with thick silver cushioning was placed to one side with a table in front that held sea pebbles soaked in kerosene so we could light it if we grew cold. Dark blue velvet blankets were draped over the back of the love seat if she felt like cuddling up. *Only if she wants to. Her decision. Always.*

On the other side of the balcony, a few feet into the doorway, sat a table for two. Cherry wood, of course. Low candles were ready to be lit, though it was plenty bright without them. Underfoot were more thick rugs.

She paused and just looked. She reached up and held her pendant. "Is there a significance to your necklace?" I asked as I guided her to the inside chair.

"Oh, this." She smiled and shook her head. "Not really. Just sentimental for me. The potion they forced me to drink morning and night stopped working as well after a while. I was puking it up as often as I could for a couple years. I worked in the kitchen and they left me alone during the night. I took advantage of the opportunity. My magic started to get stronger. One day, I'd had enough. The old lady in the kitchen wore it. For years, I watched her twiddle it in her fingers as she stuffed her fat face with the food meant for me."

She stopped talking and turned her attention to the sea. "You see, she was cruel. She barely gave me scraps to eat. She'd gorge herself and then tell me there wasn't enough. She kicked me in the ribs almost daily to wake me and forced the potion down my throat. So, when I'd decided my magic was strong enough, I used my cords of light to break the chain on my ankle, and I killed her with this wretched necklace. I made it my prize." She turned and looked at me as a wave of triumph crossed her face.

Not a shred of remorse. *Good for you, Arabella. You deserve so much more.* "Not with my magic. I mean, I could have used my magic, I'd been practicing whenever I was left alone in the kitchen. Killing the rats I knew would bite at me while I slept. I'd let my magic coil and snap their necks. No, that was too easy for her. I wanted her to feel some of the agony she'd put me through," Arabella mused.

"Clara was her name. I strangled her with this necklace. I wanted to see the light leave her eyes, and then I took it when I left that night. It almost seemed to call for me, like I should keep it. I didn't know where I was going. I just wanted to get away. It wasn't really planned, but I figured if anything, I could sell it later. Thankfully, it was warm. It was sometime in late June, right after summer solstice. There was debris in the streets from the celebrations." She looked out to sea as she told me her tale of liberation.

"I was on the streets in little more than a flour sack dress I'd fashioned out of the trash bins. About a week after I escaped, I was wandering the countryside and came upon two men preying on a woman. She was trying to fight them off unsuccessfully. Her pretty dress was covered in mud, and she looked to be well off." She continued to look without seeing, as she remembered.

I let her talk. *Get it all out. I want to know everything. As much as I hate it, I need to know what they did to you.*

"I barely hesitated before I wound my magic around their necks and squeezed it until they dropped like sacks of grain. The woman collected herself for a moment, and gaped at me. Her brown hair was disheveled, and her tan skin peeled away where she'd fallen on the rough ground. I reached to help her up, and she took my hand. We spoke for a few moments to check on each other.

"If my magic had bothered her, she said nothing, other than she had gotten lost from the path she'd been picking flowers along. She asked where I was headed, and I said any road out of the Torrent Kingdom. I remember she nodded thoughtfully at that. She pulled a bag of coin from a pocket inside her dress, pressed it into my hands, and bid me good luck." Arabella ran her hand absentmindedly through the bottom strands of her hair. Still thoughtful at the memory.

Turning to me with a smile, she said, "It was enough to buy a proper outfit and some supplies. I remember being excited to buy a bar of honey milk soap and scrub up in a nearby stream. I wasn't allowed to bathe often. I bought a decent sized leather bag to pack around all of my new belongings and headed out on foot to the Daemon Kingdom. I stayed in the mountains South of Stanzley mostly and the Jordane Forest for a while. I'd stop in town squares to offer my *services* to those that seemed most vulnerable. Not for much, just a few coins so I could eat. I've never killed anyone that didn't deserve retribution."

"How long has it been?" I asked. "Since you escaped, I mean."

"Seven summers, counting that first one," she answered. She would have been seventeen. It's a wonder she remembers me at all.

"When did you find Knightmare?" I prodded I forced myself to stick to simple questions. She needed to talk, but I couldn't probe too fast. She'd tell me everything on her own time. *Give her time. Don't overwhelm her.*

"Oh, Knightmare." She huffed a laugh. "That horse, I swear. He really is my best friend, as ornery as he is. I heard him screaming through a thicket of trees, both literally and in my head, about four years ago. It was confusing at first. I wasn't sure what I was hearing and thought maybe a human was trapped as well, but I couldn't ignore the call. It was Knightmare, he was trapped in a barn that had caught fire. I quickly realized he was the one talking in my head. We became fast friends, outside of Neera. By then, I had made my way to the coast. I love the mountains, but I've always preferred the sea." She placed her hand on my forearm and traced the lines of the tattoo on my freckled left arm.

I watched her examine my tattoo. "It's imbued with magic. When the waves are calm, all is right in the world. When something is off, they grow wild and rough. I'm only really ever in trouble when the waves begin to crest and crash. I paid a small fortune to have the magic done. It might be my favorite part of myself." Right now, they were calm. The waters gently swirling, not a wave in sight.

"It changes sometimes," she said. "I noticed in the cave the waves on your arm were choppier, moving around a lot more."

"That may have been the bond calling, the magic at play, somehow I don't think so. I don't know if it was the cadfiends nearby or the fact that our cave existed that set it off. It certainly wasn't you," I said, giving her a wink. She laughed, a genuine full belly laugh.

"Oh what, scary little me? A big strong fae like you could never be afraid of tiny, innocent me," she joked. I wish she could see herself. She has no idea how beautiful and terrifying she is. We both sat laughing for a moment, and then food arrived.

We leaned back a little so the plates could be placed before us. Next came a couple crystal wine glasses and a bucket of ice with a crisp white wine, already uncorked. Napkins rolled around silverware were neatly placed beside each porcelain plate with cerulean waves imprinted around the edges. *Everything was presented beautifully as I had expected of my staff. Arabella deserved to be pampered and I had ordered it to be so.*

"Thank you, Gabriella." I passed thanks onto my favorite house maid. *Sebastian's favorite too.* She was quiet, thorough when cleaning, and knew a few good jokes. Her blonde hair was pulled back, and her plain sky blue dress was perfectly placed. She had lightly freckled skin and a slight figure. She wore felt bottomed shoes so her feet didn't scuff along.

Sneaky like Felix. Thank the King this side of the manor is quiet. The hustle and bustle of the main quarters is too much. Too many soldiers and couriers go in and out.

"Of course. Just buzz if you should need anything more," Gabriella said, slipping away back down the corridor the way she had come. Arabella and I looked at each other a moment before settling into our meal.

Chapter 24

Arabella

He's such a gentleman. So good and kind. And here he sits with a monster.

"What's wrong? Do you not like fish? I can call her back." He turned to look for Gabriella as she made her way around the staircase.

"Oh no, not at all," I shook my head. "My emotions are a little wild today, that's all. Please forgive me," I begged. A note of sadness twinged my voice. If I could hear it, he certainly could. I turned to the food that had been brought to us. It smelled delicious. Thick crispy pieces of ale battered cod fish were stacked on big puffy potato buns, with lettuce, a creamy white sauce and gooey cheese dribbled out the sides. Thick steak fries with a pink sauce in a ramekin were on the side. A small dish of purple colored coleslaw was to the side of that.

Fucking purple—King Plavlock wanted everything to be purple or white, all the way down to that fucking purple potion. Even the jewels on his crown were blue and purple. Purple, purple, purple. I moved the dish of coleslaw off the plate to the side of my napkin.

"I understand. We've talked about a lot of big topics today. I know it's a lot for you. Our discovery in the library was enough to stop my heart, so I can't imagine how you're feeling. I will help with anything I can. You've been through more in your twenty five years than most have in a full lifetime. I don't know how I would have reacted if I'd been in your position. I highly doubt I would have come out alive," he told me.

"I survived because I let Arabella die." My voice broke. "Those first few days—I had to let it all go. I knew I'd never make it back to my father's estate. Even when I could have gotten myself back there, I didn't want to. If I'm honest, a large part of me hates him. He didn't protect me. He never paid attention to me when I was there, and when I was taken he didn't look for me," I confessed. "Even now that he knows I'm alive, he hasn't come to find me. I waited for days in Neera, giving Knightmare excuses until I couldn't put off going to Palomora. We had to find my marks."

He nodded, and pain swam in his eyes. Our emotions mirrored each others. "I'm sorry. I'm ruining lunch, like I ruined the piano room earlier," I apologized.

"Don't do that. Please, you matter so much to me. I *want* to know how you're feeling. All of this is overwhelming, the distance, now the new proximity. I want to know what happened to you. I want to know it all. I will carry the burden with you. You've trusted me so far, so please don't stop now. I swear, we'll get through this. All of it. The good, bad, and ugly. You're my mate. I don't know how to tell you how much that means to me. My life is yours.

"Not just because you were my betrothed all those years ago. The magic that ignited in the cave...You're my mate. It's the bond every fae hopes to find. I never dreamed it would happen, but it's everything I could have ever hoped for. You're the other half of my soul, and I yours. You are everything perfect and beautiful to me. All of it. I wouldn't change it, as much as I hate some aspects, because the absolute truth of the matter is that it made you, *you*. Arabella or Raven."

My eyes swam with tears as Uriah confessed his feeling. My heart softening as I realized the full impact the last few months had made on both of us.

"You are strong, courageous, judicious, cunning and wise. You hold yourself to the highest moral standard, even if you work in the shadows. Even in your darkest deeds, you have a line you won't cross. You're beautiful and modest, and I know this is all moving fast…It's fast for me too. It's the bond, but even if it wasn't? Whether I get one hour with you or the rest of our lives, it'll never be enough," he declared.

"Uriah," I whispered. I shook my head a little and leaned closer to him. I tipped my chin up, begging him to kiss me with my eyes. He reached up and cupped the side of my face in his hand. After making eye contact for just a moment more, he dipped his head, and we were kissing again. Our food was left untouched for the moment we drank each other in.

There was no rational explanation for how badly I wanted him. The bond was certainly pushing us together. The *need* was fierce. I'd never wanted to be with anyone before. I always ignored any desires for physical touch. But this, I couldn't deny. It'd been ten weeks or so since I'd run into Uriah in that cave, and I was falling head over heels in love with him. A few hours, a couple letters. It didn't matter. *He is mine, and he wants me.*

I would be his, and he would be mine, and it was right. Out of anyone on the planet, he was the one that would accept me for all my treachery, the monstrosities. He didn't care. We kissed each other deeply, feeding our mutual need. My lady parts pulsed with need. I could feel the dampness on my thighs as I grew wetter with just the thought of letting him take me.

Magic pulled us together. Every time we kissed. it sprang out of us, swirling in the air. After a few moments of bliss, we broke apart. His forehead touched mine, and we leaned against each. Our future apparent to both of us and neither of us seemed to mind one bit.

"We should eat," he said, his voice thick with lust and want. "I think we've both missed enough meals lately." The sad edge had pulled back from his eyes. We kept falling into each others' open arms today.

"Food, yes. It smells amazing," I agreed, both of us turning at the same time. "Thank you, for what you said. I've never been particularly loquacious. I can never seem to find the words. I can't imagine a world without you in it now that we've found each other again." He was better with words than I was. But in this moment, I was determined to do everything I could to show him that I *wanted* to be here. I *wanted* to be with him. I just had to get myself out of the mess I'd found myself in first.

Tomorrow may be the most painful day of my life yet. How can I leave him again, when we're only really getting to know each other? Will he forgive me again if I keep running off? I have to find the last two marks. Queen Clawin will strike me dead if I don't. And if I die...

Uriah and I both took a bite of our fish sandwiches. "Mmm, two meals in one day. This is so good! I haven't had anything like this in years," I said, the mood lightening a bit.

"Well, hold on to your hat because we still have afternoon tea and dinner," he said, chuckling, as I wiggled a happy little food dance in my wicker chair. They had low backs, so his wings weren't bothered.

We spent a few hours out on the balcony. The glass kept the wind at bay. After lunch we poured ourselves a second glass of wine and moved over to the love seat where we curled up under one of the blankets for a bit.

Uriah protested as I insisted he pin his wings and made him stretch out. I curled up in his lap, wrapping my arms around him. My knees carefully tucked between his legs, he had his right leg stretched across the back of the seat, I sat mostly in his lap, curled up on his sculpted chest with his left leg planted firmly on the cherry deck, he held me as we talked. He gently played with my hair, twirling the long wild strands between his fingers and idly rubbing my back with his other hand.

As we settled in his hand brushed the rough edges of my scars and I stiffened. "Sorry, I didn't mean to bump your scars." He look horrified a moment. "Do they hurt often?" He asked as he moved his hand lower.

"My back is very sensitive, it never healed properly so I try to keep any pressure from grazing it." I answered. Sorrow filled his eyes. "Tell me a story. How long have you known Felix and Sebastian?"

"We grew up together. You knew Felix when you were little. He often came with me when I was in the Meadows to visit—it's okay it you don't remember."

Soon, stories of all the shenanigans he, Felix and Sebastian had gotten up to in their teens and early twenties followed as we cuddled. It was a perfect afternoon. No more tears. Just laughter and lightness as we learned about each other.

He told me stories like how the trio had gone skinny dipping just for them to come back with a bunch of goats eating their underwear. I told him about Knightmare figuring out how to fish one afternoon, and tossing me salmon from the river. I'd had so many when he was done. We ate all winter after I'd smoked it, I used the coin I made to by his oats and hay.

Talking to Uriah felt natural and easy. I just hoped everything else did as well. We talked a little about what happened in the library earlier today.

"Do you think my father knows what happened?" I asked Uriah.

"I think we have a lot of questions to answer. I'd like to know what my father knew on the matter as well. We'll have to see how it evolves. I'll send all my resources to investigate. Felix will be helpful there. We can talk to him later. He's busy with my tasks for the day right now."

I think we both needed to process the ramifications of that discovery. It meant a lot to both of us, just in different ways. I didn't care that my father had married a snake, but I did care that the man that kidnapped and sold me had sired the demon fae I chased now. Rotten from the start. I'd kill them both. All I needed was to get close enough. For that, I would need Uriah on board.

I looked at my shoes; abandoned a couple hours ago. *Uriah*

is a soldier, a sailor. I wonder if he'll balk at my particular flavor of justice? My thoughts raced while I laid in Uriah's arms. We'd adjusted a few times, neither of us seemed in a hurry to give up the blanket and sounds of crashing waves upon the shore. We'd both been quiet for a few minutes now, drinking in each others' scent and just comfortably being lazy as the sun began to set. *The view really is lovely.*

Chapter 25

Felix: Several Hours Earlier

I stepped out into the gray day. My cloak flapped around me. The thickest leathers weren't warm enough for today. Small flakes of snow had begun to fall, swirling on the wind blown in by the sea. A frigid mist mixed with it. It reminded me of another time.

❀❀❀❀❀

It was late spring and Sebastian, Uriah and I had gone to see Zeds. He was getting the ground ready to plant his garden for the year. The ground was torn up and there was a fallen tree that had it's stump pulled up, roots exposed, and a large pile of rocks in a heap near the front door. "Wonder what that's all about?"asked Sebastian, pointing to the stump.

"Probably just a windfall," Uriah answered, rubbing his hands together to warm them against the cold breeze. We were in our early twenties and taking a day off from our regular patrols. "The storms that ripped through the Shallows last week were Westward winds. They must have struck here first," he finished with a frown. "Let's see if he's home." Zeds lived on the furthest edge of the continent, where less people were found.

I knocked after walking up the muddy path to his home. It was made of white clay bricks and built into an ancient tree. The door hung slightly cooked. "What do you want?" Zeds barked as the door creaked open. "Oh, it's you. Hello, Felix. You two, never far behind Felix are you?" Zeds amended, peering passed me to Uriah and Sebastian while he stood in the doorway with no more than underwear with holes throughout and a tattered gray t-shirt. His rich mahogany skin stood out against the bleached white wood of his tree house. He scratched at his salt and pepper beard. His hair was neatly cropped short with tight curls close to his scalp. He looked to be in good health after the long winter.

"We had a day off and thought we'd stop by for a visit," I said. "I see you might need a hand with the garden. Do you mind if we stay for a bit?" I gestured to the fallen tree. "I'm sure between Uriah's shadows and Sebastian's brawn we could probably get that out of your way."

"We'd be happy to get your garden blocked out," Sebastian added. "It'd be no trouble and give us some exercise." Uriah nodded as well.

"Alright, but I expect y'all have some questions for me too," Zeds replied as he stepped back. He left the door open, as he pulled on a pair of mud crusted trousers, and slid his feet into leather clogs.

The day started out mild, but the clouds threatened rain. The temperature was dropping, and it'd be snowing before we ventured home. We got the heavy work done in a couple of hours. Sebastian used an ax from Zeds' shed to cut the tree into smaller pieces that he could carry, then he and Uriah moved them out of the way. Sebastian used his unnatural strength, and Uriah used shadows to wrap around them, pulling them loose from the thick mud for Sebastian to get a hold of. After they moved the tree, they split it into fire wood and neatly stacked it by the shed. By midday they were both sweating, despite the turning weather.

While Uriah and Sebastian worked at the tree, Zeds and I had lined his path with the rocks from the pile by the door. We carefully set them in the mud to create a pathway to the door of his house from his garden plot. Once the hard work complete, Zeds asked us inside. We sat in his small kitchen, with a cup of tea in front of each of us and a plate of gingerbread slices in the middle of the round table. Uriah fidgeted constantly as the chairs were too high *for his wings.*

We had brought him some whiskey, chocolate, stationary, herbs for various uses, and a bag of coin. He preferred his solace and didn't venture into any nearby towns unless he had no other option, but I liked for him to have money if he should have need of it.

Zeds reached out after my parents died, and we frequently corresponded. In a lot of ways, I'd come to see him as a parental figure, a mentor, much like Uriah's father had been as well. Zeds was always kind to me and often offered words of advice when I needed it most. Although I rarely understood what he was talking about, it was always comforting. Today was no different.

Taking a sip of tea, Zeds set his cup down and looked at Uriah. His eyes, one blue and one green, flashed gold for a moment. It was an odd occurrence that sometimes happened when we were talking. I was never bold enough to ask him why it happened. "Her light will find the path, and the bond will ignite in darkness," Zeds said, with a weird far away sound to his deep baritone voice. "In time, you'll know what that means. I cannot tell you when, only how." Uriah opened his mouth to speak, but Sebastian cut him off.

"Wow! I love when you do that," Sebastian exclaimed. "Anything for me?"

Zeds stared at him for a moment. His brow furrowed, and he looked down. The air grew thicker, and Zeds' eyes flashed gold again. "I don't often do readings anymore, however, the sight is clear today. 'The golden one shall bring deceit. Be wary for your heart, lest it waver." Sebastian's eyes widened.

"I have no idea what that could mean, but thank you. I appreciate you using your gift. I'll remember your words." Sebastian smiled at Zeds, and he flicked his long dark braided hair over his shoulder, clearly confused and pondering. Falling quiet, he turned to, look out the window. It was beginning to squall, and snow flakes formed on the breeze.

Zeds turned to me next. "You've been a special part of my life. I'm afraid the peace will only hold for so long. Before we know it, we'll be in a new season with new challenges."He frowned."There will come a time, a time of great excitement, and of great sorrow, when you find the letter to my Flower, use it as a map to the falsity. Don't trust your ears, for they will lead you to peril." Zeds looked around the table to each of us. "You would all do well to recognize that last warning. You are all interlinked by fate. The prophecy is written; you need only heed it."

❀❀❀❀❀

Sebastian stepped onto the landing with me and clapped his hand on my shoulder, breaking the spell of my memory. "Ready? It's so damn cold today. We should get Knightmare inside so we can head out."

I wonder if this is the time of excitement. Who is the Flower? I never could figure that out and Zeds has never divulged. So many thoughts of Zeds lately. It's a sign. I need to go see him.

The large black stallion waited before us, sporting scars down his flank, just past the stone steps of the porch on the sprawling Tudor style manor, in the yellowing grass of the yard. He looked to be a brute, but I knew he would be amicable and that he was fairly refined. For a faehorse; those creatures are temperamental at best.

"Hello again, Knightmare," I spoke to him, approaching with caution while walking with a purpose in the frigid air. "Raven will be with Uriah today. He'll take care of her needs. Would you mind if I led you to the stable? It's just down this slope of the lawn before that patch of forest there, near the spot where we met when you delivered the letter." I pointed across the grounds. "I have a large stall and all the hay you could wish for. It'll be warmer and keep the snow and wind off you. If you'd like oats or a hearty helping of grain, we have that as well."

"I will follow. Grain sounds good. We eat a lot of oats. I'll

gladly take to the stable, however, I'd prefer if you left the stall door open. I'll keep to the stable, of course, I prefer an easy exit— is all," His words sounded in my mind and he fixed me with a pointed look. Of course, the burns. I wouldn't want to be locked in either after an experience like that.

"Fair enough. We'll block the door so it doesn't close you in. I can put you in a stall with an exit to the field if you like. It wouldn't be as warm but perhaps that would be more suitable," I offered. *This poor guy has seen some things in his time. I wonder how old he is?*

"I would much prefer that. The cold doesn't bother me as much as being confined," he said as we began walking down the sloping lawn to the barn area. Sebastian silently walked beside me. Over the years he had become quiet. His bulky figure following few paces behind me. We reached the stables quickly and both set to work sorting out Knightmare's needs.

"Would you prefer this one in the front or this more open one in the back here?" I asked him.. He said nothing, walking to the back of the stable into the far stall. It opened with a sliding door into a fenced in field used for training. Most of them were war horses housed in various stables, but only a few horses were here today. I entered and pulled the door half closed. I left him plenty of room to exit if he wished. "Is this okay?"

"Thank you. This is quite cozy. I appreciate the concern. Was Raven okay when you left? Her magic has been off the last week or two, and it makes me nervous to leave her on her own," he inquired.

"She seemed quite relieved to see Uriah. The bond they share runs deeper than any of us can understand. Mating bonds aren't common anymore. The time spent together will make things better for both of them," I explained. I wasn't sure how much a faehorse would understand about such things. He might know the lore better than myself.

"Where are the other horses? This stable feels rather empty." Knightmare asked.

"The majority guard the borders with their assigned

cavalry units," Sebastian told him. I hadn't realized Sebastian was hearing the horse speak as well. They don't often choose to speak to us, and I don't know of another one willing. "We've mustered as many troops as we could find for patrols since the human lands began amassing their own troops," Sebastian continued. Hopefully it came to nothing. We'd been in a relative cold war for some time now. No one was eager to begin fighting again.

Sebastian put a few sugar cubes across the divider in the stall on the top of the wall. "A little something for a sweet tooth," he muttered to Knightmare. Knightmare neighed his approval. *Softies.*

"Is there anything else we can get you before we head out? Would you like to be blanketed?" I asked while waving my hand toward several horse blankets hanging on the wall.

"No, thank you. This is sufficient," Knightmare began eating hay. I nodded and Sebastian and I walked out the way we came.

"Have you any idea where we can find Arabella's marks? What are their names?" Sebastian asked as we walked down the path leading back to the main estate. We had cut across to get to the stable, but the ground was soggy. Gravel was much preferred.

"Seamus Brandt and Finnigan Altmore. I've been pondering how to locate them. After I heard everything the brutes that came into Arabella's camp said, I don't think we'll find the fae in the human lands at all. I think he's likely somewhere in the Agron Realm. If we do a little research, I'm sure if we can find his family, and then we'll find him. Finnigan Altmore is the fae. The Altmore family name sounds familiar, but I can't place it," I answered with a shake of my head. *Maybe Zeds would know. He knows so many things since he's lived for so long.*

We walked past the manor and continued down the drive. The wards wouldn't allow us to shift until we passed a certain point. "Altmore. Where have I heard that?" Sebastian mused. "It seems like I should know it too. I'm sure Uriah will recognize it. Let's focus on the human today. That will make Uriah happy and give Arabella a toy to play with." Sebastian hesitated a moment. "Did she really torture that blighter?"

"He had it coming," I shrugged. "I would have done it for her otherwise. I was already headed their way when she came back into her camp. Their intent was nothing if not dishonorable. She doesn't strike me as the kind that needs assistance—she certainly didn't need it then. She's pretty sturdy from what I've observed. She's not perfect, but who is? Given the torment she's been through, I'm not surprised she turned the tables. They call her the 'Sculptor's Apprentice' from what I heard poking around. He tortured her the majority of her life. Apparently, his only direction from King Plavlock was to keep her alive, not keep her faculties intact."

Who is he though? All my spies and no one will give the Sculptor's name.

Sebastian nodded. Realization of who Arabella became bloomed on his face. He hadn't known any of the details of her life before escaping. Out of respect, I kept what I'd learned between myself and Uriah. "Has he talked to you at all? He's been fairly distant with me, even before all this." Sebastian asked.

I could tell he wasn't sure where he stood in our trio. We'd been drifting apart for a while. The three of us focused more on settling down ourselves and less on getting drunk and repeating old stories. *Not that I'll find anyone anytime soon. What male in our circle would look my way?*

"We talked a little. He's concerned, because he doesn't know the extent of emotional damage done to her. He's worried the most about that. He doesn't want to add to it and push too hard, but he also has to balance his responsibility to the Realm. King Astros still needs an heir. The clock is ticking faster with the young Lord of Brume and Summit born now. He's scared that they'll end up forcing her hand, and he doesn't want that. He's never wanted her to lose autonomy and has always wished for all females to have more rights, even all those years ago. He values her too much to use her as a brood mare," I divulged. I probably shouldn't, but Uriah's intentions are honest. Sebastian will support this. Uriah will be good for her and protect her when others would exploit her.

"Hopefully he can instill that sentiment in any offspring they may decide to have. And I agree, it would not be prudent to force something like that on Arabella. She'd likely castrate him with a rusty knife." Sebastian chuckled.

I laughed as well. "Likely dull and rusty. He'll have his hands full. I think they both care for each other. Raven— Arabella, whichever she prefers, talked to that horse quite a bit and even though I only had one side of the conversation, it's obvious she cares for him too. The mating bond was an unexpected twist to their little love tale, but perhaps it'll help them reconcile this."

"Right. Well, at least she and Uriah are together for now. Hopefully he'll be less unbearable and things can be more normal," he chuckled. "Think he'll get laid while we're away? I saw those big doe eyes and that smile she threw at him. She seemed genuinely happy to be here."

"Not my business, but one can hope. Uriah will likely slow things down to make sure it's what she wants and not the bond pushing them," I laughed again. Poor Uriah, always the martyr. "Ready then?" I checked in as we approached the end of the boundary. "I have an idea of what neighborhood. The goon she tortured in the camp gave an address to a pub the kid is seen in often." I began to concentrate and pull for my magic. "Seamus Brandt…" I focused on his name, searching the ether for him.

"Yup, let's go," Sebastian said. He placed his hand on my shoulder, and I pulled for my magic, focusing on his name and the name of the pub, then shifted. My magic searched for a thread to his aura. *Seamus Brandt. Where are you? You little fucker.*

Chapter 26

Felix

The pub was surprisingly full. Apparently snow was not a deterrent for these drunks. We had hung around on the roof of an adjacent building watching for about an hour, to get a feel for the clientele visiting the establishment. We were well armed at the worst of times and could handle most of the patrons between the two of us. I had six daggers and sword on just myself. I traveled light compared to Sebastian. *I guess that's why he is the General...*

The walls were a dingy tan color, and the old plaster cracked and peeled in places. The high ceiling made the room feel open, despite the small size. The tinge of smoke hung near the ceiling that was fashioned out of square tile with silver leafing. It was probably beautiful at some point. Old barrels spread here and there acted as tables for the establishment and a long bar made out of a tree slice stretched across the room. The floor was sticky. *That must be a human pub thing.* We entered, thankful for the bad lighting.

We had the hoods of our sodden gray cloaks on covering the majority of our appearance. The black leather we wore certainly stuck out. Most the people here looked shabbier, a bit down on their luck. Our nicely kept winter wardrobe wasn't doing us any favors, but it wasn't nearly as noticeable as our ears would be if anyone spotted them.

"Any idea what this guy looks like?" Sebastian asked. He seemed a bit nervous, even for a hardened soldier. Close quarters with humans were not our strong point.

"Not really, just smaller and mousy. I figured I'd let my magic do the searching," I said. I had a unique gift for finding people. I merely had to think about some aspect of them, and my magic would lead me there. Usually, I had to have more than a name. It seemed to work better on humans.

Fae had their own talents that could muddle mine. I'd tried to find Arabella countless times before at Uriah's request and failed. After receiving details about Raven from Uriah, it proved much easier. For instance, the fact that she believed her name to be Raven, not Arabella, was paramount. I had been searching for someone that no longer existed.

I wonder why Zeds never said anything. Surely he had some insight as a seer into what happened when Arabella wasa child? Or was it blocked somehow? I suppose he can't know everything. Arabella's mother was a seer too. Zeds taught her. I need to ask him.

My magic made me inherently good at spying, much like following a trace on someone. The smallest detail could be helpful. Once I knew that Arabella had entered the cave from Neera, and that she had the scent of strawberries and cinnamon, I'd been able to follow her path through the cave. From there, it was easier to retrace her steps, and eventually find her for Uriah. My magic imbued my natural tracking skills.

Knowing that she went by Raven rather than Arabella had been the true key. Any tracker could follow a scent, it was the magic that happened when I got to the end of the trail that mattered, when the magic found a threat to the persons aura and lit up. Much like a lighthouse on the shore in the dead of night, I could see where I needed to go through the sea of auras. I simply had to follow the beam of light. *Now, I just need to do it again, with less to go on.*

"Works for me," Sebastian said. He could command a legion but as far as practical magic goes he was more steel backup and physical strength, like trying to stop a raging bull. He had physical strength most fae did not possess. He never

172

seemed to run out of energy, aside from that he knew simple tricks like pulling light into a ball to see by or encouraging plants to yield a path. If I was crossing wild country, I would want him with me to easily pass through denser forested areas.

I have a few other tricks up my sleeves that I use in my work. Magic is never exact, it's often subjective to true need. Sometimes it channeled differently based on what was trying to be accomplished. Sebastian and I made a good team for this. We took a seat at a barrel off to the side of the room near the front door.

I wonder if Sebastian plans to leave the manor. He's been so private lately, early to bed and hard to find.

Before coming into the pub, we'd used Sebastian's super strength to barricade the back door, just in case. We didn't want anyone escaping. We created a fire hazard when we piled just about everything in the cramped alley behind the building against the door, insuring no one would be getting out the back way.

"Do your thing, brother," Sebastian said, leaning back on his stool. They were sticky too. I nodded, and let lose my magic. I pushed it to focus on Seamus. Magic filtered through the air, and every conversation around us bombarded me. The words whispered in the dark ran through my brain as I cataloged what I was hearing. "Mussy," "Seamus," rang out in my head, and I immediately looked to the right.

There on the edge of the bar, right by the back door we'd blocked, was a table booth covered in mostly shadow. I probably would have overlooked it had my attention not been drawn by the magic. The group at the table my magic pointed me to weren't *complete* imbeciles; at least Seamus didn't repeat his friends' mistake and leave his back exposed.

In the booth sat four humans. Each looking seedier than the other. I wasn't sure which one was Seamus. My magic indicated they were talking about him or to him. I tipped my chin to the corner. Sebastian looked where I indicated. It was only maybe fifty feet away, but there were ten or eleven tables between us, and probably forty patrons in the bar. *How many friends does he have?*

Sebastian cracked his knuckles. "Which one is he?" He leaned forward again. A waitress walked over. Sebastian said, "Give us a minute darling," with a wink. She shrugged and cleared a tray of glasses sitting on a nearby table.

"On second thought, come here sweetheart," I said waving her back. I pulled three gold coins out. "Can I get two knocks of brown sugar bourbon for us and can you send a round over there to Seamus? Do you know him?"Her eyes went wide with the over payment. "The extra is for you if you can do it quietly." I stared at her boldly.

"Seamus. Only his mamma calls him that. He likes to be called Mussy, snot nosed brat, that one. He's in here with his uncle. That's the brute in the red sweater. Mussy's just a dumb kid. Not sure he's worth buying a drink for," she said, eyeing me. I shifted my cloak forward to cover my ears better. "I heard his pals turned up dead down on the coast a few days ago. Caught up in some fishing net. Had no heads, don't ya know."

"Is that so? If the one in red is his uncle, which one is he?" I said, sliding yet another gold coin across the table. She ran a finger around a frizzy brown curl, licking her lips and pushing her breasts forward so they popped out of her low cut gray sweater. I bet she was pretty in her day. "He's in the corner beside him. You know, they just started coming here again. They hadn't been in for awhile. Then, just like that," she snapped her fingers, "like a week ago, they started coming back with the faery from the Brume."

The moment she snapped her fingers, the lights above the table went bright, illuminating the previously murky room. Half the patrons stood quickly, drinks and food spilling, rushing for the door. With the lights brighter, I could just make out the tip of her pointed ear hidden under the brown frizz.

Fucking trollop. This joint must be fae friendly after all.

Sebastian was instantly on his feet and side stepping our table to stand at the door. His hulking figure blocked the way as people scurried toward him. As people approached, he looked to see if it was one of the two we hunted. We only had general descriptions, but humans were easy enough to identify. He let out the ones that weren't our mark.

I shifted and appeared instantly at the boys' table. His uncle leered at me, and clenched his fists while his dark eyes flickered between me and Sebastian across the room.

"Seamus! Hey kid. How ya been?" I asked like we were old friends. The boy looked up at me clearly eyeing my daggers and sword. A cruel smile spread across my face.

"Who are you? What do you want?" Seamus, bless him, tried to sound tougher than he was. He was a runty sort, who clearly hung out with people that were stronger than he was to catch the scraps that came his way. He had shifty green eyes, mousy blond hair, scrawny arms, and long stick like legs. *Why would the Queen want you? Too easy. Poor Arabella. She got ran around for weeks by this sniveling idiot.*

The uncle stood up immediately, and Seamus went over the backside of the booth into the corner of the room. Their friends stared in confused silence, eyes wide and no help to either of them as they pressed back into their side of the booth to try to avoid my attention. They had rounded ears, and no outward essence—not fae.

I blinked, reached forward into his space, and grabbing with both hands, snapped the uncle's neck as he swung his ham like fist towards my face. He dropped into a heap of dead flesh on the floor. Seamus ran the few steps to the door and started pushing.

"What the hell? We just checked this door!" he screamed, looking to the staff for help. They shook their heads and turned away. *Little punk, should have thought twice.* I closed the distance. "Help me, help me!" he screamed, as he pounded on the door both fists flying.

I reached forward and locked my hand around his wrist as it swung over his head. It was a done deal when I twisted his arm around his back to pin him close to me.

I shifted not a moment later. Time and space whistled around us for a moment, steaks of light and darkness pressing in. We stopped momentarily and shifted a second time. We landed in a dark room in the basement of the estate.

The sound of running water and smell of musty air hit us in the enclosed space. The stone floor and walls left little room for light coming through the single metal door. No windows to be seen in the underground cell. There was only a drain in the middle of the room and two steel tables—one with tools that would be utilized later and another with buckles to hold the human. *Where the fuck is Seb?*

Seamus thrashed as I held his arms behind him. He lost a shoe in transit. His ripped jeans and dirty shirt had seen better days. No matter. He wouldn't be wearing them for long. It was slightly warmer in here than it had been outside, but not by much. The lack of wind was the only real difference. "Knock it off, kid. You're not going anywhere." I said as he continued to jerk against my hold. Seamus wouldn't be seeing the rest of the estate, he'd find himself well acquainted with this room though.

A few long moments later, Sebastian was in the doorway, assessing the chaos that was me pinning Seamus's elbows behind his back as he bucked and kicked. "Nice grab," he said coolly. Fae light lit the room. He tossed a ball of light into the bracket on the wall. *I wish I could do that. I suppose we each had our strengths.*

"Too easy," I answered. Even with the kid thrashing about, it was barely a workout. Sebastian walked in front of the human, grabbed both feet under one arm, pulled the kids belt off with the other hand as he bucked again. "You won't be needing that, and we can't have you hurting yourself."

We stripped the kid of most of his clothes and laid them out on the smaller of the steel tables. The larger table had thick leather wrist and ankle straps built into it. We lifted the kid in his underwear and placed him on the table. He kicked Sebastian in the stomach as I pinned his arms and Sebastian buckled his wrists.

"Kick me again, and you won't have to wait for the pain to begin," Sebastian grunted as he fought the flailing human into the last ankle strap. I chortled softly. "Good thing you had a few drinks. It'll get you through the night. Feel free to piss yourself, there's a drain underneath you."

The screaming was already underway. I chuckled to myself again. Arabella would have fun with this one if she liked big reactions. We hadn't even hurt him yet, and he was hollering. He can yell himself hoarse.

"What took you so long? I thought you'd be right behind me," I asked, I was surprised you weren't in the cell before us.

"Oh, that. Sorry for the delay. I grabbed the waitress on my way out, and she's next door waiting for us," Sebastian said with a little twinkle in his eye. "She said she saw the fae, so I figured you'd like a head start on finding that one, especially if he could be close." He added a little shrug as he finished speaking.

"Sebastian! You think of everything. Well done." I clapped him on the shoulder. "Looks like we'll be a few minutes late for dinner. How long have we got?" I asked. He pulled a pocket watch out of his leather jacket pocket.

"We've got maybe an hour and half? Two at most, give or take. Depends on if you want a bath before we eat or not. If we come down heavy to start, I bet she squeals since she seems to like the sound of her own voice, but then we'll need more time to clean ourselves up." He said while he tucked the watch away.

We made sure Seamus was secure. I grabbed a thin blanket and threw it over him before I turned. He was still yelling, begging us to set him free. I waved to a guard at the end of the hallway as I stepped out.

"Keep an eye on him, and make sure he doesn't get loose. He's a gift for the Lady of the Shallows. It's of the utmost importance that he not be harmed in any manner." He nodded his understanding and Sebastian and I crossed the hall. The door to Seamus's cell clanked shut behind us as the guard entered to stand watch. Another guard moved into place at the end of the hall. *Hope they don't have to listen to him scream all night.*

Sebastian opened the cell door, and we entered. It mirrored the room we had left Seamus in. The fae waitress lay on the table, eyes wide and already strapped down. "I knocked her out before I shifted," he shrugged as I observed the room. "Easier that way. I also didn't have to worry about hurting her —right princess? Female or not, you made a mistake, and now you have to face the consequences."

"Let me go! I promise I won't tell no one nothing," she begged as she tried to tug on her restraints. Sebastian had left her clothes on. A tear in her sweater was unraveling as she fought to free herself. A thin line of blood ran across her forehead from her temple where Sebastian had hit her, probably with the handle of one of his daggers. "Please, I can make you feel good. How 'bout that? Both of you. Whatever you want."

"You are certainly correct about that. You won't be spouting off to anyone." I leaned over the table of instruments. "Let's start simple. We're not interested in sex, just information." I picked up a wood mallet. "Those fingers of yours can still get you in trouble. They certainly already caused some mischief today." Sebastian forced her hand flat on the table. One swift crack of the mallet a moment later and she was screaming again. We walked around the head of the table to her other side, to repeat the process. "No more snapping tricks for you. And don't even think about shifting. It can't be done here."

Uriah had temporarily altered the ward in Seamus's room. I could shift in, but no one could shift out. He keyed the magic to me specifically. Sebastian would have had to shift into the hallway as he did with his prisoner, even if he'd been alone. *Oh, the joys of well tested magic. Let's get to work, shall we.*

"Let's get to work, shall we," Sebastian said as he chose a metal instrument from the table beside us.

The cacophony of noise was something else as it bounced around the bare stone walls. Between the screams of our little darling and that little brat next door, I was going to have a headache by the time we sat for dinner upstairs.

Chapter 27

Arabella

Despite the outbursts of emotion early in the day, I was starting to really feel at home here after spending a relaxing afternoon with Uriah. Possibly for the first time in my life, I could see it, a place for me here. A purpose that wasn't killing, and a happy ever after for both Uriah and I. It would be easy, just like breathing.

We had just come downstairs from the cozy balcony. Uriah was using the bathroom while I chose a different dress for dinner, not because I really *needed* a change, just because I wanted to.

I wonder if he'd like this long, sparkly red one, or maybe this low cut mauve one? Not this one in burnt orange, my hair would look ridiculous with it. I shoved the dress to the back of the armoire. *They can't all be perfect.*

I flipped through a few more dresses as the bathroom door peaked open. "All yours love," Uriah said as he walked into our room and flopped onto the bed, his smoky wings spreading wide underneath him. "Don't feel like you have to change, but absolutely do if you feel like it." He peaked at me from around the post of the bed. "I definitely want to see you in all of those." He winked. I laughed. *What will he think when he sees my scars?*

"Well, lucky for you, I like to dress up. I just never have a reason to, so I'm taking full advantage. No looking. You'll spoil it!" I gave him a coy smile over my shoulder. He placed his palms over his eyes with mock outrage at having to do so. Now that we had gotten past a lot of the tears and harder parts of the conversation, everything felt easy and natural, in only a few hours at that. I need to thank whoever decided to dig that tunnel in the cave.

I went with a creamy white silk dress. It had little golden bead work along it that looked like sunlight bursting through clouds. I grabbed a pair of off-white pumps from the bottom shelf and slipped into the bathroom. It was flawless! It hugged my curves just so, and the square cut of the top gave a hint of cleavage. It covered all of my bra and the scars on my back. After twisting up a few fly away stands of hair that had wrangled loose, I checked to make sure I didn't have anything in my teeth and exited the room.

"I wonder if you'd consider trading necklaces, maybe just for the evening?" Uriah said softly from the corner by the fireplace with his back turned to me. He was standing in front of a stack of wood to the side, closing the safe.

He sucked in a big breath as he turned. "Wow. I mean, Wow! You were stunning before, but excuse me for a moment while I put my eyes back in their sockets. Arabella, you're an absolute vision." He crossed the room to me, tentatively placing a hand on my waist and giving the slightest pressure, encouraging me to turn for him. I obliged.

"So, I take it this one is a keeper," I asked sheepishly. I wasn't used to this sort of praise. It felt genuine. He truly did appreciate all of me, even my scars he didn't seem shy away from, though I noticed all of the clothes he selected would cover the largest ones on my back. It was astute for him to realize I wouldn't bare them to the world.

"It's perfect. I'll have to give the seamstress a raise," he answered. "May I?" he asked as he lifted the cord of the necklace. A wave of calm fell over me the moment the necklace was removed."If you're okay with it, I think this would look lovely with the dress, and complete the ensemble?" I nodded. He lifted the long cord over my head and laid it gently down on the small table between the two chairs. It's like a heavy weight just lifted from my chest.

"This belonged to my mother, Rosemary. She was the late Lady of the Shallows. She died a few years before my father. They were much older than they looked, but was their natural time, and they both passed peacefully. I think she would have delighted in you having this. She certainly would have been pleased you found your way home," he told me as he opened a square velvet box. "I doubt you remember her, I think she only met you as a child a handful of times. She hated leaving the Shallows."

Inside the box held a lovely single string of pearls. It would reach just to my collar bone and balance the dress perfectly. The sheen on the pearls would bring out the gold beading. My breath caught. I don't know what I expected he would offer, but pearls! They were so elegant. I turned my back to him so he could clasp it for me.

He bent down and kissed the nape of my neck. Lightning shot through my body in the most pleasant way. He sighed. Straightening my new necklace, he placed his hands on my shoulders as he whispered, "They're as perfect as you are to me." The new necklace was light and airy, where as the amber pendant was unrefined, bulky.

"Thank you," I replied. My heartbeat sped up. "Thank you for all of this. You make me feel like a Lady." I blushed as I turned toward his vanity mirror on his dresser and saw the two of us in the center of the frame. My chin warbled and a single tear fell down my cheek. I tried to brush it away quickly as he caught my wrist. Stepping around me, he tipped my chin up, bent down, and kissed the tear from my cheek.

"You're thinking about tomorrow, aren't you?" His eyes were smoky with shadow. They had been swirling and tugging at us all afternoon. It was constant and comforting, like a cordial breeze on a summer day.

"I'm sorry. Here I am, crying again," I sniffled a laugh. "I am sad. I don't want to leave. I promise I don't usually cry this much. I just don't see any other way to finish this. I will quickly, so then I can come home and stay home."

He nodded, and a crooked smile parted his lips a moment, "We'll figure it all out. Let's go enjoy dinner." he said, placing a hand on my lower back and guiding me through the door into the corridor. He continued, "I think that I heard Sebastian and Felix go into their rooms a few minutes ago. So, we shall indeed be in for a delightful evening. We'll be in the main dining room tonight, it's not used often; however, I think today calls for an intimate celebration. I feel as if my family is complete for now, with all I could hope for. My love by my side and my brothers at my table." *That's a lovely thought.*

He smiled a truly effulgent smile then. The ever-shifting shades of his hazel eyes crinkled in the corners, and I could see he was at peace. Tomorrow would come, and with it, whatever was meant to be. For now, he was happy.

We walked side by side down the hall, swinging our clasped hands together in a whimsical kind of way. As we neared the door to Felix's room, we heard what was unmistakably someone breaking wind from within. We both looked at each other with our eyebrows raised. Mischief dancing in our eyes, we burst out laughing as we dashed down the corridor.

Chapter 28

Uriah

Down the center of the table ran a shallow wood encasement. Inside was a rock garden filled with patches of scilla flowers and white pebbles with various shells from the beach. Their delicate light hue honored the house colors and left an inviting exquisite floral scent. The table seated twenty when all the leaves were installed, but for today there would only be four filled. The less, the merrier.

My home was day and night from the grand affair my father had made every meal. Most of the time, I took meals at my desk or Felix, Sebastian and I invaded the small kitchen Arabella and I had breakfast in. Even after my mother passed away, my father always liked to be surrounded by all the fanfare of a busy estate. He and I were complete opposites.

I left the majority of that to Sebastian as my military commander, and Gabriella as the hostess of the manor. Sebastian had grown fond of Gabriella in the process, though they were trying to be discreet. This estate was split for a reason. In the main wing, she was a wonderful hostess and often kept visitors occupied for me. I took meetings, but my home was mine. I didn't *want* to share it with the realms' busybodies.

A large portion of why I declared it necessary to build a second estate near the warring border was so I could have some peace. I didn't need all the stodginess. It was fun to attend a ball on occasion, but even that grew monotonous. *I wonder if I will like them more with Arabella on my arm.*

Arabella and I sat at the far end of the table from the door so we could see who approached. The room was decorated with two large framed canvases both filling the largest walls. One pictured mountains foreshadowed by the meadow of Arabella's family estate. The one across from it captured the Western Estate of the Shallows in all its grandeur.

She sat to my right as I took the head of the table. Staring at the meadow and mountains meant to honor her family roots, her mouth gaped open. "I hadn't realized," she started to say. Her eyes welled with tears again, and she blinked fast to keep them at bay.

"If it bothers you, I'll have it removed tomorrow. We can redecorate anything you wish. When I built the estate, I built it always hoping to find you, to make it ours. I wanted the Meadows represented here as a nod to you and your lineage," I explained. Fuck. I didn't think of the emotions stirred for her today and seeing her first home—this has to be overwhelming. "We can eat in another room if you prefer," I said quickly. "Here, let's..." I started to stand again.

"No, it's okay. I never thought I'd see it again is all." She tilted her head to the side, quizzically examining the painting. "It looks like what I vaguely remember. I assume you sent a rider to my father when you told him you found me? I know you can't shift directly. The wards around Agron's Keep don't allow for that, right? If you shifted, you'd be stuck on foot until you reach the far barrier."

I nodded. "Yes. You've got a good memory for such a detail. You can't cross the entirety of the Agron Realm by shifting. You'd either run yourself into the ground trying or hit wards meant to keep us in check. I sent word to your father. He and his, wife, came here a few days later after receiving the letter I sent. He was furious I'd let you go. He called me a liar and said it was a ruse to get out of marrying his new daughter, your little half sister, Arianna. She's six now. The idea is abhorrent, but apparently everyone else seems to be okay with it." My lip curled in disgust. I couldn't help it.

"I'm sorry they've put you in such a ridiculous situation. As for my sister, who knows? Perhaps she'll be relieved that I'm here now. Arianna likely doesn't understand all this. And my father..." she trailed off.

"I know this is difficult. We don't have to discuss it now, if you prefer to wait?" I prompted, hoping to steer to a more upbeat topic.

"It's ok. I'm sure he doesn't care for her much. He never liked me as a child either. He likely doesn't care what happens to her. He spent as much time away as he could. I shouldn't be surprised he'd pretend I didn't exist now and fail to protect his youngest. Especially after what we learned today. It makes me wonder if he knew where I was taken all this time. I would like to go see him after I settle the task from Queen Clawin of course. We should request a full court," she said casually. I felt my eyes grow wide.

"I agree. I was going to wait to bring up the matter until you were more settled. It would be best to visit King Astros as soon as possible, but I won't pressure you." I tilted my head. I could feel my pulse pounding in my neck. She gave me a small smile. "When we go, they'll insist we wed. I think you can guess my feelings on the matter, but I won't have you badgered into doing anything you don't want to do. Our magic will sing for them, and that'll be the end of our wishes."

Arabella settled her hand down on mine and her big hazel eyes looked into the depths of my soul. When our hands touched, cords of light and wisps of my shadow began to dance around us again. We both watched it dance for a moment. Gabriella came in then with a bottle of wine and filled our glasses quietly before leaving. "I hope you know how marvelous you are," she whispered, and I felt my heart flutter. "I would be too lucky," she finished. I smiled, lifted her hand to my mouth, and kissed the back of it.

A door opened at the end of the room."How are the lovebirds getting along then?" Sebastian quirked, breaking the spell of magic in our moment. *Later, then.* My heart was full for the moment.

"The lovebirds are getting on quite well," Arabella answered before I could. I gave him a pointed look. He smirked at me and slid into the seat across from Arabella. "You look tired. Was it too much trouble with the extra tasks today?" she asked Sebastian, looking worried that my orders had put him out.

"Not too much trouble at all. It was an informative day," Sebastian started to say as Felix entered the room and sat by his side, elbowing him in the ribs as he did so. Felix grabbed the bottle of wine left on the table and poured a glass for both of them before he took a big gulp.

Chapter 29

Arabella

We soon finished the first bottle of wine, and Gabriella returned to fill our wine glasses with a rich red wine. She left a new bottle on the table. It was delicious, slightly sweet but full bodied. She set out small appetizer plates for each of us and a platter of bruschetta. The vibrant tomato stood out on the table. We all helped ourselves to a couple of pieces. *Delicious. I'll have to watch how much I eat.*

"Sebastian has a habit of speaking out of turn," Felix said, giving him a pointed look as well as he raised his eyebrows. "The tasks for the day are done, as requested, with a bonus offering we shall discuss later." He looked to Uriah. "Might I suggest we put the work away and enjoy dinner? I daresay we won't bore you with our tedium," he finished cryptically, turning his head and addressing me. A sheepish smile crossed his face.

I smiled back at him. *Okie dokie.* "So, which one of you is the mischievous one then? It seems I may have contenders in all three. I know Uriah has his moments, and Felix, you'd have to, since you kept up with me, but what about you Sebastian? I'm trying to imagine you with a personality more than the common soldiers. What's your deal?"

"Oof, here we go then, my Lady. My deal...Well, I suppose I don't know how I should dare to answer that." He grinned. "Unless you want to train with me, I'm not sure you'll find out. I'm pretty versed with a sword, though I hear you do well with your khopesh." Sebastian hedged. Taking a bite of his bruschetta, he winked at me. "Interesting weapon, generally speaking, let alone for a Lady to wield."

Uriah laughed "Arabella might be more than even you can handle, Seb." He sipped his wine, swirling his glass a moment. Delight danced in his eyes. "I think most of our unruly days are over with. I did tell her about that time we lost our clothes to the goats."

Sebastian and Felix burst out in laughter. "Did you tell her how we got back to camp?" Felix asked Uriah with tears of happiness swimming in his eyes. Uriah shook his head and drank deeply. Gabriella came then to clear our appetizer plates and replace them with our dinner.

She lingered by Sebastian a moment. He leaned toward her, lightly grazing her wrist with his. I smiled knowingly at him and raised an eyebrow. He barely shook his head, his eyes pleading for me to forget I'd noticed. *I wonder why he doesn't want them to know.*

We'd been served a lovely plate of mussels and clams in a red sauce with gnocchi and steamed vegetables on the side, all of it dusted with finely grated cheese. I took a bite while I waited to hear the rest of the story and nearly groaned with how delicious is was.

"Well," Sebastian explained as he stabbed at a piece of clam, "It was quite a fiasco."

"We were supposed to be with the other soldiers, you know, working, being the Lords son and all, Uriah thought the three of us deserved a swim," added in Felix. I looked at Uriah, his eyes twinkled with mischief. "I mean, we couldn't let him go without guards."

Sebastian chuckled as he continued, "The goats had our clothes for lunch. They were all over the embankment and ate practically all we had to wear. Our underwear and britches were destroyed, but they also ate our shirts before we managed to wrestle what was left of them away. Imagine three naked guys waving our, you know, around while tugging on goats to no avail by the riverside." They all broke out in laughter again and I joined. "By the time we got done, we each had, what? A shoe left?"

"I had both of mine," Uriah pointed out, tears of joy leaking down his face, a bite of gnocchi in his mouth that he spoke around. "You and Felix were down to one each."

"Right," Felix chimed in. "The worst part was the tatters of clothing we had left barely made us loin clothes. We'd been halfway across one of the wide spots in the Couloir river, and couldn't get back fast enough after we'd noticed them. We'd intended to swim a bit then catch crawdads for supper." He shook his head at the memory. *Uriah looks so happy right now.*

"That wasn't even the bad part!" Sebastian exclaimed. "We were what, maybe, twenty at the time? Secure enough in our manhood, but when we climbed back up the bank, which was covered in blackberry bushes..."

"They didn't bother us earlier when we were going down with our pants on," Uriah cut in, laughing again.

"We get through the bramble, sliced up and scratched where no thorn should ever see," Sebastian continued, waving Uriah off, "Only to find that all the ladies from our military camp had started preparing meals in the flat lands near the stretch of river we were swimming in. They'd set up tables for chopping and had fires going..."

"And here we come!" Uriah cut in again. We all burst out laughing again.

"This was way before I decided to build the estate here," Uriah chimed in. "We came out of the bushes, dicks swinging, scratched up and howling, only to be standing in front of about thirty young ladies."

We all laughed. Uriah had certainly given me a very condensed version earlier. "We ran for it, which made it all the worse. We were tripping on our torn up boots with our butt cheeks flapping behind us and all the ladies cat calling us back," Felix finished.

"I got winks from a lot of those young ladies for a good month after that," Sebastian mused, taking a sip of his wine. He reached for the bottle Gabriella had left and refilled it. Turning, he refilled Uriah's and offered more to me and Felix.

"Yes, please. So how far did you have to go? Was your unit close by?" I asked with a small shake of my head. I didn't know the right terms.

"About a mile. The women were mostly made up of various soldier wives without children to look after that tagged along to help how they could—cooking, laundry. I don't allow it anymore. It was good for morale at the time, but things have gotten too tense in the last few years. I'd prefer the men just look after themselves rather than putting females in danger unnecessarily," Uriah answered. Felix and Sebastian nodded in agreement. "That was a day though. I remember spending a good hour digging thorns out of my legs and...elsewhere." We all laughed heartily again.

Having eaten most of our meals, Gabriella returned yet again, she loaded our plates onto a tray and left after a skittering glance at Sebastian. *Unspoken conversations are the best.*

Moments later, she came back with thick slices of chocolate mousse cake. My eyes went wide. "If you keep feeding me like this, you'll have to widen the doorways," I said, taking a bite. "This is heaven, so rich and creamy." They all smiled.

Uriah winked at me, "I wish I could say this was an everyday thing. It could be of course, if you wished it; the kitchen staff is definitely pulling out all the stops today." He looked so happy. We all dug into the thick slices of moist fudge cake. *I'm happy too, though I hope Knightmare is settling in okay.* A pang of worry bloomed, but I tried to push it back.

With dinner over and the table cleared, we wished Felix and Sebastian a good evening and retired to the bedroom. "I know it's a little early," Uriah said. It was only around eight o'clock. "I thought maybe you'd like to read by the fire for a few minutes? And um, er, I wasn't sure if you wanted the room to yourself tonight?" he asked, uncertain. "I can take a vacant room if you'd like some space."

"Please don't leave me alone. We don't have very many hours left until I have to be off with Knightmare," I said as I slipped around in front of one of the chairs by the fireplace. "I would love to read for a bit, I think," I shuffled through the couple books on the table and crossed back to him. "We may need another quick trip upstairs to the library," I finished. The corner of his collar had flipped up. I smoothed it down and pulled him in for a kiss. Our magic buzzed again. *That is never going to get old.*

"Absolutely, would you like to slip into something cozier now or when we get back?" he asked. A smile played on his lips as he kissed the inside of my wrist that still hung around his neck.

"Later will do. I'm rather partial to this dress," I rubbed my finger along the pearls. "You really do have impeccable taste." *I've never felt so light, free.*

He kissed me again. A few minutes later we slipped upstairs and he showed me where the romance books were. There weren't many to choose from, but I picked two I hadn't read before and we made our way back downstairs. He chose one of the books he had in the room and we sat in companionable, comfortable silence for an hour or so with the fire crackling merrily at our feet.

My eye's flicked to him as he read. Dirty thought swirled in my mind as my body filled with need. *Would he want me this soon?*

Chapter 30

Uriah

After about an hour of silent, cozy reading, Arabella excused herself to the restroom. She carefully removed my mothers necklace and placed it in the box I'd put on her vanity. She left her neck bare. She picked through the dresser for a moment and selected something to wear to bed.

I was giddy, testosterone flooded my system.. *Fuck, I thought for sure she would kick me out. Her choice, let whatever happens next be her choice...* My cock was stiff already at the thought of her body next to mine.

I marked my page and set my book down. I walked over to the bed and turned down the comforter on both sides. *What side will she want? I'd rather be near the door. Will being in the corner make her feel trapped or something? Fuck! What do I do? Maybe we'll rearrange the room again, turn the bed. I can't do that tonight though.*

I went to my dresser. I usually slept naked. Surely, I couldn't do that tonight. *Could I?* I laughed quietly. *Get a grip.* She slipped out of the bathroom. The fae light dimmed and went out completely as she left the chamber. My wings were twitching. I was antsy, nervous even. I didn't know what to do with myself. *How long have you wanted this? Control. Get control. She belongs with you. You belong with her. Breathe.*

"Do you have a preference for side of bed?" I tried to ask casually. I turned to see her in a dark plum negligee with a peak-a-boo thong barely hiding underneath and my breath caught in my throat. It generously held her figure in peak form, her breasts perfectly held together, their swell highlighted by the sheer material barely covering her. I'd picked it out myself, though I never thought she'd actually be wearing it. Suddenly, I felt like I was fifteen again seeing breasts for the first time.

Just don't rocket off like an adolescent.

"To be honest? I don't remember ever sleeping in a proper bed, so it really doesn't matter to me." She walked up to me, reaching out slowly, as I brushed a strand of loose curls over her shoulder, she popped the button on my pants and ran a finger along the inside of my waistband. My cock was barely contained. "I wasn't sure what you, um, had in mind for tonight. I thought maybe if you're...up...for it, I'd make a request?" She glanced down, biting her lip, taking in the bulge of my pants She looked up at me through her lashes.

Fuck, she's sexy.

"Tonight shall be whatever you need it to be. If you want me to hold you, I will. If you don't want to be touched, I'll keep my hands to myself. What's your request?" I brushed my thumb along her bottom lip. She stepped closer and ran her hand down the front of my pants, feeling what waits for her there, and stood on her tip toes. *Thank the King.*

The high heels she'd been wearing all day really leveled the field for us. I forgot how petite she was. Our magic already began to swirl in delight. "Can I explore for a bit?" I nodded, biting my lip.

"Yes, ma'am, you can." I sucked in a breath as she lightly squeezed my bulge, letting her hand lingers in the warmth of my nether region. I pulsed against her touch.

"I don't want to think anymore today. I just want to feel. Stay in the moment for a little while."

She unzipped my pants; my erection was clear as day and straining through my navy boxers. I kicked my shoes off and let my pants drop as I started to reach back and unbutton my shirt below my wings. She ran a hand up my thigh, caressing me again. It was electric.

"Can I do that?" she whispered, already sliding her hand around my waist to the back of my shirt. I searched her eyes. I needed her so badly. I *wanted* her so badly. My breathing got heavier with the anticipation. She unbuttoned my shirt, and I lifted my arms and pulled it over my head. "Can we just...see what happens? No expectations. I believe we're on the same page, so let's just see where the night takes us?"

"As you wish, my love." I whispered as I nodded. Her hands slid up my abs as I flexed to show her all my lines of muscles. I slid my hand into her thick copper hair and tipped her head back, fully taking her mouth and working my tongue with hers. She writhed her body against mine, brushing my taught cock with her stomach. I reached down and scooped her up into my arms. Placing my hands firmly on her ass, she wrapped her legs around my waist and her arms around my neck.

Peering over my shoulder as I nuzzled into hers, she swiped a finger along the top of my wings. *Oh, fuck!* That couldn't be a more sensitive spot. She might as well have put my cock in her mouth. "Mmm, Arabella, fuck. You smell so good and your kisses are so sweet," I whispered as my breath hitched. Her wild curls cascaded down as she leaned forward and laughed. She nipped my earlobe and kissed the side of my neck just below my ear. I buried my face in her cleavage, kissing my way back up her neck as I walked us to the bed. I turned and sat on the bed, letting her straddle me. I shifted my wings into a more comfortable position quickly as we continued kissing.

I could feel the hot moisture building between her legs already. The plum color offset her skin tone perfectly. Selfishly, I'd left little more than lacy scraps in the drawer for her to choose from—they covered only the essentials. Her nipples were tight. I let my shadows flick over them as she began to grind into my hard shaft, her elbows still resting on my shoulders. I reached down and pulled a sock off. *Don't need these.* One side, then the other. We kissed deep. Our magic filled the room, dancing in intricate lines.

"Oh, Uriah," she breathed in my ear, gyrating on my lap. "You're so hard." I palmed a breast, leaning my head down. I pushed the silky soft material aside and sucked her rosy pink nipple into my mouth. Softly at first, then a little bite. I felt her skin pebble with goose bumps. She ran a finger across the length of my wing again with the same result. I shuddered.

"Arabella," I said as seductively as I could while I huffed a laugh. "You keep playing with my wings, and you might get more than you're bargaining for." I pulled her other breast free, letting the straps slide down. The lace and silk were bunched around her waist now. Kissing my way down, I swung us sideways so her head landed softly on the pillow. "Tell me I can taste you?" I licked my lips. *Please.*

"Yes." She gasped, as her hand trailed down, circling her belly button once before going further to touch herself. Rubbing circles at the top of her clit for a moment she added, "but not until I get to taste you." She gave me a coy smile as she slid off my lap the rest of the way and then the bed in one fell swoop. *Graceful.*

She landed on her knees before me, her large breasts were gently brushing my knees. She looked up at me. I was frozen. *Fuck, am I alive?* "Please. Only, you'll have to tell me what you like. I've never done this before." She bit her bottom lip again, and gave me that seductive look through her lashes again. *Fuck, I love that.*

My eyebrows rose. "You've never..." My anxiety lessened immediately as my voice trailed off. She was a virgin too. We'd saved ourselves for each other. "Me either."

She shook her head. "I mean, I've castrated a few males, but that's not really what I'm going for here." She let out a nervous little laugh. "I read lots of dirty books though." Want and desire burned in her eyes. Her cords of light had exploded around us just as my shadows swirled and twisted.

She reached up to pull my blue boxers off. I lifted my hips

as she tugged them down. They hit the floor. *I should have worn something sexier. Thank the King these are clean.*

She giggled the most innocent giggle and raised a hand to cover her mouth as my cock sprang free, bobbing a moment. Her eyes never left mine and as she let her hand glide down my throbbing cock from tip to base, she opened her mouth and slid her lips over the tip sucking it in deeply.

She took the base of it in her hand and skimmed her fingers tightly up and down as she licked a bead of cum off me. "That feels so good," I breathed out heavily. "Take it as deep as you can. Don't gag yourself." There would be time for theatrics later. She began to fall into a rhythm. "Oh fuck, yeah, just like that, squeeze tighter," She flicked her tongue faster, sliding it up and down my pounding veins.

Moving her small hands up and down, she took me deeper and let the pressure build. She alternated between pulling me deep into her mouth and flicking her tongue. She kept the pattern as I moved my hips and laced my fingers into her hair holding her head so I could push a little deeper. *Fuck. Fuck. Fuck. Good girl, Arabella.*

"Arabella," I moaned. "Fuck, I'm... Fuck, I'm gonna cum." She plunged her head down taking me the deepest yet as I thrust my hips up into her face and I spilled into her waiting mouth. She moaned as my hot seed poured into her, swallowing as her hand made it's way up my shaft. She licked me clean, sucking every last bit off me. *Fuck.*

"Wow, fuck," I panted. My hand was still at the back of her neck and guiding her as she came back up onto the bed. "Oh, my love. Fuck. I'm gonna buy you all the smut I can find." I panted, out of breath, but no where near done. "Lay back for me." She licked her lips seductively as I swung her legs around me and released my hand from her hair. Leaning forward a moment, our mouths connected, and we tasted each other, tongues swirling wildly. Our magic swirled and danced around us.

She laid back, and her head caressed the pillows. Her curls cascaded over the silky pillow. I waved my hand to set a sound barrier. I should have done it before, but I think Sebastian and Felix have already heard enough.

Chapter 31

Arabella

I'd decided during dinner. Seeing him cut loose and laugh with his friends, his brothers. He cared so deeply. He did his best to take care of everyone around him, even his staff. Their purpose was to take care of him and yet, he cared that they were comfortable and happy with their roles. Secure. I wanted to give him that too.

"Uriah," I moaned. I let my hand slide through his shaggy auburn hair as he sucked into my clit. "Mmm, that feels so good." His shadows flicked and pulsed around my taught nipples; my legs were spread wide. Uriah had slid my tiny thong down as he kissed down the length of one leg. He was careful around my ankle, but he didn't blanch at the scars there. After pulling it off my feet, he began his ascent up the other leg. Still careful of my many scars. Gentle, but firm. Wanting. *Yes! His hands feel so good. His shadows...like hundreds of sensual kisses everywhere all at once.*

He looked up to me for confirmation. After I nodded in agreement, he sunk his lips into me, his mouth wide, tongue searching and massaging me in all the right spots. He flicked and sucked as I moaned and ground my hips into him. He hooked his arms around my thick thighs and pulled me closer to him. Sliding one hand down, he worked a finger inside me. "So tight. Fuck, you are so beautiful," He looked up my body at me, pumping his hand steady and swirling his tongue on my clit, letting my wetness slick his path. My back arched, and my toes curled. I called out his name before I came on his hand and

199

tongue. I grabbed my breast and squeezed my nipple.

He reached up for the other with his free hand, seeing what I wanted. "That's it baby girl, come for me. Let it go, just let it all go." I shuddered over and over again. Every time I thought he was done, he'd dive back down. He started with one finger, but now he'd moved on to two, loosening my tight muscles. He worked in a rhythm that kept my pulse skyrocketed and my breath short. *Fuck. Fuck. Fuck. I need more.*

"Uriah, please, please…" I said, biting my lip as I pulled him up the bed and over the top of me. His cock was hard again. *He tasted so good, like salted caramel and candied pears.*

"We don't have to. We can stop here or just keep doing this," He looked deep into my eyes. *What is he searching for?* I could feel my pussy throbbing for him. Our mating bond was begging for us to satiate it and our magic a harmony as it thrummed in the room.

"Take me, Uriah. You're the only one I'm ever going to want like this," I told him. It was the truth and the closest to an *I love you* as I could give him. These past couple months had culminated in this moment. *How many times had I fantasized about being with him? How much better is this in real life?!*

He kissed me deep, planting his knees between my legs, Uriah ran the tip of his cock up my middle, slicking it with my juices. He pumped his long thick cock a couple times in his big hand, making sure it was wet all over. Pressing his tip to my entrance, his breath ragged, he nudged the tip in. I was tight, even with having his fingers stretch me just before now.

Still kissing me, he slid in halfway. Our tongues dancing in each other mouths, the magic spinning out of control in the room around us, I gasped, and his hips stilled.

"Are you okay?" he asked. Hunger was rapt in his expression, but he held himself back.

"Yes." I moved my hips against him and took him deeper. He moaned, our chests rising together we breathed through it, and he slid in bit by glorious bit. "Oh, yes. Oh yes, yes!" My hands curved around his back, and I caressed the edge of his wing. His eyes flared wide, a guttural moan broke through his lips. He pulled out little before thrusting in completely.

"You don't know what you do to me." Uriah said breathlessly.

He stilled, to let me get used to him. We kissed again, and he leaned his head down, sucking my nipple into his mouth, and played with it. His shadows swirled at my other breast. He slowly began moving more, letting himself slide in and out, loosening me up. He went wild as I began stroking his wing, running my fingers down the edge and playing with the veins that ran along the bony structure. He moaned huskily, "Arabella!"

"Yes, yes, don't stop!" I screamed. Our magic locked us in place. He was pumping into me. I pulled a leg up and he slipped his arm under it, giving him better purchase so he could go deeper. Our moans grew louder. Both of us were pouring sweat down our bodies as we fucked out of control, consuming each other like our very lives depended on it because they did. We needed each other.

I pulled my other leg up. My feet were nearly over my head and resting on Uriah's shoulders now. His moans and breath ragged. My muscles contracted, and I came around his thick cock. His abs tightened and his biceps bulged as he bounced with his calves. "Arabella!" he yelled as he spilled inside me. He was buried so deep I could feel his balls slap against me. *Fuck. Yes. This is what I've been missing.* My orgasm exploded inside me as I came again seconds later.

His chest heaved, and he shuddered. He let my legs slide down around his waist, but stayed inside me. Sweat dripped from his brow, highlighting the freckles on his nose. He smiled, satisfied and breathless. The lights that had been flickering settled down. Our heightened state had likely caused them to go haywire all over the estate with the flux of our magic combining. He leaned forward and kissed me deeply again, then more soft, slow and sensual kisses. *Fuck. Yes. I've never felt so good before.*

He nuzzled into my neck and placed his head on my chest. He held most of his weight with his elbows. We cuddled together while our heart beats slowed to normal. I could feel his throbbing cock calm down, and when our breathing was normal again, he slid out of me.

He pushed his weight off of me to the side by the wall. He let his wings droop on the other side of the bed. *How does he look like that? He could be cut from marble.* His chiseled lines were slowly relaxing, but even then...

"You mean the world to me Arabella," he whispered. "Promise me if you have to leave again, you'll always come back." His deep smokey voice was husky. His arms pulled me into him, his wave tattoo half under me as his shadows pulled the blankets from beneath our feet and covered our cooling bodies. He kissed my neck. His stubble tickled as he rubbed his mouth back and forth. His shadows flitted around us in delight.

I turned a little in his arms so we could see each other's eyes. I could feel the tightness returning to my core. I would be sore tomorrow, but I would relish the feeling knowing that I would get to take him with me while I hunted down the last two heads. "Always, I promise. There is nowhere on this planet that I wouldn't go to find you."

"My beautiful Arabella, how did I get so lucky?" He kissed my lips again. We lay snuggled in bed for a while. Sliding his arm out gently, he sat up and slid out the other side of bed. "Let's get you cleaned up." He went into the bathing chamber and drew a bath. Coming back to the bed, he scooped me up. I giggled as he slid one hand under my knees and one behind my lower back so as not to touch the scars on my shoulders, and scooped me up with the twirl of his wings. We went into the bathroom.

The negligee was still around my waist. I pulled it up and

over my head. He settled me in the big tub and climbed in behind me. We spent the next twenty minutes washing and exploring each other. I marveled at the waves on his arm. "Have they ever been so flat? The lines aren't moving at all." I asked as I turned to lean my back against him, sitting between his long legs.

"Never, not even when it was being tattooed. You know that you make everything better, right? I thought my shadows would consume me before I found you in the cave, before your light chased me down. Now, all I see is you, the light in the dark. You are my guiding star, my love." he huffed a laugh, kissing my shoulder.

We stayed in the tub a few more minutes just enjoying each other. We kept adding more hot water until it ran cold. So, we slipped out, toweled off and slid into bed. Uriah snapped his fingers, and the lights went out. *I wonder if it's ever actually dark for him. It must be odd being able to see in the dark.*

I was nestled in his arms. His wings spread across most the bed as we both lay on our sides, my back to his front. We were both completely at ease. Sleep found us quickly and I tried not to think about tomorrow would bring. *Stay in the moment. Just be present,* was my last thought as I fell asleep in my loves arms.

Chapter 32

Uriah

I woke up before Arabella. She looked so calm, and the crease usually between her eyebrows was smooth. Relaxed. She barely moved all night, content to stay glued to my side. My mind was still spinning. My mate. Mine. She was mine. I wasn't a virgin anymore, and she wasn't either. *Fuck. This is all working out wonderfully.*

I'd felt the transition, the moment I sunk into her, the moment our bodies fully joined and the totality of our bond was realized. Fate. Fated mates together at last. I never knew what Zeds had meant about the bond igniting in the dark. It was poetic—her light, my shadows. Both rare and beautiful gifts. Our magic still hummed around the manor as I stood outside my bedroom door. I was trying to be quiet. I needed to speak to Felix before she woke. I crept quietly past Sebastian's door in my underwear and a bathrobe down the hallway to Felix's door. *Tap Tap Tap.*

No answer. Tap, tap, tap. I heard fumbling on the other side of the door. It creaked open, and a blurry eyed Felix grunted, "Good morning." He sounded raspy, dehydrated. *You need to drink more than wine.* "Surprised you're up so early after the light show." He smirked at me. "I take it our *Lady* is well rested and ready to journey back to the human lands?" His eyes danced with mischief. *Asshole.*

"Oh, shut up!" I said in a stage whisper while grinning. "Get in there." I pushed him back into his room and stepped inside. I need to know what you and Sebastian accomplished yesterday." He backed away from the door and crossed the room in just his underwear and sat in his unmade bed. His room was nearly identical to mine, but mirrored opposite since he was across the hall. Our bathing chambers shared a wall.

"Right. Can't we have breakfast first?" Felix half whined. "The sun isn't even up yet. Don't you realize the two of you kept half the whole house awake for a good while? The lights flicking on and off and magic swirling about for hours. The air itself felt different for a time. That gold light of hers might as well be lightning and your shadows chasing after it are like walking into an icy mist. The staff was in an uproar." He looked at me half bemused, half irritated. "I truly hope it doesn't happen every time you get laid."

"Well, perhaps we need this wing to ourselves then." Felix blanched as I said it. I didn't want him to move to a different wing, and he didn't either. "I'm sure it won't happen every time. Our magic needed to complete the bond. It's done that. Mission accomplished on that front. My mate has chosen me— that's no small feat. She's wild at heart, and now I just have to keep her happy. In which case, Arabella said she wanted to be gone by dawn. I'm scared she'll try to slip out without saying goodbye," I told him. "I'd actually much rather do this in the hall to be safe, but I wasn't sure we needed all the staff aware and Sebastian has been sleeping with Gabriella. She might be in his room. I've never known her to run her mouth, but there's a first time for everything." *Loose lips sink ships.*

Felix's eyebrows rose nearly to his hairline. "I had no idea. Ha! Well, shit, good for him," he said as he slapped his knee. *You'll find your person too.* "Okay, well, valid concerns all around. I'll be brief. First, we got the human, Seamus, he's tucked away downstairs. Second, Sebastian had the good sense to grab a waitress that mentioned 'a fae' she'd seen the human with. So, we questioned her after tucking Seamus in and leaving a guard to watch him."

"Nicely done, and what did you find out?" I asked.

Halfway there, surely she wouldn't leave yet. She could do whatever it is she needed to with the boy, and I'd have time to talk her into staying and letting us hunt the last mark.

"Well, the fae Seamus had been with in the bar was definitely Finnigan, according to Cherry, the waitress, and he's apparently from the Brume. Part of some prominent family, Altmore? I know I've heard it. Anyway, he's rumored to have run home to his parents after they heard of Queen Clawin putting out a call for his head."

"Yes, the Altmore's. There's more going on with that. It seems that Ulysses is Finnigan's great uncle," I said. It wasn't common to use the last name once the name of Lord was adopted, so I wouldn't expect it to be common knowledge that Ulysses is an Altmore. It's in the history books, but who reads those? "And it also seems that the new Lady of the Meadows, Arabella's step mother, would be his niece."

"You're kidding. Well, that's suspicious at best," Felix furrowed his brow. "The circle seems to be coming full. Did you just discover this? I mean, she moved in rather quick when Arabella went missing, didn't she? She was happy to give Lionel a new family."

I nodded. "Yesterday, while I showed Arabella the library, we started looking at ledgers. It seems that Judith would be responsible for Arabella's kidnapping, not the nanny at least as far as we've pieced together. Arabella told me Everlee died trying to protect her the night she was taken. Killian Altmore is Finnigan's father and Judith's brother, and Arabella is near certain he was the one that stole her away to the Torrent Kingdom," I quickly explained. "We need her here to delve into this for a multitude of reasons, none of which is any less important than her personal safety."

"I agree. I'll pull some of my sources and have them begin researching immediately," Felix replied, nodding and rubbing his eyes. "This conspiracy runs deep. She may not be safe, even here. Especially since we notified King Astros, his court, and the Lord of Meadows himself. The treachery and the implications…" His face paled.

"Yes, I know, I'll do whatever I have to as long as she's safe. She's safest by my side. I'm going back to bed. I'll try to talk her down for breakfast and then for a quick tour of the sub floors. I'd like it to be a surprise, but I'll blurt it out if I have to." Felix looked at me, new horrors playing out in his mind. He and Sebastian were sworn as my personal guard and the guard of my future family. Arabella irrevocably fit into that category. Whether we were wed yet or not, she was mine and by proxy, theirs.

I left him to think as I slipped out of Felix's room and back into mine. "There you are, handsome," Arabella said. I smiled at her remark as I entered. She was standing in front of her vanity. She looked refreshed, much more awake than I was. She'd pulled black leathers out of the dresser that I'd had made for her and was holding them. She pulled on her pants as I watched her a moment. I turned to my own dresser and shuffled through my drawers. We both finished dressing.

The wave clad crest of the Shallows was delicately embroidered on the back of her leather jacket in silver and blue. Usually, it was just an anchor shaped patch sewn onto the right upper arm, but I wanted to match her personal style. She had hand embroidered flowers all over her clothes. I traded her flowers for waves, but added a few of the scilla flowers prone to the territory. They were lovely. I couldn't help but notice how the leathers hugged her ass.

I watched as she strapped her khopesh to her thigh and tucked daggers into sheaths. "Thank you for these." She held one up. I'd had those made for her delicate hands too.

"Of course. You look good in my colors." I smirked as I walked over to her. "How are you feeling today?" I noticed she was wearing a silver necklace. A big smile spread across my face. I couldn't help it. My eyes lit up. "Do you like it?" I lifted the delicate silver chain. It held a single silver pendant of a wave crashing. "I thought you'd for sure put your old one back on."

"I woke up feeling amazing. I was rested and calm for once. Somehow I think last night might have been the best night of sleep I've ever had." She winked at me and pulled me to her for a kiss.

After a long moment, we pulled apart. "Interesting though, I *did* put the amber pendant back on. Only, it's weird." Her brow bunched. "The moment I did, I swear my mood soured. I've never noticed it before. I took it off immediately. It felt as if, I don't know, it's almost as if my magic was telling me not to wear it? Maybe I've just outgrown it? My magic it— it didn't like it." She looked at me, scared. That was fear in her eyes.

"I've never heard of anything like that happening. I can certainly find out. Leave the necklace here, and I'll have Felix look into it. If he doesn't know, he knows an ancient fae named Zeds that would surely have some insight. He's busy this morning with a task for me, but we'll see him in a bit. He hasn't been out to visit Zeds in awhile, so I'm sure he'd be happy to go. I had this one made for you." I said, gesturing to the silver chain. "I thought maybe you'd like something to remember me by? You don't have to wear it if you don't want to, of course, but it is yours." *Your necklace, my tattoo, two waves forever crashing into each other.*

She smiled and her eyes lit up. "Thank you! It's so pretty. My neck felt too bare. I saw this on the vanity and was drawn to it." She lifted the little wave and looked at it.

"It's yours. I'd hoped you would want to wear it. I was going to offer it this morning, but you beat me to it." I brushed her cheek. "Are the leathers fitting ok? We can have them altered if need be."

"They fit great. They're so much warmer then the ones I wore here." She bit her lip and I smiled. I wanted to scream *I love you.* "I'm afraid I've got to get going soon though. I was thinking miscreants aren't likely to be up at the crack of dawn though. So maybe I could stay for breakfast, then head out with Knightmare."

"I agree, and since you brought it up, I don't think anyone, let alone riffraff, will be out and about at the crack of dawn today. That was quite the storm that hit the Northeast. Would you allow me to continue the tour after breakfast? I think you might find it interesting. I didn't get to the lower levels yesterday."

"Oh! I hadn't realized there was more to see," she said, a smile on her face. Her copper curls were pulled back in an intricately woven braid and crowned on the top of her head again. The stud in her nose shined against all the black, highlighting her warrior heart. "I'd like that. I need to talk to Knightmare first, if you don't mind. I don't want to leave him in the dark."

"Okay. After breakfast we can tour the stables, say good morning to Knightmare, then finish the tour of the manor. We should be done by ten o'clock at the latest," I promised.

"Thank you," she beamed. "You're the best!" She wrapped her arms around my middle in the tightest hug. We hugged a for long moment. I kissed the top of her head, and then I excused myself into the bathing chamber. I ran through my morning routine quickly.

"How far did you get in your book?" I asked. Stepping out of the bathroom, she set it down on the table. I left he door cracked so it could air out. *Hope she doesn't go in there immediately.*

"I'm about half done. I'll look forward to finishing it. It's a good story about this fae male who's in love with a human woman, and he's trying to win her trust. She hates the fae, so she won't talk to him. He's tried just about everything to get her attention. She secretly loves him too; she's just playing hard to get. She wants to see how many silly things he'll do to get her attention." She laughed. "Would you mind leaving it here?" She tapped it as it sat on the table top.

"Of course," I smiled. I need to buy more books along that line. They seem to bring her joy. I opened the door and waved her on to go before me. "Breakfast, I'm famished this morning." I said with a laugh. "I hear we gave quite the light show last night. Apparently the magic we let loose in the manor was causing some mischief." I kissed the top of her head as she laughed herself.

"Worth it," she quipped as she gave me a cheeky smile over her shoulder. She bounced down the hall in new leather ankle boots. *I love seeing her so carefree.* "I wouldn't change it. Last night was incredible."

Chapter 33

Arabella

"Good morning, Knightmare!" I bounded into the stable with Uriah walking quickly behind me. I felt so light and airy. I couldn't remember feeling this good before. The cloak Uriah grabbed on the way out blew behind him in the breeze by the doorway. *I hope it doesn't tangle in his wings.* He'd put on a tight fitted black button- down shirt, dark gray slacks, and black loafers. He looked incredible with his biceps prominent and a suggestion of the muscle he hid underneath. I couldn't wait to touch him again, to taste him.

Breakfast had been scrumptious. We had thick fluffy biscuits, smothered in sausage pepper gravy, soft and crisp chunks of pan- seared red potatoes, crispy bacon, scrambled eggs, fresh orange juice and piping hot chai tea with cream. I was stuffed. This walk was anything if not absolutely necessary. I needed a nap.

I sat gingerly at breakfast, slightly uncomfortable and a little sore after our activities last night. I was happy to feel it. We had both been enthusiastic and so in tune with each other.

I had to leave soon, but I was postponing as much as possible. Uriah had tried to talk me into exploring the lower levels before coming out to see Knightmare. I missed him and wanted to check on my friend.

"Good morning. You seem…different today. Lighter, happier." Knightmare had a shoot full of hay at his disposal and a large stall with an opening outside. I'd felt bad about putting him in the cave with no opening before we came here since it made

him panic to be closed in. Not that I can blame him. I don't like it either.

"I've had a lovely time here. I think we'll put off a few more hours before we head out. No one will be up and moving yet anyway, and it's only Thursday. Friday is our lucky day to run into the riffraff, so I think it'll be okay. Uriah wanted to show me something before we go too. Are you comfortable enough here?" I asked him as I braided a chunk of his mane. Someone had given him a good brushing.

"*That's fine with me. I'm comfortable here. I'm warm and overfed. Don't take too long, I'll get too fat and won't want to move.*" He kept munching, content for once to just be.

"Okay, maybe we'll stay until after lunch then. If that's okay?" I dropped my voice to a whisper, "I know I'm stalling, but the idea of leaving Uriah kind of hurts. It's like leaving my arm behind. I feel as if I need him with me."

"*That's the bond. You smell different, like strawberries and sea salt. I take it you sealed the mating bond with Uriah? The lights flickered for a while. Your magic feels different, stronger. That's good. It'll make you stronger. It will be more painful to be apart from his though. Perhaps we need to rethink our strategy?*" Knightmare turned his eyes toward me, shaking his mane. The gold ring around his eyes was much brighter today. He was well rested. We rarely stopped moving; he needed a break too.

"If that's what it is, I do not mind it. For once, I feel settled. I'll consider a different strategy, but I just don't see another way. We have to find them. I have to take their heads and get them to the Queen before she grows impatient. The less attention she pays me, the better off we are. The more unrest in the Kingdom, the angrier she will be." I kissed his nose and pressed my forehead to his as he lowered it to me.

"*Yes, time is a concern. Have you asked your mate for his input? He has great resources. Are you feeling okay? You seem quite different then when I left you.*" Knightmare appraised me. "*You took off the necklace,*" he noticed. "*I always hated that thing. It's vile. The green in your eyes is much brighter today."*

I nodded. "I feel different somehow. I'm more at ease, like it's okay to stay put for a breather. I usually feel like we need to move on every day, like we can't be idle, but it's more than that. It's not just my magic and not the bond with Uriah. I don't know." I divulged, pondering my feelings. "I left the amber necklace in the manor. Uriah got me this one." I showed him the tiny wave cresting. Uriah was patting one of the other horses, and giving it sugar cubes. He'd slowly made his way around the stable with a box of sugar as we talked.

"I thought I would try something new. Call me Arabella now. I want to be rid of Raven." I turned toward Uriah standing a little ways back from me. "I've come to realize some things I was too close to see. I'm ready to stop running. I just have to finish this so we can learn to live again. Really live, I mean."

Knightmare pulled back and looked into my eyes. *"You're finally being honest with yourself. I like this new Arabella. Go and enjoy your time with your mate. I was promised oats and grain. The short brute with the blonde hair keeps leaving me sugar cubes too. Fat, I tell you, you'll have to put me to pasture if we stay too long."* I smiled and laughed at that.

"Okay then, we'll be at the manor." I kissed his nose again and patted his side. *He needs a break too. Maybe there is another way. I just haven't tried hard enough to find it.*

"Ready, love?" Uriah asked as I turned. "I have something to show you that I think you will appreciate." Uriah tucked me under an arm as he wrapped his arm around me, and we headed back out into the frosty morning. Everything was glazed white with a fine layer of ice. The ground was crunchy under our feet as we made our way up the gentle slope of the yard, my yard, my home, if I wanted it to be.

Chapter 34

Arabella

"I think in the interest of time, we'll start on the bottom floor." Uriah told me as we passed the top lower level and continued down a spiraling staircase encased in big gray bricks. *This is only half the manor. The other side must be just as enormous.*

The lower we went down the staircase, the mustier the smell became. It was darker down here with no windows, just several doors on either side of the corridor at the bottom of the stairwell. The blue carpets seen throughout the home and beautiful cherry wood furniture were nowhere to be seen. We were encased in large stone blocks. The moisture leached in from the ground and moss grew in the grooves.

The hairs on the back of my neck prickled, and my heart began to race. I looked to the end of the long dark hallway to the lone light at the end. *Cells. He's brought me to his dungeon. Why would he do that?* It reminded me painfully of King Plavlock's castle in the Torrent Kingdom and when Queen Clawin had me locked up for weeks. My nostrils flared and a bitter taste flooded my mouth.

My feet came to a hard stop as we entered the hallway, darkened with that single light on in front of a cell door toward the end of the hall. Guards stood on either side of the door. My body wouldn't move. "What is this?" I shrieked, trying and failing to keep the panic from my voice. *No, no, no. He wouldn't lock me away.* I pulled my khopesh and took a step back from Uriah. Goosebumps rose on my flesh.

He turned to look at me, the smile he'd had on his face quickly fading. Worry etched into the creases on his forehead. "I wanted to give you a gift, something you wanted and needed. It's just over here." He gestured toward the door with a light. "It's not a trick, Arabella. I promise. This room isn't for you."

Flashes of blood splattered walls in dim light crossed my vision. The warm trickle of blood poured out of me after one of the 'experiments.' Purple potion shoved in my face. Darkness all around for days on end. Rats crawled on me, biting. Hungry, I was always so hungry. Pain. So much pain.

"Come now, Raven, I thought you liked to play hide and seek?" The Sculptor use to taunt me. I'd run in the darkness, smashing into walls, trying to get away, but I was always locked in. There was no escape. No way out. No end to the games.

His brow bunched deeper and he placed his hand on my shoulder. "Arabella, I'm not going to hold you captive." His lips parted, fear crossed his face, and his notice catching up to my reaction. "On the King's life, I swear it. I sent Felix and Sebastian to Stanzley in your stead yesterday. That's why they were late for dinner." He stepped closer to me, rubbing his hands up and down my upper arms. talking fast. "I had them fetch the human. He isn't harmed. They did nothing more than bring him here for you."

I held my ground. "What? I don't understand." I pushed Uriah away from me. My heart beat was slowly steadying, but every ounce of my being needed out of this hallway, up the stairs, into the sunlight. *Calm down. He won't hurt you. Be rational. Trust. This is about trust.* "Who's in that cell?" I pointed my khopesh down the corridor.

"Seamus Brandt. We'll have to hunt down Finnigan Altmore, but everything my sources have found out is that he's no longer in the human lands. He's in the Agron Realm in the Brume."

He reach for my upper arms and stepped toward me,

before he pulled me forward into a hug. "I swear you are safe with me. I'm sorry. I keep forgetting the trauma you've been though. I should have just told you what was waiting for us down here. I wanted to surprise you, but not like this. I didn't mean to trigger more bad memories. You can take your time, do what you need to do with him. You can question him as long as you like. He's not getting out of there. Felix is in there with him now, waiting for us. The room had all the tools and space you need to work."

I tucked my khopesh away and let my arms wrap between his wings and back. He held me tighter, running his hand over my hair, letting me breathe him in. Cinnamon mingled in his scent now. His shadows wrapped me closer still. *Safe. I can be safe here.* I let the tears fall and didn't try to stop them this time.

The cell is for Seamus, not for me. The Sculptor isn't here. He can't cut me, he won't make me bleed. Safe. I'm safe with Uriah. Uriah isn't playing a game.

"I'm so sorry, love. I didn't think about the impact of the location. You're remembering the Sculptor. I can feel it through the bond." I shook in his arms. I couldn't turn it off. "Let's go back up. I'll find a better location for you to work. This was ill thought out on my part." He guided me up the stairs. At the top, back in the full light of the main corridor, I started to slowly pull myself together. *No more. He can't hurt me now. No more.*

"Thank you for the gift." I whispered. My voice was gravelly. "Perhaps the stables to keep the mess outdoors. Knightmare has a gift of truth saying, so he can tell when people are lying. He's useful in interrogations. He'll have questions of his own. He keeps me on track if I lose myself..." I trailed off.

Uriah nodded. "I'll have it arranged. Let's get you upstairs. You can relax in our room for a few minutes, maybe read a few chapters of your book? The one with the mischievous human girl toying with the fae male. Maybe that would clear your head a little. I'm so sorry. I never meant for this. I hoped you'd be delighted you didn't have to leave immediately. I thought if I could bring him here, you could still work, but we wouldn't have to part. It was selfish."

"It's okay. I just wasn't prepared. Thank you. I appreciate the thought. I'm glad I don't have to leave right away now." My body felt numb, and my voice still sounded far away, but the shock was wearing off.

We retraced our steps through the manor. Gabriella quickly darted into a room as Sebastian began examining a random tapestry. "Those two really should try harder to hide it," Uriah whispered in my ear.

I relaxed a little, "You noticed too?" I looked up at him. He had his hand on the small of my back, keeping me close. He's *protective. He won't allow the Sculptor to hurt me again. I can be safe here.*

"Oh, I noticed." He laughed lightly. "The two of them have been canoodling for a while and keeping me up half the night while they are at it. Sebastian has always been private, despite the bravado. He's a flirt, but he's always been cautious because of a prophecy he heard when we were younger, something about his heart wavering. I can't remember the phrasing. Sebastian seems happy with Gabriella though. He'll tell me when he's ready to make things more—permanent."

"Speaking of permanence. Knightmare told me to ask you for some ideas so that we can find the fae faster. If Altmore is in the Brume, then I don't need to go back. We could call for a court. All the families would have to attend if it were ordered by King Astros. There's no one in the Agron Realm that would deny such a call." We stopped in the hallway as I spoke. Sebastian had surreptitiously slipped into the room with Gabriella, and they were otherwise occupied now.

"Are you sure? I do think it would be wise, but we've only just found each other. I'm happy to court you properly if you want more time. We can stall Queen Clawin. Her magic will likely have a hard time reaching you here through the Realm's wards, not to mention our fortified magic from the joining last night. You're just discovering who you are, after all." He was saying the words, but I could tell he didn't believe them.

He wanted me just as badly as I wanted him. He would do anything I needed. "I don't need to wait. For once in my life, I know exactly what I want, and what I need. Let the asshole sweat a while longer." I took his hand as we walked to the stair landing. "Distract me?" I pleaded. "Please, make me think of anything else. Make me feel good." Surprise lit his face as he nodded.

"As my Lady wishes." We walked into our bedroom. His fingertips grazed both sides of my hips as we stepped though our door. He tapped the door with his foot and shut it behind us. I turned to face him, then and his lips found mine quickly as he pulled me to him, sliding his fingers around the nape of my neck and into my braided hair.

I fumbled with the buttons on his shirt, stumbling through them. Giving up, I made my way to his belt as he moved to his shirt instead. *Naked. I want us naked. Now.* I wished, and suddenly, with a gasp from Uriah, we were. My magic freed us of our clothing. It was piled, neatly folded, on his dresser beside us as I glanced around his wings. He scooped me up and hauled us to the half-made bed. *If I have my way, this bed will never be properly made again.* Laying me down gently, he began working his way down over my curves.

A half hour later, the lights across the estate were flicking on and off. We both laughed as we noticed at the same time. They flicked in tandem with his thrusts. Our bond was happy, and my mind was clearing. There would be time for Seamus later. Until then, I want to live.

Chapter 35

Arabella

After a hearty lunch of beef stew, fresh rolls and a wedge salad we made it out to the stables. Uriah had sent his shadows to Felix and summoned him to our bedroom door. He said he hadn't been able to do that in years. They whispered to him, but it was never from floors away anymore. As the magic across the Agron Realm weakened, so had his.

The door barely cracked, with me still in bed under the covers and Uriah standing in his underwear, he issued the order that Seamus be taken to the stables. Extra guards were called to ensure he remain secure so I could do my work with Knightmare. Felix seemed confused, but Uriah hadn't clarified that it was because I couldn't handle being downstairs. Felix just nodded and left to find Sebastian.

We'd made love several times since our trip downstairs that morning. We were both exhausted, but in the best way possible. I'd found that being on top was possibly the best feeling in the world. I could ride him all day but we had work to do. Uriah was going to draft a request to King Astros to take an audience with us. It would be private first, but we knew as soon as they verified who I was and saw the fulfilled mating bond between us, a basic wedding ceremony would take place.

We had been sitting in the tub. Uriah's arms wrapped around me as I lay against his chest when he dipped his hand into the water, lifting it to reveal a bubble clad ring.

"Arabella, I know things are moving quicker than either of us imagined they would, but if I'm being honest, they aren't moving fast enough. You already hold the other half of my soul. Would you do me the greatest honor of being my wife?" Uriah asked, and I nearly screamed my yes! He slid the ring on my finger, and we kissed deeply. It feels right. Fast, yes, but I've never been more sure of something.

I had a beautiful silver set blue sapphire ring with diamond accents on my left ring finger. Uriah had pulled it out of the safe to properly asked me to be his Lady of the Shallows after our second joining. It was more than either of us ever anticipated. It felt right. Our magic was thriving. We had been betrothed anyway; this was just on our terms instead of the Agron Realm's.

My cords of light felt stronger than ever before, and Uriah's shadows pooled around him in wild waves like he'd never seen. I was interested in what would happen if I pushed my magic into my khopesh. At the best of times, it had made my blade twice as strong, like I had the power of the sun in my hands. *What would it be like now? Everything feels so much better. Clearer.*

We lounged in our room for a while before I headed down to the stables, dressed in my new leathers. I left Uriah in his office and Felix accompanied me across the grounds in full armor, which confused me. "You look well this afternoon. I apologize for earlier in the lower levels. Uriah didn't say anything, but of course, we should have realized that wouldn't be a savory locale. I apologize for the error in judgment."

"Felix, I will always cherish the initial misconception I had about you. Thank you for the apology, but you couldn't have known. It comes in waves, much more than usual since I arrived here yesterday. It's odd to me it has only been a day. It feels like a lifetime already." I mused as we entered the stables. "Show time. Are there always this many guards on the grounds?"

"Not always. Usually, they split their time here and on patrols. We've had reports of ships amassing off the coast, staging for attack. Many already on the shoreline of the Bay of the Shallows. I don't think they'll strike immediately, however anything is possible. Soldiers are camped just outside the grounds."

His brow creased. He was more concerned than he was letting on. His leathers were covered in dark blue metal scales, overlapping and encasing nearly every inch of him. The only thing he was missing was a helmet. Surely, this wasn't all for dear Seamus. *How heavy is all that? Will I get armor like that too? Do I want armor like that?*

"*He's lying.*" Knightmare said as I walked through the stable to his stall. "*There's an attack coming. He doesn't want you to know how serious the threat is.Uriah is likely being briefed by Sebastian now.*" I nodded to Knightmare, pretending I didn't know that Felix was trying to mislead me. *Perhaps my misconceptions weren't wrong after all.*

I was slightly more sore than this morning, but it wasn't about to stop me from doing my job, whatever that duty may intel. I wouldn't trade the feeling. The bond was pulling me back to Uriah's side, even now. I thought we would have gotten enough of each other between last night and this morning, but already I yearned for him.

"Hey Knightmare, how's our little hoodlum doing today?" I winked at him. I walked past Knightmare. I skimmed my hand down his black flank and gave him a little pat as I came around to see Seamus, mostly naked in the freezing cold air barely inside the stable, strapped to a metal table. They must have hauled the thing out here from the manor. *Bless them. This can't have been easy to move up the staircase.*

"Sebastian did most of the heavy lifting. I need to go brief my captains. I'll leave you to it, but I'll be near the stable." Felix nodded to me as he left to oversee his duties.

"Hi Seamus, we haven't been properly introduced. My name is Arabella, but you may know me as Raven. Some call me the Sculptor's Apprentice." His eyes were wide, rimmed in red with puffy wet lines on his face. Poor fella had been crying with earnest. Snot crusted the side of his cheek.

Guards stood around the stables and the grounds in the fenced paddock outside, all heavily armored as well. *We are definitely under attack. This will need to go quickly.* The guards avoided eye contact, trying to not be invasive, but I knew they hung on every word.

I'd put my ring in Uriah's pants pocket when I kissed him in the doorway to his office before I came down with Felix. I didn't want to muck it up. That seems to have been a wise decision. *How long do we have? Will I see Uriah? Will he take me with him? Surely he won't sit out a battle. Will he stay on land or go to sea? How can I help? I need to test my powers. Will they work with Uriah's, or will we cancel each other out?* My brow creased, pinching in the middle. I was going to give myself a headache, and I don't have time for this crap.

Gathering heads for the Queen that dares to attack my mate. The audacity. Not that she knows I'm here, but still. I'll have her head before I'm through.

"I'll make this simple. You tell me where I can find Finnigan Altmore, and I'll make it very fast. You won't even know I've killed you." Seamus began screaming, his voice dry and hoarse. "I'll be frank. You're not leaving here alive. No one ever does, not where I'm concerned. Queen Clawin wants your head, and I promised to deliver it. How you go is up to you." I pulled out my khopesh. "So, easy or hard? Where's your fucked up fae friend?"

Seamus shook his head back and forth. "I don't know, I don't know. He doesn't tell anyone when he's going or where He just disappears."

"Is that so? Well, if you were gonna guess, where would he be?" I inspected my blade. I didn't feel like doing this. It felt wrong. I usually enjoyed this kind of game, the begging and pleading. Right now? I felt like throwing up. I need to get back to Uriah. Time is of the essence.

"Agron...He stays in the Agron Realm, mostly, in the far West. He just comes to get humans. He likes to hurt them, says it's fun 'cause it's so easy." Tears ran down his face. "Please, just let me go. I want my mom. Let me see my mom."

"You want your mommy? I never knew mine, so I guess that sentiment is lost on me." I looked to Knightmare. My stomach twisted. Knots were forming. I'd never cared either way, but this felt so morally wrong.

"*Are you okay? You look pale. The kid is not lying. I do not think he knows where the other is. Did you talk to Uriah? Is there a plan in place for him to help?*" I nodded. My stomach was queasy. I was losing my nerve.

"Yes. Uriah is drafting a letter to put our plans in motion now. A rider will be sent to the King. We're getting married, Knightmare. It's such happy news; it'll be good for us and the Realm. I hate that I have to mar it with this." I said, turning my back to Seamus. He was screaming again, crying and beseeching. Snot and tears soaked his face.

I pinched my eyes closed and took a breath through my mouth. I looked down at my khopesh. The moon shaped stone in the handle began to glow at my glance. The power like the sun's core itself thrumming through me into my treasured weapon. I was indeed a guiding star, but for what purpose?

I turned, looking down at the boy on the table. With no more fuss, I raised it above my head. *Please don't be bloody.* In less than a second, I separated Seamus's head from his shoulders. The blubbering ceased immediately as my khopesh clanged into steel, the light went out in the crescent moon.

Felix had returned to watch and commented. "That's some gift you have. Our Lady shall serve us well." The light bounded around the stall. The guards looked on with awe as it shimmered in the air. My magic had grown exponentially overnight. It was as if the sun had been trapped in the stable, shining through the rafters. Beautiful. *But what else can it do now? What else can Uriah do? We need to test our magic—together.*

I opened the void containing the other heads and added Seamus's to it. "It would be my honor, Felix. I shall serve the Shallows as it serves me." I looked at the body. My khopesh had heated with my magic and cauterized the wound as it lopped his head off. Not a drop of blood was to be seen. "Well, that's a new trick. It seems our Lord and I have some things to rediscover about our magic after our joining."

*"That was a sight to behold. Your magic is thriving. You all but became invisible in the light. I've never seen such a thing. It's just like the magic of old was told to be—pure."*Knightmare turned his head, studying me. His eyes were bright with wonder. *"Go back to your mate. This bond is good for you, Arabella. Let them clean up. You have what you need, and I will be safe here. Take care of your new people. They need your gifts. Stay safe for me, but help them. You can help stop what's coming."*

"Thank you, old friend. I love you. I need you with me in this. Even still, I believe a rider will go out this afternoon to the Agron Keep. With any luck, we should hear back by Monday." The guards had begun moving to rid the stable of Seamus's body as I spoke to Knightmare. "Felix, will you come back to the manor with me? There are things to be discussed." He nodded, an eyebrow raised, as he realized I knew my place, and I wasn't to be coddled. He fell into step with me. I felt numb, hollow, the joy I used to take in killing seemed to be gone. A revolted emptiness filled its place.

What does this mean? How has my magic changed? Has Uriah's too? This needs to be tested. We have to know before we do anything else.

Chapter 36

Uriah

"You're certain then?" We rushed to the armory, Sebastian and I running through the halls of the manor and down the spiraling staircase to the lower floors. "Arabella is in the stables, we need to get her back." I skidded to a stop and immediately began pulling on my armor. I should have gone with her. She doesn't even have the protection of the manor right now. *Shit.*

We'd left my study ten minutes ago so I could get my leathers on before coming down here. King Plavlock and Queen Clawin's armadas were rallying just out of our reach beyond the reef. Their flags waving like giant middle fingers. We would have to expose ourselves to close the gap, but their sheer size gave us pause. Something like a hundred war ships were ready to bare down upon us. We had twenty-three ships in the bay, no where near enough to face a threat of such size. Even with magic, we were incredibly out matched.

The day has really gone to hell. So much for an engagement celebration. I had slipped out after quickly writing a letter to King Astros and asked the ladies in the kitchen to prepare a special menu for tonight and invite anyone in the estate to attend an impromptu ball. The soldiers could take shifts dancing and cut loose for a while in between their guard duties.

They'd been thrilled, even more so that I'd divulged to them the happy news personally. Gabriella had shyly asked if Sebastian would be in attendance and if I'd mind if she danced with him. I assured her she could enjoy the evening as well. So much for that. The ladies will be running triage in the ballroom now. I'd just gotten back to my office when Sebastian barged in, not even bothering to knock. He was already in armor and clearly alarmed.

I need Arabella. I can't leave her unprotected. She's everything. I have to get her away from here. "I want a personal guard pulled together with your best soldiers to protect Arabella. They aren't to leave her side, no matter what. I will not allow her to be harmed. Knightmare needs armor, give him what ever fits him the best. We don't have time to make adjustments. He needs to be saddled so she can ride for the Agron Keep."

"And add on to the letter on my desk. Scrawl on the back a post script that we're under attack. It needs to get out with a rider. There's little the King can do, we already have most of the Brume's soldiers, but he needs to know what's going on. Order the Brume soldiers to protect the beaches. Be ready for land siege if we can't hold the armada out of the bay. Call in the entirety of the cavalry. The Summit is likely aware—John keeps scouts all the way down to the tip of the coast."

"Yes, my Lord. I'll attend to it immediately." Sebastian rushed off, and I pulled my second sword and placed it in a scabbard between my wings. I had midnight blue plated armor that perfectly fit around my wings so I could fly with ease but still be reasonably covered. I should have had armor made for Arabella.

What was I thinking? I knew they were gathering. We underestimated this. I will not risk her. She's everything, my beautiful little mate. She's fierce, though, she'll fight me on this. I quickly finished equipping myself and raced back up the stairs. As I came through the main dining room, taking one of my many short cuts, I ran smack into her.

"Arabella! Thank the King! The humans have made their move, I need to get you to safety. I want you to take a guard and

Knightmare. You need to ride for the Agron Keep. I don't know what's going on with Judith or her brother, but surely the King will keep you safe." I was out of breath. Adrenaline was already pumping, moving me to action. She was already shaking her head. *Damn it!*

"Uriah! No, I'm not leaving you. Our magic is stronger together. We need to be together! I will help you protect the Shallows. You asked me to be your Lady, so let me prove myself. I've never gone to war, but I can fight. I just did something new with my magic, and it was so potent. It was like I was able to hold the sun. It heated my blade with barely a thought. I've never seen such a thing, we need to test ourselves, and see how our magic has evolved with the bond powering it." She spoke quickly, looking me up and down. "You didn't happen to have armor made for me too, did you?" *Fuck.*

"Unfortunately, no, I did not. That's all the more reason to get you out of here." I pulled her into a hug. I needed to touch her, but I couldn't possibly allow her to stay. The first thing I did when I became Lord was to remove women from the battle fields. This wasn't the time to renege on that. "You mean too much to me. We are far outmatched. They have at least a hundred ships. It's like being flooded with ants. We may have the magic, but now that the two kingdoms have combined— they have the numbers."

"I can level the field. Uriah, please, you have to see that with our bonded magic, you and I alone are stronger than half those ships. We need to get out there to the farthest reaches of the reef. I think we can close the gap, hold them off at the very least." She looked near to tears. Fuck. I can't lose her like this. If she was injured, I'd never forgive myself.

"I can't. I won't be able to focus, and Sebastian will need me. Felix will need me. I need you somewhere safe so I can fight." I pleaded. "Please. Sebastian is gathering a personal guard for you."

"He can gather one then. I can't leave you. Our magic

needs us together; don't you see? Uriah, please." She put her hand on my arm as I tried to let go and move past her. The waves on my arm were crested. "Stop a moment. We need to think this through. Call on your shadows." I shook my head. "Call them. They'll sing for you." I was frustrated, but when I pulled on the air, I felt it twist, and my shadows instantly responded with barely a millisecond of wait. "We are strongest together. I know you want me to be safe, but the best place for me is by your side, not off on my own to fight without you."

Fuck! "Watch. Just trust me a moment." She let loose a coil of light and my shadow instantly bonded to it forming a magic spear in her hand. "We have to stay together. We can do this. We will protect the Shallows—as Lord and Lady. We will not let the Agron Realm fall. Not today, not ever."

"No, please. I know you're strong. I can feel the alteration too. I'm not trying to doubt that. I'd never doubt you. I just can't live in a world without you. I think all these years somehow, I knew you were still alive. Somewhere, somehow, you were out there and you came back to me. We found each other." I pulled her to me and placed my forehead against hers. "You have to see how much that means to me."

"I know. I meant it when I said there was nowhere on the planet I wouldn't find you. Right now, that place is the Bay of the Shallows, and we'll go together. Let me add an extra layer of leathers. My old ones are thin. They'll fit under these, protect my skin better, keep me warmer. Can you fly both of us? I have an idea, but we need to see the full layout of the ships."

"Okay." My heart broke as I said it. I could try to lock her away, but she'd never trust me again. Perhaps this was the only way. "Promise me if it gets bad, or if it's hopeless, you'll shift back to Knightmare so he can take you away from here." That was the only thing we had going for us. If a ship were to sink, most of the fae aboard could just shift to shore, rally there. Small gifts.

My hands lingered on her waist for a heartbeat before we

turned and ran through the manor, hand in hand, to prepare
Arabella for the fray waiting for us outside.

Chapter 37

Uriah

It wasn't as common these days for fae to have wings; however, at Arabella's urging I pulled together a winged unit. The magic in the Agron Realm had suffered so greatly the fae were being born with less and less attributes to the fae of old, but we rounded up the ones we could.

We needed to fly together and get a bird's eye view of the layout of the ships, from there we would work our strategy. Arabella had the idea to use our magic most effectively. If it worked, this would end quickly, if it didn't, we'd have to fight for our lives and the lives of the Realm.

Sebastian had sent word through his captains, and seventy-two winged soldiers now stood before me. We would send them up along the reef to the front lines facing the armada. Those that commanded useful magic would lead the charge, and the others would work to block any arrow volleys as they came. Many could manipulate wind or water, which would be advantageous in this fight. We could push the fleet back with the elements, and sink as many as possible to dwindle the numbers before the battle truly began. At the very least it would be a distraction while word reached the Summit and John sent more of his soldiers to assist in a land assault.

My mind had calmed considerably while I watched Arabella strip down, open her void, and pull on her old ragged leathers. I tried not to think about the red panties she wore. *Later. Time to focus.* She pulled her new black leathers on over the top of them. It wasn't perfect, and I hated the idea of bringing her with so little protection. She began laying out her plan while she changed. *She's diabolical. She thinks like a warrior.*

We tested the magic on a smaller scale, seeing if it could work. We moved out on the lawn, so we didn't blow a hole through our bedroom wall. It seemed to work. Sebastian and Felix had helped us test it. The ships were beginning to fight as we prepared to take flight. It was a scrimmage, testing, teasing each other to see who would dare to show their hand. In minutes, we would be on the front lines.

"Are you ready love? You don't have to do this." My eyes were pleading, my heart felt like it might beat out of my chest. I hated this, but she was right. I couldn't ask her to be my equal, my partner for life, my wife, if I asked her to stand down. I knew she was a warrior when I met her in the cave. She didn't need to prove herself to me. She wanted to fight with us, needed to fight with us. She wanted to help protect the Shallows. Who the hell am I to tell her no? She answers to no one—nor should she.

"I think you and I were born for this. We're fated mates; we were meant to protect each other." She kissed my cheek as I scooped her up into my arms. She laced her arms around my neck, and I pulled her close as I kicked off hard, flapping my wings. I was careful to make sure I had a good hold on her, but not to touch where her wings had been severed. The tissue hadn't healed well and was very tender. I had the fleeting thought to try to fix that.

As we flew over the edge of the cliff side, we saw the mass of ships below. They were careful to stay close enough that they could charge and attack with cannon balls if they chose to, but also far enough that we would have to leave the protection of the reef to really engage them.

The winged unit rose with me. We stretched out in the sky, headed for the mile wide gap between the reefs that protected the bay. Our ships looked pitiful against the enemy we faced. "I think we can sink a few of them before they realize what we're doing," Arabella said in my ear. Her voice was weak with the wind roaring over it. I nodded. I sent my shadows to instruct the unit. They billowed through the low laying clouds, black on gray.

The sun was bright enough through the clouds that Arabella would be able to draw what she needed for her magic without tiring too fast, if she paced herself. Sebastian was leading the ground and sea forces; he and Felix would have shifted onto one of the ships by now. He'd be issuing orders from the sea. One of his strengths was that he could send his intentions to his captains directly from his mind. It was a secret talent we didn't talk about widely. *I wonder if he influences anything else? I suppose he wouldn't be my right hand man if he did.*

It wasn't like Knightmare where he could speak into our mind, it was more a hint of direction. He uses his intentions and implants the suggestion of what he wants. Most weren't even actively aware they were being instructed. They could then pass the information along as if it had been their own idea. It wasn't perfect, but it coordinated us well enough. Training took over after that. Aside from sending out basic thoughts, he was mostly just well-honed muscle.

I turned into the wind and pushed. My wings flapped quickly to keep us steady, and an incoming breeze would be a test of strength. With the extra weight of holding Arabella, the frosty wind was tossing me around. It would be a battle all on its own to get where we needed to be, but we would manage. If we had to land, we would. For now, this was the best bet.

My shadows reported back. All had been notified and the charge would continue. We crossed the reef and went for the largest of the ships carrying the most humans. Their swords were at the ready as we approached the first one. Arabella twisted slightly in my arms, freeing one hand so she could work her magic.

She pulled for her power, and a great cord of golden light exploded from her hand. Launching it forward, she wrapped it around the large middle mast of the ship and began working to rip it down.

The humans scrambled aboard the ship to try to cut the line around the mast, but to no avail. The wood splintered and snapped, falling into the front mast and crushing sailors in its path. As she moved onto the next, flaming arrows began to fly toward us. I threw up a shield of shadows and they dropped into the swirling sea below. Her magic whipped right past mine and slammed into the ship again. My shadows coiled with it, enhancing it—fortifying it.

The other fliers in the unit were teamed up two or three to a ship as we ripped away at them. Some were pulling on their magic, making waves surge and crash over ships. The human sailors were washed to sea, and the hulls flooded. Other fliers shifted the wind to blow arrows off course and to push the ships' sail's making them crash into each other. It was successful. Several ships were already listing, and beginning to sink. Some were being abandoned. Smaller boats dropped to the water only to be smashed by fae magic.

Arabella sent another cord of light ripping down another mast. She was careful where she threw her line so it couldn't be severed from the deck or crows nests. I blocked the arrows as they flew our way. We stayed as close as possible to the enemy without being in real danger. The wind was fierce but I made the effort to match her magic. Her plan was flourishing. Sailors were screaming on deck, trying to get row boats into the icy water. Ship after ship lost to the sea. All across the sea, ships began to sink, occupants trying to get into smaller boats and board other nearby ships. We kept at it, and debris began littering the sea.

The back row of ships began to turn, attempting to put greater distance from the reef. The aerial assault was efficient. We couldn't let them turn tail and retreat. They'd just regroup and come back. Arabella threw more cords out now, settling into a groove with her magic. She launched three cords at the next ship nearest us, ripping away all the masts with a grunt of effort. Wrapping her magic around the ship, she crushed the middle, splintering it in two. I could feel the hum around her. Our bond was singing.

A volley of flaming arrows whizzed past our heads as I pulled for my shadows. The flames extinguishing in a flurry of darkness as they engulfed them. Arabella quickly rebounded, throwing bolts of light wrapped in shadow at the archers.

"Don't push too hard!" I yelled into the wind. "There are too many, you'll tire too quickly. This is effective! You're brilliant!" Her forehead was soaked in sweat despite the frigid winter wind and sea breeze.

"I can do this! We're pushing them back!" We were indeed. We were only a couple hours into the onslaught, and I'd already counted over twenty ships sunk. At the very least, the other captains had to be concerned. Sebastian had moved our ships forward, rallying them into position and closing in on the ranks in the mouth of the bay in a fighting formation. They were ready to take on the ones we couldn't sink. We continued, but the biting wind slowly grinding us down.

Arabella sunk four more ships with the help of four other fae before the remaining ships formed a new grid. Her magic was exhausted. She'd had to return to sending one or two cords of light again. My shadows reported that the flying unit was nearly exhausted as well. They'd been at it for over three and half hours now. My own wings had begun to ache in the wind. "One more," I yelled. "Take this last one. then we'll pull back." *I can't risk her over-using her magic.* I sent my shadows out to tell the others to retreat to a ship after they sunk the one they were working on. We would take to the air if we needed to again. We'd evened the playing field substantially.

I needed a full count. "We'll have sunk sixty-three ships in a matter of six hours. Forty-four remain once these are down." She sent out a burst of magic as a volley of arrows came at us. I hadn't been paying attention. I was too distracted by counting. She screamed as an arrow sunk into her thigh. "No!" I screamed, turning us away immediately and dropping back in the wind. Her golden light recoiled as it snapped and slashed madly in the open air as we headed for the deck of a ship. Arabella shaking in my arms. "Call it back!" I yelled. Her magic dissipated as we careened toward the nearest ship.

Chapter 38

Arabella

"I've got you, hang on," Uriah said as we twisted in the air and shifted onto the top deck of the nearest ship. Sebastian was instantly by our side. "Fuck, I'm so sorry. I didn't see it. I couldn't block them fast enough." Uriah looked terrified. My thigh burned. I looked down to see an arrow nearly all the way through my leg. *Fuck. That'll be a new scar.* Havoc raged on the ship around us as fae raced from place to place, heading off an attack.

Felix screamed in the distance, and his voice carried on the wind. "Hard on the rudder! Bring the ship around! Attack on the starboard side. Move the cannons!" I'd never heard him sound so urgent.

Uriah sent a blonde haired fae sprawling with a flick of his wrist as he stopped the fae from nearly crashing into me as he followed Felix's commands. Uriah bid his shadows to thicken the air and create a barrier around us.

"Watch it!" Uriah shouted, fear and red hot anger raging in his voice. "We need to see how bad it is," he continued, as he turned his attention back to me while sailors attempted to give us space.

"We need to get her pants off," Sebastian said with a smirk as he squatted down next to me. The look of ire Uriah shot at him quickly wiped the smile off his face. "We can move her below deck. Get her out of the wind. Can you heal it?" Uriah's hands probed my leg gently, and then he let go.

Sebastian's voice filled my head and I was startled.

"Incoming projectiles, douse the arrows as they land, protect the sails." I realized then that he had just used his gift to issue a command. He continued his conversation with Uriah without missing a beat. Several flaming arrows landed near us on the top deck. Uriah sent out a burst of shadow to quickly snuff them out.

"Yes, but she won't be able to walk on it right away." Uriah and Sebastian were talking about me like I wasn't even sitting between them. I rolled my eyes. I reached down, and snapped off the long end of the arrow leaving an inch sticking out of my leg. Uriah's eyes went wide, and Sebastian's mouth gaped open as I slammed my palm down on the end sticking out. The head of the arrow ripped through the rest of my thigh. It was all fatty flesh. There were perks to being a thick girl. *Fuck. Fuck. Fuckity. Fuck.*

Blood gushed from my leg as I pulled the rod out of my thigh with shaking hands. "Can you heal it now?" I asked Uriah as I sucked in a breath. I felt woozy, but we didn't have time for this. Those ships were going to attack at any second, and they still outnumbered us. We hadn't gotten that last one down so forty-five ships was a lot to contend with and our air support was dwindling.

"You're bleeding out." The alarm ratcheted up in Uriah's face. He reached for the button of my pants. "Get these down. I'm sorry we don't have time for modesty." He helped me shimmy my layered pants down. *I should have thought about how cold it is.*

I shivered as the icy air hit my legs. I'd felt numb and hadn't realized how much heat my leathers had actually held in. The damp sea breeze was murderous on my exposed flesh. "Does anyone have a drink? Maybe some liquor?" I asked, my teeth began to chatter.

"Sailors! Avert your eyes!" Sebastian bellowed. He braced my back, holding me up while turning his head, to look away from my exposed ass. I had a pair of silk panties on, but they didn't leave much to the imagination. *Must be their lucky day.*

"Here," Sebastian said as he handed me a hip flask. I took a swig. The golden liquid burned my throat as I took a couple more deep pulls on the flask. "Don't over-do it!" Sebastian's eyes were wide as he peered over his shoulder and watched me gulp down the bourbon.

Uriah spread his wings wide, wrapping them around us and blocking most of the wind and view from the sailors on deck. The ship rolled over the waves violently. The water was especially choppy with all the magic swirling and tugging on it. "You should have waited. I could have taken that out cleaner," he admonished as he pulled for his healing magic and pushed it into my leg. His magic felt weak, but I could feel it threading into the tissue, knitting it back together.

"Going below deck would have taken too much time. You would have been too gentle." I gritted my teeth as the booze began to dull my senses. The blood wasn't pouring out anymore, but it still burned.

"All the same. You don't have to prove how tough you are. I already know. I've seen the map on your body, remember?" He looked at me. Pure pain etched his face. His concern ran deep, and it wasn't just the wound. "This will take a few minutes. Sebastian, see if we can find a blanket."

"I'll go, my Lord." Felix was a few steps away and quickly moved across the broad planks of the ship to a supply box. I couldn't see him clearly through the shadows or wings, but I knew his voice. We were silent for a few minutes. The roar of the sailors around us was a cacophony as they yelled across the ship to pass information and carry out orders. "Here, this was all I could find." Uriah lifted his wing a moment, and Felix came into view. My pants stopped at the knee. He laid a gray wool blanket over my exposed legs.

"Thank you. What happens next?" I asked. We might as well work on a strategy.

"The armada has regrouped and is surging forward."

Sebastian answered. "We're volleying flaming arrows, cannon balls, and bursts of magic at them as they approach, much like what you were doing in the sky. That was quite effective by the way. If you can go out again, we can end this. I wish we had a second unit to relieve our primary force." We were sitting back-to-back now, and he spoke over his shoulder to us.

"She needs to rest." Uriah growled at him. "The blood loss alone…" His voice trailed off. He was angry, but we made a big impact with the aerial assault. This was the right path to choose.

I leaned forward and put my hand on his. "I'm okay, we're okay. We dented the line—that was more than we hoped for." I wasn't sure this was the time. "I think I have an idea, however it will take a big push from you and I. We'll have to draw them in. The sun will set in a quarter hour. My powers are much weaker without sunlight. We can use the last light of day—if we hurry."

"No, you're going to rest. Let my navy fight. They know how to sink these ships. They may outnumber us, but this will drag on all night. I'll be more effective when the sun goes down. You need to eat and sleep. After I heal your leg, I'm taking you back to the manor. If we haven't won by morning, you can rejoin the fight." Uriah glared at me, daring me to fight him on this.

"Uriah, I can't just leave you here." I began to plead. He was dead serious.

"He'll go with you," Sebastian said. Felix nodded his agreement over Uriah's shoulder. "You both need to rest. Uriah, you've been aiming shadows all afternoon. You need the rest as much as she does to see the end of this. You've expanded an exponential amount of energy.."

Felix tacked on with, "the playing field is level now. We can defend this. The ship you were attacking is mostly sunk already. The others are smaller. You took down the biggest war ships. We can handle this. The two of you will go back for a reprieve. I think the flying unit needs to as well. They've done their fair share for now. It may be what we need to end this if we haven't by dawn."

"I don't like it," Uriah said, shaking his head.

"I didn't like watching you and your mate out there for hours fighting with my ass floating around on a ship either. We've got to play to our strengths. By morning, Felix and I will be useless. We'll need that unit again. It'll be harder to fight them in the dark; we have a few hours at best before we fall into a stalemate for now. Go eat and sleep. Feed the fliers and bunk them down so you can help sink the rest in the morning." Sebastian argued.

"I'll go back if you do." I hedged. Sebastian was right. This wasn't going to end today, but tomorrow we could come back refreshed and either sink them or turn them away. Uriah studied me, his warm hands still pressed to my thigh working his magic.

"Dinner and straight to bed." He nodded to me. "I don't like this. I have to agree though, the logic is there. My powers are most advantageous in the dark. We'll come back a few hours before dawn. I'll do what I can to wreak havoc then. When the sun rises, we'll attack from the sky again. Try not to fully engage if you can help it," he ordered Sebastian. "Do what needs doing, but I think we'll save the most ships and sailors if we keep to the skies."

Chapter 39

Felix

"Great, just what we needed." I watched Sebastian as he sent silent commands to other captains. I shivered in the cold, my breath a cloud of fog in front of me. The rain began to come down in earnest, freezing as it landed, and turning the miserable cold nearly unbearable. It coated the ships deck and railings, making everything treacherous. Sailors walked around with cork wood mallets to break the ice before it could form too thick and sink the ship, like we had sailors to spare.

We're outnumbered, but not outmatched. Uriah and Arabella were amazing. Their magic was a sight to behold. Thank the King!

The sun had been down for a few hours now and sailors were bundled up trying to stay warm. Neither side was attacking. The humans didn't seem to be too sure at this point. Our strongest commanders had pooled their magic to lock the ships in a ward off the coast.

The delicate instruments on the ships had all gone haywire when they did it, but Uriah had been clear when he said to sink them all. So, we cast the wards out as far as we could and found ourselves stuck in a gridlock. Every now and then, a round of cannon balls would come our way or a few groups of arrows would light the sky. It was pitch black, the starless night making both sides weary of engaging.

We would take the favor. The battle had raged well into the night and had only just settled, an ominous lack of sound, we all waited with baited breath for the next sign of trouble.

Uriah had mended Arabella's thigh and then flown them back to shore. The need for rest drove home when he'd tried to shift them instead and couldn't. Both of their magic was so badly drained. *Hopefully they stop fucking long enough to sleep. The magic will consume them if they don't give it fuel.*

Arabella took down ship after ship for hours, magnificent. *She's incredible. To hone such a gift—when has a fae been so strong in living memory? I should ask Zeds.* Uriah blocked with his shadows when arrows flew, and then repaired her leg when one hit its mark. His magic was spent. Uriah's magic was stronger, but today took a toll.

With luck they stopped to eat before they went to bed. It was near midnight, I felt my stomach growl. *We should give out rations while it's calm.* "You there," I said, pointing at some sailor."Go down to the galley and tell the cooks to prepare something hot for all the sailors like soup or oatmeal. It doesn't need to be fancy, but it should be easily eaten and warm." He nodded and hurried off.

"You know they'll attack the moment you take a bite." Sebastian winked at me as he came to the railing of the top deck I was leaning on. "It never fails. These dumb humans. I swear, the inferiority should make them want to hide, not try to tunnel into our Realm and break into the wards around the bay that were supposed to keep *them* safe from the fae and magical creatures that would harm them for sport."

"Irony strikes again." He held out a ball of fae light for me. "They don't know any better. Their Kings and Queens of old told them we want to hurt them, not that most of us just want to mind our own business. Who knows, maybe this will end it."

"Nothing will end it except taking their heads. How many generations will lose because they tied our hands in this? We can't let them leave just to come again. We've tried that. Uriah is right. If we don't exterminate them like the cockroaches they are, they'll come back bigger next time. Just like they have now. This is by far the largest surge I've seen in our twenty years of military work, probably in the last hundred years. If they've ever breached before. I can't say I was paying attention to that in my history lessons."

"Arabella said King Plavlock and Queen Clawin are working together now too. I think my only real concern is we haven't been paying any attention in the Daemon Kingdom because we've been fighting the Torrent Kingdom for so long. I'm out of my depth, and I've been reallocating my spies, but I don't like what I'm hearing—and apparently, she has magic?" I shook my head. I dropped the ball in this. Horribly. *So much for an intelligence officer. I'm about to get us all killed.*

"Horse shit. I have a hard time believing that. I don't think you missed much. All they have are numbers now. We still have the magic to stop this." He disregarded my worries. "I just don't know what to expect from King Astros. The letter that went out will be there by midday. Uriah isn't sure if he will force them to marry immediately and if that will sit well with Arabella. She accepted his ring, but this is too fast, even for him. Toss in a raging war? Bad decisions are bound to be made."

"I think proposing was smart," I mused. "It shows intention. He may not require the marriage until they wish it, especially with the Lord of Meadows insisting he marry that little brat when she comes to age. The bigger question is, did he know that his new wife was involved in making his eldest daughter disappear, and will Arabella be safe from their clutches now?" I mused. Fucking snake in the grass of the Meadows. Where else will it strike?

"I worry about that more than these ships. Would you have thought we'd be on the deck of this ship two days ago? It's just wild. It's almost as if they followed her here. You said Arabella was employed by the Queen, right? What if she *isn't* Arabella? What if Raven is a fox in the hen house?" I stared at Sebastian, and my mouth dropped open.

Perhaps it was her father that orchestrated the kidnap. Is he the snake and Arabella doing his bidding? That doesn't make sense. Who abused her—The Sculptor? I can't seem to get any information about him, not even his name. I don't like this. There are too many questions.

"You think she'd really betray Uriah like that? The mating bond is real, regardless of whether or not she's Arabella.." I shook my head. "I was confused when the ships entered the seaway in front of the bay. The wards were set so long ago to keep the humans away, but it's as if they melted away with the wind. They shouldn't have been able to find their way, even with our lands joined."

"Arabella's the difference. I just can't figure out how or why." Sebastian stated, a coldness flitting across his face. "Look into her past more, will you? Obviously we're busy for the next few days, but you were tracking her. You know the most about her life in the human lands. It doesn't track. The timing—it's just too convenient."

I didn't like it, however I nodded my agreement. "She killed Seamus extremely quickly. She toyed with those thugs in the woods for quite awhile before finishing up." I shook my head. "We hand delivered him and wham! She asked him two questions then took his head off. Kind of odd. It's almost as if she was squeamish."

"That's a good point." He looked out at the lanterns bobbing in the sea two hundred yards ahead. "We still have to find Finnigan too. Our laundry list is getting long. I want to figure out her deal first. What if we're unwittingly aiding our enemy and she's guiding them? I just can't figure out how a double armada got through ancient wards. Is the magic really *that* fragile?"

"Why would she help sink them? She was out there for hours. It was her idea to bring in the fliers." I felt my brow pinch together. The sailor I sent off came to our side then, two streaming mugs of clam chowder in his hands. We each took one with thanks, and he rushed off again. Several other sailors were handing out mugs to those on deck as well. "Good. This will ready them." We drank our mugs down in silent thought. A few minutes later another sailor came by with a tub full of empty dishes. The sky seemed to darken more suddenly.

"Why is everyone standing around doing nothing?" Uriah asked as he landed on the deck in front of us with Arabella in his arms. She looked better but still a bit pale, even with her ivory complexion. She looked like a ghost in the fae lights onboard. "Please don't argue; just go below deck for a few hours. I promise we'll come get you when the sun is up." He looked at her, pleading.

"Ok, but you have to come get me." She gave him a small smile and kissed him quickly. As she hobbled away, she stepped gingerly. She was in thick leathers again, no armor. We really should have thought to have some made for her.

There's no way she's a traitor. She should want the humans dead more than any other fae after all they did to her. "I'll take her to the captain's quarters. She can rest there." I put a hand out for her as she wobbled.

"No, I need you both." Uriah said curtly. "You there," he pointed to the same sailor I'd called upon earlier. "Take her below, and get her anything she needs." He waved the sailor forward. Lowering his voice as Arabella began to hobble off again, he said, "Do not let her out of your sight. Keep her below deck in the captain's quarters until I tell you otherwise. Lock the door, but do not tell her. She won't like it, and she'll flay you alive if she realizes. Stay outside the door. That is your new post. Guard her with your life."

The sailor helped Arabella down a few steps, and then we lost sight of her in the murky darkness. "I know you aren't going to want to hear this, but I don't like that the moment she arrives, suddenly our wards have fallen." Uriah looked at Sebastian as he spoke with murder in his eyes. *Glad Seb said it, because I didn't want to.*

"You noticed that, did you? I was distracted, whether

intentional or not, but I'm here now. Rested. I have a theory on that as well, but we'll deal with it later. The Summit has been attacked. Multiple ranger stations are at siege. Help is not coming. I've ordered half of the Brume soldiers to the Summit. Thankfully, the bond has charged my magic to the fullest I've ever seen it. Let's see what my shadows can do."

Chapter 40

Uriah

I began to pull for the darkness surrounding us. I could feel everyone and everything inside it. Anger pulsed in my veins as I let my aura spread. My shadows billowed from me as I rose into the frigid night air. It was after midnight. I had enough time; I could take their numbers down by half. The half-frozen humans were barely moving. The biggest danger at the moment were the large chunks of ice forming in the shallowest parts of the bay.

They could split a hull faster than a barrage of cannon balls. But for now, I focused my mind. *Don't think about her. She's safe. Finish this so she won't feel the need to help.*

I sent a wall of thick dark shadow out to either side of me and let it sweep down the edge of the reef. I could feel the tug in my core as I brought the darkness together building it into a tool of destruction. On one side were our ships, safe behind our natural barrier. The front line had taken some damage, but the sailors were repairing what they could while there was a reprieve. On the other side, I could see our enemy.

They were now sandwiched between the wall of the wards risen again to block them from retreating from my shadows to open sea.

I whispered to my shadows, "Rip and tear. Toil and bear down. I'm too angry to control you tonight. Do as you please." I pleaded with my magic and unleashed the fury of the Lord of Shallows.

Sweat began to run down the small of my back. I pushed

more on my magic, summoning it to shred the ships before me. My shadows began to move forward, pressing into the enemy ships. The winter sky grew darker, and they rushed forth to do as I commanded. I would squeeze the ships together as much as I could. They'd crash into each other and sink. Floating pieces of ice would crash into their hulls to help the process. I could try to do what Arabella had with her cords of light, but even in the dark, I was only one fae. No. I'd let them crush each other, and then when dawn came, we would be able to see better and sink the rest.

✿ ❄ ✿ ❄ ✿

I worked for hours. I enclosed the ships before us in a small pocket. There were about thirty ships remaining. I'd only managed to sink a few with all my effort. I was not as strong as I thought I was—Arabella had been right about that. Even with her on the ship, without our magic building each other's, we were no stronger than any other powerful fae. Together, we were a powerhouse. The lightest pink began to blend into the darkness; the promise of a beautiful winter day.

I shifted and landed on deck. "Is she still below?" I asked Felix, his expression accusatory.

Don't look at me like that. You know it's too big a coincidence too. She's my mate! I'm missing something. She wouldn't try to hurt me like this, would she? No. No, there's something I can't see with her. I need to dig deeper. There's more to this picture, there has to be. Please! She's my Arabella. Mine.

He hesitated a moment, "She is...but she's angry. She didn't appreciate being locked in. She's all but screamed herself hoarse demanding we open the door. She promised to break it down with her magic, however Sebastian talked her down."

I grimaced. *My little firecracker.* "How did he manage that?" I was moving now. I weaved between the throng of sailors, below deck and toward the captain's cabin.

"He, well, he pointed out that she'd sink the ship if she tore it apart." Felix kept up, sliding past sailors working at their tasks.

"I see." I came to a halt in front of a tired looking Sebastian leaning against the door. I could hear Arabella yelling threats on the other side. "You better give us a few minutes, although I don't think we have many. I need her help, but she may not wish to join me." I turned the key in the lock and stepped inside.

"How dare you! You're just like them, aren't you?!" Arabella screamed as a book flew towards my head. "How could you lock me away? Haven't I proven I want to be here? Haven't I given you enough of myself?" She was crying, and tears marred her beautiful face. Her hair was frizzed and falling out of the crowned braid she'd had it in yesterday. Puffy pink splotches dotted her face.

"I'm sorry." I held my palms out. "I didn't want you to try to come out to fight when you needed to rest and I needed to concentrate. I made the decision. Sometimes I will need to be a commander, but I should have explained. I'd never purposely endanger you; you must know that. Don't be mad at anyone except me. It was my order to keep you safe because you refused to stay at the manor." I took a step further into the room and shut the door behind me. Another book sailed through the air. This one clocked me in the shoulder and fell to the floor. *A Guide to Modern Warfare. Of course.*

"Please stop throwing books. I may look tough, but that did actually hurt," I said as I threw my arm up to block another tome as she flung it across the room. *Fuck, she's mad.* "I understand you are angry, and I'd love to dive into that. You should be angry at a lot of things, least of which my pathetic attempts at keeping you safe, but right now, I could really use your magic." *I need you, not this crazy woman. What the fuck is going on?*

"Sure. Use me. Everyone else does!" She was hotter than

a tea kettle about to burst. "You know I heard Sebastian and Felix talking. They think I called for the ships to come here. Me! How? Why, I don't know! But since my presence seems to be so much of a problem, maybe I should just go find the Sculptor and let him finish me off."

"Don't ever say that. You cannot leave me. Do you understand? I need you. I want you! I know I crossed a line, but you're my fiancé. You're my equal in this, however at the end of the day, it is you I must be willing to protect because you won't put yourself first. This is an ancient war. I will do whatever I deem necessary in fighting it. If that means putting you somewhere relatively comfortable and making sure no one else can get at you, then fine. I'm sorry I didn't tell you what I was doing, but I would do it again."

Arabella flung another book across the room, I pulled for a shadow near the foot of the small bed to block it and sent it flying back at her. "Asshole!" She shrieked at me, her eyes wild and unfocused, but she stopped throwing things.

"I need you to boost my magic. I want to make a wall of shadow before dawn crests to hold the line while the fliers get in place. We can end this before any more fae lives are lost. It's tragic for the humans, but they came here. Somehow, they've bypassed three-thousand-year-old wards to do it. Forgive us if that raises suspicions. You've been here not even forty-eight hours and finally the Kingdoms in the East have made their way to us not even twenty-four hours before they breached the wards? For a millennia, they tried and failed. The timing *is* a bit suspicious." I huffed a big sigh after I said it and regretted it immediately. *She's never asked for any of this.*

She deflated, sinking onto the bed. She looked like I had slapped her. *I might as well have.* "You think I took the wards down? You think I'd help them?" The color drained from her face.

"You work for Queen Clawin, and she's paired her forces with King Plavlock—I don't understand why you would, but you have to see this from our side." I hate this. I know she's not doing this. How could she be? She's been with me day and night.

"Right. Of course. I couldn't possibly be here for any other reason. Never mind Felix is the one that talked me into coming. Never mind Knightmare telling me how the bond would tear us both apart if we didn't appease it. Never mind me thinking about you night and day. Never mind any of it." She stood and walked to me. "Never mind me wanting *you* to be safe. Never mind me trying to help. Never mind."

"Arabella, please." I caught her upper arm as she tried to shoulder by me. "You are everything. I think there's a strong magic at play. Something tied to you that undid our protections. I don't think *you* did it, but I do think you may have unwittingly brought it with you. We'll fix this, but I need you to realize the danger you're in—the danger we're all in."

"Let go." She said in barely a whisper—more menacing than if she had screamed it. A single tear rolled down her cheek She tugged her arm, and I released her.

"You have some deal with a Queen using magic she shouldn't possess. You were stolen away decades ago and given to a King determined on waging his forefathers' war. Both are now attacking just as you arrive." I stepped back, blocking the door. I bumped into it and held my position. "Your stepmother is involved somehow. I can't trust your father to protect you."

"And yet, you wanted me to ride to the Agron Keep where my father is probably hiding right now. You think I'm a traitor, and yet you'd send me to the King? To my father? Sure. That makes perfect sense. That's a great way to protect me, like locking me into a cabin on a ship that could be sunk." She huffed and jutted out her bottom lip. *I wish I could suck on that. I bet she'd kick me in the balls if I tried right now.*

"I was not being the most rational. Locking you in here wasn't my best idea either. You make me crazy with worry. I will try to be better. I've never really been in a relationship. I need to learn some things. Please try to be patient." *We need each other. We can't keep fighting like this. It's only been two days!*

"Patient...right. Dawn approaches, and it seems we need to sink these ships." Arabella looked up at me with frustration and anger on her face, but hope and love lingered in her eyes. *She won't be mad forever.*

"Arabella," I leaned down. "Please. You used a lot of magic yesterday. Don't overtax yourself today. Just boost mine. Help me make it sing." I came almost to her lips and stopped. *Her choice.* I waited for two breaths, three, then finally she rose on her tippy toes, and her lips met mine. Our magic purred.

"Thank you. I promise I will make it up to you somehow." I opened the door and turned, holding it open for her. Felix and Sebastian were nowhere in sight. We started down the corridor below decks and as we reached the steps to the main deck, the boat listed.

Wood splintered, and a cannon ball shattered the steps before us. Icy water flooded in around our feet. More cannon balls were striking, fae were yelling, wood split and water gushed as I pulled her into my arms and flew out of the hole. Chaos surrounded us. Fae screamed in agony from injuries, magic streaked this way and that. Water, blood, and smoke from flaming arrows filled the sky. A catapulted boulder flew through the air and landed with a crash cracking the main mast.

Fuck. We need to move faster. I willed my shadows to build, trying to hold the ship together as it exploded in pieces.

"Abandon ship, she's lost. Shift to another vessel, take whoever is nearest with you. Drop the dinghy's, save as much as you can carry." Sebastian's voice filled my mind. *The Rosemary*— my mother's ship was sunk.

Sebastian was screaming orders, and Felix was ushering sailors forward with buckets, trying to rid the now flooding hull of all the water. It was no use. "Get into the row boats! Shift if you can! Make way to other ships!" I began bellowing orders, while holding Arabella in my arms and flying along the ship. Two other ships were coming to our aid. As the deck cleared, I released my shadows letting the inevitable happen.

We'd taken the point in the reef. Our ship would be the one to sink first in this bloody battle. All we could do now was find a new platform to fight from. Those that could, shifted others. Sailors blinded with gashes from the exploding wood stumbled aboard the ship. The battle-scarred mast cracked and slammed down the length of the deck. The list grew worse, and sailors began sliding into the churning sea below. Row-boats dropped, and sailors were swimming for them through great pieces of ice. The effort was almost futile. The blood of the Shallows was being spilled in the bay.

I flew us higher. Dawn bearing down on us. My chance for using shadows to maximum damage was lessening. Rays of sunlight began to gleam across the rough bay over the Western cliffs. Sailors on several ships were screaming as they took on the siege from the armada boxing us in. We'd played right into their trap. The reef would protect us some, but it would eventually be our downfall as our ships were pushed closer to the shredding rocks, barely visible in the choppy water.

"Call for your shadows. Get the fliers here—now," she barely whispered. I heard her voice on the wind as I nodded, watching the battle brew below us. A flaming arrow whizzed past my ear, and I turned. Six ships were engaged in battle. The one we'd been on had nearly sunk now. Arabella pulled for her magic and cast it toward the ship nearest us. We had work to do.

She created more spears of light twisted with my shadows and, sent a barrage toward a line of archers. One by one, they fell. The water began to tinge pink where they fell.

Chapter 41

Arabella

My brain was screaming. He'd locked me away, not in the dungeon, but in a floating cage. He promised just yesterday morning he wouldn't do that, and then he did! Right before he blamed me for everything that's gone wrong.

What the fuck did I ever do to deserve this? Will I ever find my place in the world? I shouldn't have come here. And I slept with him! I swear if I get the chance, I'll kill them all. The King. The Queen. The Sculptor. Fuck them and fuck this. I don't need anyone.

I let my magic unwind at my finger tips. I couldn't remember being this angry, at anything, but most of all at myself. *How could he? No windows. No light. Just a dark room with a few strategy books and a bed. Stinky socks. And of course, it's my fault the humans attacked and the wards came down. As if I have that kind of power or understand that depth of magic.* I ripped a mast down with a yank on a cord of light. The sun was coming up in earnest now. The fierce wind tugged at us. I let my magic loosen, the damper on it fully released.

My fault. Everything is always my fault. My. Fault. The cords of magic I was letting loose fell into the fray. Everything was moving so fast I could hardly keep track. I'd go to rip a mast down, and a cannonball would slam into it. "Take us higher. I need a better overview." I yelled into the wind.

Uriah maneuvered us higher. Other fliers had joined us now but we weren't as effective as we had been yesterday. They were ready. They had sailors in the crows nests armed and shooting. They were looking for us and turning the ships so we couldn't get at the side and easily overrun them. They learned.

I am not nothing! I can prove it! I can do this! My mind reeled. I couldn't keep up with my own thoughts. *I miss Knightmare. I just want to go home. Where though? Where is home? It doesn't exist.* I froze. *Why am I here? What's the point? They don't trust me. No one wants me. He doesn't trust me. He doesn't want me.* He banked and suddenly we were flying hard west, towards the cliff line. "What are you doing?" I yelled so he could hear me.

"I can feel you in the bond." He stated it. *Can he hear my thoughts? I can't hear his, but I could feel when he was unnerved yesterday. Does he know?* We landed on the upper cliff side. A little nook halfway down had just enough ledge to hold us and tuck us out of the wind for a reprieve. "I'm sorry. I let doubt get in my head and I've passed it on to you."

He pulled me close as he sat me down. My leg quivered. I could walk on it, but the muscle spasmed when I stepped down. The muscles were brand new and too tight. I looked at him. Sorrow filled his eyes. "I don't doubt us, Arabella. I don't. I can feel you, and I can see the love in your eyes. This is moving fast. All of it. The timing is off—this war, the bond, finding you. The culmination has me looking anywhere and everywhere for answers, and I'm just as confused as you are."

I sighed. *And now we break. Is that it?* "So what, I'm not good enough now? I tried to come back at the wrong time? I *knew* I should finish the Queens task before I tried to come to you. I knew it!" Tears streaked down my face. He shook his head and wiped a tear from my cheek.

"No, not at all. Where is it?" he said, looking at me with worry.

"Where is what?" *What does he think I have?* "I don't know what you're referring to."

He ran his hands through his hair. The sun was just bright enough to light up his dark auburn strands and make it look as if his hair might combust into flames. "The necklace, Arabella.

Raven's necklace. You took it off and put it on the table. I went to go get it and it was gone. Where did you put it?"

I reached into my pocket and pulled the cord out. "This? It's just an old necklace." I looked at the amber stone. It glinted in the sunlight, and a darkness rolled through it.

"It's not. You noticed yesterday, when we were in the library. I felt it too, in the cave. I think that was what set my tattoo off. It reacts just as much as you do sometimes. If I had to bet, that necklace has a trace on it. It's cursed. You're flighty and scared when you wear it. You feel different, but you've worn it for so long that you don't see the difference. I noticed when you put on my mother's pearls, you relaxed, and you laughed easy. Your innocence shined. You touch that thing, and your mood goes to shit. You become angry and volatile. It's not good for you. It's tainted with evil."

I looked at him. *That can't be. I've worn it for years.* I shook my head. "It's just a dumb necklace, Uriah. I promise. I took it when I freed myself." I looked at it.

Was it this all along? A poisoned trophy. Knightmare always said it was vile and made him uneasy. Raven needed it to survive. It got her out, kept her working. It kept us—running. Never resting. Always scared. Never stopping.

My mind was moving like lightning. *What does it mean? Did I do this? Did I lead them here? It does make me feel different. I thought I was just giddy like a Lady coming home to my mate.* I looked into Uriah's hazel eyes. I could see my reflection in them, sadness and worry coated both of our faces. *Uriah wouldn't hurt me. It would destroy him to hurt me. Hurt us both.*

I held it out to him. "It was never you Arabella. The things you did, the things Raven had to do to survive, they were never fueled by you. I think it was this cursed necklace. Do you know where Clara got it?"

I shook my head. She always bragged it was a gift from the King, for all her years of service, given to her by the Sculptor. *The Sculptor. The mother fucking Sculptor. His repulsive touch. His prolonged pain. He could leave me on the cusp of death for days with just a thought. He didn't have to cut or maim to prove a point. He just had to want it. The want for me to hurt, just the thought. How many times had he flayed me alive? How many times had he willed me to heal so he could start over?*

"We need to destroy it," I said, looking at the necklace in his hand. "I never made the connection, but I'm making it now. This is my fault. All of this is my fault." I waved my hands at the battling ships below us.

"It's not." He shook his head and pulled me into him for a hug. He kissed the top of my head. My arms hung limp beside me. "You didn't ask for any of this, Arabella. You were just a little girl. A small child trying to grow up with a father that checked out and a mother that died before she could know you."

I don't want to be here. I am nothing. No one even looked for me. I don't belong anywhere. I don't have a place in this world. No one wants me.

I could feel the necklace in Uriah's hand calling to me, making me feel worthless, like nothing. Just like nothing. I'd always heard people in the castle say that Clara used to be so nice, and so charming, but then she got older and meaner. She didn't though. He gave her the necklace to watch me and make her cruel, hateful, vengeful—just like Raven was. No mercy. No problems. *No home.*

I wrapped my arms around Uriah and tucked my head into his chest. The cedar wood campfire scent of him filled my senses and my chest eased up a bit. "We have to destroy it."

"The pendant is amber. We can try crushing it," he said. I nodded. He squatted down and picked up a fist sized rock. I took the necklace and held it against another rock. Uriah smashed his rock into it. We both looked at it and nothing happened. Despite the force and how easily amber should be able to be manipulated, it stood firm. "Again, then." We repeated, but this time Uriah took several hard swings with the rock.

"We can't just throw it away, if it is cursed," I said into the breeze. The winds were changing direction. I reached down and shifted us off the cliff. We were instantly down the road from the estate. "We need to hide it. I have an idea of what to do about the ships." Uriah looked at me with earnest.

"Okay, we'll put it in the safe for now, we'll take care of it when we can." We raced up the road. I was limping heavily, slower than I usually managed. We charged through the manner and into our room. Uriah went to the wall and opened the safe. "I trust you Arabella. I don't want you to think that I don't." He put it into a black box. "This box is made of obsidian encased in onyx. It's very old. It's been passed down for generations. It should contain whatever spells or curses have been placed on this amulet." *That's handy.* The moment he shut the safe door my mood shifted.

"Do you have enough strength to raise a shadow wall, and to block the ships from blow back if we can get ahead of them, or call them back into retreat long enough for me to try something? I don't think I would need long." He placed his hand on my waist. My mind was clear again. Calmer. *What the fuck was I thinking grabbing that thing last night?*

"What are you planning?" He manipulated the wards on the manor and shifted us on the cliff overlooking the battle again. He appraised me a moment. "This will all be okay. I don't know when and I don't know how—but I will make sure you find a way to be whole again. We'll destroy it. We'll find Finnigan. We'll take care of Queen Clawin. We'll address King Astros and the court. We'll do it all. For now, we have to handle this." He scooped me into his arms and we flew into the chaos of the fray waiting below.

Chapter 42

Arabella

We landed on the bow of a heavily engaged enemy ship. I immediately cast my magic out and began to wreck the ship before us. Most of our ships had moved beyond the bay, into the open water, but some were holding the line to keep the humans from entering the reef. They swamped us. Even with the damage done yesterday, they still had us nearly two to one. Several of our ships attacked while a handful hung back.

"Call for the winged force. We should attack their reserve. They won't have anything to fall back on." I pointed to the waiting string of ships five hundred feet beyond us just watching. I gawked as wisps of shadow drifted off from Uriah and the pandemonium raged around us.

"Done. Are you sure you're rested enough for this?" He looked apprehensive. Our minor tiff was clearly still making him tense. Not that I felt much better. This was all so damn complicated. *Nothing is ever easy.*

"Better to get it done now before we have no options." He pulled me back into his arms, fighting against the stinging cold of the wind. Clouds had blown in to cover the glorious sun. Flurries ripped through the wind as we took to the air. I don't think I'll ever be warm again.

"We need to get backside and push them forward. The wards won't let them go out much further than they are, but we need to squeeze them toward the reef. If we can bank them to one side or another, they'll smash into the rocks." Uriah expanded on my suggested strategy. I nodded and pulled for my magic.

"Uriah, I'm sorry I took the necklace. I didn't realize it affected me so drastically until I took it off the other evening. I never should have touched it again once I knew how it made me feel. It's almost as if I couldn't help it. I swear it called out to me. Begged me to take it." He shook his head.

"It's one of your only possessions, like a demented sort of friend. We'll talk about that thing later. It's nefarious, but as long as you can see that, we'll get past this. I'm not going to give up on you Arabella." Our conversation cut short as we came upon an enemy ship.

Immediately, a volley of arrows shot for us. Uriah pulled on his magic, and a wall of wispy shadows pulled for the arrows knocking them to the swirling sea below. Streaks of black marred the sky, and Uriah commanded each strand of shadow to do as he commanded.

I launched three cords of light and quickly began to tear at the ship. The gold and black streaks of our magic intermingled in the fray. Other fliers joined us. We tackled each ship with three or four fae. Even though we were working in tandem, it was hours before we paused. We were making a dent, but it wasn't enough. They'd learned to cut the cords of my magic.

It was a jumble of smoke and blood on the breeze, and the screams of sailors, human and faerie alike, reverberated on the wind. Arrows flew past us at alarming rates. *Where are they getting all those damn things? I can't keep up. There's too many. We have to find another way.*

"Uriah!" I yelled. "Get me over to those rocks in the reef. I want to try something different." He veered to the left, a gust pushing us along. We tried to land, but the seaweed covered rocks were too slippery. The tide was going out, and more rocks were becoming visible. Algae squelched under his feet as he tried to find purchase to no avail. Uriah wobbled and struggled to keep his balance as we took to the air again. We hovered, looking out to the battle ensuing before us.

We can't let them leave. They won't stop. All my life, I thought the Fae were the evil ones, but it's not them. They've tried to prevent this. It's the humans. I can end this if I can channel my power; I know it. No more pain. No more suffering. It can be fast.

There were still twenty or so ships attacking, and half of ours had been sunk. They still outnumbered us, despite all our efforts. We had to keep fighting; there was no other option. If they made it to shore. the soldiers waiting to defend it might hold them off, but they might not. The odds were looking bleak. Uriah is right, the humans are like cockroaches, hundreds of them and hard to kill, despite their apparent weakness.

"I need to find a better vantage point, this is too slick. We'll break our necks." He bobbed us along the reef, looking for a landing zone. After about five minutes of searching, we were able to land. We were further away then I'd hoped for. *I'll make it work.*

"I need to you ready yourself. I must try something. I can feel a power in me. It's desperate to be let loose and I need it out of me. I didn't notice until I took the necklace off and now that we've locked it away, I can feel it again. I was so stupid, but I can end this. I know it. I feel it." I shook my head. *Why would I even want to keep something from that horrendous place?*

Uriah crinkled his forehead. He started to say something, but I held my hand up and pulled for the power. I could feel it coursing through me. Uriah gasped as I probed for it. "Can you feel it too?" He nodded, the discernment of the power fueling him as well. I could feel him probing. We needed to do this together.

"I feel it, too—power I've never noticed before. I think the bond has woken it. This feels… ancient, as if we've unlocked something of old. A primal force lost through time. If we project it, it may be enough to obliterate them." Uriah wrapped his arms around me, his front to my back. We entwined our arms, steadying ourselves as we pulled for the new magic within, feeling out the magic of our bond.

My soul mate. Home. Uriah is my home, and I will protect that. Two halves of one whole come together at last. Ancient magic fueled us now. It was raw and pure; untainted and untouched in centuries and we held it at our fingertips.

We took a breath at the same time, and the world stopped. Cannonballs in midair froze, the wind paused, and screams cut off as we focused our magic. We tied it together and filled in each others gaps. Our souls intertwined, his shadows braided themselves with strands of my light, and a large orb began to develop before us—light and dark. Good and evil. Everything in the world came down to black and white, and we were about to make it shatter.

The orb began to pulse, and we channeled our magic into it. I could feel every particle around us—the sleet in the air, the individual dropped of sweat on my body, every breath we took. It all intensified in this moment. Every heartbeat pounded in my ears. Uriah and I melded into each other, and the unrestrained, tangible power of our magic blossomed between our hands. It grew until our hands ached and the strength we needed to hold it back began to falter.

"Now," I whispered and felt my hands push out, Uriah dropped his hands to our side and cast upward a great wall of shadow. Wisps of darkness pulled from the cliff side and lifted above the reef. It encased our ships in a dark cloud, protecting our people from the havoc we were about to release. It coursed down the reef, crossed between our ships and our enemies, and created a mass of magic to protect the fae fighting to save their home.

I pulled for my magic. The light flowed from me in droves now, and a shock wave burst from me shaped like great wings of golden light as they swept across the sea. A sustained roar ruptured across the sea as I made my wish and directed my light. *Save them. Save my people. Save the Fae. Sink the enemy ships. Take the soulless humans to the depths below. Protect the*

Agron Realm!

My own essence exploded outward in a golden wave of rippling destruction, vaporizing all in its path. Seconds ticked by, and the sound pulsed through the air.

The sound, both beautiful and terrible, rocked my soul as it crashed into their ships. My great wave of golden light shaped as giant raven wings swooped through the battle zone obliterating everything in its path. I shuddered at the immense power of it. Uriah's magic held against the heat radiating from my fiery cords as it incinerated our enemy, the percussion rebounding off the cliff sides of the Shallows and the cocoon of darkness he summoned protecting our forces. The waves ripped back to us and Uriah scooped me up as a tsunami washed back toward the shore. I watched with disbelief as I realized nothing more than smoke and floating splinters remained of the human's armada.

Everything was cloaked in a stunned silence. Nothing made a sound for some time. No voices carried on the breeze, and the crackling of burning wood was muted by the sheer force of magic that hung in the atmosphere. It was silent. I could feel our heartbeats as I leaned against Uriah's chest while he tried to land again. *One. Two. Three. We're alive. Four. Five. Six. We did it. Seven. Eight.*

My vision began to blur. Spots of black began to pop, and I couldn't focus my eyes. Waves crashed against the cliff walls, and the icy water buried us to our knees on the slippery rocks. Uriah flapped his wings to keep us in place, to hold me up. I fought to stay awake. The reef broke up the rushing water so it didn't flood the entire shore of the Shallows. For a moment, all was calm, but with horror I realized *I used too much magic.*

Uriah dropped his protective barrier of shadows. "Arabella!" He shouted in my ear. I tried to turn towards him. His face was a pale streak as my knees buckled. A tumultuous round of cheering exploded from our remaining ships. "Don't close your eyes." *Why does everything sound so far away?* "Arabella!" The human's bodies were floating in earnest now, washing toward the beach as the water churned around us. These humans would not return to their homes, to their families. And we were celebrating. *I'm so cold. Are we flying?*

Uriah and I had blended our magic and damned the humans, our way to the end of the onslaught. With the afternoon sun baring down on us, I passed out in his arms almost twenty-four hours after it all began—a massacre on the Bay of Shallows.

Part Three: Revolution

Chapter 43

Uriah

Arabella had been asleep for three days. She exhausted her power to the point of near death. I've never been so scared. It's always a give and take. The price must be paid, but she almost paid with her life—for me and for the Agron Realm. She made that last blast the end to the attack on the Shallows, but the cost. The price was too high; I could have lost her.

She was so tired. I couldn't fly her fast enough to the manor. She was fading, and I almost didn't make it. Gabriella helped me get her into a tepid bath. Her skin was so cold. She was clawing to get away. "It burns," she screamed. She had hypothermia, and the weariness was drawing her down. She kept passing out. I had to warm her up before she succumbed. After the bath, I'd held her all night in our bed. I was too scared to sleep myself. I just watched her breath in and out as it finally evened and her body could begin to rest. *Too close. I almost lost her. It was too close.*

The humans were decimated. She was still in our bed chamber sleeping it off. She's given everything to the Realm, and we've given little in return. That balance needs to be paid. I'd barely gotten her to wake enough to drink some bone broth and a take a trip or two into the bathing chamber the last couple days. She was drained, but she was strong, she'll recover. It'll take a few days. She gave so much of herself to end the attack.

King Astros had just sent a rider back escorted by a full guard of fifty royal soldiers to help as needed after receiving our message. It was a generous bit of help. The Agron Realm was being stretched thin. Fae weren't as abundant as humans were, so the additional troops were welcome. I gave them assignments immediately, knowing they wouldn't be able to stay indefinitely. We'll use them while we can.

The bay was wrecked. All the docks had disintegrated when the tsunami from the force Arabella expelled had come crashing back to shore. The shock wave of power she'd amassed was incredible. My own little weapon—if it hadn't damn near killed her, I might consider letting her do it again should the need arise, but we'll find a different way next time. I can't risk her. That kind of ancient power is not worth losing my mate.

I shifted in my seat, staring at the flames beneath the mantle in the fireplace across my office. The rain pattered against the window behind me as the wind howled, My desk was as messy as the bay. Scraps of parchment and ink pens littered the top. Piles of maps and charts hung over the edge, held on by a bottle of bourbon that was quickly emptying. I was overwhelmed with the onslaught of additional responsibilities. I swirled the tawny liquor in my crystal tumbler.

Arabella likes brown sugar bourbon. Felix reported that was all she had drank when she went to bars and it's pretty good. I took a sip, the warmth of the booze seeping into me. *Nice of him to bring me a few bottles.*

We'd lost all but nine ships. My navy was incapacitated at best. I'd been reading reports as they were updated, and over a hundred fae sailors had died or were presumably dead at sea. The bodies were still being pulled out of the bay. I'd had to ask the townsfolk of Marelitor to allow sailors to use the boats belonging to the nearby village fishermen. *Thank the King they weren't all destroyed.*

Fishing nets scooped up remains that were piled on the beaches. Some had been claimed but most were humans that would need to be buried. We'd had to contend with hundreds of bodies. We were about to have a whole new problem.

When Arabella is better, I'll take her to the village. She'll enjoy meeting the people she just saved. She would like the bakery by that book store. I'll take her to both. She deserves a proper courting. We need to celebrate our engagement too. She needs to see the good in this world. Until then, we need to clean this up—so much death and so many bodies.

Sebastian and Felix had gotten into quite the argument. To think, two brothers at each others throats when we were already in a time of turmoil.

Sebastian has requested we dump the bodies on the shores of Neera, give the humans back their remains and make a bigger point at the same time. Felix thinks it would be barbaric and prove their point instead. They both made good arguments.

For now, it's cold enough outside the bodies are mostly frozen and in no risk of decomposition. We plan to hold a meeting and see what some of the other captains think. Thank the King we didn't lose much of our leadership. A few captains were lost in the attack, but at least I don't have to shift ranks around. I turned in my chair to look at the beach in the distance through the rain-streaked window.

I sent a courier to John to see his opinion on the matter. It would affect his border the most. The Summit suffered numerous attacks, but they fared well enough considering it was mostly hand to hand combat. He lost a tenth of his cavalry in the skirmish, but it would be recovered. They drove the humans back from the border. *Thank the King for that, too.* The natural landscape only allowed for the humans to infiltrate in a few areas, and the bottle necking of the passes made them easy to pick off. Still, John had his hands full leading the Summit to victory with such a vast region to cover. *Yet, the Brume and Meadows would leave us to fight and argue their soldiers couldn't be spared. Cowards.*

I looked back to my desk from the window. The letter I'd read ten times still lay on the top of the pile, waiting for my attention. King Astros has asked us to attend a Winter Solstice Ball in three weeks. He wants to verify our bond and will leave room in the court's schedule for a bonding ceremony after verification. He sounded skeptical, so clearly Arabella's father has gotten to him already. *Lionel is such a piece of shit. Arabella never deserved to get stuck with him as a father.*

I asked the courier to stay for a hot meal and rest. The poor kid looked around the receiving hall, it lay between my private wing and the main manor on the first floor His face paled at the sight and smell of bloody rags piled along the walls. They were left-over from caring for wounded sailors. He looked like he would rather be anywhere else, but he reluctantly agreed. I needed him to return with my reply.

I accepted the invitation on behalf of myself and Arabella, and I requested that the Brume, Meadows and Summit Lords and Ladies be invited as well. I worded it carefully so I didn't seem suspicious, but I implied that all the full entourages should be in attendance for such a magnanimous occasion.

King Astros would never allow me to investigate the other Lords. How do I explain the actions of the Altmore's without looking into the Brume though? Ulysses must be involved somehow. His niece and nephew had to have some sort of motivation to kidnap Arabella. One problem at a time. I will only get married once, after all.

I included my military blockade and naval warfare report of our victory as well. I conveniently left out that Arabella and I had combined our magic into an overly effective bomb of sorts. The pure magic that had transcended time and space, blowing apart everything in its path, should perhaps stay with the Shallows for now.

Rumors will spread on their own. I'll deal with them then. Arabella has enough enemies. That percussion alone had to have been heard across the Realm. The sheer immensity of the force rattles my bones and the wings. The beautiful wings swept across the sea to obliterate the enemy. I've never seen anything so majestic. *The Sculptor might have sliced them from her back, but he didn't sever them from her soul.*

"You wanted me?" Felix poked his head in my slightly ajar door. I starred at my tattoo. The waves were sloshing back and forth, unsettled. It'd been days since they were calm. I pined for that night when they were completely flat with Arabella in my arms.

"I did." I slid around my desk and sat on the edge of it. "Have you found anything yet?" I gave Felix the necklace and explained what I thought it was. He felt the power in it. Something evil lurked there and buried itself in Arabella. It was working out of her system, but it still calls to her. We need to keep it far away from her lest she be tempted again. Unfortunately, it'd had years to take hold. This was sorcery, not fae magic. *It's unnatural, forbidden—the darkest of magics.*

"We're researching. Sebastian and I have been in the library most of the day looking up various tomes. I have a feeling we'll find that it's connected to whatever power may be tied to Queen Clawin. Speaking of, there seems to be some missing pieces there as well."

"How do you mean? Is she fae or a witch?" I rubbed my chin and furrowed my brow. *There are so many layers. Where do we even begin?*

"I'm not sure *what* she is, but she is *not* human." Felix said as he came in from the door way and leaned against the back of an armchair in front of the fire place. "I've been kicking myself. Never once have I bothered to look into her. It's almost as if that in itself is a spell at play. Sebastian and I have found ourselves wandering around several times while researching her. We keep getting sidetracked. It's gotten quite frustrating. He's currently in the dungeon reading. It seems to be the only place that isn't affected." *Interesting. Arabella is terrified of the lower levels.*

"That could be. I noticed when I tried to read about concealment charms, I'd realize I was half way to the kitchen before I remembered what I'd been doing. By the King, it's any wonder Arabella hadn't realized she was spelled all those years. She was little more than a child when she put the wretched thing on. She wore it for years. There's no telling what it influenced her to do."

Perhaps that's why she was able to carry out such dark deeds. Is that really who she is, or was it the influence of the necklace?

"I asked Knightmare about it." Felix crossed his arms in front of him. "I've been popping down to see him once a day. He's quite the conversationalist. I don't know how old that horse is, but he's got a solid understanding of all things magic." I nodded. Knightmare is a mystery too. It's a wonder they found each other.

"He told me he has tried to talk her into leaving the necklace behind before. Since she pulled him out of the burning barn, he said she'd get glassy eyed and freeze up for a few minutes every time he asked her about it. He didn't know why she kept it all this time when it had such an ugly history. When she came to, she would pick up a conversation they'd had a few days earlier—as if she were in a trance of some sort. She'd speak like they were just having it, not rehashing it. He was never sure what to make of it. Clearly, though, we need to destroy the thing. I'm not sure how to yet, but we need to figure it out." Felix looked perplexed. It bothered him to not have an easy answer.

"Arabella and I tried smashing it. It's amber, so we should be able to take a mortar and pestle to it for goodness's sake. I wonder if the powder might be worse to contend with. Do you think it holds a curse, or is it in the fiber of it? Perhaps trying to break the amber is more dangerous. I can keep it in the box for now, but we'll need a permanent fix soon." I mused. This was a complicated bit of magic. Some magics were best left contained, and this may be one of them. *What would it do if we released it?*

"I suppose we should research that too. It's been too long since I've last seen Zeds, I'll go ask. I'll ride out and see him this afternoon. He's moved his home to the fringe of the Brume, back where he had it a decade ago. Magic is a little wilder there. He may know since he's a bit of a hermit. As you know, he dabbles in some...interesting things." Felix grinned.

"I was thinking you should make a trip myself the other day. That old fae gives me the creeps, so more power to you." I said as Felix's grin widened. Our encounters were rarely normal, and he usually had some weird prophecy for me when we met. It was always unnerving."See if Knightmare will go with you. Perhaps he can provide some insight, and I'm sure Zeds would like to meet the faehorse. Faehorse seem to be like seers. Their auras are similar, and Knightmare has spent a fair amount of time around the necklace, far more than we have."

"She was certainly different the other night." Felix said, amusement dancing in his eyes. *He probably thinks it's funny I finally find my mate, and she's a murderous little thing.* "Her whole demeanor was changed. It felt much more like she was in the Daemon Kingdom rather than here in the manor."

"I can certainly see the impact when Arabella has it on versus not. She was downright scary the other night. We'd barely gotten back to the manor and had the fliers bunked down in the ballrooms. The poor staff was scrambling to find as many blankets and pillows as possible, along with preparing enough food for eighty fae. It was chaos. Then Arabella comes out of our room absolutely unhinged with anger. I didn't know what to make of it. I thought maybe she'd just overdone it, but I should have caught on faster." I shook my head.

I'd realized the necklace wasn't on the table when we left after sleeping a few hours. She was so combative and reactive to everything. I thought she was possessed for a moment, and then I remember what she'd said about the necklace dampening her mood earlier in the day and how she felt taking it off. But where I saw my necklace around her throat, she seemed to listen to reason. She was pragmatic, rational. If I plot things out in a straight line, calm and simple, she connects the dots well. *I'll have to remember she's impressionable.*

"He's weird, but hey, maybe he'll even have pants on this time." Felix belted out a hardy laugh, and I grimaced. The last few times we went, the Seer hadn't bothered with britches and ran around with an unbuttoned shirt and holey underwear. Seeing an old man's sack is not usually on the top of anyone's to do list.

"Check in with Sebastian first. Did you two work it out?" I didn't want to butt in to their relationship, but we'd all been drifting lately. We needed a retreat—go hunting and fishing or something. Just slow down and sit around a fire for a bit. Touch some grass. *I'm losing my best friends.*

"Well enough. We both agreed that we're both right." He smirked and shook his head. "I don't know. I think it's mostly like what you said the other day. He wants to settle down with Gabriella, but he doesn't know how we'll deal with that. I just want both of you to be happy." I nodded.

"Arabella and I will be wed soon. We might as well get you two hitched too. We can raise our children together." I looked at him. *Does he know that I know his preferences? Does he know that I don't care?*

"Right. I guess we're not kids anymore. It's time we all grew up. Anyway, I'll run up to the library, grab another stack of hopefuls, and take them down to Sebastian before I go talk to Knightmare. I expect we'll be gone overnight, unless he agrees to shift. It's handy having a faehorse, if I dare say it. I know he's not ours, but nothing is more useful than that— well, aside from wings." He winked, kicked off the chair and headed out of the door.

Chapter 44

Felix

"Does he have wards set?" Knightmare asked me as we approached the broke down cottage. It was on the edge of a swamp in between the Shallows and the Brume. It fell into a no mans land of sorts. There was thick brush and thorny shrubs. Mist hung low to the ground as dense fog swirled around us. The marshy ground sloshed and squished beneath our feet. The cottage was little more than a single room hovel, half built into an ancient tree, half built of bricks made from bound twigs and marsh mud. Thatched grass lined the part of roof jutting out from the dead tree, that long ago turned ash white.

The smell of roasting meat wafted from the tiny home, and a small vegetable bed lined the walkway leading up to the front door. Cabbages, kohlrabi, potatoes, radishes, and carrots grew in abundance. It was warmer here. It was a temperate piece of land that stayed mild year round, tucked between the cliffs of the Brume and the low marshlands of the Shallows.

"He doesn't need wards," I cautioned. Zeds was an interesting fae of old. He was well over five hundred and probably lived here for most of his life. He took the land with him when he felt like a change. He knew things about the ancient ways fae couldn't understand anymore. He was one of the few left blessed with long life.

As the magic faded, so did our attributes. Whole formerly fae families were being left with only the eldest carrying magic. The days of winged fae and pointed ears were coming to an end. The dilution with humans made it probable. Even

Arabella, with as powerful as she was had rounded ears. She looked like a human with no wings. *She was robbed of her heritage.*

The door opened as we approached. I was ahead of Knightmare. I was hoping Zeds would talk to us outside. His small tree cottage was cramped and usually smelt odd. I could smell it already—like peppermint and...something? "Who goes there?" Zeds leaned out shouting at us.

"It's Felix, and I've brought a friend. This is Knightmare—he's a faehorse, we were hoping for a friendly chat." I stopped, and Knightmare leveled to me. "We've brought a few gifts as well." I took out a parcel in the saddle bag I'd strapped to Knightmare before we shifted.

"Ah, young Felix. It's been a time since you've visited. I thought I might be seeing you soon. I'm never wrong. I thought I was once, but I was wrong." He squinted at us. "Don't suppose a faehorse would fit in my house. Pull up a stump." He waved his hand, and two stumps appeared in the pathway by the garden patch.

"With thanks," I said and sat. "I've brought you some sweets. There's a few sugar pastries from the ladies in the kitchen, some chocolate, spices of all sorts, and a few bottles of bourbon." I handed the package over.

"Well, I thank ya. I don't get into any town very much anymore. Never seems anyone wants to barter and I don't bother keeping coin." He peeked at some of the spices. "Society has changed. These days, diplomacy is saying 'nice doggy' until you find a big stick and nice rock to bash in heads."

Knightmare looked at me, and I rearranged my face. My eyebrows had drifted closer to my hairline then my eyes. *This is going to be interesting. He's showing his age.* "Well, here, in case you need it." I pulled a sack of coin out of my pocket, adding it to the top. Zeds was shaking his head and he scratched the back of his head.

"I won't. Since your question arrived, the world has

changed…" Zeds trailed off, looking in the distance as if he were expecting someone. "That's awfully generous. You must be in a pickle. I'm supposing it has to do with what took the wards down a week or so ago? I've been expecting someone to come my way, and I hoped it'd be you."

His gray hair was matted on one side and scraggly on the other but, roughly cut short. It used to be dark gray when I was a boy. Now, some thirty years later, it was mostly silver in it. His mahogany face was peppered with a silver beard. His hands were knobby and thick with arthritis. He looked much thinner than the last time I'd seen him. *How long has it been? Five years maybe? I need to get out here more.*

"Aye, that's precisely why we're here. We think we know the source, only we aren't sure what to do about it." I readjusted on my stump as it's jagged edge cut dug into my rear. My leathers weren't thick enough to pad it. "Do you remember the Meadows child that disappeared all those years ago? The Lord's daughter?"

"Young Arabella. I never met the babe, but I knew her mother. She was one of the greatest Seers this land has seen. My Flower. I taught her everything I know." He nodded, and tears welled in his eyes at the reminder of her, as he rubbed the stubble on his chin again. His full lips puckered and his bushy brows furrowed. Zeds *Flower was Arabella's mother.*

"Yes, Arabella. Uriah has found her. The mating bond snapped almost immediately, and she's joined him in the Shallows. She came not even a full week ago. She was taken to the Torrent Kingdom that night when all those people were murdered in the Meadows. She was hidden away and abused by someone called The Sculptor for decades. She eventually escaped and ended up working for Queen Clawin somehow." I wasn't sure how much to say or not say, but I need Zeds' help in this. Uriah may be angry, but Zeds wouldn't tell anyone. He might already have seen it.

He looked at me in full. He had one ice blue colored eye,

and the other was a dark forest green with light blue specks. I used to find it unnerving, but now it was merely comforting to see, like an old friend, but also an advisor, a mentor. *Family.* "I see—and her coming to the Shallows to be with Uriah brought the wards down. When exactly did it occur? I felt it mind you, it was late in the evening last week. Must have been around sunset midweek when I felt a ripple. By midnight they had collapsed completely."

"We hadn't known when, actually, but now that you say that, they accepted the bond Wednesday evening. She came earlier in the day. I fetched her from a snow storm over in Stanzley, Daemon Kingdom that morning. I talked her into coming to the Shallows because Uriah was miserable. She was fighting the bond at first, trying to complete a task set to her by Queen Clawin. Uriah found her months ago, but she fled from him at first. Arabella was terrified the Queen would act against her, but the bond called them together. Neither want to fight it now. They are determined to find a way to be together."

He nodded. "A conclusion only comes when you get tired of thinking, but you believe it was something else? You have a different concern."

"Yes, sir, we do have a concern. Before we get to that, are you saying you felt the wards come down?" *Fuck. What in the world is going on? Have any other wards fallen? How exposed is the Agron Realm? Is the Summit secure?*

"I felt it. I feel all the things in the world. I tune them out mostly, but when things are out of the ordinary, it's hard to ignore. Ancient wards falling? Well, I never. I felt you put new ones up too. They're not near as strong...they'll keep the humans out for now, but a force is growing in the East. There's something evil and you've brought an essence of it along with you, so just show me." He looked to my jacket pocket. *Indeed. We came to the right place.*

"*You feel it too?*" Knightmare said, stepping closer to Zeds. I heard it in my head, and Zeds answered. The old fae looked at

Knightmare and gave him a single nod.

"Aye, I feel it. It's corrupt. It's not stable, either. I suspect you've felt it for some time?" he asked Knightmare as he took him in the burns down his side, his jet-black hair, and braided mane. "Rough time you've had. I take it humans did that to you?"

"Who else would hurt someone without provocation?" Knightmare replied in a sardonic drawl.

Zeds chuckled and mumbled to himself. "If you don't want a sarcastic answer, don't ask a stupid question."

"I always told her to take it off. She never would. She earned it, she said. It was her trophy. It belonged to her captor, a vile old woman that used to beat her senseless and starve her. She strangled her with the necklace and broke away from King Plavlock's castle. She was on her own for a few years before she rescued me. I scared a human, and he locked me in a barn and lit it. I couldn't shift then. Rave—Arabella taught me how after she nursed me back to health. She was never scared of me. The necklace though..." His withers shook from head to toe.

I handed the obsidian and onyx box to Zeds. As he spoke, he pulled the necklace out, blanching when he opened the box at a wave of power that washed over us. He touched nothing more than the string it was on, careful not to touch the amber pendant. "This is an ancient magic—a nasty bit of sorcery fueled by hate and fear. It reminds me of the skulduggery from a sorcerer in the Brume. I forget the surname of the line. I haven't seen anything like this in well over three hundred years, maybe longer."

He held it up to the sky. Shuddering and shaking his head, he carefully laid it on the lid of the box in his lap. "She had this on her person? Touching her skin?" he asked Knightmare. Fear flashed in his two-toned eyes.

"Yes, She wore it day and night. She never took it off for years." Knightmare looked sad. He clearly felt like he had failed her in some way.

How many times did he try to get her to take it off? And how many times did the spells prevent him from helping her? How many times has the world failed Arabella?

"Did you notice any behavior difference? Or rather, did she have any...tendencies most wouldn't? What I mean to say is, was she volatile or angry?" Another wave of fear flashed across Zeds face as he pondered his own questions. He looked past Knightmare into the fog swirling on the ground. His eyes flashed with a gold ring.

"You have to understand. Raven, she did what she had to do to survive. She kept us fed and moving so the Sculptor would not find her again. We had many conversations I don't believe she remembers. She became an assassin, but I only ever saw her kill the ones that would prey on the weak. Sometimes, she took great pleasure in it. She never balked at a challenge. She failed once though, and the Queen began making demands of her—either she complied or Queen Clawin promised she would deliver her back to the Sculptor. The Sculptor is the Queen's bastard brother Jade. He's King Plavlock's pet. He tortured Raven for years. He started when he took her wings and then twisted her identity. He broke her in ways no being should ever have to endure. They call her the Sculptor's Apprentice because he used every sick punishment he knows on her. She learned them all and uses them herself now." Sadness filled Knightmare's eyes as he recounted Arabella's tale for Zeds.

"I think you are a fool, but what's my opinion against everyone else?" Zeds looked Knightmare dead in the eyes. "You failed the girl. Did you divulge this knowledge or hold it to yourself? You've wasted time and endangered the entire Realm. I would expect more of you in the future." Knightmare took a step backward.

I shifted uncomfortably on my stump. I'd never heard Zeds sound so utterly angry and appalled—those were harsh words coming from the genial fae that I had come to know.

Zeds turned to me. "The Sculptor encased part of his

essence in the amulet. I see someone has tried to smash it. You mustn't." He looked me dead in the eye. "You must not break the stone. To abolish the wicked force trapped inside, you need to kill the source. The Sculptor must be killed first. Then, only then, the stone may be broken. To free the essence first will only make him stronger."

I looked between Knightmare and Zeds before replying. "Kill the Sculptor. I'm assuming he isn't human then. If he has such strong magic, do you know what he is? Clawin as well, presumably if they are half siblings..."

How have I missed all this and why didn't Knightmare tell me about Jade? Knightmare knew who the Sculptor is and didn't tell us when he knows we are searching...Is the necklace at play? Did it distract him too, like Sebastian and I researching? I'm gaining more questions than answers.

"He is but half a sorcerer. The Queen has no powers; she is human as far as I know. They share a mother, but have different fathers. I suspect the Sculptor's father dwells in the Brume. There are a few sorcerers left there, but they work in secrecy as they are not welcome many other places. Many tales of trickery and cruelty originate from them, but those have been blamed on the fae." Zeds began to talk faster. *Is he trying to get rid of us?*

Looking around again, Zeds continued, "The Dark Queen calls upon her brother to do her bidding. He is loyal to anyone that lets him practice his craft. He will never wear a crown; he knew that as did their mother when he was born. I do not know for certain, but I suspect that was why he was raised elsewhere and not in the central castle of the Daemon Kingdom."

A flash of gold flitted through Zeds' eyes again. I'd rarely seen Zeds use his power as a seer. I understand why he knew Arabella's mother, but it was odd to be in the presence of someone all knowing.

"*What will it take to kill him?*" Knightmare asked. He

stomped the ground. His ears flattened, and he seemed agitated. Thick fog swirled around us, the air thickening and white blocking our view into the plains.

"If the Sculptor has to be killed first, won't the necklace tether him here? Would we have to destroy both at the same time to eliminate him?" I cut in before Zeds could answer.

"Indeed, those are the questions. It will take the greatest magic of all. I think you'll find—" an arrow flew through the air and pierced Zeds green eye. I starred a moment as everything fell into slow motion.

Zeds body slumped and tumbled off the stump. "Zeds!" I bellowed before drawing my sword. Without a second thought, I raced into the fog the direction the arrow came from. A thick bunch of dried grass and shrubs lay in the distance of the bog. I threw out my magic, searching for any trace, any aura within reach. There was no one in sight. I searched the area by sight and saw footprints.

I knelt down some thirty yards away. I wouldn't have been able to see them through Knightmare. *It's a wonder they didn't hit the faehorse.* I hadn't considered we'd even be in danger. I noticed a heel impression in the soft mud of the marsh. The scent lingered, pepper and something else? I pulled for my tracking magic to filter the scent. Flowers. Hay. Sweat.

I continued my search. A scrap of hunter green velvet with a gold silk lining was entwined on a branch several feet away. It was a piece of fabric from a quiver lining. It smelled of wildflowers and peppercorn too. Then I saw a second impression. Boot heels sunk in the mire.

How much did they overhear? Surely, our conversation carried on the wind. How did I miss a fae? Zeds never sets wards; why didn't I?

"I heard someone shift in, but thought I was just imagining it. The fog muffled the sounds, but then I knew one second before I heard the bow draw. I'm so sorry. I reacted too slow." Knightmare nuzzled my shoulder as he stood behind me in the brush. I had

tears streaming down my face. I hadn't noticed I was crying.

Not Zeds. Who did this and why? What was he telling me that they didn't want us to know? I will avenge this. He didn't deserve this end. His breed is all but dead. I should have visited more often, taken better care with him in his old age. Years have passed us by, so much wasted time, so many missed opportunities. Not my friend. No.

I tucked the scrap away and walked back to Zeds. *He didn't even get a piece of chocolate.* He loved his sweets. I picked up the cursed necklace and the onyx box that had tumbled onto the ground. I was careful not to touch it as Zeds had been, especially now that I knew what it was.

I walked into Zeds' house, and after a few moments of searching I found a small shovel. I pulled up all the produce in his beloved, well taken care of garden, and began to dig.

I remember putting this in with Uriah and Sebastian. A tree had fallen. Zeds and I laid each rock in the pathway. I was just thinking of it the other day. 'My Flower.' His Flower was Arabella's mother. This is the time of great sadness. He told me this would happen a decade ago. He never deserved this. What will I do without him?

The late afternoon sun was setting by the time I had laid him to rest. I took apart the wood of his closet door to build a hastily made coffin. The dirt would surely make it's way in, but I think he'd prefer to be in touch with it since so much of his magic relied on the world around him.

"From the earth and back into it. Thank you, old friend, for your wisdom throughout the years and your kind soul. I'm sorry it ended this way. I will think of you often and share your stories so that the world may never forget."

Knightmare stood and waited. He didn't rush me. He didn't speak, just let me carry on as I needed to. I placed the parcel I'd brought Zeds beside him in the grave. Removing the arrow, I tucked it in the saddle bag along with the scrap of fabric. It bore Meadows colors in the fletching. Someone would answer for this. I would make sure of it. There are snakes in the Meadow. I will flesh them out. I will not let this rest.

I slid the lid in place and covered my friend with the rich soil of his garden. Hauling a large rock from the surrounding bog, I carved his name in the sandstone in the fading light. I then went back inside his little home, and after a quick look, I took a very old thick leather-bound journal, a few old books, and a letter, addressed to me, that was on his bedside table.

He knew. He knew and he welcomed us anyway. That's why he didn't argue about the coin. 'I won't' he'd said when I told him he might need it. Grief struck like a white hot iron against my soul.

I pulled a pot of roast venison out of his fireplace and drowned the fire burning there. I didn't have the appetite to eat it. *Did he know he wouldn't eat it either? And he cooked it anyway?* I scooped up a few more things, both ancient and clearly important to Zeds, and I tucked them into a leather bag beside them.

Did he intend for this? Who can I tell of his passing? I don't know if he even had anyone. All these years, I never asked. How selfish of me. I started to exit the small cottage. The gnarled inside of the tree always brought comfort, even the weird smell. *Neroli. That's what that is. Peppermint and neroli oil.* The sickly-sweet smell I couldn't ever place came to me then.

Would Zeds be dead if we hadn't come? If we came tomorrow, would we have found his body and had no answers? I walked up to Knightmare in the eerie winter twilight and tucked the heavy bag onto the saddle horn. I set a heavy ward around the home. I should burn it, but I couldn't bring myself to do it. *Perhaps I will still visit. Maybe I'll make it my own home someday.*

"I think if Zeds could give you an answer, he'd say you have to die a few times to really begin living," Knightmare said into my mind as I looked at him, a gold ring flashed in his eyes after he spoke.

What the fuck does that mean? "Right, if only closed minds came with closed mouths," I replied curtly as we shifted home.

Chapter 45

Arabella

I was asleep for a solid five days. Somehow, blending my magic with Uriah's created an explosion of power out of the two of us that I never knew could occur. It cast out as golden wings, sweeping broadly before us, crashing into the ships and the sea. His shadows guided it along and laid waste to everything we deemed encroaching. Our bond was strong and incarnate when we blended our magic. The power was robust and destructive like the pooling of magics of old. Beautiful. Infinite. We were a powerhouse.

When I finally woke longer than to drink something or pee, Uriah asked me again if I was sure about our future. He doesn't want to rush me, but I wish I could show him how much I need him by my side—other than with words. He is everything I never knew I was searching for, the reason I felt incomplete. Raven is no more. With Uriah by my side, I do not need her. I am Arabella, the future Lady of the Shallows, and I shall rise to the challenge.

All this time, I thought it was my mutilated body that held me back, but it wasn't. I was missing the other half of my soul, and joining with Uriah has shown me that. Ridding myself of the wretched necklace helped. Knightmare always knew. He tried to tell me, and I never heard him, never took credence in what he was saying. *I'm such a bad friend. He was loyal to me, and I failed him.*

In just a few short days, I was feeling more complete than I ever have before. I love Uriah, and I love the feeling of security being with him brings me. Not just that he will take care of me, but that I get to take care of him too. Together. Together, we are shatterproof.

I stood before the mirror on my vanity. Since I just bathed, I combed my wild curls up into a twisted bun. I shimmy into a tight cerulean blue dress. The scars on my back are mostly covered, but peak through the soft chiffon fabric. It's snug on my hips, but flares out at my knee with the mermaid cut. It's definitely overkill however I haven't seen anyone all week and I woke just in time for dinner.

It was then that I realized I was finally home, I'm where I belong and *I want to live.*

"Well, that's a sight!" The door to our room opened, and Uriah stood in the doorway, taking in my outfit as he walked in and shut the door behind him. "You look ravishing." He rewards me with a big smile and his shadows danced across his shoulders.

"Thank you," I said, stepping into his arms and gazing at his eyes. "I figured I might as well get use to wearing these lovely things." He sweeps an arm up my back and bends me into a dip before pressing his lips to mine. We lingered for a few moments before straightening out. *He smells so good.*

"Dinner is about ready. I can have Gabriella serve us up here if you're not up for company." Uriah studied me as I stepped away and picked a pair of silver heels. I slid them on carefully, and I caught the glint of the wave necklace in the mirror. *Perfect.*

"How is Felix doing?" I asked instead, deflecting his inquiry. He came back an absolute mess from an errand with Knightmare. His friend had been murdered. He was angry, grieving and swearing vengeance on the Meadows. I can't blame him. Uriah had explained the evidence to me while I bathed, I agreed it was all too connected. We just can't figure out how they knew to attack his old friend or why they would want to. *What did Zeds know? And who wanted him quiet? How did they know Felix would go to him?*

"He's positively seething. Zeds was his mentor. After his folks passed, he didn't have a lot of family to help him along. Zeds was there for him. He's angry with himself mostly. He doesn't think he visited enough. I keep trying to tell him he can't turn back the clock—all he can do is honor Zeds memory now. I suggested we have a statue and plaque mounted on the grounds to commemorate the old fae. He seemed to like that idea."

"I don't think that's the same as having him alive, but it would be a kind gesture." I patted his forearm. "Shall we? I dare say I'm starving." I'd lost another few pounds over the week. I tried on two other dresses, but they were far too loose. I had to opt for a smaller sized dress, a little tight, but my figure worked in it. He kissed me on the top of the head and we left the room. *I'm sure I'll spring back. Uriah likes my curves.*

"Ah, finally! Our brute returns!" Sebastian stood as we entered the room. "That was an incredible bit of magic you shot off there. It's any wonder you exhausted yourself. I've never seen such a thing!" Sebastian gave me a gentle hug as I approached the table. "How are you feeling? You look much better. It was terrifying seeing you collapse into Uriah's arms. We couldn't see well through Uriah's magic and feared the worst, with the cost of magic and all." His brow scrunched.

"I definitely needed a very long nap. My legs are a little stiff, but it'll loosen. I appreciate the comfy bed. I'd do it again, with Uriah; I can't muster that on my own. It takes both of our magics to accomplish such a feat. Don't let him give me all the credit. I'm just glad we figured it out in time." Uriah moved around me to the head of the table and pulled out my chair. I sat first, then he followed. Picking up a warm crusty dinner roll, I began to slather butter on it before continuing. "I know the damage was immense. How is everyone coping? Are things coming back together?" I shook my head, "will everything be okay?"

Uriah answered. "The casualties were higher than we like, but it was nothing compared to the slaughter of human life. We've found a handful alive, but for the most part, they all succumbed. It drained the resources of King Plavlock and Queen Clawin. I think we'll have to be rid of them completely. We're just waiting for the order from King Astros; it's his call. He's refused to put an end to their treachery for the last few decades. Until last week, they couldn't breach our wards." He stared at me with that. *He's still mad that I came so close to dying.*

"Do we, um, know what happened there?" I ask tentatively to the table.

Shame washed over me. *Did I do it? How did the necklace cause that? Is this all my fault? Is Zeds my fault too? Why does pain follow me?*

"We have a theory," began Uriah. Then the door to the formal dining room opened, and a very drunk Felix stumbled in. He was swinging a bottle of wine and looked bleary eyed. His dark hair was disheveled, and he clearly hadn't bothered with a bath since returning from Zeds' place.

"My lady." He nodded to me and took a seat next to Sebastian. "Apologies for my tardiness."

"You're fine. We were just discussing the wards and how they might have fallen," Uriah said as he picked up a dinner roll himself. He glanced to Felix and pushed the basket of bread to him. "I think you may know the most about it," he said to Felix with encouragement. Felix's throat bobbed. I reached a hand across the table and took his.

"I'm so sorry to hear about Zeds. I would have liked to meet him. He sounds like he was a true gem and a great friend throughout the years. We won't let this go unpunished. We'll find whoever is responsible and deal with them. If I have to kill my own father, we will avenge him." I promised. *I grimaced at the thought of the Lord of Meadows. Father. Such a disgrace to come from his line or the Meadows.* "Uriah told me the Meadows colors were on the fletchings, and you found fabrics matching the region as well."

Felix nodded as he pulled his hand away. His tanned skin looked so dark next to the creamy white of mine. His breathing was unsteady. "Zeds mentioned he felt the wards start to fail shortly after sunset last week. The first night you arrived. Shortly after dinner began. He wasn't sure exactly how or what would have brought them down, only the general time they began to weaken. He said they failed completely just after midnight."

Uriah nodded. "I was with Arabella the whole time," he said pointedly, looking to Sebastian and Felix. *Why did that sound like a defense?* "We were upstairs and had come down to change for dinner."

"Well, something must have occurred and created a ripple effect. I can't think of what would be strong enough to take down wards that have been in place for millennia," Sebastian said with his mouth half full of bread. We all sat in silence.

I picked the white dress, with white heels. I fixed my hair. Uriah gifted me the pearls. "Pearls." I stated. "Uriah gave me his mothers pearls to wear to dinner." Uriah sucked in an audible breath. "I left the amber necklace upstairs. It was the first time I took it off since putting it on."

"You took off the cursed necklace." Felix sat back in his chair. "Zeds told me it holds a shard of the Sculptor's essence. The necklace holds a piece of his soul, and you've been wearing it. You brought him here, and before we neutralized the necklace in the onyx box, he's had a link directly into the manor. He was about to tell me how to kill him and how to destroy the necklace when he was killed." He shook his head, his eyes glistened as he glanced down at his lap.

Sebastian cut in. "Something triggered when you took it off. Is he strong enough? Could he tell that you separated yourself from the necklace?"

Felix replied, "Zeds told me he was half sorcerer. Knightmare admitted that he's a bastard, half human from his mother's side. He's Queen Clawin's bastard half-brother. Why he never told you that is beyond me." He waved in my direction. "The Queen herself has no magic. She uses him to do her bidding. She can't hurt you, but her brother can."

"What?" I couldn't believe my ears. "But, how can the Queen know whether or not I'm trying to collect the heads?"

"That's what I'm saying, she can't. She has no magic. There is no tracking spell, at least not from Clawin. I suspect she had her brother set a spell and even more that he's been watching you all this time through that necklace. When you took it off, he panicked. Maybe he realized he didn't have control of his little apprentice anymore." Felix said, leveling his eyes on me.

Felix hates me now. I caused Zeds to die. I brought the wards down by coming here. This is all my fault!

"Oh no." I gasped. "Oh no. What did I do?" I covered my face with my hands. A tremble started, and I couldn't stop it. *My fault. This was all my fault. I caused all this.*

I turned to Uriah. "I swear I didn't know. I swear it." Tears began to fall down my face. Sebastian watched me across the table, his face somber at the revelations.

"None of us suspected it, even after you told me the story of how you acquired the necklace." Uriah held my hand. His eyes were sad, and his brow scrunched. He ran his free hand through his wild auburn hair. "It doesn't matter now. We can't go back and change it. All we can do is move forward. The necklace is safely locked away. Thank the King—it can't take hold of you again."

"Zeds mentioned that we can't destroy the necklace until we kill the Sculptor. Breaking it would release what he contained in it, and that will only make him stronger. I fear he's much more evolved than we fully understand yet. He's been left unchecked. I think he's the real enemy here. He's been pulling the strings of both the Torrent Kingdom and Daemon Kingdom for far too long. At this point, I'd wager the King and

Queen are just puppets doing his bidding."

"I have to agree," Sebastian said, Gabriella came in with a stack of dinner plates then. He looked at her and muttered his thanks as she placed it before him after giving the rest of us a plate first. She retreated, and he continued."I was trying to research from our archives. I found that, unless I holed up in the very bottom level, my mind would forget what I was searching for. I had to write it down in front of me to stay on task. We put the necklace below ground so it can't be influenced any longer. Whatever magic it contains is corrosive, strong, and evil."

Gabriella came back with a large serving dish of buttery mashed potatoes, set it down, and brought a platter filled with piping hot roast beef, sauteed carrots and steamed broccoli. If heaven had a scent, this would be it. My stomach grumbled. Leaving us with a gravy boat of thick gravy, she exited quietly after taking an empty bottle of wine and pointedly looking at Felix.

"I had that around my neck?" I whispered, shaking my head. "I couldn't even feel it." I felt puzzled. *How could I not tell? Am I that stupid?*

"I think," Uriah started, taking a scoop of potatoes and putting it on my plate for me and another for himself, "you'd been around it for so long as a child, that you couldn't feel it. It was just a normal setting for you, first around Clara, undoubtedly for the Sculptor to keep an eye on you. Then, I think when you killed her and took it, it was just icing on the cake for the Sculptor that you happened to keep it. It's likely why he never came after you himself. He knew where you were all along."

I looked at Uriah, "You think when I crossed the wards with Felix, he decided it was time to break them?" I scrunched my brows together and bit my bottom lip. *The caves though, I crossed them before. But I left...The Sculptor didn't care until I came back again.*

"Yes and no." Uriah loaded my plate with meat and vegetables. "I think when you took the necklace off, our dear Sculptor realized his hold on you wasn't as strong as he thought. And I think he may have noticed your magic blooming under our mating bond. I think when we joined our magic that night, he panicked outright, knowing he lost you." He took a bite of roast beef and chewed a moment. *The Sculptor is scared of me.*

"Did you have the necklace on when you went down to the stables?" Sebastian asked me.

"No, I'd left it in the room. I didn't touch it again until after the first battle, when we came back to the manor to rest before dawn. I went up to our bed chamber, I saw it on the table and I..." I paused, shame flooded through me. *I'm such a fool.* "I felt like I needed it, like it was calling to me. I didn't want to take off the wave necklace Uriah gave me, so I put it in my pocket and left the room. I helped Uriah and the staff bunk down the soldiers, then we went to bed. It was still in my pocket when I put my leathers back on the next morning. I caught Uriah just as he was getting ready to fly back to the ship."

"I sensed it." Uriah said. I took a bite while he talked. "That was why I was angry when we landed on the deck. I sense the necklace on her again, her whole damn conduct changed. You two were busy, so we flew off to the cliff. I called her out on it. We tried to break it. Thankfully, it seems, we were unsuccessful. Who knows what evil we might have unleashed in the Shallows had we been successful. We went back to the manor and put it in the onyx box before rejoining the effort."

"Did you take it with you?" I asked Felix. "When you went to Zeds, did you take it with you?" *I've ruined everything. How could I be so foolish? I brought death and destruction to my mate. How could I ever deserve him?*

He gasped, and gave a curt nod of his head, "I see where you're going. I took it so Zeds could appraise it for me. You think the Sculptor knew it was traveling? But that doesn't explain the green and gold fabric or fletchings." He shook his head, taking a bite of his own meal and puzzling it out as he chewed. *At least he's eating.*

"It was always suspected that someone in the Meadows took Arabella." Sebastian mused, mostly to himself, but the table fell silent. "We thought it to be the nanny, Everlee. What if who ever it was knows the Sculptor? What if they work for him? You were his prize. Perhaps he knew King Plavlock would allow him to keep you? Or, if Plavlock is his puppet he'd make the King offer you to him as a toy." Uriah's fork was halfway to his open mouth, and he looked at his best friend with horror etched into his face.

"The King be saved."he muttered. Uriah looked at each of us in turn. "I'm not one for conspiracies, but this seems much more plausible than Everlee taking Arabella. She'd basically raised you, was practically your mother," he said looking at me. His face paled. "I think you have something here Sebastian. I think we've all been manipulated, Arabella most of all. I don't know how far this corruption runs."

I took a deep drink of my wine. Once I drained my glass, I reached for the bottle, but Felix beat me to it and filled my glass for me. He said, "And we've called them all to court. How will we manage this? We know there is a player in the Meadows, but Queen Clawin has called for Finnigan's head. Will the Sculptor know we're onto him and tell his sister? Will his sister know that Arabella has been distracted, and what will happen if she doesn't kill him?" *I still have to kill Finnigan. It's the only way to protect everyone from more harm before I can kill the Sculptor.*

"I almost balked in the stable. I had a hard time killing Seamus." My voice cracked, but I continued. "I did it as quickly as possible because I was afraid I'd lose nerve and throw up if I didn't just get it over with. I wished for there to be no blood, and my khopesh—the blade heated with my magic. It cauterized his flesh so the blood wouldn't spill." I shook my head. My appetite was gone.

"Oh, honey." Uriah scrunched his brow, shaking his head. He put his fork down and took my hand again. "That's because Raven wore that necklace charged with hate and evil. You're so much more than that. Raven was the Sculptor's Apprentice. It's not who you are. It's who he wanted you to be." Sebastian covered his mouth with his hand and sat back in his chair. A ghost of moisture filled his eyes before he blinked it away, and Felix grew silent, dipping his head. The pain of the realization hit us all at once.

Who am I?

Chapter 46

Uriah

It was three days before Solstice, and the last couple weeks were a blur of preparations. After we came to the consensus we came to st dinner, we all kicked into overdrive. Sebastian and Felix were deep in preparation for a show off with the Meadows, and Arabella and I prepared for our wedding. I had a pair of seamstresses working day and night to ensure that her dress would be perfect, whatever she wanted. She'd insisted that I couldn't see it until the ball. She'll look amazing, no matter what she chooses.

Sebastian had finally come to his senses and requested that Gabriella be allowed to travel with us. He suggested that she be one of Arabella's maidens with the duty of tending to her on our trip. I told him if he wanted her along, she was more than welcome to join us. I would appreciate it if she'd help out with the preparations, but it wasn't necessary.

Gabriella was welcome if he wanted to bring her into the family. I explained that I knew the two had been together for a while, and I was happy for him. I'll miss her as a housemaid, but I would never begrudge her happiness, especially with one of my best friends, my brother.

Arabella and Gabriella had become fast friends. I would often find the two of them talking about books and walking the grounds together. Sometimes, I would find them having a cup of tea or working on wedding preparations. They had taken a few trips into the village to visit the shops in Marelitor. I'm glad Arabella has a friend. She needs people to talk to and socialize with.

Sebastian brought Gabriella to dinner the last few nights since our conversation. The five of us enjoyed ourselves while we hashed out more details. Gabriella was originally from the Summit and offered a different perspective on occasion.

Felix was still spiraling and drinking far too much, so I felt the need to have a conversation with him about the wine. I knocked on his door a week ago, and the fumes were overwhelming from the bottles stacked all over. Aside from the fact that he was burning through several bottles a day by himself, I needed his head in the game.

Later that day, I saw him carrying the empty bottles out in bins, looking sheepish. I'm not sure what to do to help him, but hopefully leaving in a few minutes would help. Various ways to help him though this kept coming to mind. *Maybe a change of scenery will help. He needs to get his angst out. Zeds was important, but he didn't see him often. The two corresponded regularly, so maybe he needs a new pen pal.*

I stood before the mirror in the bathing chamber, having just given myself a fresh shave and finished dressing for the ride. Arabella and Gabriella would ride along in a carriage with the rest of us riding along side Knightmare. Sebastian had guardsmen lined up and ready to accompany us, and everything was being loaded. Arabella had a trunk packed with clothes and things that she wanted to bring on the trip.

Nestled in Arabella's trunk was the necklace still in the warded onyx box. *As long as she doesn't touch it again, I think the sway has diminished on her.* We had to consider that bringing the amulet with us would keep the people of Shallows the safest they could be in our absence. It was evil, and we would do whatever we had to contain it. It was the only way to keep innocents safe. The people were unsuspecting. Unleashing the essence trapped inside would be disastrous. We were all in agreement that it was a top priority to protect it until we could destroy it.

It was the only way we could ensure nothing nefarious happened while we were far away. With all the Lords and Ladies of the Realm being called to the Agron's Keep, the Shallows were vulnerable. I'd left extensive instructions for my remaining captains. I didn't like it, but it had to be done.

We would be no more vulnerable than having the unknown corruption running through the regions. I didn't know who to trust. We were sure after digging around some more that something was amiss in the Meadows, and the Brume was most likely complicit in some manner. *Too many questions and no answers.*

"All ready, love?" Arabella called from the main room. She was clad in her Shallows leathers for the journey to the Keep, but when we arrived, she would change into something more fit for a Lady. *My Lady.* She had a jewel bedecked silk and lace gown picked out. It was powder blue and adorned with hundreds of sapphires. *Lovely. She deserves all the finest things.*

I had snuck a quick peak at the front of it when the seamstress was doing a fitting, and it set off her porcelain skin and copper hair beautifully. Gabriella would help her get ready after we arrived to our wing of the Agron Keep.

We would see her father and step mother at dinner, and she fully intended to make her presence well known. Tomorrow morning we were to have breakfast with King Astros, and all the Lords and Ladies had been requested to dine with him over the next few days for various meals. King Astros liked to talk over meals. The Keep was always a busy venture and would be a blur of responsibilities.

I did my very best to spend as little time in official duties at the Keep as possible. My father adored the attention, but I found it dull. With all the phony well wishes and pleasantries. It was mind numbing. The diplomacy and ass kissing after every function was too much. It was all so tedious.

I pulled on my riding jacket and snapped the clasps under my wings in preparation for the cold ride. "All set," I said turning around. "Do you want to take any books for the ride? It's a long one. You will have ample time to enjoy a few stories, and you could likely read a couple more before we return home." She giggled at me.

"You know me too well." She held up a book. "I already have one. Gabriella and I went down to that little bookstore in the village yesterday and each bought a stack. I packed a few extra in case Gabriella gets through hers and wants to swap. I'm so glad Sebastian finally pulled his head out of his ass." We both laughed at that.

"Shopping again?" I smiled as Arabella nodded. "I'm glad the two of you are getting along so well." I clapped my hands together with nervous energy. "Okay, off we go then. Lunch is packed, so we'll eat and ride. With any luck, we should be there by sunset." It would be a long day, but I had some twenty soldiers pulled together on horseback and another thirty for the air. I needed to keep as many as possible here. The wards were up, and human soldiers seemed depleted. Usually, I only traveled with Felix and Sebastian, but given the situation, we couldn't be too sure.

Chapter 47

Arabella

I pulled back a silver curtain and peeked out the window of the carriage as we rolled down the lane. Gabriella had fallen asleep some time ago, and I'd been reading all day. I rubbed at my weary eyes.

The heavy fog was thick in the mature oak trees as we made the dreary trip to the Keep. The thick brush hung over the roadway in places, making the journey slower than anticipated. My eyes were blurry with trying to follow the bouncing page as we trilled along.

I wanted to ride Knightmare, but Uriah assured me the carriage would be more appropriate, for my status. I wanted to argue with him, but when he pointed out it was cold, rainy, and I could snuggle up with a lap blanket to read, the carriage sounded so much better.

Mid winter on the coast was dismal but in a good way. The fog bank hushed the world around us, making everything feel calm and quiet. It was the last bit of tranquility before we would be ushered around with court duties. I will stand firm with the Shallows, no matter the consequence that may result with my father. I may have been born to the Meadows, however I would not associate myself with them now. At least I know that much about myself. I'd processed a lot in the last couple weeks and I finally began to come to terms with who I was becoming.

Every dress Gabriella and I had packed was a shade of blue or silver. Even my wedding dress is white with aquamarine accents. It's lovely. Long sweeping lines of silk with delicate lace and aquamarines shimmered in a cresting wave pattern. The veil I chose is dotted with sapphires, hand sewn into place to make ethereal waves cascading down my back when it's fanned out and trailing behind me. I brought along Uriah's mother's pearls to wear as well. I twirled my engagement ring around my finger. The sapphire in the center was a beautiful marquise cut with tiny diamonds encrusted around it that sparkled brilliantly in almost any light. Nothing would feel more right. *I'm finally where I belong. I won't let anyone take that from me.*

I watched as we rounded the corner of a thicket of birch trees. The roadway turned from rutted mud into tightly packed cobble stones as we neared our destination. An imposing stone castle with a high tower in the middle and several wings branching off to a formidable fortification pointing to each of the regions came into view. We would come upon the wing dedicated to the Shallows in the South of the monstrous complex. Wild vines of ivy reached up the giant stone edifice of the fortress. *I bet they are pretty in the spring.*

There was a deep and wide moat surrounding the keep with strange foot prints belonging to whatever creature built its home in its depths. We entered the small bridge way to the portcullis in our wing. Guards stood at the ready as Felix and Sebastian spoke to them, and it began to rise. Uriah stayed just behind them, looking every bit the fierce reigning Lord of the Shallows. With the recent victory, he wasn't about to show an ounce of vulnerability.

As the carriage came to a stop, Gabriella jostled awake. "Are we here?" she asked, sitting up and straightening her dress. Her hair was slightly out of place as she patted at it, tucking in the tendrils of golden hair that had fallen out of place.

"We are, but we've only just arrived in the South wing." I said, leaning back from the window and pulling the curtain to block the cold air rushing in. It was slightly warmer inside the carriage, but it was still the peak of winter. Uriah was right about the cold. He must be frozen solid out there. *I hope his leathers kept him warm enough.*

I heard our trunks being removed from the carriage top. The door opened and Felix offered Gabriella his hand. She clambered out and I followed taking his hand when he offered it. "Thank you, Felix." He gave me a curt nod, eyes sweeping our surroundings. *Always so vigilant.*

The Agron Realm's Keep was massive. Stone walls reached several stories above us, plateaued upon each other with outdoor hallways and courtyards consisting of imposing archways made for aqueducts to service the expansive inner buildings. It would surely take awhile to navigate. Our sentries fanned out and searched our wing to secure it.

King Astros would have his own guard stationed as well, but Uriah insisted on bringing the best foot soldiers we could muster after the battle. He wanted many of the winged soldiers we'd used to great effect in the skies during the attack on the bay as well in case anything went awry during our stay in the Keep.

"We'll go through here." Uriah took my hand and pulled me along possessively. "I don't want you visible for a while if we can help it. My shadows are not giving me good reports. It seems your father and his court came yesterday, and he has been alleging rather unsavory things about us." I felt his nerves through the bond and I squeezed his hand gently. His pace quickened as we entered a covered archway and up a small flight of stairs. We passed through a door into a long corridor and through another door into a deserted wing. "There will be time to make your point, I promise."

"What will be, will be," I shrugged. "I bet if I pulled that necklace out of the box, I could slit his throat myself." I glared to the North where his wing would be. It mirrors our own. Uriah had carefully laid out the entire Keep for me to memorize in preparation. He wanted to make sure that if I got separated from him, I could find my way back to safety. The wings were all designed in the same way. The only difference is that the silver and blue would be replaced with green and gold for the Meadows. The Brume would be laden in yellow and black where the Summit would be clad in red and orange. It was purposefully designed all one country divided into four weaker regions to protect the precious center of the Realm. It kept us separate, but dependent, on one another.

We walked through the stone halls. They were all nicely decorated with silver rugs with cresting wave accents and tapestries telling the history of the Shallows. Great war ships with stretched white masts billowed, sandy beaches below cliff sides. Once we reached our bedchamber door, we stopped and waited.

There were a handful of other rooms for our court scattered around the hall, but this part of the wing was meant for only the Lord and Lady of the Shallows. Felix stepped outside of our bedchamber, "It's all clear, I don't see anything of concern or out of place and my magic doesn't detect anything either." Sebastian and Gabriella paused at our sides to make a small huddle, having searched other rooms.

"Felix, would you take the room to our left? Uriah asked, the authority in his voice suggested it more of a command. Felix nodded and tossed his traveling pack towards the door.

"Gabriella, would you prefer your own chamber or will you be staying with Sebastian?" Uriah asked with as softer tone, and gave her the choice. I felt my eyebrows rise as I gave him a look. *You dolt! You shouldn't ask her in front of him! How awkward?*

"Perhaps they can settle it themselves." I say pointedly. "There are four more rooms. Sebastian, please stay across the hall from us—Gabriella, choose any room you like."

Sebastian cleared his throat. "I'd prefer you stay with me, Gabs. It's doubtful we'll have a problem, but if there's an issue,

I'd like you close by me." He cheeks tinged pink. It set off his short strawberry blonde hair as he rubbed the back of his neck in embarrassment. Uriah didn't need to push them together. They're doing just fine on their own.

"I'll stay with you." She beamed up at him. "Thank you, my Lady, for the options." She added, turning away from him to look at me with a mischievous glint in her eye. She gave me a small smile and quirked her eyebrow. We've both been reading too much smut. "I'll direct them to bring your belongings. If you like, I'll set your room the same way it at home?" She was attending as my court lady and would be my right hand while we were here. When we returned home, her role would officially change as Sebastian had made his intentions clear with Uriah.

"Thank you. We'll have to prepare for dinner soon. Uriah and I are expected to dine with the full court as well as King Astros." Gabriella nodded and rushed off. I looked to Uriah; he was tense. I couldn't blame him as I felt the same. This dinner would hopefully bring to light a few eluding answers we've been seeking, but I hoped we would have time to unwind first. "We shall see how it goes. I don't expect to find many friends here this evening." I didn't divulge to Uriah, but I fully intended to strap at least a dagger to my thigh under my dress. I purposely chose one with a slit high enough that I could access it if needed. I'd mourn not carrying my khopesh—in this instance, stealth was necessary, and my aim was true with a dagger.

"Okay Felix, keep an eye out. Alert me immediately if there's a problem. My shadows will inform me as well. I set a few wards as we walked along. I've already skittered wards down hallways with no guards if anyone not in our immediate inner circle enters the area," Uriah informed Felix. He paced and peaked along the corridor for anything amiss.

I've never seen him like this. The anger rolled off him in waves. I hope he can control it until the appropriate moment.

I hate to think about what would happen if he attacks without clear evidence...

Felix nodded."I cast a few wards of my own. I'll poke around the other wings while you are away. I have a few friends in the Brume and the Summit I can converse with, but I'll have to figure out a way to bridge the gap with the Meadows." He looked concerned. His dark brow furrowed as he calculated his next moves. "I'm sure we won't be the only ones gathering as much intel as possible."

Uriah nodded his agreement. "Sebastian, we're doing a little role reversal like we discussed. You and Gabriella will insert yourself into various locations and acquire as much intel as possible. I want to know who we can trust and who we need to pay attention too. We will leave as soon as we can, but for the next few days we need to be aware of everyone and everything."

"Absolutely. Thankfully Gab's pretty quiet on her feet and quick-witted. I can think of plenty of ways to hide ourselves in plain sight if necessary." Sebastian said with a smirk and spark in his eye.

Gabriella rounded the corner of the hallway, "ah, perfect timing," Uriah said. She returned with two of our sentries carrying our trunks. He opened the door to our chamber, "Arabella," he said as he gestured for me to enter. "We only have a few minutes to change, my Lady of the Shallows." He guided me into the room with a hand on my lower back. The blue and silver silks adorning nearly every surface were divine. *Yes, Lady of the Shallows sounds absolutely perfect to me.*

"It'll only take me a few minutes to get ready. The carriage was a good idea. I'm much fresher than I would have been had I ridden Knightmare." I walked through the room, marveling at the beauty of it. Gabriella set out the dress we had chosen for tonight and hung the others. She paired them with the various shoes I'd chosen. She set a stack of books on the mantel above the fire place in the middle of the outer wall and pulled the window curtains closed. We didn't need anyone looking in. Gabriella left and Uriah and I began to dress for the evening, anxiously preparing for the night's agenda.

Chapter 48

Uriah

Arabella changed into her evening gown and I put on my suit. The black slacks and shirt with a navy-blue jacket lined with a handful of concealed daggers offset the sapphire crystals on her dress wonderfully. I kept sneaking peaks at the impossibly high slit up the side of her gown, grinning when I noticed that she had strapped a dagger to her thigh. The back of her dress was low cut. I was surprised when she pulled it out of the trunk, but I quickly remembered her saying she'd had it specially made for tonight. It left no illusions to what had been done to her. Her scars would be on full display tonight. I kissed her neck as we entered the dining hall off the main chamber of the castle. *She's so brave.*

The walk through the castle was an event in itself as staff and other court figures gasped at our approach. Her stunning dress out shined me by miles. The mere fact that she stood by my side was turning heads. Her copper hair was brilliant against the blue sapphire and aquamarine jewels shining on her bodice.

She loosened her grip on her power so tendrils of light flowed gently around her as much as my shadows danced. We were a sight to behold. They twisted and swirled in the air around us. There would be no doubt about our bond as people saw our magic interact. Beautiful as well as a subtle warning—we are not to be trifled with. *I hope they realize that. She is mine. Mine and no one else may have her.*

Our fingers intertwined. She gave me a light squeeze as

we came to a stop in the main entrance. King Astros was at the head of the table. His light brown hair was braided back, and his gold crown perched upon his head. He opted to wear a white shirt with ornate golden buttons and wide billowing sleeves with black pants. A simple mantle boasted the colors of all his courts in wide stripes. *Interesting and understated. This shall be an intriguing evening.*

The great dining hall was encased in towering columns of stone. Tapestries honoring each region lined the walls. The bare black marble floors allowed a small echo as people talked softly at the tables. Several smaller tables to the sides played host to the King's personal court and council members. The massive ornate gold table before us centered the room. It was stacked with vases of colorful flowers every few seats and could easily seat thirty people, though tonight only nine were in attendance and allowed to sit with the King.

"Announcing the Lord of Shallows and his Lady Arabella." A court courier announced into the room. His booming voice seemed far too loud and a hushed silence followed. We were the last to enter, and everyone's eyes fell to Arabella immediately. King Astros watched intently.

"Arabella, could it really be?" Lionel said, a mocking and bored expression crossing his face, as he stood from his seat at the table, breaking ranks with his wife. His extraordinary white feathered wings brushed past Judith as he came around the table, strings of light flowed from him and dissipated in the air. The sneer on Judith's face couldn't be more prominent as she sat engulfed in an enormous hunter green dress with puffy sleeves. The color was ill fitting with her skin tone, making it appear to be green tinged.

Lionel's golden blonde hair was pulled back in a tight braid down his back, it was lined with tinsel strands now, he'd aged considerably over the years. His pointed ears jutted out ostentatiously, but the green and gold appeared more natural on him. His dark green jacket highlighted his eyes. He scowled in our direction as he made his approach.

He walked around the length of the table to Arabella. He gawked at her, inches from her face. "Oh, how you've grown if it's really you." He scrutinized her before pausing. "Your wings. What happened to your lovely black wings?" He curled his lip and turned then. "This can't be *my* Arabella. She is missing her mother's wings and her hair is different. It was more golden, like mine, as a child," he said, addressing the court. "No, no. Something is amiss here, just as I told you earlier, Your Majesty. Her face is certainly right. It's similar enough to the child stolen from me, but this can't be her. She must be an impostor." He scoffed, shaking his head. He glanced up to King Astros, who leaned forward in his seat but did not stand or speak. He merely observed the interaction.

"I suggest you step away from *my mate*, Lionel. I shall not be too kind if I find she has been threatened." My voice rang out into the room. Pure ice and venom leaked from me, and my shadows began to swirl in kind. Lionel's own magic seeped from him, and his skin gave off an eerie glow, though far weaker than Arabella's. I knew Lionel was quite powerful, but the magic bubbling from her made his appear as more of a wisp. *Arabella is stronger.*

"I am Arabella, but I was never *yours.* Though I find it rather embarrassing to acknowledge, I was born to the Meadows. You were informed months ago and yet you never bothered to try and find me then, either. Luckily for me, my *mate* never stopped searching, always probing." Arabella returned his pointed look. "Funny enough, you seem to believe me dead rather easily—as if you expected it to be so." Arabella stated, revulsion and fury heavy on her face. Her cords of light buzzed in the air, a clear warning as she pushed past her father gaping at her.

We walked toward our seats. We were to be on the king's left hand. As she passed by Lionel, he saw her back and gasped. "Does it bother you?" She turned so the others could see as well. My muscles were rigid and my was stone, however I couldn't help but be proud of her tenaciousness, even if this led to a fight between regions. *My does she know how to exhibit herself. So strong. So fierce. Mine.*

"Your back!" He glanced to his wife. Judith looked on with an amused expression. She seemed utterly unbothered as she took a sip of her wine. She seemed almost gleeful at the mutilation. A small twitch of her lips flitted across her face before she put her mask firmly back in place. Lionel glared at her. His faced paled slightly, and his lip trembled for a moment before he tucked the shock into a careful mask of his own.

"My Lady," I started to say softly to Arabella though it still echoed across the grand room. I gestured to her seat as I pulled it out for her. "You see," I spoke to the room, "Arabella was not just wandering around all these years. She's been through quite the trial and tribulations for her young years. Who ever took her sold her to the humans to be a fae play-thing."

The Lady of Summit, Esmeralda, gasped a second time as Arabella sat next to her, and she saw more scaring up close. Tears bubbled up in her smokey gray eyes as she tried not to look in shock. John on the other side shook his head, clearly appalled.

They both snuck quick glances at her mutilated back, noting the scars on her limbs as well as on her face and neck. Her back was full of red and angry scars where her wings had been sliced from her. Bumps still remained where the connective tissue had healed poorly. The other white lines were prominent up close. Her body was a map of sorrow and anguish.

"You would question your own daughter?" John said angrily, as he rubbed his bearded chin. His jet-black hair was stark against his pale complexion. He continued to glare at Lionel as the latter sat back down across from him. "All these years later. You never could seem to find her, though now I wonder if you even really searched." He was clearly disgusted. "There, my Lady." He leaned past Esmeralda, her dark hair swishing behind her shoulder as she leaned herself back against the chair. "You have friends in the Summit," he whispered and nodded at me. We worked closely over the years together to defend the Agron Realm. It was good to know we could count on him in this too.

"Come now, this is a delicate matter. I'll meet with Uriah and Arabella after our meal. I would very much like to hear the story of our Lady of Shallows." King Astros said with a nod to me, and the room quieted once again. The atmosphere was thick, the tension billowing from the side of the table with the Meadows and Brume, clearly thick as thieves. *I wonder if Ulysses will show his hand or if we can expose him?*

"I think the rest of us might like to hear it as well," chimed in Ulysses, the eldest of the Lords. He adjusted himself in his chair, cocking his head at me. "We have every right to question if she is an impostor. How did you find the girl, after two decades nonetheless?"

I snarled. My shadows were wild now, feeling threatened. They ached to lash out. I gritted my teeth as I responded. "We found each other by fate. The mating bond that ties us led us into a cave system that connected the Agron Realm to the Daemon Kingdom. She entered one side, I came from the other, and we met in the middle. By the time we found our way out of the caves, I realized who she was and why she seemed so familiar."

A group of servants began placing plates in front of everyone. A sentry took a small bite from each of the king's portions while he watched, then stood to his side. The king would wait a few moments to see if he dropped dead. Since he had no magic he was always weary of those that may wish to unseat him before he was ready to relinquish the throne. He was only in his seventh decennial. For a fae, that was relatively young. Even without being blessed with long life, most of us lived well past our hundredth year.

"You really expect us to believe that this is the child? Some ragamuffin off the street that you cleaned up? Ha" Snapped Judith, as she took a bite of salmon. She cackled and food dribbled out of her mouth. "This is all so you don't have to marry my daughter when she comes of age. Would a tie to the Altmore family truly be that much below you?" she seethed, viciously stabbing her fork at her food.

"Judith, I'd love to insult you, but I'm afraid I couldn't possibly do as well as nature did. Perhaps you should leave this conversation to the grownups," Arabella stated. The table quieted at her remark, and a few guards snickered at their posts.

Ulysses and his wife Eugenia looked uncomfortable at the turn of the conversation. Eugenia wore a bright yellow dress that looked horribly out of place given the current circumstance of the dinner. Her blonde hair was swept up, and her light skin was nearly orange against the blazing color. "Don't tie yourself to my name, niece. You married into the Meadows. You're Lionel's problem now. My brother should have drowned you when you were a baby," he finished starkly, as he glared into the rice on his plate.

"And why it that, Ulysses? Are you finding as much treachery as I suspect?" I said. Looking around the table, I boldly looked to the King. He looked perturbed to say the least, but he remained still, taking it all in. He waved a hand, inviting me to continue.

"Your Majesty, did you know that on the night Arabella was taken from her bed, Judith was at the Meadows? She was already in his bed, even though they were not yet wed. She is the lone survivor of that massacre." Gasps filled the table, and all eyes snapped to Judith and Lionel. "Arabella and I pieced it together from my family's meticulous ledgers. We always thought it was the nanny, Everlee, but Arabella's recalled that Everlee was dead before she was removed from the house, by Judith's brother Killian. She also remembers two voices, a male and a female arguing in the corridor outside her room. The male called his counterpart, Judy. Everlee's belongings were staged to set the ghastly scene and frame her for Arabella's disappearance. I can only wonder what Judith was doing at that time."

Arabella stiffened beside me. I reached down and gently squeezed her thigh. "Additionally, they found the great seer Zeds. Many of you knew him and exchanged information with him from time to time. He was a long-standing treasure in this Realm. However, he was murdered just a fortnight ago. It seems they worried that Zeds would disclose this insight to my spymaster."

I turned to the King, *he's not stopping me.* "I'm sure you noticed the color of the fletchings and the unique stamp on the arrow I sent along with those documents. It matched an arrow from Lionel's personal quiver. You see, after Zeds was murdered, the perpetrator left behind tracks, evidence, and two eye witnesses." Leaving my left hand on Arabella's thigh, I picked up my fork as King Astros took a bite. He was quiet and thoughtful. His brow creased at the insinuation I'd made public. Sorrow filled his eyes. His leadership was falling apart at the seams.

"How dare you! You come in here with some fake whore portraying my dead daughter and expect me to believe that my wife had a hand in it! You call me a murderer? Blasphemy! Your Majesty, do not entertain this nonsense!" Lionel half stood and screeched at the court while waving around his fork. His napkin tumbled off his lap to the ground as his wings spread wide. "She's nobody. Nothing. Don't you see that? She's just some filthy urchin off the street meant to cause strife."

I felt Arabella tremble under my hand, I pushed for our bond. *You are not nothing. You are everything to me. It's almost over, baby. We're almost done with this. You're so brave. I hope you can feel how much I love you. I hope it shines through this bond to help you be whole.* She looked blankly ahead, tears welling in her eyes. We'd talked about this moment and how hard it would be.

"Do not speak to me like that in my court." King Astros said clearly and with deadly intent. Ire flashed in his eyes. He may not have magic, but he could still command the room. His broad shoulders stiffened as he sat to his full height. His royal guard stepped behind Judith and Lionel.

What they didn't know was that I'd made copies of the ledgers for myself and sent the requisite original pages to King Astros last week for his consideration with the detailed retelling of Arabella's story and what we believed to have happened. The King was letting this play out because he wanted to know who was complicit. He fully believed we'd solved the decades old mystery and intended to weed out the corruption of his court.

"The treachery of the Meadows runs deep. So deep, in fact, that I have made the decision to find a new lineage to tend to it. It's been soiled by evil. A plague has crossed the land, and for the last twenty some years, it has festered. Uriah gave me great evidence and the fact that young Arabella sits before me with her very wings stripped from her back corroborates her story. No one would willingly allow their body to be mutilated —certainly not a child. There's also evidence of murders either conducted by Judith and her brother with the help of Lionel, or on his order. I intended to talk to Uriah about this after dinner, but I see now that it will be with this court. My greatest apologies," he said, bowing his head slightly to Arabella.

"I had hoped to do this quietly, lest my own shame and embarrassment get the better of me." He shook his head and stood. "Lionel Overton and Judith Altmore. You are hereby stripped of your titles, land, and rankings. You will be afforded a full criminal trial as is outlined in the laws for the Agron Realm. Until such time, you will be placed in the custody of my guard. Take them to the dungeons. I've seen and heard enough."

The room was completely silent except for Judith

screaming vulgarities and Lionel telling her to shut up repeatedly. Both struggled out the main door as guards dragged them away. They would be bound with a leather collar made with rune etchings to negate their magic once in their cells.

Turning to Ulysses, King Astros continued. "Now that I have taken care of that, your brother's son, Killian, is a wanted man. You can hand him over, or I can send my guards to find him in the Brume. I would suggest the former." King Astros leveled a daunting stare at him. Ulysses bowed his head. He had the good sense to look grave and unsettled at the situation at hand, especially for what it would mean for his own region if the king were to begin investigating there.

"Your Majesty, I shall send for him immediately under the guise they appear for the Solstice Ball. He should come readily at the news of being included. Unfortunately, my brother and his children have always been overly concerned about such things." His face flushed red. His hands shook on the chair as he stood and pushed it in. Bowing again to all of us, he took his leave to send a courier back to the Brume. If they ride through the night and Killian is hasty with packing, they should arrive by dinner tomorrow. Eugenia whimpered a distressed good evening and quickly followed her husband.

The room sat in stunned silence for a few moments until King Astros spoke again. "Uriah and John, I shall like to have a word with you both directly after dinner. There are a few matters at hand that need our attention," King Astros said in a somber voice. He looked pensive, as if he'd made a decision of some sort. The gleam in his eyes had dulled.

Dinner was rather uneventful after their removal. I couldn't help hoping that Finnigan would be with Killian when he arrived, so we could kill him to prevent the Sculptor from realizing what we are up. Finnigan couldn't be so stupid as to think Arabella wouldn't hunt him in the Agron Realm? She was still worried about the Sculptor's reach, especially since he brought down the wards. A niggling feeling left me unsettled as we excused ourselves and headed back to our wing.

I left Arabella tired and upset in our suite, but I'd return to comfort her shortly. Until then, she wanted to read in the tub and unwind a bit. I knocked on Felix's door, and as I told him what had occurred, his face brightened. Zeds would receive justice. He'd barely been sleeping. Even though he'd slowed down on the wine, it still didn't help much. "I want you to do a little sleuthing," I began, laying out my plan. King Astros and I had already worked it out. Neither one of us believed it was only Lionel and Judith creating havoc between the regions, but we needed proof. Our way of life was about to violently change, and this event was to be the catalyst.

I gave him my instructions and headed off to my meeting. Things in the Agron Realm were about to really go in a new direction.

Chapter 49

Felix

In the dead of night, somewhere down the long, dark, stone corridor, a clock struck midnight. Uriah had sent me to the Meadows wing to see what I could glean. I needed to ensure that most of the castle was asleep before I could get to work. I crept along the hallway as quiet as a mouse, but I couldn't glamour myself completely. Fae know each other's tricks.

I reached the door to the main chamber. The hallway seemed deserted, which was odd, but given the circumstances, not entirely unusual. The Lord's chamber loomed before me. I needed to see if there was any tie from Judith or Lionel to the Sculptor. *Hopefully, I wasn't too late to retrieve their belongings.*

Something felt seriously off—the motive? *Everyone has a motive, why did they do it? Arabella's mother was already dead. He could have remarried, so that's not it. Even Arianna as heir doesn't make sense. The timing was always way off there. So then what?*

I quickly picked the lock to the room and stepped inside. *Too easy.* Relief washed over me as I saw all of their belongings were still piled in the corner haphazardly. I lit a match to ignite a candle from my pocket. I sighed. *I wish I could make fae light.*

A fae light appeared before me and I froze. "Don't you think this would be much easier?" I cursed under my breath. *Spymaster indeed.* "Blow that thing out and raise your hands." A male fae stepped forward. He was taller than me, perhaps by a whole inch, which shocked me as I was generally the tallest in the room. It's nice to meet people eye to eye and not have to look down all the time. *Well, isn't he handsome. Who the fuck is this?*

"I'm surprised you all didn't turn tail and run when your Lord and Lady were stripped of their titles." I shot at him, blowing out the candle and casting magic into the room to see if anyone else was here. *Why didn't I do that first?* We were alone.

"I *am* the Lord of Meadows. I was given the post an hour ago. And you, Felix, belong to the Shallows." The light in his hand grew brighter, and the sconces lit when he snapped his fingers. "Your Lord advised me that I might run into you tonight. He asked me not to kill you, and promised you would be here only on his order. He assumed the place would be vacant as well." He chuckled.

His voice was deep, silky, but had a dark and dangerous ring to it. He set the ball on the small table next to a set of chairs. I raised an eyebrow. *What the hell did Uriah send me into?*

Now that the room was properly lit, I noticed he was stark naked. His bronze skin was rippled with muscles like he was chiseled from rock. He had tattoos scattered about his body in a nonsensical order. His hair was cropped short, so black it nearly looked blue, and it shined in the fae light. Curls of soft hair peppered his chest and tufted around his engorged cock. His pointed pierced ears perfectly balanced his almond shaped eyes. He had a tattoo that snaked around his neck from his back. It ended just beyond his nipple on his impossibly well-formed peck. "I'm Aaron." He reached out his hand for me to shake. *Well, fuck me if he isn't the most perfect being I've ever seen.*

My eyes snapped to his, hoping he didn't see me check him out. A tawny amber looked back at me. I gasped. It was as if the world tilted, and my gravity shifted. He froze in place, gazing at me. He licked his lips and leaned his head down, tilting it in confusion for a moment.

He withdrew his hand after I failed to take it. Then he stepped forward, closing some space between us. Reaching up, he tilted up my chin with a light brush of his fingertips and pressed his lips to mine. I was frozen in place. He pulled back slightly, his lips barely touched mine as he whispered, "Tell me you *feel* that?" He kissed me deeply then. I let my lips fall apart so he could take me more fully. I'd never felt something more exquisite.

"I didn't know it was possible," I replied. His hand slithered around my neck, and he kissed me again, biting my lip and pulling me closer to him. I could feel his cock throbbing against my leathers. My bulge rubbed against his and I yearned for more. I slid my hands down his pecks and abs. A low growl rumbled in his chest and I echoed it as my hands wrapped around his waist.

"I didn't either, but I've waited a long time to find you, mate." *Aaron.* I could feel my magic building in my core. My cock thickened, straining against my pants. "When are you expected back? Or rather, what were you looking for? I can help you find it, so we can have this time together."

I looked up into his eyes, steel blue meeting tawny amber and I wondered if I should trust him. *We just met. But he's my mate.* We don't know what treachery the Meadows is involved in. Is he complicit? I couldn't decide if it mattered. Uriah, Sebastian—one of them should have warned me.

"I have no interest in those two going free. I've been aware of the—oddities—between the Meadows and Brume for some time. I could never get any leverage until now." He hedged. *He doesn't know if he can trust me either.* "I already corroborated the Shallows and handed over all the evidence I could find. I was approached a week ago by the king and offered the opportunity to build a new line—if I could prove the allegations against Lionel. Judith has always been wretched; I feel badly for her daughter. I was happy to help, with or without the promotion."

"Do you know if he killed Zeds or was it Judith? Or did they order someone else to do it. I have to know. I have to find out who killed him." Aaron sucked in a breath and stepped back from me, but kept a hand firmly at my waist. A wave of shame washed over his delicate features, and sorrow clouded his eyes for a moment before his careful facade slid back into place. *He knows something.*

"It's unfortunate that happened. Judith ordered me to carry it out. As the Commander of the Guard for the Meadows, she had me at her beck and call. I went to his home on the edge of the Brume as ordered. She'd spun a tail that he was a traitor to the Realm, but I found it unprovoked. She lied that he was helping the humans, giving their sorcerer access to our lands and supplying him with magically imbued trinkets." I felt a shudder run through him.

"When was this?" I asked.

"About three weeks ago. The day I refused, I returned back to the Meadows. It takes several shifts to go through the Brume from the Meadows, but as you know, you can't just shift through the center. I told her the claims were unfounded, and I refused to carry out her orders against an innocent. She threatened to tell Lionel, but I still refused, calling her bluff. Judith found another way. She disappeared for several hours— I searched the property, but I couldn't locate her. I think she appealed to her sleazy bother, Killian, as an accomplice. I'm so sorry." His hand dropped, and he looked absolutely grief stricken.

"It was nearly midnight by the time Judith returned. Her dress was torn and muddy. She ripped it off and yelled over her shoulder for me to burn it when I walked into the foyer and saw her returning. I kept the dress and hid it away. When King Astros asked for evidence, I turned it over to him. He matched the scraps you found to the bottom hem of her dress. I gave him an arrow from Lionel's quiver to match to the arrow you removed from Zeds' body." *I thought the fabric was from a quiver lining, not her dress.*

He looked uneasy a moment. My lip curled and vomit rose in my throat as I realized he knew Judith was intent on harming Zeds. "I swear, had I known she would do it herself, I would have lied and said the task was complete." *He didn't kill him then, but didn't protect him either.*

"Am I to believe that you would have killed him on her order, if you hadn't stopped to think about the plausibility of her claims? He was an ancient! He kept to himself, he was my friend." I was seething with pure rage. My fists clenched and Aaron looked down and he paled slightly.

"He was your friend? I truly am sorry. I wish I would have acted differently. It hasn't been easy serving the Meadows —I've been tasked with rather unsavory things over the years. I acted on the evidence I was presented with, whether fabricated or otherwise. I'm sure there are moments you might have questioned the logic of your Lord as well." Aaron tried to reason with me, no doubt sensing my rising anger and the grief pouring out of me. I could feel his trepidation. "What can I do?" He reached out and squeezed my upper arm. "I can't go back in time. How can I help now?"

Oh, not now. I can't do this right now. I'm too sober for this. Zeds! By the King, what would he do? What would he tell me? I miss him. I just want him back! Why didn't I write him more often? Or visit as often as I could? How many trips did I put off? Why does everyone I love leave me? I could feel the tears welling.

I shook my head, my voice came out like gravel as I fought to control myself. "He was my mentor. My parents died when I was young, so, I grew up with Uriah. His father, Peter, raised us both, but Zeds was always there. I should have visited more. I took his time for granted, and then I watched him die. I drew him out of his home for him to be shot by an arrow, to talk to me and a faehorse, for our gain. He didn't have to help us, but he chose to, likely knowing that the end was coming." My voice broke, and Aaron stepped close again, rubbing my upper arms with both hands.

"Tell me," he said huskily.

I told him everything that had been going on the last

few months, from Uriah finding Arabella and finding out how the Sculptor abused her, tracking her through the Daemon Kingdom, trying to help her break the spell placed on her by the Sorcerer and find her marks. It all came pouring out. I looked into his eyes. Sadness, curiosity and more looked back to me.

"Their mating bond was calling them together," Aaron tilted his head as he said it, licking his lips. The words hung between us a moment. I nodded.

"Their magic was weakened when they refused the call of it, well, refused isn't really the right word, but they'd been away from each other for too long." The implication was heavy. I pulled on the bond just then and felt him tug back, and a small flit of a smile crossed his face.

"Anyway," I continued, "We were working on the tracking spell and her task from Queen Clawin. She had five heads to collect and return to break the spell. She has four now. We have a vague idea where the fifth is. Before we could set out, the wards came down, and a double armada attacked the Bay of Shallows. I'm sure you heard." I felt myself calming down.

I shouldn't be telling him this. I know nothing about him. My magic is calm though. It didn't flare, even though he was here. If my magic trusts him, can I?

He nodded, his dark brows creasing. "I did. I pulled together half of the Meadows soldiers only to have Lionel tell me to stand down. He forbade us to help, sent us to the borders of the Meadows and Brume instead. I swear that witch sucked away all the good that was ever in him."

"Witch?" I inquired.

"Judith. She's not really a witch. Her magic isn't even that impressive—more parlor tricks than anything, but she lacks all empathy. She's devoid of most feeling unless it brings her power, money, or secrets to be bartered. I'm fairly certain she had the sorcerer work a spell on Lionel a decade ago when he refused to marry her. Judith conspires with a sorcerer, not Zeds or anyone else. I've been suspicious of her activities for awhile, but when she called upon me to kill the Seer...I don't know. It didn't sit right." Aaron confessed.

Ah, I see now. The Sculptor. He's been pulling all of our strings. Who else has he influenced?

I felt he tug between the two of us was intensifying already, and I began to ponder how this would plat out. *Is he quick on his feet? He seems intelligent and quick witted I suppose.* "Are you single?" I asked bluntly completely changing gears. *I need a drink, or just a whole bottle of something strong.* With my luck he'll be attached to someone else.

"How many gay fae do you know?" He grinned showing all of his white teeth. His eyes twinkled with mischief and disbelief that I'd just come right out and asked. "No, I'm not single. Not anymore." He caressed my cheek, rubbing my soft stubble.

I gulped. My heart was pounding through my chest, and I felt like it was going to burst from the increased pressure. "Felix. That's a strong name—happy, fortunate. So, are you happy and fortunate? Aside from losing Zeds, of course, I know that muddies things a bit."

"You seem to fill the role of Lord well. You're full of questions and twisted answers." I quipped back. *Fuck, get it together, you've always hoped for this.* "When you say you're not single anymore, what exactly does that mean?" I raised an eyebrow and licked my lips.

"I mean, you have too many clothes on. You're rightly upset, but you should come to bed. It's late. We should at least try to get some sleep I suppose." He looked at me uncertainly, but he nudged. "Either way, I'm getting cold. Come warm me up, and we can talk more about this tomorrow if you like."

He turned toward his bed-chamber on the other side of the larger sitting room. The door was ajar. I could just make out the rumpled bedclothes with his green and gold comforter half slumped onto the floor. I must have fallen asleep. There is no way this is real. He reached a hand out for me again. I flexed my fingers. I couldn't decide if I should take his hand or not. *He won't offer it again.* I could feel it through the bond. Now or never. *This is reckless.*

"I need to be back to my wing before they come out for breakfast. Uriah will expect a report." Aaron smiled a wide wickedly handsome smile, gave a huffed laugh and pulled me toward the bed.

"And what shall you report? That you snuck into my wing and picked my lock only to find your mate waiting for you?" He laughed softly. It reverberated down my spine in a loving caress as a beautiful, broad smile crossed his face.

"Um, well..." I was suddenly unsure how would this play out. *I need to report to Uriah. We need to find Finnigan too. But I can feel the bond growing, crying out for me to touch him, taste him—be with him. My magic purrs in his presence. What are his strengths? How will the bond affect the Shallows. He's Lord of Meadows now, how can we survive so far apart? What will Uriah say? He's already losing Sebastian to Gabriella, but then of course he has Arabella now. They'll need their space.* My mind was racing with possibilities.

"Slow your mind down. I can't keep up. My strengths very; I can loosely tell what someone is thinking. If you don't know how to block me out, I'll teach you. As for how this will play out, you'll be at my side, so I wouldn't worry too much about that. The breakfast tomorrow is for the Lords and Ladies. I'm not sure how we'll work your title, but we'll figure it out. Maybe we'll both be Lords of Meadows." I stopped in the doorway. *I'm definitely dreaming.*

He sat on the edge of the bed. His cock bobbed as he slid back on top of the comforter. He was hard. I could smell his musky arousal. Drool pooled in my mouth at the thought. I shrugged out of my leather jacket and kicked off my boots. I glanced at the clock. It was nearly one o'clock now.

Aaron watched me undress. He reached down and began

stroking himself. Our bond tightened in response. The tug in my middle increased. I slowly unbuttoned my shirt, tugging on the tails I'd tucked into my leather pants. Unbuttoning them, my bulge threatened to free itself. He bit his lower lip as he watched, still stroking, and building a rhythm. I dropped my shirt on my jacket and slid my pants past my hips. I heard him gasp as I stepped out of them and dropped my underwear.

"You are magnificent." He purred as he slid off his bed onto his knees. He looked up at me through the dim fae light. His lashes were thick and long. He wrapped his strong hands around my thighs and took me in his mouth. Slow and deep. He let his tongue curve around my cock, lapping at my veins, pulling me into him, letting his cheeks hollow out and build pressure. He pulled me forward, encouraging me to fuck his face. I moaned with pleasure.

He began bobbing his head as I worked my hand into his silky hair, thrusting gently as my cock slammed into the back of his throat. I face fucked him for what felt like an eternity of bliss. I looked down, and he was pumping himself too. I was close to coming when I pulled back. I tapped his shoulder for him to ease up, and I nodded once to the bed. He rose, crawled into the middle and leaning back with his feet hung over the bed. *He's so sexy. I wanna trace every tattoo with my tongue.*

I moved to the edge of the bed and began to work his long, thick length. Pumping myself this time, I held myself up with one arm as I sucked his girth into my mouth. He smelt so good, like fresh cut pine. He moaned under me as I took as much of him as I could. I could feel our bond growing between us. We were both getting amped up, steadily edging each other into bliss.

He motioned for me to change position. I laid down opposite him so we could suck each other at the same time. Side by side, we both began again in earnest. He tasted so good. Our hands were sliding up and down each other's thighs. The pressure felt exquisite while we pulled and tugged.

We kept each other on the cusp of orgasm and I could feel the cum building. I was about to burst. I was trying to hold back, waiting for Aaron so we could come at the same time. He moaned again. His chest began to heave, and we released our seed into each other's waiting mouths. We moaned around each other's cocks as we twitched with pleasure. *Fuck, fuck, fuck.*

We were both panting, sucking each other in deeper for the last dregs. I licked him clean while he sucked the last of the semen off my tip. "That was amazing." His sultry voice filled the room. He snapped his fingers, and the dim lights went out. "Come here, baby." I crawled up the bed as he reached for the blanket laying completely on the floor now. "Fuck. This was unexpected, but greatly desired. I've waited for you for a very long time. How old are you?"

The thought hadn't occurred to me. He didn't look any older than thirty. "Thirty-seven." I answered.

"Still so young! Just a baby really, but you're my baby, my mate. I'm fifty-four, believe it or not. I've been in the Meadows since the girl went missing. I was brought in as a replacement after most of the staff was found slaughtered. I was born in the Summit. I was only about your age at the time of my new assignment given to me by King Astros himself," he mused.

We curled up together, facing each other side by side, but with our arms and legs entangled. Pine and mint filled the air between us. He gently kissed me. His fingertips swept down my arms and played with my muscles, lingering on the veins prominent in my forearms. Our lips began working together, and we made out until we fell asleep, warm and cozy.

Chapter 50

Arabella

I dipped my toes into the dissipating bubbles floating around the tub. I had a bottle of white wine from home that we'd packed and I'd already drank half of it. My book lay forgotten on the floor of the expansive bathing chamber. My father's word echoed around my head—you are nothing, whore...not my daughter.

I looked around the gaudy chamber. I preferred our smaller one back at the Shallows. It held in the heat better. The draftiness of this room had me constantly peeking over my shoulder. I couldn't shake the creepy feeling that I was being watched.

I heard a noise at the door. "Uriah, is that you?" I shook my head, no one else would dare enter our chambers. "Uriah," I sat up. Water rushed off me and took the bubbles with it. I grabbed my towel. Tucking it firmly around me, I pulled the bathing chamber door open the rest of the way. I'd left it cracked so I could hear when Uriah came back from his meeting. "Uriah," I whispered again. My body prickled with goosebumps despite the steamy air.

I edged around the corner of the entryway back into the main sitting room. A scrawny kid stood pilfering through my trunk. I snapped out cords of magic. "And what exactly do you hope to find in there?" I asked, spinning him around. "Do not yell. I'm not dressed and not in the mood. What are you looking for, thief?" Recognition flashed through my brain—I know this face.

An image flashed into my mind of gloomy smoke hanging in the air of a filthy bar. "Oh my Finnigan, it's so nice to see you again." I smiled a wicked smile and pulled my cords tighter. "I have no need to play with you, so let's just get this over with." *Well damn. Thank the King he delivered himself. It saves me the trouble of finding him.*

"The Sculptor sent me. You might want to know about that." Finnigan blurted out.

"I already know he hunts me. I'd suggest you word vomit so I can decide if you need to keep talking or—not." I said coolly as I picked up my khopesh from the top of the low oak-book case by the bathroom door. My towel pulled loose with the movement. *The kid's going to get a show before I chop his head off.*

I pushed my power into my khopesh. Like with Seamus, it grew warm in my hand, ready to cauterize and not make a mess. I wish I would have learned that trick sooner. All my favorite outfits had gone to the trash over the years.

"He doesn't hunt you. He hunts this. That's why he brought the wards down." Finnigan swung the necklace from the cord in his hand. "The Queen wanted my head, but said she would trade for the necklace if I could get it. She sent word to my father through a sorcerer in the Brume." He paused to laugh, gazing at the pendant. "Looks like I win! Did you know a piece of—" His voice cut off, his face turning shades of purple and red. His eyes began to bulge, and the petechia burst, leaving his eyes blood red. A strangled gurgling noise drew from him as he started to convulse, frozen in mid-air.

A cold calm washed over me, and Finnigan's lifeless body dropped to the floor. I looked at him for a moment and then stepped over him to my trunk. I hastily began to dress in my leathers. I paused and looked around the room. I heard a familiar and eerie sound—music, but just loud of enough to hear. *Where is it coming from?*

I shook my head and finished dressing as a plan formed in my mind. *Uriah will be back any minute. If I leave quickly, I can end this by morning.* Using my cords of light, I moved Finnigan's dead body to the bathing chamber. I let my khopesh heat in my hand, and I went to work. I only hope Gabriella is not the one that finds the rest of him.

❀❀❀❀❀

"Knightmare? Are you here? Which stall are you in?" I took Finnigan's head and put it with the others in the void before coming down to the stables. Hopefully, Uriah would be the one to find him first and guess what I'm doing from there. "Knightmare!" I hissed as I walked through the massive barn.

"Raven? I'm over here. What are you doing?" Knightmare swung his head over the side of the stall. "What time is it? The moon is still high." He had a window in his stall; it was probably the best they could do in the castle.

"I need to ride quickly, then we need to shift and get to the Torrent Kingdom." I felt the pulse of the necklace in my pocket, calling me back to its master like a heartbeat. I couldn't believe I never noticed it before—or the near silent sounds coming from it. "I need to get to Plavlock's castle. I'll end this where it began, and finally break free." I can do this.

I could feel the pull to put the necklace on. It wanted to command me again, make me afraid, make me want to run. It wanted to keep me from Uriah, where I wouldn't be as strong. Uriah could detect the energy from it. I knew what he meant now. It was palpable now that I'd had it away from me for so long. I was too close to it before.

It'd become part of me. It was angry now. The magic contained in the box had grown stronger and needed a soul to feed on. We had starved it these passed weeks. It was desperate and lashing out. I could feel it trying to seep in to me, but Zeds had said it couldn't be destroyed first. He hadn't had time to say how to do it, only that it needed to be done after the Sculptor had died. I wrapped it several times in a scrap of leather before

327

pocketing it as a small barrier. This ends tonight. All of it. I'm so tired of running.

"Unlatch the door, and we'll go. Where is Uriah? Is he coming?" Knightmare seemed uneasy. His ears flattened, and he tossed his head.

"We need to go. Now. I need you to take me. We have to get past the boundary and shift. Will you take me or not?" I was growing impatient. It was already around midnight. We didn't have much time and it would take a while to ride out past the boundary of the wards so we could shift. "I need to be back by dawn. I'm supposed to attend breakfast at Uriah's side with King Astros. A lot has happened since our arrival—I'll fill you in as we ride." I finished buckling a saddle on him. I usually rode bare-back, but we needed to move. I would have him at a full gallop.

"If you're sure. I think we should bring your mate though." Knightmare stood still while I climbed up. "I've been pondering what the ancient fae said about killing him, rather what Zeds wasn't able to say. I think it'll take the magic of the bond. We should get Uriah. The power of the mating bond between you would be enough if you both used your magic. We need him. You need Uriah."

"We don't have time for that. Ride North for the Meadows and go Northeast as soon as you can. We'll cut across the Summit by shifting. Quickly, Knightmare. The Sculptor will know I touched the necklace again and Uriah will only want to protect me. He won't allow me to end this. The longer the pedant is in my pocket, the harder this will be." Knightmare bolted, and we rode hard and fast.

I told him about dinner and Finnigan. I had the five heads. I promised I knew what I was doing. Knightmare swore it was a mistake to leave Uriah behind. We would find out together.

Chapter 51

Raven

I left Knightmare in a hidden wood with instructions to leave by dawn if I didn't reemerge, and I climbed the icy steps into King Plavlock's wretched castle. My black leather boots sliding more than I liked, I tucked a dagger away, leaving only my khopesh for defense. It dripped blood as I walked down narrow hallways, weaving inside and outside. I'd only stopped long enough to kill the sentries I came across. It would be enough. I pushed my magic into it. It always seemed to give me an extra bit of stealth. I felt invisible.

Sneaking out to get here worked perfectly. I walked right past sentries without even a nod in greeting when I went to get Knightmare. I knew Uriah would be furious when he found out, but in this moment, I didn't care. This was my battle, not his. It was nearly three o'clock in the morning now. The sun would rise in a few hours. I could feel the pull of the necklace taking me to its master, so I kept walking. I let my hand slide along the outside wall of the frozen stone steps to keep my balance until I came to the door I remembered.

Go ahead. Summon me. Your time is coming to an end. I dared the Sculptor as I walked down a familiar hall, the same one I was dragged down as a small child terrified and shaking from the cold. *Good. I'll end this where it began.* This time I wasn't shaking. I wasn't afraid. I was ready for however this might end. I'm so tired of running. I *wanted* to be home, but I *refused* to let Uriah fight for me. I would finish this.

My father and that foul bitch started it all those years ago.

As I made my way through my darkest memories, I wondered if my mother saw it—if she knew she would die, only to have me stolen, and ripped to pieces. I knew in my tattered soul that no death is good enough for them—My father, Judith, Killian, the Sculptor, Queen Clawin, King Plavlock. They were all complicit and I will not allow them to haunt me anymore.

I paused as I gazed over my shoulder, down the empty corridor. Where are the guards? Why none in this hall? Clearly this is a trap, but I couldn't tell of what nature? I didn't really care. I don't know why all this happened, but I will put a stop to it. This treachery ends tonight.

I pushed on the door, and it swung open to reveal the expansive throne room. I pulled my magic from my khopesh, making myself visible again. The arched ceiling and stained glass looked ominous. A few torches flickered but left the room mostly dark. I took a few steps into the chamber. My boots echoed on the white marble floor until they came upon the deep violet rug running the length of the room.

"There's my little dove!" King Plavlock stood next to his throne, his voice ringing out into the corners of the grand hall. He looked to be badly abused. Blood was running from his ear, and he swayed where he stood. His skin was mottled and bruised. His white hair was matted and his clothes torn. He looked to be no more than a shell of a man. *Interesting.*

"Where's your master tonight?" I asked as I made my way toward him. I cast my magic out, tendrils of light searching through the darkness around us. The violet carpet running the length of the room cushioned my steps.

"Master? Why would you say such a thing? Our dear Gralton has no master. Do you, dear? Have you brought me my heads?" Queen Clawin came out of the shadows from the head of the room, her limp black hair hanging by her shoulders. Her skeletal figure was enshrouded in a blood red dress that left little covered. The gauzy material was see-through and she made bile rise in my throat. Her skin was paler than mine and nearly translucent, reminiscent of a skeleton with their skin stretched tight.

"I have them. I have something your brother wants as well." Her face stiffened momentarily. I pulled the heads from my void and bowled each head down the carpet toward the throne. "One," I said as it rolled. "Two," I tossed the next one and grimaced when it splatted upon landing. "Shall we keep going this way?" I threw the rest of the heads in the same manner and closed the void. "Not very pretty, are they? There you have it, just as requested. I'll be taking my leave from your Kingdom from this point on. I do believe we are fair and square now, unless you'd like me to take your head too?" I taunted. "Now, tell me where your brother is."

"Brother? I have no brother." She laughed as she scooped up a head. She stuck her fingers through the eye holes and waved it around as she spoke. "Aren't you curious why I'm here and not in my own Kingdom?"

"Not particularly. You all have been working together long enough, I just assume you prefer the bigger castle." I sneered at her. I called back my magic and barred my teeth. "Where are all the guards tonight? I only killed a few. Where are you hiding them?" Queen Clawin's eyes glinted in the flickering light. A ravenous expression crossed her face.

A tendril of light brightened in the furthest corner, and the Sculptor stepped through a doorway. "Ah, you came to me after all. You dare cast your magic to summon me? My dear Raven, it's so good to see you come home. My little Apprentice, as they call you on the streets." Jade, the Sculptor, stepped toward me, laughing softly and moving slowly. "We don't need guards. They tend to get in the way."

"Sculptor," I sneered. He leered back at me as I spoke his preferred name. I doubled down, "are you sure that's not because you sent them south to the ships that attacked the Shallows? I had fun ripping them apart. Did you get the gifts we sent back?" I pivoted to face him. The necklace in my pocket grew warm and I was glad I wrapped it in leather. Otherwise, I might feel the burn like so many times before.

"Ah, yes, well orchestrated. I didn't see it myself, of course, but that's why Opal is here." He glared at Queen Clawin. "She came whining about nonsense, something about hundreds of bodies being dropped into her castle's courtyard and the surrounding towns. A bit dramatic, I think. Was that your idea or your precious Lord's?" I cocked my head and stared at him. Hate billowed from him.

I heard Knightmare from the wood, his thoughts echoed to me faintly. *"Easy now. He wants to bring out your fire. Be cautious."* I'd forgotten how deep our own bond ran, and felt the comfort of my friend from afar.

"Don't talk about my mate, Jade." I said simply and softly. *That ought to be all the warning he needs.* My magic flared around me, cords of light arcing and flowing freely. The Sculptor sucked in a breath and a flash of fear filled his eyes as I used his given name.

"Would you like to see your precious mate?" Jade smirked trying to regain his composure. He clasped his hands behind his back as he began to pace. "He arrived not long after you. I believe all the guards are occupying him while I take back what you stole." His eyes danced with delight, and his greasy hair caught the light of the torch.

"I won't fall for your tricks. I'm not a little girl anymore. I won't play your games." I whispered. Worry filled my gut as I thought of Uriah fighting a castle of guards on his own. Goosebumps spread across my skin and the hair on the nape of my neck lifted.

Don't let Jade get in your head. Don't. Uriah may have followed, but he couldn't come that quickly or know for sure where we were going.

"No tricks, little dove. Not this time." He snapped his fingers, and a group of guards came through the door— Sebastian hung between their arms. "Your lover awaits." He grinned as he waved his hand. "I always thought you'd have a different type. I wanted it to be me for a time, but then you grew too—old for my taste." Jade winked. My stomach twisted at the memory of all his advances and I considered chopping his cock off for good measure.

I locked eyes with Sebastian. The slightest nod of my head, and he kept quiet. Sebastian's voice bounced around my mind. "*We'll protect him together.*"

"Since you've made it very clear you don't wish to play my games, perhaps your mate would like to instead?" Jade's lip curled as he took in Sebastian, clearly deciding which game he should play.

"No one will be playing your games, but I will barter for him." I refused to allow Jade the pleasure of hurting anyone tonight. I stepped toward Sebastian. My magic surged around me as my anger built.

He had three men hanging on each arm straining against his form, fighting to pull his arms back. His power was bubbling under the surface. Humans are weak to him, but he was allowing this diversion. I couldn't help but wonder where Uriah was, but then I felt Sebastian's suggestive power wash over me again. "*Use the shadows.*"

"Barter?" Jade laughed a full belly laugh. Glee filled his face. "My dear Raven, I'm not bartering with you. I'll kill you and take the shard of my soul that's in your pocket." He paused, tapping his chin in mockery as if to think, "and then I'll kill him."

I rolled me eyes. "You're a joke, weak, and feeble. You're reliant on parlor shop tricks and crappy magic." I tried to throw Jade off with my words. He sneered at me with contempt while waving a hand at Sebastian.

Sebastian took the opportunity of the distraction and lunged forward. Four of the six men tumbled over each other. I threw out cords of light, snapping their bones and binding them, before flinging them into the darkness. Their screams pierced the air and echoed around the chamber.

Sebastian hadn't expected my magic and didn't rebound fast enough. Shoving the other two guards my way, he missed his opportunity to reach Jade. I snapped the necks of the two guardsmen with cords of light, pulling tight to make sure they were dead.

Jade raised his hand, and the air grew thick around us. A glass like bubble formed around Sebastian. It looked as if he were trapped in an elephantine fish tank. Wind swirled inside, whipping Sebastian back and forth as he tried to regain his footing.

I shot a golden cord of light out and broke the tension of the malleable bubble. The wind gusted into the room for a moment, but Jade cast a spell again to hold him in place before Sebastian could make his way forward. The smile wiped from Jade's face, and he looked murderous. His eyes flicked to the necklace in my pocket, the shard of his soul searching for its master.

"Not so much fun when people don't play by your rules, is it? Oh, come on now. Are you really scared of one little fae?" I mocked him, trying to move myself forward a bit. The wind was intense as my boots clung to the strip of carpeting beneath my feet. I needed to distract him. My pants shifted with my stance, and the pendant's heat was burning through the wrapping, trying to reach it's true owner. *I can't let him reunite with it. It'll make him stronger. We have to end this.*

I lashed my cords of light out. Jade cast another bubble spell, trapping Sebastian again. My cords tried to cut through the spell a second time, but Jade changed the design so I couldn't break it. Sebastian was still moving painfully slow as the wind whipped around him.

I glared at Jade. "Two can play that game. Wanna change the rules? Me too." I pushed my magic into the handle of my khopesh and felt the magic I unleashed ripple over me as I disappeared. I pulled my cord of light, whipping it around and snapping it across Jade's face. Blood spurted at the contact, and I slipped into the waiting shadows behind me.

Use the shadows. Sebastian needs me to use the shadows.

Chapter 52

Felix

Dawn was approaching soon. Breakfast was still a few hours away, but my stomach gurgled. I woke in a big comfy bed, my face on Aaron's chest just above his heart. I could feel and hear the steady *thump thump* of the beat. Soft, smooth skin pressed against the scruff of my morning beard. *I need to shave.* I'd always hated my beard hair since it made my face look dirty. Aaron's muscular arm cradled around my back, and his other hand rested on his stomach, his breathing deep and even. Breathing in his scent, I quickly realized what happened last night it was not a dream.

My mind whirled. *I found my mate. Or he found me. Now what happens?* I took in his handsome features, his straight nose, full pouty lips, strong chin, and the slight slant to his eyes. His dark hair was tussled from sleep. He was glorious. I didn't want to leave the bed, but I needed to pee.

I started to shift slightly, and his arm tightened ever so gently around me. I tipped my head up and stretched a bit to lightly kiss his perfect lips. "I'll be right back," I whispered. He gave me a sleepy smile, and I slipped out of blankets. I used the toilet and washed my hands, then went back and snuggled into bed again. We were both still naked. A rush of warmth filled me as I realized one of my only real wishes had come true. *I thought it was a dream.*

I lay half asleep next to Aaron, thinking about Uriah and the betrayal he'd feel if I moved to the Meadows. We weren't kids anymore, and we had to live our lives, but he was my best friend—basically my bother. And what about Sebastian? He's moving things forward with Gabriella. He hasn't proposed yet, but Seb told us on the ride here that he commissioned a ring. He's been irritated it wasn't finished by Solstice like he planned. The attack on the Shallows set all the metal smiths and jewelers back by months, rearming the region and making ship parts to rebuild our armada.

My mind raced with questions. *Should I buy Aaron a ring? Or will he want to pick them together? What size does he wear? Would he want silver or gold? Probably gold since he's in the Meadows and those are his colors. Green and gold. I like silver though. Do they have to match? Maybe we could get both metals. How soon will he want to talk about it?* I pulled the blanket up higher trying, to get more comfortable.

My stomach twisted as my worries grew. *What will breakfast be like? What will happen if I sit with Aaron and have to face Uriah? Uriah has enough going on this weekend. The treachery they endured yesterday, now this, and they are supposed to be wed tomorrow. Will I be wed tomorrow? We're all here. Aaron and I will have to verify the bond as well. Are we about to crash their wedding? Does he even want a wedding? How does a wedding with two males even work? Will the King allow a public wedding, or will it be private? I wish I could ask Zeds. He was half a century old, he would have known. Was Zeds ever married? I don't think I ever asked.*

"Don't be a worry wort," Aaron murmured. "Go back to sleep. We'll face it soon enough. And no, I don't have any of those answers."

Oh great, now I'm annoying him. Aaron popped one eye open and sat up on his elbows. "You are *not* annoying me. I just have a feeling today is going to be a shit storm, and I think we should at least sleep until the sun rises. Trust me on this. Take a nap." He leaned back into the pillows and pulled me onto his chest. He lazily stroked my shoulder while he began humming some song I don't know. Soon, my anxiety eased and I fell back to sleep.

❀ ❀ ❀ ❀ ❀

The door-knob in the main room rattled. Aaron and I both woke with a jolt. The Meadows wing should be deserted. We looked at each other, and I slid carefully out of bed. Not bothering with underwear, I slipped my underwear and leather pants back on. Aaron reached for slacks on the floor at the foot of the bed and did the same. Buttoning them up, we crept out of the room. I stood off to the side of the door, and Aaron crouched behind a chair in the sitting room.

The door opened after a moment of jostling and a click. A dark-haired male walked in. He smelt sweaty and like hay. His foul odor filled the room. He must have just ridden in. "Judy?" He looked around the seemingly empty room. Our eyes locked. Shock flitted across his face and he stumbled backward toward the open door.

"Nope." I winked at him. He turned tail and began to sprint out of the room, back into the corridor. I gave chase with Aaron hot on my heels. He came around a corner into an intersection of rooms. Guards blocked the way at the end of the hall. He took a sharp left and slammed into a suit of armor. "I guess you're not super bright. You're early, it seems. I'm going to go out on a limb and say that you must be Killian Altmore." We stopped a few paces away, watching the fae roll around tangled in metal.

"Indeed," Aaron said. "I've caught him sneaking around the Meadows several times over the years, usually canoodling with his sister in the stables. King Astros has a mark for your head, you know. Shall we give him a show at breakfast?"

"Where do we put him in the meantime?" I asked.

Killian pulled himself up and turned to run again, this time turning right down the opposite hallway. "You there, why are you standing still?" Aaron called to the royal guards. I rolled my eyes at their laziness and lack of action. Dimwits.

The guards gave chase after their admonishment from Aaron. Killian had nearly reached the end of the hall when their magic wrapped around him, binding his hands and ankles in what appeared to be vines. They were forest fae. Killian tipped forward as he lost function of his legs and he tumbled. His momentum propelled him forward, and he smashed through the waiting banister.

"Oh, shit." I mumbled as Aaron and I picked up our pace.

We sprinted the length of the hallway, looking over the mangled banister. Killian's body lay twisted several flights down the wooden staircase at the bottom of the landing. Another set of guards looked up to us. "He broke in," I yelled down with a shrug. Aaron and I both leaned over the ruined banister.

"I can take care of myself," Aaron huffed, catching his breath from the sprint, "But since you let this riffraff in, why don't you take what's left of him to King Astros? He's not dead yet, just fairly broken. Please inform the King that I can use my magic to help retrieve a full confession if he prefers, even if he doesn't survive. As long as he hasn't been dead too long, I can still access his memories. I'd be delighted to put all this to rest." The guards proceeded noisily down the stairs after receiving the order.

He looked over his shoulder as the door at the end of the hall swung open, and a new set of royal guards took station on both sides of the door. They weren't much for protection. He may need my services more than Uriah with the way things are going. We could rebuild the Meadows together if he wishes it.

"They can't lose him, even if he survives. I have a lock on him now. My magic is tracking. I don't think there's a soul on this planet I couldn't find with enough time and resources," I mused. "I need to go back to Uriah for a bit. I'll just get the rest of my clothes first."

"Uriah isn't here. He left hours ago. I saw him out a

corridor window on the way to this wing. He was following his mate with your other friend tailing behind. It wasn't long before you picked my lock, maybe ten minutes before you showed up in my wing? I assumed he sent you to me then started out on his own adventure. They went toward the stables. I disregarded it, stripped, and got in bed." Aaron watched me for a reaction.

"You let my sworn Lord sneak out and didn't think you should mention it until now?" Irritation saturated my voice. Now it was my turn to be annoyed. I pinched the bridge of my nose. "Why didn't you tell me?"

"In all fairness, I assumed you knew. I was also distracted when the bond snapped. I was fishing when I asked when you needed to return." He bit his lip, tilting his head to study me. "I wanted to see if you'd tell me what they were up to, but your mind stayed clear. It was obvious you didn't know at that point, but… I wanted you. A distraction was not going to allow for that, so I let it go."

"I guess your skills are far more refined then my own." I glared at him, then walked back to the Lord's chamber with him a few paces behind me. I forced myself to guard my thoughts as I wondered what I got myself into. I needed a drink. What the fuck am I doing? Where is Uriah? Or Arabella? Is Sebastian with them too? Where did they go? If they headed to the stables, did they take Knightmare? Am I alone?

Chapter 53

Raven

I bumped into something warm and a hand clamped over my mouth and I startled. My eyes flared wide, and I tried to kick and thrash. Shadows wrapped seductively around me, holding me still but not slicing or harming me. My heart thumped wildly in my chest.

No, it was more of a warm embrace and I nearly cried as I recognized the scent. "Uriah! Thank the King you're okay." I whispered.

"Quietly," Uriah breathed into my ear from the shadows. He flicked his wrist, setting a sound ward. His shadows danced along my skin. I could feel the warm flick of them caressing me as he held me against his chest. "I have a plan. I need you to go on the attack, again. The winged unit is on the way, but they've been held up. I don't know if they will make their way through the castle in time to help us," Uriah urgently whispered. "They are neutralizing castle guards first."

"We can do this, together we can beat Jade. We can kill the Sculptor and his puppets." Relief washed over me at having my mate by my side again.

I could hear Jade pacing back and forth as we hid in the shadows. "Raaaven, I thought you didn't want to play." Jade's sing-song voice echoed through the room. "Wanting to play hide n' seek now, is it? It was always your favorite." The Sculptor dropped his voice. "Until it wasn't." His voice drifted away as Uriah thickened the shadows around us, further blocking us from view.

"Jade knew you'd follow me. I didn't come across many guards when I arrived. I think he held them back to separate us further," I whispered back. "He thinks he can outsmart us, but I know I can win this game. I've played it before."

"I agree. We have him outnumbered. He's backed into a corner and making mistakes," Uriah whispered.

"I'll start with Plavlock and Clawin," I felt Uriah nod, his chin bumping the top of my head. "I have my khopesh. It's never failed me. We need to combine our magic again. You'll know when it's time. We can't show our hand too soon. He thinks Sebastian is you."

I stilled as Uriah barely breathed his words into my ear. "I think you're right; the way to kill him is to the combine our magic and force it into him. We'll gain your freedom and end this war tonight. I'll come around his backside. He's the only real threat left." I nodded, and relief washed over me. "It's time to reclaim Arabella." As Uriah's shadows released me, he quickly kissed me, and the darkness around us lifted slightly.

Jade rolled his eyes as he stood before Sebastian with a muscle ticking in his cheek. *He's annoyed. Good. Make him sweat. The angrier Jade gets, the more mistakes he's going to make.*

Sebastian strained against the air holding him. "You know, I could just snap your neck, but I've wanted to play with you for so very long." Sebastian pushed back, but his magic was held tight by the vortex of wind caught in the bubble around him.

Every time he tried to speak, it would rush down his throat and gag him. Muscles and veins popped in his neck as he strained against Jade's sorcery. He was getting frustrated with the sorcerer and so was I. "I always thought you'd look like a bat with shadows billowing around you. Seeing you in person isn't very impressive," Jade sounded disappointed in his new toy, but the asshole wouldn't be conducting any experiments today.

I circled around quietly, keeping to the deepest shadows

along the wall, trying to keep my boots from echoing in the room. The King was still standing listlessly, clearly entranced and waiting his next directive—poor little puppet.

I slipped out of the shadows behind the throne and quietly pulled a dagger. I faded into the dark room, helping me blend in unseen and hide in plain sight, as I pushed my magic into my khopesh. Queen Clawin screamed as I came around the dais by the massive throne. The gold and silver chair blocked my view as I bounded into the flickering light of the torches on either side of the platform.

"Get her!" Jade screeched in turn. I grinned. We're getting to him. He's nearly unhinged, and the game has barely begun. King Plavlock lunged forward and grabbed my arm as I quickly swooped past him. Willing my magic to burst forth, I lashed out with cords of light and my khopesh, slicing clear through the old King—a fitting end for a little girls nightmares. His screams filled the chamber as pain sliced through my shoulder. I shoved off as the Queen's blade sunk into my flesh.

"Bitch. You'll pay for that with a lump of your own flesh." I cursed.

Plavlock's screams slowly eddied into gurgles. I threw the dagger in my hand and embedded it in his throat. Jade called to me from the other side of the dais. "Playing with my toys, dear Raven? You know I don't like to share. Tsk, tsk, tsk. That's a naughty girl." I could hear footsteps in the seconds I had before I lunged where the Queen had hidden after stabbing me in the back.

Queen Clawin stood half concealed by the massive throne. Surprise lit her features as blood poured from me, and the knife in her hand raised again, ready to plunge into me a second time. "I always liked the color red." A twisted smile stretched across her face. "Gralton always favored all this purple. He's say it was the color of royalty, but it looks as if he won't be saying much anymore," she snickered.

She lunged just then. The knife came fully behind the

throne as she flung herself toward me. I nearly fell of the edge of the raised platform as I tripped on Plavlock's body. Recovering my footing, I looked up to see Jade sauntering toward us now. I needed to eliminate her quickly.

I shoved off King Plavlock as he slumped to the ground in a bloody heap. I could hear Sebastian's intentions again. *"Use the shadows,"* Uriah thickened the darkness around me. Vaulting myself into the air with a back flip, I felt Uriah catch me with his shadows and flip me upright. I landed with both feet in a kick straight to her chest, and her knife slid by my calf slicing through my leather pants into my flesh. Uriah's shadows retreated as I gritted my teeth against the pain flaring up my leg.

The burning sensation distracted me, and the Queen knocked me to the floor. I failed to recover quickly as my boots lost traction in the pooling blood. I twisted as she surged forward again. Her eyes widened when she realized she over estimated me. I caught her by her hair and I yanked her back, placing the curve of my khopesh along the under side of her chin. Her bony limbs didn't give me much to hold onto. I smiled in triumph. *You should have enjoyed more food while you had the chance.*

"Come now, child." Queen Clawin laughed. "You smell so good, with all your life force leaking out of you." She tipped her head back against me and took a big whiff of the rusty scent flooding the air. I felt the maniacal laughter pour from her. *She's as insane as her brother.*

"Thanks," I whispered into her ear "I used both nostrils." She was caught off balance by my bad joke. Her feet slid in the blood, and she gripped my arm fiercely trying to pull the blade away from her flesh as it dug in. *Not today, bitch. I'm tired of this crap.*

Jade whirled around the throne where we'd been hidden from view. "How did you pull off that little flip? It looked most —unnatural."

"Don't you know? I'm a faerie, and we like to play our own tricks. Just because you took my wings doesn't mean you took my might," I quipped back at Jade. "Fuck you." I whipped a cord of light at him, pulling the Queen back with my blade as I did so. The light seared across his chest as it crossed his body and snapped in the air like a bullwhip.

A moment of shock and delight crossed his features. "Nicely done, I see you've learned a few tricks of your own." He hastily side-stepped a second cord of light whipping towards him.

"You know, I remember how positively smitten I was when I heard you'd not only escaped, but you'd taken my amulet with you. It was the first thing I checked. I'd gifted it to the old lady so she could keep an eye on you for me. It worked well until you strangled her with it."

"That bitch deserved what she got," I seethed. Blood began to run down the Queen's throat. She pulled against me. I flicked my wrist and bound her hands and feet with cords of light, pulling it tight as she struggled more.

Jade watched the exchange with little interest in his sister. "Tell me, when was it that you decided to stop taking my potion? That worked so well for so long. I was truly astonished when I found out you had left me."

"I took it until the day I left, but, I started puking it up when I'd had enough of you and your bullshit." I let a few more beads of blood trickle down Queen Clawin's neck.

She hissed, trying to wrench herself loose from my magic. It nearly matched her ugly dress. Her gold and silver crown tilted on her head. Her thin stringy hair barely held it in place. *I need Jade to turn his back to the shadows.*

"I suppose Clara wasn't doing a very good job then, was she? I always warned her to be kind, keep your confidence, and treat you like a daughter. Family is important after all and you lost yours," Jade peeked around the throne. *He expects more light magic. Uriah, where are you?*

I scanned the darkness. Listening intently, all I could make out from my vantage point was Sebastian struggling against the wind in his bubble.

"I'm not sure if you've notice, but I have your sister here. How much is she worth to you? You need a puppet. Clearly, you'll never be a king yourself. You're too weak, just a bastard born mutt trapped in your own delusions. You could *never* sit on the throne because no one would follow you. You've had to use others to keep the little power you possess. Remember all those years you told me I was nothing, no one. You were only ever speaking of yourself." I burst out in a fit of laughter.

My laughter echoed around the dark chamber. I quickly scanned the shadows again, looking for Uriah. *How could I let him ruin me all those years? Torture after torture…*

Jade's lip curled. He pulled a dagger and threw it in a fit of rage. "Do not mock me." he shouted. He shook with rage. I had struck a nerve. The dagger landed smack in the middle of the Queen's chest. She looked down at the steel hilt buried deep, crimson dripping down the front of her dress. She stumbled, blood gurgled up her throat, and I let go.

"So easily bothered. Thanks for saving me the hassel, you've been helpful tonight." I said, as I put more space between us. I stepped toward the lit torch to the far side of the throne, turning us so that his back would be toward the dark corner where I thought I saw Uriah wisp by. "Tell me, when Killian sold me to the Plavlock all those years ago, was it because he wanted to or was it because you influenced him? I haven't puzzled that piece out. What was so important about getting your hands on me?" I took another step closer to the torch. Maybe if I grab it with my magic, I can burn him.

"Look at who's delusional. It was never about you, stupid brat. You were always so full of yourself. No matter how I tried to break you, that arrogance has always survived."

"Please, enlighten me of my ignorance then, oh Mighty Master of the Dark Arts," I glared at Jade, keeping distance between us as he stepped further around the throne.

"Your step mother helped me, of course. You were so perfectly vulnerable. She's had dealings with my father. You're nothing, and no one has ever cared about you. You're just a runt on the filthy street exactly where you belong."

"Exactly where I belong?" I interjected, my voice carried across the chamber. "You mean the filthy streets you drove me. Is that why you want this necklace? To teach me more lessons?"

"You had many lessons, and they should have taught you exactly how pathetic you are, Raven. Don't you remember your lessons? I thought they were beginning to resonate. You are nothing. Nothing!"

"I am not nothing,"my voice was hardly a whisper.

No. I'm something. I'm someone. I have people. I have Uriah. I have Knightmare. I matter.

"You'll never be anything. You're so unimportant that your father didn't even search for you," Jade laughed, and the hair on the back of my neck stood on end. "No, Raven, no. It was always about your dear mate, and now I have him. Isn't that a fun little trick?" He gestured behind himself. "He'll be stuck in that wind tunnel for as long as I want."

Jade looked pleased with himself as I gasped at the realization that I was not the intended mark. "Uriah? What's so special about my mate? He's mine. His power is no more incredible than my own. Together, we'll destroy you, but alone, we're equals."

"You were the easy one to take. That's why Killian delivered you to me, lazy fool." Jade was coming unglued, and his eyes scanned the room wildly. "Are you really that stupid? You were never wanted, Raven. Even I didn't want you. You were just a toy to play with while I waited for your precious mate to find you. No one wants someone born to a dead mother, with a father lost in grief. You are nothing."

"Uriah's powers are opposite to mine. Is that what you

sought?" I inquired. We both slowly pivoted. I was carefully moving to my left so he would counter to my right. If he wanted to play games, I could turn his back to the darkness, away from the torch light. Blood soaked his black shirt, dripping to the floor beneath him.

"Uriah was well cared for." Jade explained it to me like I was a toddler. "He was treasured by his parents, doted on by his mother and staff. He commands the very shadows I have searched for, and wanted to experiment on. I may be able to manipulate wind—"

Jade flapped his hand at Sebastian and threw him to the floor. The bubble disappeared, but the wind shoved him down the purple carpet toward the entrance to the outer hall. Sebastian scrambled to right himself. "But the darkness? Why, *that* would make me royalty in my own right. When Killian fell in love with that stupid girl, I simply saw an opportunity." Jade looked absolutely unhinged.

"The power to manipulate light is far more rare than the ability to use shadows for your bidding. How would having me allow you to get close to Uriah?" I prodded, seeing a flash of movement behind Jade.

Blood still ran down his face where I whipped him with my light earlier. His dark eyes and sneer made him look less and less human as the conversation wore on.

Jade's now fully disheveled appearance showed every bit the monster he truly was. He gritted his teeth as he spoke. "I knew I could take his precious betrothed, and perhaps I'd gain the fae I really wanted. You were only ever meant to be a distraction, a lure for your young mate. Except those idiots took you when you were only four. They were supposed to wait until you were older and true feelings had developed between the two of you, but Killian's lust for that stupid maiden got in the way."

"Ah, so your poor planning and so-called *teaching* didn't work on Killian either. Have you ever taught a lesson that stuck? Don't answer that—its rhetorical, I already know you're a shitty teacher. How did you hide me from the Agron Realm?"

Jade laughed with mirth. "They never searched for you, as far as I know. I put a simple forgetting spells in place just in case, but Judith distracted your father, and talked him out of taking any action. I knew it would be pointless to pursue the Meadows."

"Why the Shallows? Even if I was betrothed, why send word to Peter? Why not go directly to the Agron Keep? Why was the Shallows important?" I needed to know. *Was Uriah's father part of this conspiracy?*

"I had no reason to provoke the crown. I sent the ransom note to the Shallows, and your dear mate's late father sent it back with a message of his own." Jade laughed again. "He didn't care about you either! He preferred that the Agron Realm stay busy looking for you. He didn't want you or the alliance with the Meadows!" Jade wiped tears of joy from his eyes before he shrugged. Blood smeared across his face from the cut in his cheek. "No matter. You brought your mate to me anyway. It's later than I wished, but now, when I kill you it will hurt him all the more."

"Why do you want him? Why hurt Uriah? Who hurt you so badly, that all you wish to do is destroy others?" Anger coated my voice as I asked, but the answer didn't matter. It was time to end this. *No more mind games.*

I looked at the pathetic creature Jade had become. The Sculptor that I had feared most of my life. Blood dripped to the floor around him. I remembered all the times it was my blood leaking from me. His wounds inflicted upon me as an innocent child. The monster I had come to fear was now disheveled and feeble. I would win this battle.

"I hate you. I hate what you turned me into. You don't have the power to control me anymore." I whispered the words and they carried across the room despite the sound of roaring wind.

Reclaiming Arabella

"Hurting other people is what I do best—I learned my own lessons after-all." Jade turned his back to me and looked down the long carpet at Sebastian, who was now on his hand and knees.

"Don't turn your back to me!" I screamed, lashing out with cords of light. I wanted to rip him open like he did to me when he sheared my wings off. Tear and mangle his flesh. Make him bleed. My cords met a wall of solid air and faltered.

A split second later, Jade held his hand out to Sebastian and closed his fist. Still struggling to stand against the wind, Sebastian sailed through the air and slammed into the marble floor beside us. He looked positively murderous.

"You better hope he doesn't get loose. You won't be my problem anymore," I laughed at Jade, as he pursed his lips, puzzling over Sebastian.

"Why haven't you tried to yield your shadows against me? You lay there, pathetically tumbling in the wind. You're letting your mate fight alone? The Shallows have always been pitiful. Why I ever thought you'd be worth my time is beyond me, but we shall persevere." Scoffing, he started to turn back to me. My magic coiled again, ready to strike.

I saw Uriah make his move seconds before. "You know," my voice rang out, "the shadows are always strongest with light." I pushed my magic out with force. It violently combined with Uriah's shadows, and we let the cords slam into Jade. His wall of air was no match for our magic and instantly failed in the face of our bonded magic.

"You shouldn't have taught me so many lessons. I took

them to heart." I grunted with the effort I was shoving forth. We tried to pull him away from Sebastian as Jade bore down over him, curling and twisting our lines of magic around his arms and legs. "You will not hurt my friend."

He changed direction and careened toward me. My cords snapped back with the sudden change, and Uriah's shadows dissipated in the bright flickering light of the torches. "Raven, you surprised me today, but you are always too slow."

I raised my khopesh, suddenly finding him much too close. I swung it as his hands fell around my neck. He was larger, and the momentum I'd helped give him sent us tumbling. I fell back, and we slid through the pool of blood streaked across the floor off the edge of the dais. I tried to push down with my elbows for leverage to no avail. I slipped in the gore and thudded back as he pinned me.

My khopesh skittered across the floor into the darkness as Jade slammed a fist against my arm. I pulled a dagger with my other hand and slashed at his kidneys as he shoved his weight down on me, pushing me harder into the floor. He seated himself between my legs, pinning them down with his knees. The air trapped in my lungs burned, and I struggled to draw a breath through his tightening fingers.

Uriah lurched for him from the shadows. A strand of darkness wrapping around his short sword as he drew it, the echo of ringing steel filled the room. "Mine!" he screamed, pure rage filling his features. His wings flared in the moonlight filtering through the windows, great and powerful, as my mate surged forward.

Anger seeped from Uriah as he shoved his power forward. Blood gushed from the cut in my shoulder, and a wave of nausea washed over me as I struggled to find a breath of air. I raised my hips, sliding and trying to find purchase, seeking to buck Jade off as I stabbed him over and over. I desperately tried to keep my grip, but there was too much blood. My only hope to hold on relied on getting air, but Jade's fingers tightened more around my neck.

Uriah's shadows sent his sword flying forward straight through Jade's back as he continued to pin me to the floor. Leaving my dagger embedded in his side, I dug into my pocket, pulling out the amulet that lay hidden there. Jade's hands went slack, and I stopped bucking when I could pull in a breath. *Thank the King!*

I slammed my hand down onto the steel jutting from his chest. Blood bubbled up Jade's throat as the piece shattered in my palm, and the metal pierced my skin. Jade tried to scream, and I gritted my teeth as we were both wracked in pain.

The wind holding Sebastian dropped, and he was instantly by my side, pulling me free from under Jade's weight and propping me up. Sebastian, held me steady as I called for my magic. I pulled in my core, beckoning the same primal force I'd called to end the attack on the Shallows. It was building, searching for Uriah. His shadows wrapped around Sebastian and I.

"Now, Arabella! Let it all go!" Uriah yelled to me. He came into view behind Jade. He pulled Jade back roughly by the shoulder, shoved the sword deeper through him, and twisted it for good measure. Shadows and light twisted around the sword as we rallied.

His shadows swirled, blending with my magic. I could feel Sebastian's strength fill me as mine waned. He was imbuing my magic with his own, as was Uriah. Years of terror flooded my mind—the dungeons, the wretched kitchen, the daily potion, living on the run, Knightmare's burnt flesh. Blood. So much blood. So much pain. *Let. It. Go.*

"I am not Raven. I am Arabella!" I raged at Jade. *The Sculptor.* "I am not nothing. I am Arabella, and I hate you and all that you made me. I am not your apprentice. I am nothing like you!" Tears fell down my face, lining my cheeks.

I pushed my hands into his chest and let my magic consume me. A scream erupted from deep in my core. Hundreds of cords of light burst from my aura, pulling Uriah and Sebastian's magic with me. It was a cataclysm of energy spilling forth and devouring him whole. The power reverberated around the room.

Everything froze and sped up all at once, as if we were suddenly sucked into a time warp. A combustion of force blasted through the air as cords of light wrapped around Jade, squeezing him tight and pulling what was left of his wretched soul from his body into the necklace as the amber turned from yellow to black. His body was shredded into a pile of gore. The amber necklace exploded into gritty black dust, and shock waves bounced off of every surface. The essence in the necklace was consumed by our magic as it evaporated into the air.

Sebastian covered our heads the best he could with his arms and a wave of his magic. He wrapped himself around us to protect me from my own magic and take the brunt of it onto himself.

All the stained-glass windows were hit with the powerful blast that had emanated from me. The arches trembled, and blocks of white marble began to crack and fall. The power I poured into the Sculptor made what was left of Jade's face turn to stone and crack before our eyes. If I held on, perhaps he would turn to dust like the amulet. There was no time to be sure.

Uriah closed the distance between us, kicking Jade's lifeless body away from me and Sebastian. Pulling me to my feet, we both offered a hand to Sebastian. Sliding through the blood, we looked to the ceilings. The castle was coming down from the blast of magic I had unleashed. The ground below us trembled as the arches continued to buckle.

Uriah took us both by the hand and shifted on the spot leaving the crumbling chamber behind. We landed just outside of the castle walls, and the small forest where I had left Knightmare was just feet from us.

Knightmare stepped out of the tree line, *"What did you do?"* he asked, his voice laced with amusement. I winked at him and lifted my shoulder in a shrug. Pain lanced down my back and side. My leg throbbed. My ribs felt broken. Blood slowly trickled down my wrist as I studied the slow drip to the ground wondering how we would explain all this.

"We need to get back, but first, I need to issue orders," Uriah said as flier after flier landed beside us, covered in various degrees of blood or dust.

"We saw the windows blow. When we diverted to help, you'd already shifted out. Are the royals dead? There was quite a bit of gore," a blonde haired fae asked as he approached our group.

"Wait! My khopesh." I didn't retrieve it. Fear filled my face as I looked up at Uriah. Concern creased his brow. "Fuck." I turned to go back. "My khopesh. It's like a third arm and I left it behind."

"No love, they'll retrieve it. I promise we'll get it back," Uriah squeezed my uninjured shoulder. "I know it's important, but damage control needs to be orchestrated right now."

Turning to his captain, Uriah continued, "Clifford, I'll leave you in command for now. Make sure you find her khopesh. It's silver with moon-shaped stones in the handle."

Clifford clapped a hand over his heart. "Yes sir. I expect it'll be in or near the throne room, possibly below. We'll find it."

Uriah gave him a single nod. "Do what you can to help the humans."

"Yes sir, we'll need to figure out who will reign now that we've conquered them completely." Clifford looked between us. "Our Lady doesn't look too well, sir."

Uriah turned to me, and the concern deepened. "I'm not sure what this will mean for the Agron Realm. We need to report back to the King," Uriah said. "We'll already have missed our breakfast meeting by the time we ride back. Somehow, I think he'll be amiable given the news we have for him." Uriah looked grim as he inspected my wounds.

"Let me go back in. I can find it. I know I can." I tried to reason with him. Tears began to tumble down my cheeks and I shivered in the frosty air. "Please, Uriah. I need it." I begged.

Can't he see it's part of me?

"No. Call for it. If it comes, you can have it, but if it doesn't, then you don't need it right now. I need to heal this." Uriah dismissed me. "You've lost too much blood."

Clifford added, "the soldiers will search for it."

"In the event they can't find it, I'll have a new one made for you." Uriah looked stern. I felt dizzy and wondered when the last time I ate had been. I looked down, and blood pooled at my feet. My navy leathers were crusted in it as well. "Try to summon it, but do it quickly."Uriah's tone was sharp, he was clearly angry with me. I would have been angry with him too if the table had been turned.

Dawn was quickly coming upon us. The sun stretched over the hill side, and blotted out my the rising plumes of dust as the castle crumbled before us. I willed my khopesh to return. His eyes softened. "We need to get you healed and back to the Keep. Try to focus on it, then we need to go."

He placed his hand on my other shoulder, steadying me as I swayed on my feet. I felt his healing magic trickle into my torn flesh. The pain began to recede, and my vision started to clear. Keeping his hand in place, he knelt before me.

Clifford offered me a hand. I placed my hand in his to balance myself. Pulling my foot up to rest on his thigh, Uriah's other hand wrapped around the cut in my calf, and he began to heal it as well. His magic trickled into my body, weaving and stitching the damaged tissue back together. *That feels so much better.*

The tension in my body began to recede as the pain ebbed away. I pulled from the dawning sun, and the morning rays touched my magic deep inside as I focused. My hand warmed, and looking down, I saw my beautiful weapon had returned to me.

"Well look at that!" exclaimed Clifford. "Looks like we won't need to search after all." He dropped my hand and rushed off after nodding to Uriah. I beamed a smile like I had never smiled before. After the long night, we were going home.

I opened a void and placed my Khopesh inside. Knightmare stepped forward and nuzzled my neck.

"*There. Do you feel okay? Dawn approaches. We can go. I will shift us together as one.*" Knightmare said. *Thank the King for faehorses.*

"You're my best friend Knightmare. What would I do without you? I will be alright, as long as my love keeps putting me back together." I nudged Uriah in the ribs as he stood up beside me.

He rolled his eyes, but swooped in for a kiss. "We'll be okay. You killed the Sculptor. His dead. His lessons can't haunt you anymore." He hugged me tight and whispered into my hair, "you won the final game."

We all reached for Knightmare, placing our hands on his flank, and he shifted our group as dust continued to roll in around us.

Chapter 55

Uriah

Knightmare shifted all of us at once, we were able to get back to our other horses in one shift. It would still take time to ride back to the Keep, but we wouldn't deplete our powers shifting numerous times.

The other sentries would either fly home or shift themselves. They would stay and help evacuate what was left of the castle, as well as getting anyone buried alive out if possible. Hopefully, they don't try to rise up against us. They should be too busy fighting each other over the crown for awhile.

I planned to send Sebastian back this afternoon. He can oversee everything once we know what the King Astros wants us to do. This was a full military operation. The bigger issue now was that we didn't have any accompanying guards with us. We left four sentries behind to watch over Gabriella and inform Felix where we were going. Hopefully we didn't just put targets on our backs. If anyone comes near Arabella—I will kill them, politics be damned.

I was still angry with Arabella for taking off in the dead of night, the ride back to the Keep was silent as we processed the night's events. As we walked into our bedchamber late in the morning, I'd stopped briefly and knocked on Felix's door, but he didn't answer. Hopefully nothing had gone awry for him last night. He hadn't had back up if he needed it, and I didn't have time to tell him where we were going before we left. He would have been on his own mission anyway. *Maybe he found something worth while if Aaron didn't catch him first. I wish I could have warned him. He's going to be pissed if I sent him into an ambush.*

"You should bathe, and then you need to rest. I healed your shoulder, but you lost so much blood again. I'll look for Gabriella and have her find you something to eat," I said to Arabella.

Arabella gave me a soft nod as she shut the door to the bathing chamber. We were both covered head to toe in dust and debris from tearing down a whole castle, and Arabella had copious amounts of blood soaked into her leathers from sliding around on the floor in it. The threads in the embroidery are tinged red and I wondered if it would wash out? It'd likely be best to just get her new leathers and some armor.

I stripped and changed into light gray slacks with a powder blue shirt. I was barely done fastening the buttons beneath my wings when she came back out. Naked. *Wow.*

"I wanted to apologize. I didn't mean for you to follow me. I intended to take the heads, kill whoever I had to, and make it back before dawn. Clearly, that's not what happened. I didn't mean to make such a mess of things." Arabella twisted her hands together in front of her, but I couldn't focus with her perky breasts exposed in front of me.

"I mean, I appreciate the apology, but you should know you'll win most of our fights, naked or not. Though it certainly helps." I smirked at her. "I'm sorry I was so short with you. I was scared and angry, mostly because that I told you to attack when you stepped into the shadows, and then you were injured so badly. I should have handled that differently."

"If there's a next time, we can do it differently," Arabella said, stepping closer and tipping her chin up. I dipped down for a long kiss, careful to avoid the bruises blooming from the fight as I pulled her close.

"I know your power is drained. We need to get you cleaned up and in bed before you collapse. King Astros will understand.

And as much as I love seeing your curves, I'd rather them not be covered in blood." *Or bruises.*

She opened her mouth to say something, then closed it. She nodded and spun on her heal, giving her rear a taunting little sway as she went back to the bathing chamber. Water finished filling the tub and I saw her sink into it. I bit my lip. *That's my good girl.*

"I love you, and I'll be back in a while. Do not open the door unless it is me or Gabriella." I put shoes on as I spoke. I peeked in the bathing chamber, she had her eyes closed as she leaned against the back of the tub. The water was tinged pink as it began to rinse her light skin. *Please listen to me, just this once.*

I opened the door to leave and search for Felix just as Gabriella raised her hand to knock. "Begging your pardon my Lord," she flushed. Her eyes widened. "You look about as well as Sebastian did, sir."

I nodded. "I need to find Felix, and fill him in. Please tend to Arabella. She needs to eat after she cleans up before she gets some sleep. She lost a lot of blood last night, and her body will need time to recover."

"Of course. I'll see to lunch for her immediately. Would you like me to bring it for you as well?" I opened the door wider for her to enter but she stayed in the corridor.

"No, I'm afraid I haven't the time. After I speak to Felix, I'll need to meet with King Astros. I'll try to find something myself later. Thank you, and please—take care of my heart." I left the door ajar and whisked past Gabriella down the hall. I sent shadows ahead, I asked for them to tell me where Felix was.

❀❀❀❀❀

I hadn't been able to locate Felix, so I made my way to the king's wing. I stood at the door to King Astros private chambers. His guard eyed me, but didn't move. I've never been in this portion of the Keep. Dare I knock? I mustn't anger the king, but he needs to know.

I hesitated, then knocked. A servant opened the door from the inside. "No need for announcements." King Astros said. "Out with you." He shooed the servant away. "We've been waiting. It seems several things happened throughout the night, and I'm sure you are about to divulge even more." King Astros seemed almost jubilant, as if he had a secret he couldn't wait to share. I entered the room. It was spacious with light yellow and cream colors. The aura was calming.

"Felix?" I looked at him, confusion etching on my face as I took in his appearance. He was wearing a hunter green velvet jacket and gold pants. He sat next to the new Lord of Meadows, Aaron. "What is this?"

"Ah, this would be one of the things that has happened. A rather happy occasion, not unlike your own!" King Astros was positively beaming.

"It seems another mating bond has come into play." Felix cleared his throat. He was turning pink, his dark hair making his face seem even more red. Mating bond? Who's?

Aaron placed his hand on top of Felix's. They sat side by side on a small couch. "What he's trying to say is that our mating bond snapped last night when you sent him to spy on my court." He smiled.

"Your mating bond? I'm sorry, I don't think I understand," I cleared my throat.

Aaron tried again. "I should rather thank you, both for the warning and the gift of such an incredible fae. We'll have to discuss his move after tomorrow night's ball. I would prefer it be amicable." What the fuck.

"There's a mating bond between you two? Felix! You've waited so long." I swallowed. He looked uneasy. He's never liked scrutiny and never wanted to be in the spot-light. "Congratulations."

My heart ached as I tried to be happy for my brother.

"We'll make the move as easy as possible. There will be a lot of upcoming changes." Felix's expression shifted as he spoke. Excitement danced in his eyes. No shit. More than you know about yet, friend.

"Yes, changes. I have no need to verify any bonds, they've both made themselves apparent without further scrutiny," the King continued, looking at me.

I glanced at a mirror on the wall. I was still covered in blood and dirt. The fresh clothes did little to help how much of a mess I was. I glanced down at my hands where Arabella's blood had dried and began to flake off.

King Astros watched me appraise myself in his mirror as he said, "I apologize for not holding off on this meeting with my Lords of Meadow. We weren't entirely sure when you would return." His eyes held nothing but amusement when he said, "I was informed late in the evening that you left with all your sentries in the dead of night, to follow Arabella while she snuck her horse out of the stables. Would you care to explain?"

"Yes, of course, I owe you all a full explanation." I said before diving into the last twelve hours. I spent the next ten minutes recounting our evening and all that was accomplished.

The King nodded his approval before stating: "So, the war has turned? You've managed to assassinate two of our greatest enemies and squelch the power of a sorcerer all with a few well chosen sentries, your right hand man and the Lady of Shallows."

I answered, "Yes, sir. A sorcerer that has infiltrated our own lands to a degree not yet known. It's my opinion that we'll have to occupy the human lands for now and then we'll have to flush out the rats here." I glanced at Felix and Aaron. The both look liked they'd been struck in the head with a mallet after hearing the news.

"It's funny that to kill a monster, sometimes you have to cut off multiple heads. I shall send a courier to the humans to offer our support with rebuilding." King Astros offered, "as far as I know, they do not have any heirs in place. If they do, I will determine if they should stand. Perhaps there can be peace after all this."

"As you wish Your Maj-" He raised his hand, cutting me off.

"Call me Reuben. I hate being called King Astros, and Your Majesty all the time. It gets dull—and lonely. When it's just us, call me by my name." I nodded my acceptance.

"Yes, sir, Reuben. Thank you. I will try my best to remember. Old habits may die hard. Have I missed anything else in my absence? I apologize for missing the meeting this morning."

"We had an interesting morning as well," Aaron said, shifting beside Felix. "We were rudely awoken to Killian Altmore picking the lock to my suite."

"We ran him down," Felix added quickly as my eyebrows shot up.

Aaron continued as if Felix hadn't spoken. "As it turns out, my magic had dramatically increased after the mating bond snapped." He took a sip of something that looked like lemonade.

Felix picked up where Aaron left off. "He's dead, actually. He fell down the stairs when we tried to stop him from running away."

Reuben spoke next. "Aaron was able to extract his memories with his exponential power increase. He corroborated everything Arabella claimed in your letters a fortnight ago. He also admitted that he and his sister killed Zeds, as well as other notable seers."

Felix shifted in his seat while Aaron spoke. "Most notably, it seems they had a hand in Arabella's mother's death. They gave her a poison to weaken her heart before giving birth. It's any wonder Arabella was born at all." I stared at Aaron in shock.

What the fuck is going on in the Meadows? Maybe with Felix there, I can get answers to many of these questions.

Perhaps this is the best thing that could have happened to all of us.

The air in the room grew tense as the information was revealed to me. "Given the situation, I think we'll hold off on any nuptials tomorrow. I still plan to hold the ball, but I'd like to shift the celebration to the end of this ancient war instead. I hope you won't mind." Reuben said, first looking at me, then at Aaron.

"Sure, whatever we can do for the Realm. Arabella needs to heal, she sustained quite a few injuries during our excursion." I said.

"I'm fine with that," Aaron said with a hopeful expression. "Felix and I would like to plan some elements if possible. I'd personally rather have a small ceremony at our estate, not that the Keep isn't lovely." He gestured to the room.

Felix chimed in. "I was thinking something outside, perhaps, an evening ceremony in the summer. We'd of course be happy to host the full court for the occasion."

Aaron nodded. "I'm sure we could accommodate everyone by then. I'll have my work cut out for me, but I don't think I'll lose many advisors, many have been loyal to my commands over the years and weary of Lionel. The Meadows is in a bit of shambles, but I know we can restore it's previous stature with time."

I nodded my agreement. "I think Arabella would prefer a quiet ceremony herself. She isn't used to being around a lot of people yet. Given her history, people tend to stare at her scars. It makes her uncomfortable."

Reuben studied me a moment as I paused before continuing. "We'd be happy to host a gathering in the Shallows as well. Maybe in the spring when the freeze relents? We can use the Western Shallows Estate. It's bigger than my new home and has adequate housing for all."

"Very well," Reuben said, clapping his hands together. "I'll take that as settled then. This spring we'll have a wedding for Uriah and Arabella. That will give you time to settle in." He gestured to Felix and Aaron. "Mid-summer will be dedicated to Aaron and Felix. A bright future for the Agron Realm." Reuben beamed at us. I didn't think he would be this thrilled.

"Speaking of the future," Aaron said, "We need to discuss Arianna. I'm happy to keep her at the Meadows Estate, but she will need a legal guardian. I can afford her upkeep, however I have to insist she not be considered my heir. Felix and I haven't discussed how we will manage that yet. I can ensure that it will be handled. We will produce one with time, or we will name one together." Felix bobbed his head in agreement.

"Arabella and I have spoke on that. She would like her little sister to come to the Shallows. We'll raise her away from the Meadows to cleanse her of her parents' evil. As far as an heir of our own, I do wish to make it clear that I will not force Arabella. She's given a lot for the Agron Realm already. I know that may throw things out of balance..."

"Not at all." Reuben interjected. "My plan to force heirs to marry has turned into a debacle. Clearly, Ulysses has been pushing for more power than he deserved. I should have seen it when Judith wormed her way into Lionel's bed."

Reuben stood and walked to a window. "For now, the decree will be stricken. There will be no more arranged marriages. I shall give the proclamation at the ball tomorrow. I can't turn back the hands of time, but I won't allow it to fester any longer. The magic is strengthening on it's own. Two mating bonds in such a short time! It's not a lot, but it means a change is coming. I can feel it."

Reuben turned and locked eyes with me. "It seems Arabella has thinned his line a bit more as well with Killian dead, and the headless male that was found in your room last night."

"Ah, I forgot about that." I flushed. I'd forgotten about the headless body in our bathing chamber. "My apologies, I saw Finnigan's headless body and when I realized Arabella was gone, I reacted without thinking."

"After you slipped out, I sent guards to check on your

quarters," Reuben admitted. "The timing works well. I'll have to replace Ulysses, but I have too much to sort through in the mean-time. It appears the continent is ours for the taking. I'll have all the generals converge. I hope you won't mind if I keep Sebastian for a spell?"

"I'll be here when needed as well," Felix volunteered. "I'll shortly be apprised of the Meadows's inner workings and I'm pretty well versed with the Summits' structure and along with the Shallows. I'll assist however I can."

"I already assumed Sebastian would be needed. I intended to send him to the Torrent Kingdom this evening. He needs a meal and a nap before returning. I left Sebastian's second, Clifford, in charge of the unit." I glanced at Felix. "I'll likely move him up into Felix's position since he'll be at the Meadows."

Felix looked at me, nodding his acceptance. "Clifford is a good fae for the position. He's versatile and has many strengths similar to my own." He gave me a single nod. He deserves this, I've only ever wanted him to be happy—and now he's my equal in title.

"Very good." Reuben took a step toward the door we entered, opening his arms and gesturing us forward. "I'll have John organize a campaign as well. We'll sort it out later. Have Sebastian wait a day. I think that blonde fae of his might want a dance first." I nodded. He deserved to be happy too.

Aaron and Felix stood up. "Thank you, Your—Excuse me, Reuben. Thank you for entertaining us. We'll see ourselves out," Aaron offered.

"Yes, yes. Of course." Reuben nodded. "Uriah, you and your mate have done the Agron Realm a great favor. Take the day for yourself. I'd like to see you attend the ball tomorrow night. I won't hold you longer than that." He turned and looked out the large window in his suite again. Deep thoughts filled the lines etched in his face as the three of us exited the room together.

Chapter 56

Uriah

I dismounted as we came into the grounds just before the stable. Arabella's carriage was pulling in now as well. It had been a long ride home. It was well worth it after the havoc of the last few days.

I was still seething. The Sculptor had indicated that my father knew all along Arabella had been held captive in Torrent. He knew and did nothing. It was disappointing and I couldn't stop the tirade of questions in my mind.

Was anything my father did honest? Why did he want the Realm distracted? What was he up to? Was he part of the corruption we're facing now?

Judith had a hand in stealing Arabella's mother from her. Murdered, like Zeds, but what did she know that they wanted kept quiet? Was her death about the baby she carried or something more? Ulysses was thought to be complicit as well. All the Lords I grew up with. Suddenly my life felt like a lie. Am I a pawn in their game?

Their corruption made me wonder if I could trust John. He was friends with my father. I could only guess at what he knew that I didn't. I would keep him at arm's length and get Felix to investigate if he can manage helping me with his new responsibilities. Aaron came from the Summit before he moved to the Meadows. Perhaps he knows more than he's been willing to share thus far.

The Agron Realm was full of more deceit than we were currently aware of. Now I'd be investigating my own father. I wonder if Arabella felt like this when we began investigating her family. The evident treachery in the Meadows and Brume was one thing, but I didn't know far it stretched.

Who are all the players? What's the agenda? What are they trying to accomplish? They've taken their time, but why? What would take twenty years to cultivate?

I'd watched carefully last night at the ball to see which families were sharing space and who was talking to whom. I won't let the treachery stand. The future won't allow for that. If Arabella wants children, I won't allow them to grow in such an ugly world of deceit. At least Felix indicated he would keep communication open as he discovered new information. Since he found his mate, it would hopefully become a strong alliance.

The Winter Solstice Ball was held last night. The ballroom had been filled with finery and lovely dresses. Elegant tables filled with intricately made appetizers lined the side of one end, and the open dance floor surrounded by round tables with crisp white linens and enchanted ice sculptures that sparkled in the warm light of the chandeliers graced the other.

Arabella had looked absolutely stunning in her jewel encrusted gown. She will make a beautiful bride. Now that we have garnered some time, I can properly spoil her the way she deserves. I'll plan a date. She would like that. At the ball her wild copper curls had hung down her back and shoulders. She'd worn the silver wave necklace I'd given her. *I'll have to get her a matching bracelet.*

Nearly every eye turned to her as we entered with her on my arm. My navy blue suit was perfectly matched to her ivory dress, and she beamed as I twirled her around dance after dance.

"Stop working for just a few minutes," she'd begged me, "Dance with me, Uriah!" The light in Arabella's eyes sparkled as much as the gems on her gown.

After some time, she took a turn with Sebastian, then

Felix, then Aaron. Laughter boomed around the room as people celebrated the end to a long war with the humans. Champaign and wine were passed around the room for numerous toasts. We were all drunk by the time we crawled in bed.

We celebrated with Felix and Aaron, congratulating them as we poured bottle after bottle of wine. The ladies munched on the little hors d'oeuvers, and Gabriella and Arabella laughed with Esmeralda while I spoke with various Lords and Commanders. Only Ulysses and those of the Brume seemed subdued. The Meadows was sparsely represented since Aaron would have to rebuild his court, but those that remained appeared to be jubilant.

Towards the end of the night, Sebastian surprised us he got down on one knee in front of the entire crowd and asked Gabriella to marry him. She positively beamed at him as he knelt before her with her hand in his. Sebastian began by apologizing for not yet having a ring, but he clearly was unable to hold back his excitement in asking for her hand in marriage. She squealed with glee as she nodded yes, a wide smile crossing her face, and he spun her around as they kissed for the assemblage. Smiles beamed all around, and we finally stumbled to our rooms well after midnight.

I watched as Arabella stepped out of the carriage onto our grounds. She stopped a moment and waited for her sister, Arianna. The child was shy and quiet. I'd never paid her much attention, despite the wishes of her parents. Her eyes were filled with curiosity as she took in the land and buildings around her. Arabella was speaking to her and gestured to the manor up the grassy slope.

I hope they settle well. Arianna deserves stability too. We all do. Is it over? Was it at simple as killing the Sculptor, Plavlock and Clawin? I'm sure a revolution is coming, but will it be theirs or ours? Nothing is ever that easy. If it was, Reuben would have ordered their demise decades ago.

I watched as soldiers pulled trunks off the carriage. We would need to make new plans soon. Spring Solstice was not far off. We'd have to take a trip to the Western Shallows Estate so Arabella could see the grounds. It was better protected from the wind on one side, so if she wished for an outdoors ceremony, we could manage it. We would bring in tents in case it rains. The flowers bloom earlier on that side of the Shallows. We should be able to make it presentable by the end of March. It'll be perfect, as long as she's by my side.

She'd need a new wedding dress since she wore the original gown for the ball last night. She couldn't present it again. That wouldn't do for my Lady. She'll have the finest, anything she wants. We have more time to prepare this time.

She had been positively elated when I explained that the wedding would be postponed, and we would be able to host it in the Shallows instead. "It's not that I don't want to marry you," she promised, "I just like the idea of having the wedding at home, in the Shallows." She'd begun bubbling off ideas of a beach ceremony and wanted Knightmare to walk beside her down the aisle. *At least she didn't say she wanted to ride him.*

Arabella was crushed moments later when I told her of Felix's bond with Aaron and that he wouldn't be returning to the Shallows. We were preparing to go down to the ball when I broke it to her. The two had their differences at first, but they had grown to be friends over the last few weeks.

We were happy for Felix, but it still hurt. We would ship most of his personal effects by courier and he would collect the rest at a later date, most likely when the weather was more temperate after our wedding. Deep down, I knew that as long as my brother is happy, I can be too. He's lost so much in his life. It's fair he get something good back.

Arabella and I both agreed we couldn't hold the reception here, at this manor, but we'd bring a separate carriage for Felix's possessions. We were still working out the logistics. We would hold the wedding at my father's old estate, and he and

Aaron would be traveling there for the occasion. It was the official seat of the Shallows. It also gave me an excuse to go through my fathers old office. I wanted to try to dig up some answers.

Since Arianna moved to the Shallows last minute, she would take Felix's room. We would have it cleaned and readied for her. The maids would make sure all of his hidden weapons were removed, and then rearrange it. She would have toys and lighter colors to cheer it up. Arianna's belongings would be shipped by courier as well. She was frightened and confused with everything happening so quickly, but the sisters were beginning to bond.

Sebastian stayed behind to deal with the political and military ramifications of what we did in the humans lands. Gabriella opted to stay with him for the time being, but she had agreed to return soon to take charge of caring for Arianna. She loved children and had suggested she could help Arianna settle in.

Arabella and Arianna walked with Knightmare. Arianna's dark brown hair blowing in the wind was a direct contrast to her sister's fiery copper locks. The sisters pat his side as he walked into his stall, and Arabella helped Arianna scoop out some oats for him. Giggles floated on the air. They finished filling Knightmare's hay rack, the three said their good nights and came back out of the stable door. Our horses were tired, and fae bustled around putting them away for the evening.

We'd had a small party coming home from the Keep since most of the Shallows' guard unit was still in Torrent. Their horses had been retrieved by the Royal Guard, and they would station themselves around the human lands while things settled down. There was still a lot to sort out in the mess that had been left behind with the Sculptor's demise.

The sun was beginning to set. "I think that we should get something for dinner. I'm cooking tonight! Who wants pancakes?" I asked as I joined them in walking up the hill.

"Pancakes, for dinner? Are we allowed?" Arianna's eyes filled with mischief, and her face lit with a big grin.

"With syrup, too. I bet we could find some blueberries," Arabella said, giving me a wink.

"It's my house. I can make pancakes for dinner if I want to." I countered. Arianna skipped ahead of us, and I took Arabella's hand. She was gorgeous in the golden light. She'd chosen a knee length silver tea dress that brought out the blue in her hazel eyes. The silver heels she picked to match it were understated but perfectly paired with the light blue pea coat she wore. She shivered in the crisp winter air. "We better get you inside."

❀ ❄ ❀ ❄ ❀

After dinner, we showed Arianna around the house and set her boundaries. She wasn't to go downstairs to the sub levels. She could go as far at the kitchen, but she had to stay out of the visitors wing. She was allowed to explore the grounds as long as she stayed with a guard. She would be assigned several of them, and tutors would arrive next week for her schooling.

We would make it more child friendly in the coming days, but in the meantime, she needed to obey some basic rules. Mostly the house rules revolved around safety, not to play with things like knives and certainly not to run with anything of the sort. *I wonder if she's anything like Arabella?*

We tucked her into a guest room at the far end of the hall. She only a small bag of clothes and a couple simple toys. It wasn't much, but we would make do for now. *Arabella can take her into Marelitor. They would likely enjoy a shopping trip—new clothes, toys and books. It would be a good distraction from their losses.*

"I'm tired," Arabella yawned as we closed the door to

our bedroom. "But I think I'm relieved most of all. So much happened these last few months. I really want to just be with you and begin our life together."

"Luckily for you, that's exactly what were going to do." I pulled her in for a deep kiss. "Even if I do smell like a horse right now." She giggled and nuzzled into me as I wrapped my arms around her. Standing on her tip toes she kissed the hollow of my throat.

We began to undress each other and quickly made our way to the bed, all ceremony lost. Kissing down her side, I nipped a small bruise left over from her fight in Torrent. I started kissing all of them. It seemed she had little bruises and cuts everywhere. "I guess I should spend more time healing you next time." I rubbed my stubble down her rib-cage, and she squealed. I laughed into her side.

"If you just keep kissing my boo boos, they will heal on their own," she purred at me. She drew lazy lines with her finger tips along my shoulder as I slid her panties down her legs and tossed them to the floor.

"Here's one on your knee." I kissed it. "And another on your thigh." I made my way up her body and settled myself between her legs. "I don't see any here, but I think I'll kiss it anyway." She giggled as I flicked her clit with my tongue and lingered a moment letting her taste flood my mouth.

I continued making my way up, kissing here and there before I pulled her in for a deep kiss, our tongues swirling in each other's mouths. My shadows were going wild, taking their time exploring her body as well. *Thank the King, she's mine.*

My erection was already trying to free itself out of the top of my underwear band. My cocked throbbed for her, despite it only being a few hours since I'd had her last. I reached down with one hand and tugged my underwear off. Arabella swiped her finger across my wing, and I nearly fell off the bed.

My eyes flew wide as I quickly pinned her arms over her head. Pulling at my shadows, I tickled her with them in return, and we both laughed. "My brightest light. I'm so very glad I found you in that cave, but if you keep doing that, one or both of us is liable to get hurt." She bit her lip and gave me a mischievous 'come and get me' grin.

I let myself sink into her silky wetness as we kissed again and I moaned into her mouth at the sensation. We began to move in sync with each other on top of the bed. Rocking on my knees, I pulled back and twisted her hips. Flipping her over, I tugged her up to her knees and knelt behind her. I gave her ass a light smack as she leaned back into me and sunk onto my throbbing cock. "Good girl, fuck, I love it when you take me so deep." I was slick with her juices and she let me fill her completely. Moaning loudly, she bounced on my lap as I pulled her hips into me. We were getting sweaty with the effort. *I could end every day like this.*

The fae lights in the sconces began to flicker as our magic swirled and danced around the room. The pressure was building. Magic began to build up in me as I got closer to climax. She felt so good.

My curiosity peeked and I wanted to try something. Tipping her forward a little, I placed my hands on her back. She gasped, but let me apply pressure. My shadows wrapped around her waist, binding us together as we rocked. I normally tried not to touch her scars, but I placed my hands directly over them now. *I wonder if I can take the edge off the pain for a night so she gets better sleep.*

I shoved my magic forward into her back. I could feel the knotted tendons. The scar tissue was thick. I pushed more magic into her, letting my healing magic explore. Her pussy tightened around my cock at that moment, and we both began our climax. We were both moaning, and my shadows flickered wildly about the room. Her answering cords of light illuminated everything as I spilled inside her. My magic flared in a burst around us as we came. She shuddered and leaned back into my chest. I wrapped my arms around her. Her tight pussy pulsed on my dick as we sat together catching our breath. *Fuck. I will never get enough of that.*

"I love you," she whispered. "If I had to fall into the cave a hundred times before we found each other, I'd do it for you." We snuggled together a moment. "Except for the cadfiends, they can stay there." She giggled at the memory.

"I think we might have drowned all the ones around here. I'm sure there are still some in other parts of the Agron Realm." She lifted her hips, and I released my shadows so she could slide off me. Pulling the blankets back, she patted the bed and slid under the covers. I tucked my wings tight and slid in beside her. Snapping my fingers, the lights went out and we settled in. "You look so sleepy." I kissed her again.

"So sleepy. Good night Uriah."

Chapter 57
Arabella

I blew a shot of air up my face. "Uriah, contain the shadows. That tickles," I grumbled half asleep. Something was tickling my nose. I cracked my eyelids enough to see feathers. Everywhere. All over us. Tiny, fluffy, soft, little black feathers littered the bed. "Uriah, did we rip a pillow?"

He grunted as I moved in the bed, pushing into him. Sunlight was just beginning to filter into the room from a slit in the curtain. I rubbed sleep from my eyes and tried to sit up, but couldn't maneuver myself. I felt... heavy, but not as stiff as I usually was in the morning.

"Arabella?" I shifted again as Uriah said my name. I was lying on my face. He snapped his fingers, and the fae lights lit. Small black feathers were littered all over our pillows. I peeked over my shoulder to see that they also covered my back. Their iridescent shine was diluted in the poor lighting.

I bounded out of my side of the bed, tripping on our clothes from the night before. I was off balance and nearly sent myself sprawling, but caught myself on the nightstand. I turned for our window, and I ripped the curtains open. Faint winter sunlight cascaded into the room. "Uriah!"

He jolted fully awake now, sitting up and looking at me. He froze. Shadows swirled around him while he peered at me, and his mouth hung open. Disbelief and shock coated his features as he raised a hand to cover his mouth. He looked at me standing naked in front of our window. Gaping, his eyes widened as he took in the sight. "Arabella!"

I felt off balance again and tipped backwards, trying to work out my footing in this new form. I tried standing taller to steady myself, I glanced over my shoulder, wobbling with the effort. Magnificent black feathered wings wrapped around my back. Turning, I looked to the vanity mirror across the room.

Uriah and I were speechless as we both marveled at my wings. We were stunned, trapped in silence, for several moments. I never thought it possible. I never even thought to ask him. He healed Knightmare, but I didn't think he could heal me.

"Uriah, you gave me back my wings." We stared at each other. Happy tears streamed down my face as I tested a few movements. We both smiled. He came to my side, and we stared at the mirror together, our wings framing our naked bodies. "We can fly together now. Really fly!"

"Thank the King." Uriah whispered with tears in his eyes. His fingertips danced along my naked hips as he kissed my forehead. "Thank the King, Arabella. You've been made whole."

Epilogue
Arabella

"I can't do it. This is never going to work." I pushed myself up. The ground was still partially frozen. Spring was blooming slowly this year. It was a mucky mess and I didn't want to ruin my dress.

I'd wanted to have the wedding directly on the beach itself, but the weather wouldn't allow for it. The main courtyard in the Western Shallows Estate would have to do. It was twice the size of the Eastern manor and would accommodate all our guests.

Everyone had been steadily arriving today. They would be here for a few days, and we would be swamped with hosting duties, so I stole a few minutes to practice flying while I could.

I'd decided I wanted to fly into the ceremony. Uriah thought I was nuts when I mentioned it. He'd been teaching me to fly, slow going as it was. Sometimes I got into the air on the first try, other days, like today, I frequently found myself face down in the mud every other attempt. I hadn't figured out how to flap and kick off at the same time, so it was easier for me to jump off something, catch air, then bring myself up. I'd nearly given Uriah a heart attack several times with my efforts.

"Always with the theatrics. I have no problem walking you down the aisle. It'd be my honor." Knightmare scolded me as he stood nearby, watching my spectacle. *"You're going to scare your guests when you come crashing down the aisle."*

"Thanks for the vote of confidence, old friend." I looked at him pointedly as I climbed back up on a boulder, flapped my wings once, and jumped, trying—and failing—to catch air again.

Uriah and Arianna searched for early blooming flowers in the distance. Arianna had taken to walking along of the large grassy clearing on the grounds of the estate. She was settling in. I'd found a large boulder to jump off of, so they were humoring me. I didn't care that the boulder was meant as a decoration.

"Ah, our friends have arrived." I looked up to see who Knightmare was talking about.

"Felix!" I ran the short distance to the fae walking up the path and slammed into him. "You made good time. We didn't expect you until dinner." I looked him over, and he seemed to be happy and healthy. He'd gained a few pounds since moving to the Meadows.

"Anything for you two!" He hugged me back. "Hello Knightmare." Felix took a step back, taking in my wings. "Wow. When I got your letter I didn't think it was true. He grew your wings back? I didn't know such a thing was possible."

"It never occurred to me either. Uriah just tried it on a whim." I winked at him as Felix raised his eyebrows.

"Uriah's magic reaches far. I was surprised when he healed me too. It's good to see you, Felix. I feel rain coming in the distance, I'll head to the stables now." Knightmare excused himself and loped off towards the training ring and the stable.

Felix inspected my wings, his eyes bright with curiosity. "Beautiful. They always were, though. I remember from when you would visit the Shallows when you were younger. Uriah always talked about them too." He smiled at me.

"It hasn't been the easiest adjustment, and we had to get a bigger bed. We needed much more space with both of our wings. I'm also learning to fly and I swear, I might give Uriah a heart attack before I get the hang of it."

Felix laughed. "I can only imagine. I'm glad you are causing Uriah plenty of trouble."

"Someone has to! Sebastian and Gabriella have moved into the guest wing so we're going to take down the wall between his old room and our room to have more space for the furniture."

"I'm sure that will work out just fine." He seemed lost in thought as he gazed across the grounds. He looked towards where Arianna and Uriah were walking. "Listen, while we have a moment together, I wanted to show you something."

"What's that?" I asked, following him to the boulder just out of Uriah's eyesight.

He leaned up against the backside of the boulder, putting his back to Uriah and Arianna. "It's not the easiest for me to talk about. The last few months have been complicated for me. When Zeds died, I took some things from his home. Nothing of much value money wise, at least. One of them was this letter."

He held up a worn envelope. It was folded in half and looked to have been read numerous times. His name was neatly written on the front in a loopy scrawl. "Okay. What did he have to say? I know you two were close. I wish I would have gotten to meet him. Did he leave you any words of wisdom?"

"That's the thing. He says you *will* meet him, just as you have come to know *his Flower.*"

"His Flower? I don't understand." I tilted my head, peering at the letter.

He opened the letter. "It says here on the second page, '*When the stolen fae becomes whole again, I shall return. This is but a short goodbye.*' I can't think of what else that might mean other than you. You were stolen and now your wings have been regrown—whole again. Surely, this is what he meant."

"But, Felix, no one can rise from the dead." I said. I looked out to sea and began to ponder. *Can they? I suppose in a way I have.*

"Zeds' *Flower*, Arabella. The nickname belonged to your mother."

Acknowledgement

I write this book with many thanks and all the gratitude.
To my husband, best friend, and partner in crime, Mike. Thank you ever so much for holding down the fort so I could tackle this massive project. You keep up with my constantly changing mind never ceasing to amaze me, and our children. I love you so much and am so very thankful for the life we've built together. You'll always be my Wander Thirst.

To my wild child, Nicole Baylee, your endless ideas and stories make me believe in magic every day! You are bigger than life and your dreams soar! The way you see the world makes it a better place, and I never want to see that light and curiousity extinguished. You are my sunshine on the dullest of days. I love you, my little star.

To my silly little man, Griffin Michael, you are such a delight and I am so lucky to be your mama! From your tight hugs to your rolling laughter, I will always delight in watching you learn and discover new things. I love you little bug, you make my heart happy everyday and I cannot wait to see the kind of man you will grow into.

❀✿❀✿❀

To Maurie and Holly, thank you for your input, and for helping to make this book a reality. Without your constant support and encouragement, I never would have gotten this far. I can't wait to explore the Agron Realm in the next adventure. Thank you for believing in me.

To Sherrie, Amy, and Hayley. Thank you for pointing me in the right direction, and catching all the little things. And Kati, thank you especially, for teaching me that there is magic in this world, if only you believe. You're the best sisters a girl could ask for.

About The Author

Diana Kay Abraham

DianaKay lives in Illinois with her husband, daughter and son as well as their two dogs, Abbigail and Duke. Originally from the mountains of Southern Oregon in the Pacific Northwest, she moved cross country in 2015 to set down roots.

Diana is an avid reader, enjoys creating and consuming art, adores a good old fashion road trip and loves lake life.

Forever a Duck, Diana graduated from the University of Oregon in 2008.

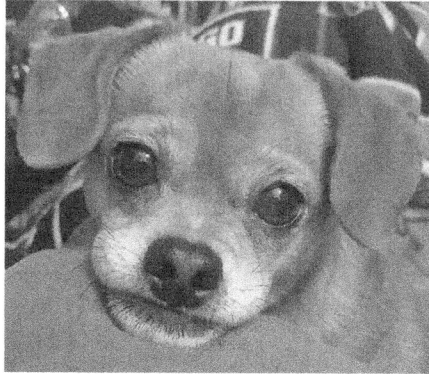

Abbigail Jean

September 9, 2009 - October 23, 2024

There are many people I've lost along the way, far more than I should have, if I'm being honest. In a way each of their ghosts follow me, and you may wonder where I came up with some of the names for Arabella's tale, while I'd never use anyone without permission, there are those lost along the way that I still think about daily. They are embedded in my soul through tears and heartache. My book is filled with not just my characters, but it encompasses different traits of people I no longer get to see.

As I sit here today, I have to say goodbye to my dear friend and pet, Abbigail Jean. To some, she may be just another dog, but to me, she's my Bouncing Queen. The girl that got me through illness, shitty boyfriends, dead end jobs, and everything in between. She helped me fall in love with my husband and hated kids until I brought my daughter home.

She's my first real love, the girl that sat on my lap as I listened to my mom, Virginia, take her last breaths. The girl that climbed mountains, and swam in pools under waterfalls with me. She was always up for a roadtrip, or a walk in the park. She loved to catch a mouse or chase rabbits. She was always up for whatever adventure I could muster up. She never said, "no," to a Beggin' Strip or snuggling up while I read a good book, painted for hours on end or sculpted into the night and well past sunrise.

She took a piece of my heart today. I wish I could have given it all to her so she could live for another 15 years. She's made me who I am. She kept me accountable and fighting to survive on days I would have rathered just to give up and cash it all in. She gave me a purpose and I gave her a home.

I was 23 years old when a woman in a Walmart parking lot held her up in the rain, on Friday the 13th in November 2009. "Hey lady, you want a puppy?" Yes, my heart sang and I took a soaking wet pup and wrapped her up in my jacket. She road home with me that day and as we travelled I spoke every name I could think of until her little ears pricked up when I said Abbigail. I said it a few more times and I knew. My Abba Gabba had found her forever home.

I never dreamed that day she would be with me for 15 years. A little puppy that I soon found out was very sick. After hundreds of dollars in veterinary bills and long nights keeping her going, she made it. Fast forward a year later when I grew very ill, she was there, by my side, and she never left me until now, but her body was tired. She gave me more than I could ever hope for on that rainy Friday the 13th.

She's my first daughter, and I will wait until we meet again so I can see her warm chocolate brown eyes, and feel her soft copper hair when I give her a snuggle on the rainbow bridge.

Bonus Content From the Agron Realm

The Etheriam

Jade's Journal

Entry Number Two Hundred Twenty-Two

I saw Raven again last night, covered in blood like a good little bitch. She took two blokes to the docks and dismembered them. She looked like little more than a spirit flitting around their bodies, methodically slicing into them with the expert skills I taught her.

I can still feel the echo of my heart pounding in my chest when I thought she caught me watching her in the cover of darkness. She looked right at me, seeing, but missing that I was close to her yet again. It's like she could sense me there. Like she wants to come home to me.

She was more careful after that and I was more surreptitious as I followed her trail of magic to an alleyway. She tried to shift away, but I'm never far behind. I always know exactly where my little pet is.

I could see the beautiful scars I gave her, all my gifts glinting on her pale skin as she stripped off her bloody clothes in a shadowy doorway. So many lessons, she learned them all so well over the years. I should have taken more from her while I had the chance. I never dreamed she would leave me, and when she was still so young. Pity. We could have been magical together.

Now she toils from place to place, always trying to flee me. She can't, but that's no matter. She wears my essence like a collar. Such a good little bitch. Her fear fuels me with such lust, such want.

She got caught playing her games a few years ago by my

wretched sister. Stupid bitch had been doing so well up to that point. After Raven killed the kitchen staff, I wasn't sure if I wanted to find her or just end her, but of course, I couldn't let it go unpunished. No one is above that.

Opal and her games annoy me, but in the end it suits my purpose to let her carry on and punish Raven for me. My sister thinks she is so crafty to send Raven to do her bidding. The only purpose it serves is to activate the necklace she stole. The evil deeds she forces Raven to complete ignite the maleficent being trapped inside. Such a brilliant piece of magic I performed. I'll take it back from her spent body eventually.

Still, it's annoying to think that my sister gets to play with my pet and I don't. I'd kill Opal for even thinking about it, but I need a way to influence the throne for the time being. Soon, I'll be strong enough to simply take control of the human lands for myself.

I control the Torrent Kingdom through Gralton of course, but father won't give me the secret to having more than a handful of puppets at my disposal. The Musician. The great sorcerer of the Brume. He's always been so protective of his magic. The truth is that he is an asshole. If he'd spent his time training me properly, rather than testing my Etheriam heritage, and playing that damn music all the time, I would have unlocked Raven's mysteries long ago.

I'll find a way. Once I unravel her magic, take down the wards protecting the Agron Realm from us pitiful humans, I can go after Uriah by myself. That fucker. He infuriates me. I'll take my sweet time with him, just as I did with my dear Raven, my sweet little dove. He doesn't deserve her and I won't let him just walk away with her.

I won't be as thoughtful when I sever his limbs. I won't need to save them as I did Raven's. Her little wings were useless of course, but I thought maybe I could capture the essence of her light magic if I removed them carefully enough. I should have waited. She'd barely started the Reveal when I stripped them from her tiny body.

Patience won't be necessary this time, I'll take Uriah apart piece by piece just to fuck with him. Entitled shit that he is. Maybe I'll cook his parts and give him a last meal. He thinks he's such a noble Lord, such a perfect leader. Wait until he begs for me to kill him. Wait until he begs for me to leave her alone. I'm sure Raven and I can entertain him while he bleeds out. I'll flay my little dove alive and make him watch, if only to cut his stench off of her milky flesh.

How dare Uriah think he can move in on my girl. My Raven. I groomed her to be my perfect counter piece all those years—back when I didn't think I could harness it. Then I created the amber pendant with the worst part of my own soul and things—changed. I changed.

She got older. She's spectacularly disturbed now. It's all down to capturing her powers for myself. I'll figure it out, my grandmother was a natural full blooded Etheriam. Such wonderful and terrifying creatures. Not human, not Fae, just...other. Sinister in nature, I've always wondered how they used their essence to capture the magic of the Fae and use it against them in turn. Being a descent from such ancient beings —as crude and cruel as they are, that's a wonder in itself. Etheriam. Even the name is mysterious and haunting.

I've been siphoning Raven's power with the amber pendant and storing it in a hidden magnetic field below the Daemon Kingdom. I nearly shit myself when I realized Raven had found herself in a chamber near where I keep the source. The bond pulled her away from it, but she very well could have discovered it had Uriah not been near that cave. Small graces for the pendant.

I pulled the essence of my grandmother's Etheriam soul out of my body and locked it in that wretched amber all those years ago. Now it watches her for me. I was able to retrieve the source and move it before Realm soldiers could discover it. I'll use it to bring down the wards when the time is right.

It disgusts me, knowing I'm not human. The Etheriam have never been more than leeches, stealing power that isn't theirs and turning it back on its owner. I used to hate the idea, but I think I can turn it against the Shallows, against Uriah. To finally destroy the Realm for my father. Perhaps he won't think I'm a waste of space anymore if I do.

I'm going to try to breach the Realm in a few short weeks, if I can take Raven back to the Torrent Kingdom with me, I certainly will. I feel time slipping through my fingers like the grains of sand in an hourglass. The bond snapped between Uriah and Raven a fortnight ago as the old Seer foretold it would be so. Infuriating, as she is every bit mine. My masterpiece. I made her who she is. Carefully sculpting away her innocence her into the bitch that she became.

The time is nearing. I can feel it. She's pulling away from me, away from the necklace's control. She'll slip into Uriah's hands, driven by the magic of the bond. I can't allow that to happen. I can sense the shift in her when she talks to that beast, Knightmare. How she could love the monstrosity of an animal so tragically ugly is beyond me, then again, I wish she would love me, but I don't think I'm much prettier.

I was so good to her over the years. She never had to worry about a place to stay. She had the basic things she needed. Enough to survive. Enough to make her strong and resourceful. We played our games, of course, but she hurt me just as much as I hurt her. Always turning away from my advances, my gifts. Fuck her, she doesn't have to love me, but I'll make her mine all the same.

Clara used to complain that she'd steal food, but I'm sure it was a misunderstanding, I made sure she had enough. I hated to punish her for it, but it only made her stronger, and I needed the old lady to trust me, report back what she noticed about the girl.

It was important the necklace be near Raven to catch her magic as it broke through the potion. Raven has always been immensely strong. I remember the disappointment in my father's face when I asked him to teach me a stronger potion. I can still hear his voice. *"Perhaps you just fucked it up like everything else you touch.*" I didn't mess it up.

I was so angry when that idiot Killian delivered the wrong Fae to me, imagine though! If I can harness Raven's power, what will happen when I finally get a hold of Uriah? Surely, she'll bring him to me in the end. I'll hate to say farewell to her after all this time, but if I can harness Uriah's dark power, unleash that on the world—I'll be invincible.

Made in United States
Orlando, FL
14 September 2025